A GIRL LIKE YOU

BOOKS BY MICHELLE COX:

The Henrietta and Inspector Howard Series

A Girl Like You
A Ring of Truth
A Promise Given
A Veil Removed
A Child Lost
A Spying Eye
A Haunting at Linley
A Christmas at Highbury (a holiday novella)

The Merriweather Series
Matched in Merriweather
Uncovered in Merriweather

Standalone Novel
The Fallen Woman's Daughter

A GIRL LIKE YOU

A HENRIETTA AND INSPECTOR HOWARD NOVEL

BOOK 1

MICHELLE COX

Michelle Cox

Copyright © 2025 Michelle Cox
First published in 2016 by She Writes Press
This edition published in 2025 by Woolton Press
Grayslake, IL 60030
www.michellecoxauthor.com

All rights reserved. No part of this publication may be reproduced, stored in a retrieval system, or transmitted in any form or by any means—electronic, mechanical, photocopying, recording, or otherwise—without the prior written permission of the publisher, except for brief quotations used in reviews, articles, or scholarly works.

This is a work of fiction. Names, characters, places, and incidents are either the product of the author's imagination or are used fictitiously. Any resemblance to actual persons, living or dead, events, or locales is entirely coincidental.

Library of Congress Control Number: 2025902198
Print ISBN: 979-8-9880097-6-4
Ebook ISBN: 979-8-9880097-7-1

Cover design by Kari Brownlie
Interior design by Danna Steele

Printed in the United States of America
10 9 8 7 6 5 4 3 2 1

DEDICATION

To my husband, Philip Cox

I can find no better words than those of A. A. Milne, who touchingly said in one of his own dedications: "It would be my present to you, my sweet, if it weren't your gift to me."

Thank you, Phil, for everything.

FOREWORD

I didn't originally set out to become an author—or even to publish a book.

Around 2012, after years of volunteering, raising my family, and occasionally writing stories about the people I met while working in a nursing home, I reached a turning point. One of my kids had just been diagnosed with ADHD, and I panicked a little. I began reading everything I could on the subject, which only served to make me wonder if there was something perhaps wrong with *all* of us . . .

In all seriousness, though, I felt the need to hit the reset button. I quit all my volunteer positions to focus more fully on my family. But once things settled down—faster than I had anticipated—I suddenly found myself wondering if I should go back to previous pursuits, or if I should start something new. Maybe even try writing a book.

I had studied English Literature in college—after a detour through pre-med—and though I'd always loved writing, I didn't have the confidence back then to pursue it seriously. Now, however, I thought I might try. I privately mulled it over for a while, during which time four different people from four completely separate parts of my life oddly approached me and said, "You should write a book." If I was looking for a sign from above, this felt like it.

So I decided to try—not with the goal of getting published or building a writing career, but simply to see if I could sit in a chair long enough to finish a manuscript.

Turns out, I could!

I then hesitantly gave the finished product to friends and family to read, and they all claimed to love it. So much so that they urged me to try publishing it, even though that had never been my intention. Having heard how difficult it was to get a book published, I wasn't sure I wanted to step into that world. Still, my early readers persisted, and eventually I begrudgingly decided to give it a try.

As predicted, it was every bit as difficult as I'd imagined. After a year of querying that first (very long) book and getting nowhere, I decided to start over and write something new—something shorter, faster-paced, maybe a little sexier.

Needing at least a small kernel of truth to get my imagination going, I turned to my nursing home stories and selected one that had always been a favorite. It was the story of a woman born and raised in Chicago who had lived through the Depression and had some amazing tales about her life in the 1930s and '40s. Her name was Liberty Adelaide Appleby, and every chance she got, she loved to remind me: "Once upon a time, I had a man-stopping body and a personality to go with it!"

I couldn't help but use her as the inspiration for my fictional heroine, Henrietta Von Harmon—and ***A Girl Like You*** was born.

I originally intended ***A Girl Like You*** to be a standalone mystery, but by the time I reached the end of the story, I had fallen in love with my own characters. I couldn't bear to say goodbye, so I decided to turn it into a series. I'm so glad I did.

This new edition of *A Girl Like You* marks the relaunch of the entire Henrietta and Inspector Howard series, with updated covers, polished interiors, and light edits throughout.

Whether this is your first time meeting Henrietta and Clive or you're returning for a reread, thank you for being here. I hope this series brings you as much joy in reading it as I've had in writing it.

— Michelle Cox

CAST OF CHARACTERS

THE VON HARMON FAMILY

Henrietta Von Harmon: Vivacious, determined taxi dancer; eldest of eight living children and the family's main breadwinner
Leslie (Les) Von Harmon: Henrietta's deceased father
Martha (Ma) Von Harmon: Henrietta's chronically depressed, critical mother
Eugene Von Harmon: Troubled brother; oldest son in the family
Elsie Von Harmon: Shy and sweet younger sister
Edward (Eddie), Herbert (Herbie), James (Jimmy), Doris and Donny (twins): The younger Von Harmon siblings

THE NEIGHBORHOOD

Stanley Dubowski: Neighbor boy devoted to Henrietta; Elsie's love interest
Mr. Hennessey: Owner of Poor Pete's; father figure to Henrietta

Mr. Dubala: Tailor; Elsie's employer
Father Finnegan: Priest at St. Sylvester's Parish
Mr. Welters: Regular at Poor Petes
Mrs. Hradek: Neighbor of the Von Harmons
Mrs. Ludmilla and Jack Jankovic: Neighbors of the Von Harmons
Mr. Sneebly: Bookie
Mr. Arthur Cartwright: Owner of the Electrics
Frank Schwinn: Owner of Arnold, Schwinn, & Co.; Les Von Harmon's boss

THE POLICE

Inspector Clive Howard: Reserved and principled Detective Inspector with the Chicago police
Clancy: Bumbling precinct officer
Kelly & Charlie: Undercover officers

Jones, Murphy, Henderson, & MacKenzie: Police officers

THE PROMENADE

Polly Shoemacher: Henrietta's friend and fellow taxi dancer
Mama Leone: Gruff floor matron
Mickey: Bartender; Polly's love interest

Jack: Another bartender
Mr. Mercer: Absentee owner of the Promenade
Artie Karzan: Clarinetist in the band; Henrietta's initial love interest
Al Karzan: Artie's brother and band member
Reggie: Doorman
Edith: Ticket booth attendant
Casanova: Regular dance patron with wandering hands

THE MARLOWE THEATER

Mrs. Alice Jenkins: Dictatorial manager of the Marlowe
Esther: Crabby Irishwoman; Mrs. Jenkins's right hand
Neptune: Owner of the Marlowe; suspected of running a prostitution ring
Larry: Greasy, slow-witted custodian
Lucy Szweda: Usherette; Henrietta's protector and friend
Gwen: Usherette; Lucy's love interest
Rose: Usherette; part of Lucy's gang
Ruby & Agnes: Usherettes; members of the secretive White Feather Club

Sam & Ed: Bartenders
Tony: Musician
Vic "Snake Eyes" Martelli: In league with Neptune
Libby Shoemacher: Polly's missing sister and Rose's love interest; presumed dead
Iris: Missing usherette; presumed dead
Carlo & Frankie: Bouncers
Mable & Dorothy: Usherettes
Evelyn: Dancer seen going beyond the green door
Ida: Girl in line for auditions at the Marlowe

CHAPTER 1

Henrietta stole another look at her compact before she snapped it shut and hurried out from behind the bar. The gilding around the edge was worn from overuse, but Henrietta didn't mind. It still did its job, and, anyway, it had been a gift from one of the regulars in lieu of a tip, an old-timer whose wife had died several years back. It was obvious that the compact had been hers, but Henrietta had accepted it gratefully, gently squeezing the old man's hand in payment when he had offered it, milky-eyed and shaking, happy that someone seemed to want it at last.

She weaved her way gingerly through the tables where the crowd—mostly men—sat at low, battered tables throwing dice. The next round was starting, and as the house twenty-six girl she was supposed to not only keep score but to encourage drinks as the night wore on and inhibitions lowered.

"Who needs a refill before the next round starts?" she called out. Several men at the back table put up a thick, callused finger to indicate they were ready for another, Henrietta pulling out a tiny pencil from behind her ear and scribbling down their orders in a small notebook she kept in the front pocket of the worn, faded blue dress she always wore to work.

"What about you, Mr. Welters?" she asked, coming up behind an older man with snow-white hair, though he was probably not yet fifty. "Care for another?" she asked with her familiar smile.

"When you gonna call me Welty, like everyone else?" he said with false petulance.

"Just doesn't seem right somehow," she teased, "you being my elder, you see."

Mr. Welters laughed out loud until it ended in a coughing fit. "You're a little fox, that's what you are," he said clearing his throat. "A real vixen! Go on, then, I'll have another. But don't think I don't know what you're doin'."

"Course you do!" she called out agreeably as she made her way back to the bar to give the order to Mr. Hennessey, the sole bartender as well as the proud owner of Poor Pete's, the establishment in which they both currently toiled.

Mr. Hennessey winked at her as he patiently pulled the Pabst tap and adroitly poured whiskeys as the pints filled. Henrietta leaned against the dark walnut bar, waiting for the drinks, her eyes straying for a moment to the bank calendar hanging just above Mr. Hennessey's head on the far wall, squeezed in between a rack of peanuts on one side and a crowded shelf of genuine German beer steins on the other. The calendar read January 1935, but it was hard to believe a new year had begun. It seemed like only yesterday that she had been helping Mr. Hennessey hang a few strands of Christmas garland and some rather thin sprigs of holly between the bottles of booze on the top shelf, which, being expensive, usually lay undisturbed for most of the year, anyway.

"Not too many tonight, is there?" Henrietta asked him with a shrug. "Think people are taking a break after the holidays?"

"Naw. It's the damn coppers. Pardon my French," Mr. Hennessey said with a nod of deference. "You know how it is. Cops come in, break up the twenty-six. People stay away for a while, but then they finally come back. Just a matter of waitin' it out."

"Yes, but the last time they were here was right around St. Nicholas Day, I think. It's January now!"

"Well, you know," he shrugged apologetically, "it's been cold." He looked out the tavern's little window at the snow softly falling. It made a pretty picture despite the iron bars that ran across the window. "Here, get these out, girl," he said, hurriedly putting the last glass of beer on her tray. "Almost time to score."

Henrietta quickly delivered the drinks and then rifled through her pocket for her notebook. "All right, then!" she called out. "Table one, what's everyone got?" she asked and methodically worked her way around the room until she had recorded everyone's score.

"Ooh! Mr. Mentz! That's your second one!" she said enthusiastically to a middle-aged man in the corner, who had just declared that he had gotten a perfect twenty-six. "You're hot tonight!"

"Always am when you're here, Henrietta!" he shouted back, beaming and looking around at the crowd for acknowledgement of his high score. Only Mr. Welters blearily raised his glass in salute.

"Anyone else?" Henrietta called out.

Disgruntled mumblings were the only response.

"Okay, then, Mr. Mentz, that's a free drink for you; what'll it be?"

"Schlitz!" he answered. "Make it strong!"

The crowd snickered at his joke, as only beer or wine, not hard liquor, were offered as the prize for throwing a perfect twenty-six with the allotted ten dice. Almost any corner bar in Chicago offered a game of twenty-six, though sometimes a game could be found at the back of a cigar store as a quick alternative as well. It had been just over six years since the crash, but people were still struggling, and a game of twenty-six made for a cheap form of entertainment among working people—those who had a little bit of cash to spare for a drink and a laugh, as it cost only a quarter a game to get in.

Somehow, though, the police had gotten it into their heads that it was illegal—which it wasn't, everyone knew—but they broke it up from time to time anyway, saying it amounted to gambling and possibly racketeering with possible links to the mob. It infuriated Henrietta whenever they busted it up at Poor Pete's, as Mr. Hennessy ran a straight establishment, though she suspected he had been approached more than once to become a part of a bigger network. He would have none of it, though, and was determined to stay independent. Henrietta was proud of him for it, though she could see by the bags under his eyes from time to time that it worried him, especially when particularly unsavory types wandered in for a "little chat" about expanding his horizons, extra protection, and various other shady prospects.

Mr. Hennessey was an older man in his fifties or maybe even sixties. Henrietta wasn't sure exactly; she was notoriously bad at guessing ages. He had graying hair that he wore in a crew cut and a thick gray mustache to match his thick, round body. He was married, of course, and had children, but they were all grown up. Henrietta didn't know much about them except that his daughter lived out east somewhere and one of his sons had died in the war. He never spoke much about his other son, and Henrietta did not like to ask. All in all, he was well liked, and Henrietta thought him a good businessman. He could be harsh with the occasional customer who got out of hand, though his sleepy corner bar was not the type of place that usually attracted young hotheads. But he had a softer side, too, especially when it came to Henrietta.

He had hired her when she was just fourteen to scrub the floors before Poor Pete's opened each day at noon. It had been a favor, as he had known her father, that is, before he had killed himself just about four years ago. Mr. Von Harmon had been a regular customer, and Mr. Hennessey felt it was the least he could do to help out the wife and the large family he had left behind. Not long after the "accident," Henrietta had turned up out of the blue, asking if he had any work.

"You're Les Von Harmon's kid, aren't you?" he had asked as he wiped his hands on the dirty towel hanging from his belt loop.

Henrietta merely nodded. She had come to the back door, and Mr. Hennessey had let her come in, though he suspected she was probably underage.

"How old are you?" he asked, peering down at her.

"Almost fifteen."

"Sweet Jesus," Mr. Hennessey had whistled. "That all?" Mr. Hennessey had let his eyes briefly, albeit uncomfortably, travel over her body and knew in that moment that this girl's life was either going to be a heaven or it was going to be a hell, for he had not seen this kind of beauty more than a couple of times in his whole life. She had long, thick auburn hair, which she wore loosely tied up; a heart-shaped face with perfect alabaster skin; full, pink lips; blue eyes that seemed to light up each time she spoke; and an already fully developed body with ample breasts and a slight swell at the hips. She had been dressed plainly in a cotton dress, but her beauty radiated nonetheless. She had the body of a woman that men look back twice at, a body that even made women comment.

"I know I'm young," she said in a cheerful, pleasing sort of voice that oddly mesmerized him, "but I'm a real good cleaner, Mr. Hennessey. Please, I . . . we . . . need the money. I'll clean the bathroom, too. You don't want to be bothering with that, now do you? Let me do it for you . . . please . . ."

"Well, I don't know," he said, scratching his head. His wife would be upset if he took on another employee, but he felt he owed it to poor Les. He had been drinking at Poor Pete's that night. "I suppose we could try you out."

"Oh, thanks, Mr. Hennessey!" she had said, two dimples magically appearing as she shyly smiled at him. Mr. Hennessey felt himself unwittingly blush.

"You come 'round about ten each morning and get everything ship-shape. How's that sound?"

"Oh, thanks, Mr. Hennessey! Want me to start now?" she asked, eagerly looking around.

"No, come back tomorrow," he said hurriedly, shooing her out the door, knowing his wife was due any moment.

Henrietta came back promptly the very next day and every day after that for the next two years as the bar's cleaner, Mr. Hennessey's wife eventually coming around to the idea and actually becoming fond of Henrietta, too. In time, as she grew older, Henrietta naturally progressed to being a waitress, and then Mr. Hennessey had allowed her to try her hand at being a twenty-six girl, for which she was very grateful, as it meant more money that she could then hand over to her mother. As a twenty-six girl she got a percentage of the house's profits for the night as well as any side tips she collected. Mr. Hennessey was happy to share the profits, as he knew it was Henrietta who had slowly boosted his clientele, word of the pretty twenty-six girl at Poor Pete's getting around. Many men showed up each week just to be the object of her smile or the receiver of a little wink before they trudged home to their own wives or lonely beds. There were only a few times that anyone had tried an advance on Henrietta, having drunk a bit too much, and then Mr. Hennessey had thrown them out without a moment's hesitation.

In truth, a caress on the arm or a pat on the bottom never really bothered Henrietta that much, but Mr. Hennessey objected in the strongest of language, having grown fiercely protective of her as time had worn on, like the father she no longer had. Henrietta, in turn, trusted him completely. He was one of the few men who never tried to take advantage, never looked at her in a suggestive way, never let his fingers stray.

She had grown used to men staring at her, not that she particularly enjoyed it, but she did enjoy the doors it seemed to open, to the great annoyance of her mother, who preferred what hard work could get you in this world rather than what usually came from having a pretty face. Henrietta, too, would have preferred to get by on her wits alone, but times were hard, and she figured that she had to use what she had been given. Her mother seemed to resent her good looks, however, perhaps because they reminded her too much of her father, Henrietta reasoned. She missed him terribly, but they weren't allowed to talk about him; her mother forbade it.

Though her mother might think otherwise, Henrietta was no stranger to hard work, often taking the morning shift as a waitress at various restaurants—although she had lost count of how many—before reporting to Poor Pete's each night. The problem was not in procuring a job, which seemed to plague the rest of the country; it was in keeping the job. No sooner had she learned the ropes somewhere than she would inevitably be fired for slapping some greasy owner or telling off the cook for pinning her up against a wall for a "little smooch" when he thought no one was looking. Inevitably, then, when she turned up back at home before she was due, her mother would moan, "Oh, Hen, not again! What'd you do this time? Why can't you ever just get along? A girl like you should be able to keep a job!" and before Henrietta could explain fully, her mother would hand her one of the crying twins while she went to tend to the other one.

But that was just the problem, Henrietta would sigh resignedly to herself as she awkwardly attempted to rock the crying baby in her arms. She wasn't that kind of girl. Several times she had tried to explain to Ma that men had tried to take advantage, but her mother usually responded with something like, "Well, Hen, that's the way of the world; better get used to it." This always left Henrietta somewhat confused. Surely her mother wasn't advocating that she be a "loose" woman, that she let men get away with fondling her; after all, she was always going on about women who had lost their virtue. But then why the disappointment when Henrietta took the moral high ground? What did Ma really expect of her?

Whatever incoherent message Henrietta got from her mother, she decided early on of her own accord that she would try to remain "good." Isn't that what her father would have wanted as well? And if she didn't, what lay ahead of her? No decent man would take her then, she guessed, and in her heart that was what she wanted, though she didn't exactly want to become her mother, either, trapped in a little apartment with eight kids to take care of. No, she resolved, she would not just "get used to it," as her mother suggested, and would instead let the chips fall where they may.

Mr. Hennessey was always so much more understanding. "Lose another one, did you, girl?" he would ask if she showed up earlier than usual for her shift. "Ah, well, Henrietta. You stick to your guns! Something else will turn up. You wait and see. You've always got a place here, you know."

Henrietta would sadly smile her thanks while she got out the bucket to start the floors. "Yes, I know, Mr. Hennessey," she would say wistfully, wishing her mother would adopt the same attitude. Her mother had never been the same after her father died, and it was almost as if Henrietta had lost two parents that awful night.

Her father had been employed at Arnold, Schwinn & Company on Courtland and Lawndale. He had worked on the line making their world-class Excelsior-Henderson motorcycles, but after the big stock market crash in '29, the dice seemed loaded for him. Two years after the crash, in 1931, with the company dragging along, Frank Schwinn had called together his department heads and coolly announced that they were closing the motorcycle line and focusing only on bicycles for the foreseeable future, effective immediately. Les Von Harmon, along with 452 other men, lost his job that day, and rumor had it that Les, impossibly in debt from gambling, had stood outside the Schwinn mansion on Humboldt and Palmer for hours, hoping to catch a glimpse of Frank Schwinn to beg for his job, any job. After hours of waiting, he apparently gave up and made his way to Poor Pete's, where he drank himself to near-unconsciousness and then stumbled back to the factory and hung himself in the maintenance shed.

Father Finnegan at St. Sylvester's had been surprisingly very kind, recording Les's death in the parish record book as heart failure and allowing him to be buried with full rites in the cemetery as a favor to Ma. He and several ladies from the bereavement committee had often visited Martha Von Harmon after that, offering what help they could, but Ma was fiercely independent and refused their prayers and sympathy, though she was forced from sheer desperation to take the collection they had brought.

They had likewise received a note of condolence from Arnold, Schwinn & Company, but nothing else. Ma had thrown it into the fire. While Les had been alive, they had at least enjoyed a certain level of respectability, living in the company apartment building on Humboldt in Logan Square on Chicago's northwest side, not too far from California and Milwaukee. It was a unique neighborhood in that it was a quite sought-after address of some of the city's more wealthy, with their large mansions surrounding Palmer Square proper, and yet it was also home to various poor immigrants and laborers living in the surrounding streets.

Though the Von Harmons themselves were working-class, Les Von Harmon had often entertained his brood with stories of how, back in the old country, somewhere called Alsace-Lorraine, the Von Harmons had been part of the landed class, the "gentry," as he called them. In fact, he had delighted to tell them, they were almost a part of what one could call the ruling class and had enjoyed a sophisticated existence. Les frequently regaled them, as they ate their meager suppers, with stories of their lost wealth and the luxury they had once enjoyed. That is, until Les's great grandfather had thrown it all away, so the story went, when he fell in love with an American woman whom he met while she traveled through the Alps with her family. The young couple, unable to live without each other, had eloped and ended up in Chicago, attempting to create a new life, which had been difficult without any money or family to speak of. But they had toiled on, happy at least in their love, until the present-day Von Harmons had taken the stage, though Les and Martha's union was perhaps not so romantic as their predecessors'.

Ma had usually rolled her eyes whenever Pa told the story of their aristocratic roots, but Les had taken great pride in it, which was why it seemed all the more tragic somehow when that pride wasn't enough to sustain him at his own moment of crisis. Les, it seemed, had perhaps taken after his great-grandfather more than he realized and had chosen to escape, desperate, from the only world he knew, to the great sorrow of those left behind.

After Les's death, the Von Harmons had been consequently reduced to extreme poverty and had had to move to a smaller apartment on Armitage with just four rooms. At least the ladies from St. Sylvester's left them alone now, Ma had said. She possessed a stubborn pride of her own, though she never spoke that much about her own family, saying that it really didn't matter where she was from. Something always told Henrietta, though, that perhaps she had once come from money. Just the way she held herself and the way she spoke certain phrases seemed different somehow from their neighbors, as if she were from another world, too.

When Les died, Martha was just one month pregnant with the twins, never having had the chance to even tell him she was expecting. Unable to go out to work after they were born early, whimpering into the world, she had taken in mending and washing and had instead sent Henrietta out to be a cleaner, at least to begin with. Elsie,

Henrietta's younger sister by two years, left school as well and managed to get a job sewing at Dubala's Tailor Shop around the corner. Eugene, just thirteen at the time, was still in school, as were Eddie and Herbert, while Jimmy and the twins, Doris and Donny, were at home with Ma. Henrietta, being the eldest, was of course the one upon whom Ma relied the most for their meager income and to go down to the armory each month on North and Kedzie to stand in line for the free food given out by government agents to the city's masses after the country had plunged into the Depression. Ma just couldn't bear to hold her hand out, but she compromised with her better feelings and allowed Henrietta to go in her place. Henrietta didn't really mind. In fact, she could never understand why her mother balked so at getting free food—all the neighbors did it—and it was a chance, as they all stood in the long lines, to exchange goods or strands of gossip while they waited, though it had admittedly been difficult at first.

Though only young when she first started going, Henrietta had quickly become aware of a certain stigma that seemed to have attached itself to them in reference to her father's suicide. As time went on, she had learned to ignore any whispered murmurings in the armory line, brushing them off with the appearance of nonchalance. She never mentioned the stares and the whispers to her mother, however, who would not have failed to see the ridiculous irony in the situation, the supposedly once-great Von Harmons brought low by the selfishness of a weak man. Somehow, though, Ma seemed aware of the stigma anyway, which perhaps was a reason for her predilection for staying indoors, a habit over the subsequent years that began to border on reclusiveness.

The assumed attitude of indifference that the young Henrietta had developed, combined with her natural flair for the dramatic, proved rather helpful for her, however, in the various jobs she seemed to find, or, rather, which seemed to find her. Two summers ago, for instance, she had worked during the day for a Dutch rubber company at their booth at the World's Fair before her shift began at Poor Pete's. All that was required of her was to wear a Dutch girl costume and hand out neatly printed fliers extolling the virtues of said rubber company. It was wonderfully easy, though it took an age to get down there on the streetcar as well as to braid up her hair and tie it in loops. It was worth it, though, as she had gotten to see the whole fair on her lunch breaks and because it had led to yet another job.

As the fair was winding down at the end of the season, a man had approached her as she stood handing out fliers and had asked if she would come work for him at Marshall Field's as a curler girl. Henrietta had been hesitant at first, not knowing what a "curler girl" was, but in the end she had agreed to come on a Wednesday morning, the one day she had off each week from the fair, to investigate. She was immediately put at her ease as the job itself seemed innocent enough. All she had to do was look pretty and demonstrate to customers how to apply Baldwin's new hair curlers on a willing assistant. Her model, it turned out, was a girl named Polly, who luckily—but unbeknownst to the customers—already had naturally curly hair.

Henrietta loved performing in front of this built-in audience and found that she had a bit of talent for the stage, never mind that she wasn't particularly skilled as a hair stylist, and Polly became what Henrietta never seemed to have time for, a friend. Henrietta still worked there on Saturdays before heading over to Poor Pete's, and it was Polly who was now encouraging her to try being a taxi dancer with her instead of working at Poor Pete's as a twenty-six girl. Henrietta considered this prospect yet again as she carried out the second round of drinks, glancing back at Mr. Hennessey as she did so. She couldn't imagine leaving him after all he had done for her, and yet it was hard to ignore the money Polly claimed to make.

"You do as you like," Polly had said about a month ago as they shared a seat on the elevated train headed north from State Street, where Marshall Field's flagship was anchored, "but I don't know how long you're going to waste your life in that dump."

"Polly!" Henrietta said with mock irritation. "It's not a dump! It's quite charming, actually!"

Polly grinned as she blew her cigarette smoke straight up above them. Polly reminded Henrietta of a pixie of sorts—petite, with blond curly hair cut short just above her shoulders, and with fine, delicate features, not unlike Carole Lombard. She wore heavy mascara, which made her lashes look unusually long and accented her big brown eyes perfectly. "Really? News to me! Even the name's awful. Poor Pete's? Come on, Hen! Come to the Promenade with me. The music's swell, and Mama Leone's always looking for new girls; you'd be perfect. You'll make loads more money . . . isn't that what you're always on about?"

"But I've told you, I can't—"

"Yes, yes, I know. You can't dance very well. But it's like I've said, it hardly matters. It's not Buckingham Palace. Most of the clods that come in there just want to hold a pretty girl in their arms for a few minutes. Nothing to it!"

"Yes, but . . . Mr. Hennessey. I just don't know . . ."

"Look, doll," Polly said, getting serious. "You've got to look out for yourself, you know. You don't worry about Mr. Hennessey; he can look after himself. You worry about you and all those brothers and sisters of yours."

Unfortunately, she had a point. "Maybe. I'll think about it."

"Well, don't think too long; you don't know when a good thing might pass you by," Polly said, standing up to get off at her stop in Lincoln Park. "See you next Saturday, then," she added, giving a quick wave before stepping off the train. Henrietta watched her blend into the crowd before the train pulled away to head north toward Logan Square. She envied Polly sometimes, living alone in her own rooms, with apparently no family or cares to weigh her down. She was her own woman, it seemed, able to come and go as she pleased. Henrietta had sighed as the train lurched forward. It wasn't just that she couldn't dance well or that she didn't want to be unfair to Mr. Hennessey, though both of those things were true; it was that she wasn't sure she wanted to go down the road of being a taxi dancer. Wasn't there something wrong with dancing with men for money? Mightn't it lead to more unsavory things?

She had put Polly off for weeks, but as Mr. Hennessey counted out the night's takings on the bar after the last man had stumbled out, she winced at her little pile and knew that Ma would be disappointed tomorrow. She had made a few dollars in tips, but it wasn't much.

"Sorry, girl," Mr. Hennessey said as he slid his pile of change off the bar and plopped it into the hulking black cash register at the end of it. "It'll pick up. Just gotta give it some time. Just gotta wait for the cops to back off."

Henrietta felt a burst of anger as she slipped her share of the money into her dress pocket next to her notebook. Didn't the cops have anything else to do? Shouldn't they be out catching gangsters or some such people instead of breaking up twenty-six games in corner bars on side streets? It just seemed unfair, wrong somehow.

"I know, Mr. Hennessey," she said, giving him a weak smile as she slipped on her coat and wrapped a scarf knitted by Elsie around her neck. "See you tomorrow."

As she walked home in the freezing January night, however, she ruminated on what Polly had said. Perhaps she should listen to her. Christmas had been terrible this year. Not only were there no presents except a bar of chocolate and an orange in each of their stockings, which she herself had insisted on buying, but the flu had hit them hard. Herbert had nearly slipped away from them to join Pa in his bed in the graveyard, and Eugene was still very weak. He had also quit school this year but had so far only found work as a box burner behind some of the shops along Milwaukee. He had been hoping to get on at Sulzer's, the electrics factory on Western, but each time he inquired, he was told there was nothing yet. Ma kept urging him to ask for a job at Schwinn, seeing as it was the least they could do, but Eugene always refused. He was generally quiet, but he could be stubborn as well. So far, the twins had escaped the flu, but when Henrietta had left for work tonight Ma was fussing over them because she thought they might have a low fever. Henrietta prayed it was nothing serious and resolved to stop by Gorski's tomorrow to see if they had any beef soup bones so that Ma could make them a beef tea. The money in her pocket wouldn't go far, though. She sighed and remembered that their charge bill at Schneider's was higher than it had ever been. The last time she had been in, Mr. Schneider had given her a look, something between frustration and pity, as he agreed to put the small pile of things she had set on the counter on their tab once again.

She could kick herself now for buying the oranges; she should have gotten them each just a chocolate bar for Christmas. Ma had told her at the time that she was being extravagant, but she hadn't listened. As she turned the corner onto Armitage, Henrietta decided reluctantly that she simply couldn't wait any longer for business to pick up at Poor Pete's; she was going to have to put her reservations aside and go see about the taxi dancer job.

The problem was what to do about Ma.

CHAPTER 2

As expected, Polly had been delighted when Henrietta had turned up inquiring about a job the very next week before the Promenade had opened for the day. Polly had happily led her across the dance floor to the tables at the back where Mama Leone, the floor matron, could be found. Mama Leone had a tiny office in the backstage area, but she preferred instead to sit at one of the tables in the elevated back row, just off the dance floor, where she could presumably see the whole expanse of the hall, thereby keeping better tabs on the girls. In reality, however, she spent more time reading cheap novels and smoking.

As they approached the table littered with various newspapers, empty highball glasses, and ashtrays, Mama Leone looked up, annoyed, from the crossword puzzle she was attempting.

"Who's this?" she asked with a scowl, peering at Henrietta. She reminded Henrietta of a bulldog of sorts, short and squat with rolls of fat around her neck and bottom teeth that protruded out beyond her mouth in a permanent sort of grimace. "Whoovya drug in now, Polly?"

"This is Henrietta, the girl I was telling you about. She's wondering if you have any openings."

"Can't she speak?" Mama Leone asked, settling back heavily into her chair to look Henrietta over.

Henrietta held out her hand to shake Mama Leone's. "Pardon me, Miss . . . Miss Leone," Henrietta stumbled. "My name is Henrietta Von Harmon. Pleased to meet you," she added nervously.

Mama Leone did not take Henrietta's outstretched hand but instead looked at it with a type of disgust. "No need for niceties. Or brown-nosin', for that matter. What'd ya say yer name was? Henrietta? That'll do. And it's Mama Leone to you; I'm no 'Miss.' Never was."

Henrietta lowered her arm and awkwardly folded her hands in front of her, feeling Mama Leone's gaze upon her.

"Turn," she barked.

Bewildered, Henrietta looked at Polly for direction, who twirled her finger in a circle to show Henrietta what was expected.

Slowly, then, Henrietta spun around and looked back at Mama Leone hopefully.

"How old are you?"

"Twenty," Henrietta lied.

"The truth."

Henrietta felt her face grow warm at having been discovered in her attempt at a lie. "Alright, I'm nineteen. Honest."

"Ever work as a taxi dancer?"

"No."

"But she's a twenty-six girl!" added Polly quickly.

"What's that matter?" Mama Leone said, still staring at Henrietta.

"Just that, you know, she's used to working with the public . . . with men . . ." Polly's voice trailed off.

"You'll do, I suppose," Mama Leone said, glancing back at her crossword. "There's no hanky-panky, though," she said looking up at her again sharply. "Got that? That's what you want, there's other places."

"No, of course not," Henrietta replied nervously. "I . . . I prefer it that way."

"Yeah, I'll bet," Mama Leone said sarcastically.

Henrietta felt herself blush, but she did not respond with the angry retort that had come into her mind.

"When can you start?"

"Any time, I suppose."

"Tomorrow night, then. Polly, you show her what to do."

Excitedly, Polly grabbed Henrietta's hand to lead her to the backstage lounge, but Henrietta merely bit her lip, stunned that it had been that easy and wondering if this was what she really wanted after all.

"Wait . . .," she said, turning back toward Mama Leone. "Don't you want to know if I can dance?" she asked.

"What the hell does that have to do with anything?" Mama Leone answered irritably, looking up from the crossword she had already returned to.

"Told you," Polly whispered as she led her away to show her where she could store her hat and purse and change shoes.

"But that's so soon . . . what am I going to tell Mr. Hennessey?"

"Oh, God, why are you always so worried about him? You're becoming an awful bore, Hen," Polly had said.

As it turned out, Mr. Hennessey was very understanding when Henrietta told him the next day, which somehow made it worse. She had slowly made her way to Poor Pete's that morning and had sat opposite him at the bar as he went through his morning routine of unlocking the cash register and lining up glasses near the taps.

"Well, I figured you wouldn't stay 'round here forever," he had said with a wry smile after she broke the news. "Just glad you stayed with me for as long as you did."

"Oh, Mr. Hennessey, I wouldn't do it if I didn't have to; you know that, right? Maybe if things pick up, I could come back . . ."

Mr. Hennessey sadly laughed. "I don't know if that's ever going to happen, girl, but you're always welcome." He wiped the bar with his towel, thinking. "Don't know what you're gonna tell your ma, though. Thought about that?"

"Over and over," she said glumly, rubbing the ridges on the bar's surface where the varnish had cracked. "I know she'd never approve of me being a taxi dancer; it was bad enough when she found out I was a twenty-six girl," she said, looking up at him. "If it hadn't been for Mrs. Hradek blabbing her mouth off to her, she never would have known."

"What are you going to do, then?"

Henrietta looked at him sheepishly, "Tell her that I got a job at the electrics? Night shift?"

Mr. Hennessey looked at her skeptically. "Think that's really gonna work?"

"Well, what choice do I have? Polly says the hours are very late at the Promenade, later than I get off from here, plus the time it takes me to get back on the trolley or the motorbus, depends on what's running that time of night. It'll also explain the extra money I'll be bringing in. Hopefully," she added with a smile.

"Don't you think she'll find out? I'm sure she knows people who work there."

"Not the night shift. That's mostly men. Oh, I don't know! I'll cross that bridge when I come to it. It's the only thing I can think of right now!"

"Well, good luck to you, girl." Mr. Hennessey had come out from behind the bar and kissed her on the top of the head. "You've always got a place here, remember."

Henrietta couldn't help but wrap her arms around his stout body, trying hard not to cry. "Maybe I could stop by sometimes . . ."

"Sure you can. Hope you do," he said, smiling sadly at her. "Go on, then! Better be off! Don't want to be late on your first day!" he said, attempting to be cheerful.

Henrietta patted his arm. "Thanks, Mr. Hennessey. For everything," she said quietly and walked slowly to the door.

"Good luck," he said with a sad smile, and held up his hand to shield his eyes from the blinding winter light, reflected off the snow piled up outside, that shone in as Henrietta opened the door and slipped out. The door thudded behind her, and the interior of Poor Pete's seemed all the darker to Mr. Hennessey as his eyes readjusted. He sighed, then, and went back to wiping the bar.

It had been strange at first—dancing with men for money—but Henrietta found she rather enjoyed it, actually. She didn't know what she had been worried about; it was terribly fun if she didn't think about it for too long. She had taught herself to see it as Polly did—simply as getting paid for an evening of dancing. It was better than demonstrating curlers or even keeping score for twenty-six, and she made loads more money. She still felt guilty about lying to her mother, though, especially when Ma had been so proud of her when she had told her she had gotten a job at the electrics. Ma had even baked a small cake to mark the occasion, to the great delight of the whole family, except Eugene, of course, who was very grudging in his congratulations, having failed so many times himself to secure work there.

Henrietta left the house at about four in the afternoon now and didn't usually get home until after two in the morning. It was a long day and night, but Henrietta was used to being on her feet. The problem was her clothes. She couldn't very well leave the house all dolled up for a night of dancing when Ma believed her to be working in a factory, soldering radios. After a bit of thought, she had come up with a way to get around it by wearing an old pair of boots and an old flannel shirt and overalls of Eugene's when she left for work and changing into a dress and high heels in one of the back rooms of the Promenade once she got there. Polly had taken her shopping after a couple of weeks of earning some money, and she was able to find three dresses on sale at Kaufmann's that she kept and rotated through at the Promenade, using the sink in the bathroom to occasionally wash them. No one seemed to care that she hung them out to dry in the back storage room or that she kept some of her belongings there. On the contrary, it rather seemed to amuse Mama Leone.

"Hidin' out are ya? Like a gypsy, aren't ya?" she would wheeze in place of a chuckle whenever she saw Henrietta's laundry hanging there.

Henrietta tried to ignore her. Though Polly seemed able to brush off her rough comments, Henrietta found this more difficult to do. Try as she might to figure her out, Mama Leone remained an enigma. When she hired her, Mama Leone had warned Henrietta that there was to be no "hanky-panky," and yet Henrietta had never seen her enforce this policy, seeming instead to turn a blind eye most of the time. Consequently, Henrietta had been shocked on her first few nights by some of the goings on and on one occasion had slapped a man's hand away from caressing her breasts, his hot breath in her ear, causing him to grumble loudly enough for Mama Leone to overhear. Mama Leone had waited for him to move on to a different dancer before taking Henrietta by the wrist and leading her to the side of the dance floor.

"What the hell do ya think you're doin'?" she'd hissed at Henrietta. "He's a regular, ya know!"

"What do you mean? He . . . he tried to rub my . . . rub me! Didn't you say—?"

"Listen, sister. Get this straight. A little feel here and there ain't gonna hurt nobody, see? We've got to keep 'em coming back; make 'em feel special, understand?"

"But I thought you said no 'hanky-panky' . . .," Henrietta felt silly saying those words.

Mama Leone had wheezed out a laugh. "That's not hanky-panky, you stupid girl! I thought fer sure you'd know more than that by the looks of you."

Henrietta wasn't sure she knew what she meant, but she felt she should apologize. "I'm . . . I'm sorry. I didn't realize . . ."

"Well, now you know. Now get back out there," she said, dropping Henrietta's wrist in disgust. "Some girls is never grateful for a job."

Henrietta had then looked across the room in an attempt to find Polly, rubbing her wrist as she did so. She finally spotted her standing over by the bar, her favorite place to loiter when she wasn't dancing. Henrietta was pretty sure she was sweet on Mickey, the bartender. He was a rough Italian character whose hard edge behind the bar was certainly different from Mr. Hennessey's friendly style. He seemed to like Polly, too, but then again, he seemed to like a lot of the girls.

When Henrietta approached, Polly was whispering something to Mickey but stopped when Mickey nodded his head toward Henrietta. Still smiling from what Mickey had just said to her, Polly turned to face Henrietta as she came up.

"No partner?" she asked, surprised. Henrietta was very rarely without one.

"I've just been chastised," Henrietta answered, furtively looking back at Mama Leone, who was already settled back at her table with a novel. "For slapping some idiot's hand for taking advantage. It turns out I'm the one that got reprimanded, though!" she said with disgust.

Mickey laughed, and Polly merely smiled.

"I thought she said no hanky-panky," Henrietta said in an accusatory way.

"She always says that to the new girls. It's some kind of front. But a feel here or there or maybe a quick kiss in a dark corner isn't really what she means," Polly explained. "In fact, she encourages it, as you've found out. She means no going all the way with some chap in the back, for instance."

"What?!"

"Well, as it happens, it has been known to occur," she said, giving Mickey a look.

"Does Mama Leone know?"

Mickey laughed again.

"Of course she knows," Polly explained patiently. "She's willing to allow it, but she gets a cut, if you know what I mean."

"But that's . . . that's like prostitution, isn't it?"

"Some might call it that, but some might say they're simply providing an extra-long dance, if you know what I mean," she grinned. Henrietta felt herself blush and looked over at Mickey.

Smiling to himself, he moved to the other end of the bar, where customers were waiting for drinks.

"Have . . . have you?" asked Henrietta tentatively, just above a whisper.

Polly shook her head. "Naw, it's not for me. Sometimes, though, girls don't have a choice." Her face had looked sad as she said it. "Come on, let's get back on the floor before the ol' bulldog chases us."

Mortified by the knowledge that some of the girls were having relations in the back with the customers, Henrietta reluctantly allowed herself to be led by Polly back onto the floor but was unable to shake the feeling that she was somehow tainted, too, now, just by association, and felt jumpy the rest of the night.

Henrietta quickly learned the ropes from that point on, and at Polly's suggesting, found her own ways of dealing with "gropers," as the girls were wont to call them. To be fair, Henrietta had never minded a little wink or a touch at Poor Pete's when Mr. Hennessey wasn't looking. Indeed, she found she liked the attention from men, even craved it sometimes, but here, without Mr. Hennessey to watch over her, and where attentions were indeed encouraged, she worried that things might get out of hand, and very quickly at that. She did not want to find herself backstage one night becoming absolutely the woman of loose morals her mother seemed to suspect her of already being. It was difficult sometimes, though, if the band was playing something romantic and the man she was dancing with was even the least bit handsome, to not give in to more than innocent flirtatiousness, but Henrietta had only to remind herself, then, of her father to reaffirm her desire to remain virtuous.

To that end, she had already discovered certain strategies that helped. For one thing, she made sure that she always stationed herself at a place on the floor farthest from where the bulldog sat perched behind a cloud of cigarette smoke. If a man's hands did start to roam while they danced, Henrietta made sure to "accidentally" step on his toes and then make a big fuss and apologize loudly for doing so, which usually resulted in embarrassing the culprit in her arms enough to stop any more surreptitious attempts. After that, if they were regulars, they usually went for someone else more obliging. The girls made up nicknames for some of the more arduous—Chatterbox, Ticky, Chummy, Rough Hands, and Casanova were just a few. Henrietta avoided them like the plague.

Polly had been amused by her tactics.

"Well, I don't care what the ol' bulldog says, I'm not letting any man grab at me!" Henrietta had responded.

"Good luck, doll!" Polly merely answered. "But I don't know why you're saving yourself."

Henrietta chose to ignore this. "Aren't there any men that come here just to dance?"

"A few. The shy ones, mostly. Can't get a date or are practicing for their sweetheart. Most of them are just farm boys up from the sticks looking for work. Lonely, I suppose."

"I'll be on the lookout for those," Henrietta said, observing the room with her hands on her hips.

"I prefer the married ones," Polly said absently, patting her hair in place as she observed herself in her compact mirror.

"Married? Why would married men come here?"

Polly had laughed at her naiveté. "Oh, Hen, you've got a lot to learn."

"Places, girls!" Mama Leone shouted.

Henrietta adjusted the little pouch she wore around her wrist to collect tickets in. The band was just finishing their warm-ups as the lights dimmed, and the first men of the afternoon would soon make their way into the Promenade Club, tickets purchased for a dime each jostling in their pockets. Henrietta had been here for almost two months, though it felt much longer. She smiled as she heard the band begin. This was her favorite time, just at the beginning, when the night was still full of potential.

As Polly had promised, the music was an added benefit to the job. She loved hearing all the bands, but the Rhythm Section was by far her favorite. As Mama Leone signaled the two doormen lazily hanging about to open the main doors, Henrietta glanced over at the band, hoping to catch the eye of Artie, the clarinet player. Sometimes when the Rhythm Section stopped for a break, Artie would make his way over to her and buy her a soda. He was always trying to get her to drink something stronger, but Henrietta usually refused, knowing she had to keep her wits about her. She liked the attention, though, and had even let him kiss her once or twice when he had led her backstage. Breathing hard, he had tried to press her for more, shockingly pulling her to him so that she had felt his hardened, excited state through his blue serge pants, but, flustered, she had gently pushed him away. He had been irritated with her then and had angrily sulked until she reminded him that the next set was starting soon, and he had reluctantly slunk back to the stage, lighting a cigarette as he strode off, puffing so deeply that his cheeks hollowed. Still, she was crazy for him, despite his rough kisses and injured sensitivity. She adored watching him play.

"Casanova's here," Polly whispered out of the corner of her mouth. "And he's headed this way."

Henrietta groaned and turned to avoid looking in his direction, only to find Mama Leone staring at them.

"The bulldog's watching," Henrietta whispered back, and both girls falsely smiled at the approaching Casanova as if on cue.

Grinning sardonically, Casanova held up his ticket with an air of superiority as he neared. He was admittedly a fairly good dancer, but his forehead was overly large, making his eyes look small and too close together by comparison. His hair was always greased back, and he sported a pencil-thin mustache, which Polly felt sure he drew on each night. Besides his strange appearance, however, he likewise had an uncomfortable way of grasping his partners too tightly, making it difficult to move, as if he were about to devour them at any moment.

He was making his way over to them, looking right at Henrietta, but before he could reach her, a younger man, almost a boy, really, raced in front of him, his ticket haphazardly in hand as he rushed up to her and held it out.

"First dance?" he panted, looking triumphantly behind him at Casanova, who scowled momentarily before instead turning his attentions to Polly.

Henrietta rolled her eyes. "Oh, Stan," she said putting his ticket in her pouch. "I told you not to waste your money this way. I'll dance with you at home if you like."

"Not a chance," he said as he bashfully held out his arms. "And have all the fellas see? Nah! Not on your life."

As they awkwardly made their way onto the dance floor amidst the other couples, the band imitating Bing Crosby's "You're Getting to Be a Habit with Me" in the background, Henrietta spoke again. "You really don't have to do this, Stan. I can look out for myself, you know."

"I'm not so sure about that! Oh, Hen, why do ya have to work here? Why couldn't you just keep your job at Poor Pete's? That was bad enough, but this?"

Stanley Dubowski was her neighbor one street over, whom she had met one evening coming home on the streetcar after a long day at the World's Fair. She had still been dressed in her Dutch girl costume, too tired to change, with its wide, blue skirt puffed out from the layers of petticoat underneath, and beautiful patterns embroidered on it in rich reds and yellows. On top of the dress, she was required to wear a starched, old-fashioned white apron trimmed with eyelet lace, and her braided hair was pinned up underneath a starched white cap.

Stanley had almost fallen off his seat when he saw her, pinching himself to make sure he wasn't dreaming that a fairy-tale character had come alive, especially when they both got off at Armitage and Kedzie. He couldn't believe his good fortune that they shared the same stop, wondering how he hadn't noticed this divine vision before, and mustered all of his courage to approach this beautiful creature, insisting that he walk her home, lest she fall prey to some unseen dragon that perhaps had come into existence along with her. Amused by his offer, Henrietta, with a quick flash of her dimples, had nonetheless told him "no thanks," and attempted to go on her way. It was obvious to her that he was several years her junior, and, upon first glance, annoyingly resembled an excited puppy, with his short brown hair accentuating the rather large ears that stuck out from under his cap, as he dogged her home, not taking no for an answer.

Though she said very little to him on the walk home, by the end of it he had fallen hopelessly in love with her, a fact which he revealed to her every other week or so. Henrietta, of course, took no notice of him, except when he made a nuisance of himself, which, unfortunately, was often. He had a bothersome habit of popping up out of nowhere as if to protect her from whatever dangers he imagined lay all around her, and she suspected him of secretly following her home from Poor Pete's from time to time. Ironically, he was employed at the electrics in the warehouse on the day shift and often used his precious evenings off to follow her.

"I've told you before, Stan, I need more money," Henrietta said as she twirled him past the stage, glancing up to see if Artie was watching her. "Well, I don't exactly, but Ma does. And, anyway, don't you have anything better to do?"

"That's another thing. Your ma would die if she knew you were here."

Stanley was now familiar with all of Henrietta's family, having introduced himself to her mother and all of her various siblings in an attempt to endear himself to them as a way of strengthening the bond, however imaginary on his part, between him and Henrietta. He was quite the family favorite, bringing sweets for the little ones and offering to run errands for Mrs. Von Harmon.

Suspicious at first, Mrs. Von Harmon had eventually warmed to him and had even begun to invite him in for a cup of coffee from time to time, during which she had, uncomfortably for Stanley, asked all about Henrietta's progress at the electrics. Stanley, not wanting to let his girl down, had been as evasive as he could at first, but then decided to jump over the cliff of morality for his love, and out-and-out lied to Mrs. Von Harmon, telling her how well everyone thought of her Henrietta down at the electrics. He could have left it at that, but, caught up in the deception he was weaving, he related with a sigh of pleasure that Henrietta had just been named the "top solderer"—a position he had just invented on the spot—and had been personally congratulated by the owner of the electrics himself, one Mr. Arthur Cartwright. Mrs. Von Harmon had consequently beamed with pride.

"Stan? Stan!" Henrietta repeated. Sometimes he did that, just seemed to stare off into space, to Henrietta's great annoyance. He still reminded her of a big puppy, always panting around her, it seemed, always wanting her attention. For the most part, she accepted it good-naturedly, but occasionally it annoyed her, like now, when she was trying to work and he was just getting in the way. Or when he went around and had coffee with her mother, which just gave Mrs. Von Harmon one more thing to complain to Henrietta about.

"Stanley was here again last evening," she would say when Henrietta woke the next morning. "Such a nice young man. Thinks the world of you, he does. Might want to think about that, Hen. Don't get many chances like that in life," she would say bitterly.

"Ma! He's just a kid! You do realize that, don't you?" Henrietta would invariably answer. "He's probably around Elsie's age. He should go for her."

Elsie was the second eldest of the Von Harmon family, at the tender age of seventeen, and was still employed as a seamstress in Mr. Dubala's shop around the corner from them. While it didn't bring in much money, at least the job was steady and reliable, much like Elsie herself.

"Well, he's got a man's job and that's all that matters, Hen. Age doesn't come into it," her mother would reply.

"Stan!" Henrietta raised her voice to knock him out of his stupor. "The dance is over! If you don't have another ticket, I've got to move on to the next customer. Mama Leone is watching!" she hissed, releasing herself from him and eyeing the somewhat bemused-looking gentleman standing nearby, clearly waiting for her. "You'll get me in trouble one of these days, Stan."

"Gee whiz, Hen. You really know how to cut a guy up," Stanley said disappointedly.

"Business is business, Stan. I've got to make a living. If you want another dance, go buy a ticket. Otherwise, you'd best be off. Don't you have somewhere to be? I'm sure your mother is wondering why you're late getting home."

"Next!" roared Mama Leone. Stan jumped and backed away slightly.

"Sorry!" he said, nervously looking in Mama Leone's direction as the man waiting took Henrietta in his arms and began dancing with her. Stan watched wretchedly for a few painful moments and then finally slunk off.

Henrietta's new customer was someone she had never seen around the Promenade before. He was definitely not one of the regulars; she would have noticed him. He was about a foot taller than her—just the right height for dancing—and had a nice build to hold onto. He had wavy, chestnut hair that would probably curl up if it weren't for the heavy amounts of hair cream applied to it, and warm hazel eyes that reminded her of a fall afternoon. He was clearly much older than her, a hint of gray showing just above his ears, but Henrietta thought him very handsome just the same. He had an air of authority to him; he reminded her of someone, but she just couldn't place him.

"You'll have to forgive me," he said, his voice deep and resonant. "I'm new to this, so you'll have to inform me if I'm going about it all wrong."

Henrietta smiled up at him. "Oh, you're doing just fine," she said, giving the hand that held hers a little squeeze. It never hurt to give the new ones extra encouragement. She breathed in his smell as he held her close and found it oddly enticing—crisp linen muddled pleasantly with pipe tobacco.

"May I ask your name? Is that allowed?" he asked, attempting innocence.

"It is allowed," she said as he twirled her gently. The band was playing Louis Armstrong's "You Are My Lucky Star," one of her favorites. Tonight was going to be a good night; she could just tell. It always hinged on the first dance of the day, and this one was turning out swell. Stan's didn't count, of course.

"So, are you going to keep me in suspense for the whole of the dance, then?" he asked, a smile lurking behind his eyes.

"It's Henrietta," she said, flashing her dimples. "Henrietta Von Harmon, but most people close to me call me Hen."

"Why on earth would anyone want to compare you to a chicken?" he said with a smile as he neatly spun her again. "You seem much nicer than that."

"Bet you say that to all the girls," Henrietta said smoothly, laughing a bit. Out of the corner of her eye she glanced at his left hand and saw that he wore no wedding ring. She smiled to herself.

"I shall call you Miss Von Harmon, if you don't mind," he said, not unkindly.

Henrietta raised her eyebrows. "That's rather formal! We are dancing, you know!"

"All the more reason, I should think. Besides, I'm a formal kind of guy, at least in the beginning, anyway," he said added, smiling down at her with such a warm, easy smile, as if they were already old friends.

"Well, what's your name, then?" she asked.

"Clive. Clive Howard. At your service."

"I suppose I should call you Mr. Howard, then," she said teasingly.

"Perhaps you should," he said as he twirled her again.

"You're no fun at all!"

"I apologize," he said, with a deferential tilt of his head that made him seem very wise, yet teasing at the same time. Henrietta found it oddly attractive.

"I'll let you off," she answered, giving him a little wink.

"Thank you," he said, coughing uncomfortably through a smile. He was toying with her, she was certain, and she wasn't sure how to proceed.

"Nice place," he said abruptly, looking around, though instead of observing the other couples, he seemed peculiarly interested in peering into the shadows.

"I suppose so," she said, watching him.

"Been here long?"

"About two months."

"Good pay?"

"Better than what I made at Field's or as a twenty-six girl. That's good money, but this is more steady. Don't have to worry about cops interrupting business."

"I see," he grinned at her. "So . . . a taxi dancer, a twenty-six girl, and whatever it was you did at Field's. You don't seem old enough to have had that many jobs, not unless you were only at each for a day or so. How old are you, anyway?"

Henrietta laughed. "Don't you know it's rude to ask a woman her age? And if you must know, I've had plenty more jobs than that!"

"Such as?" he asked keenly.

"Well, I've been a waitress half a dozen times. And two summers ago, I worked the World's Fair. That was a hoot. I had to get dressed up as a Dutch girl every day and hand out fliers. Nothing to it, really. Oh, yeah, and a couple of times I was a coat check girl for Mr. Sneebly. He's a bookie," she said leaning closer to him conspiratorially. "That is, until Mr. Hennessey found out. He was awfully furious. Said I could get in a mess of trouble that way."

"Doubtless this Mr. Hennessey was correct. But where would you have met a bookie?" Clive asked curiously.

"Oh, he used to come in from time to time to Poor Pete's. That's where I worked as the twenty-six girl. Mr. Hennessey banned him after that, but wouldn't you know, right after that the cops started messing with us. Mr. Hennessey was convinced there was a connection."

"There seems to be no end to this Mr. Hennessey's wisdom," he said, an amused look in his eye. "Any side jobs here a girl could pick up?"

"No," she answered slowly, as a disturbing suspicion occurred to her. "Hey! You aren't some kind of cop, are you?"

Clive laughed. "A cop? Nah. Not me. Just a regular joe. Came in for a dance with a pretty girl is all," he said, giving her his warm smile. There was something about him that made her heart beat a little faster. Something that drew her to him in a way she couldn't quite explain.

"I've never seen you here before," she said, trying to play it lightly. "You say this is your first time?"

"Why, yes, as a matter of fact. Thought I'd try my luck, as they say."

"Luck doesn't come into it that much, I don't think."

"No, I suppose you're right," he said thoughtfully.

The dance ended then, and out of habit Henrietta began looking beyond him for who her next customer might be. Before her eyes could settle on anyone, however, Clive had produced another ticket and was holding it out to her. Eddie Duchin's "Lovely to Look At" had started up.

"One more?"

"Why not?" she said, not being able to hold in her smile. "Let's go." She held out her arms to him, and Clive held her more tightly this time.

"Say, you're pretty good, once you get going!" Henrietta exclaimed over the noise of the band. Clive didn't answer. They were very near the stage again, and though Henrietta was oddly enjoying Clive's company, she couldn't resist looking up at Artie, who gave her the slightest of winks. Henrietta smiled and looked guiltily back at Clive, who seemed regrettably to have observed the whole exchange.

"Friend of yours?" he asked calmly.

"In a way," she said, nervously smiling up at him.

"You ever looking for new girls?" he asked.

"Why?" she asked suspiciously.

"Just that my sister's looking for a job."

"Oh, I see; that's why you came in. Looking for a job is all. Funny, I didn't think you were the type to come to a dance hall."

She was vaguely irritated for some reason, but a part of her felt sorry for Clive and his sister. Times were hard, and people were desperate for work. It must be hard for him to ask; she herself had been in the same position many times before. "Well, as it happens," she answered kindly, swallowing her own selfish disappointment, "Mama Leone's always looking for girls."

"She's the boss? This Mama Leone?"

"Yeah, she's over there in the corner, see?" Henrietta indicated with a nod. "At the back table reading the newspaper?"

"Her?"

Henrietta laughed. "'Fraid so. We call her the bulldog. Tell your sister to watch out around her."

"Why's that?"

"Well, she likes to bark if she thinks you're dallying around."

"And she keeps a close watch on the girls, does she?"

"Well, that's just the thing. She says no fooling around, if you know what I mean—no bodies touching—but she turns a blind eye as long as she gets a piece of the action."

"What do you mean?" he asked interestedly.

"Some guys are regulars, you see. They like a little smooch here and there back behind the stage, or more, if you know what I mean . . ."

"Go on," he said, steadily, his eyes narrowing.

"You sure you're not some kind of cop?"

Clive merely stared at her with an arched eyebrow, his head tilted to the side again, and she felt her heart speed up a second time. "You were saying?" he asked, and she couldn't help but go on.

"Well, some girls don't mind a little action because they get little gifts or extra money on the side. You know, it's a way to earn a bit more. They have to give Mama Leone her share, though. In return, she lets them get away with murder. That and she gives them extra work."

Clive looked over at Mama Leone again before looking back at Henrietta. "Such as?"

"I don't know, really. I think waitress jobs, 'cause I heard her talking about costumes once. I made the mistake of asking if she'd consider me for the extra work, but she said I wasn't the type. 'Yer not what they're looking for,' she told me."

"Who's they?"

"Beats me."

The dance was ending, and Henrietta found herself hoping Clive would produce yet another ticket, but he didn't. He merely looked at her for a few moments before saying, "Thank you, Miss Von Harmon. You were lovely," and gave her hand a final squeeze.

"Don't you want another dance?" she said, giving him her best smile that she knew accentuated her dimples.

"I only wish I could. I must get back, though," he said sliding off.

"Another time, then?" she said to him eagerly, even as the next man handed her a ticket so that she had to poke her head around him to see Clive as he backed away, casually holding up one hand in a gesture of farewell.

"Perhaps."

"Tell your sister to try the electrics on Western. Or better yet, tell her to come round here, and I'll put in a good word for her," she called after him.

"I'll do that."

"Next!" shouted Mama Leone, causing Henrietta to jump as she held out her arms to the next man.

CHAPTER 3

By the time Henrietta got home, she had nearly forgotten about her encounter with the intriguing Clive Howard. She had a lot on her mind, and on top of it she was pretty sure Stanley was following her.

She never felt afraid on her walks home, with or without Stan trailing behind, even though she sometimes didn't leave the Promenade until midnight or one in the morning. She let herself into the apartment as quietly as she could, draping her coat on the back of a chair and slipping off Eugene's boots. Despite the short respite from the heels she always left stored in the back room of the Promenade with her dresses, her feet still ached by the time she got home.

She took out her coin purse and tried to quietly dump its contents on the table so she could count them. Before she did so, she stood up, turned on the gas, and lit a match to heat up the old kettle for some tea. Ma always made sure it was full of water before she went to bed and had a mug set out, ready, not out of any kind of thoughtfulness, but so that Henrietta wouldn't have to bang around any more than was necessary and wake anyone.

No matter what she did, Henrietta could never seem to please Ma. Even with the fictional job at the electrics and the increased money coming in, Ma still seemed to find fault with her. As she grew older and her knowledge of the world grew, too, Henrietta found herself wondering from time to time if Ma had been this way with her father, and whether it could have had anything to do with him taking his own life. Had he been so worn down by never being able to please her that he simply couldn't face her when he lost his job?

No, it was too horrible to think like that! Henrietta scolded herself. And yet, she couldn't quite shake the nagging suspicions that crept into her mind, unbidden, from time to time. Perhaps there was something in her that reminded Ma too much of him, so much so that she tended to take out all of the anger and the grief, the utter exhaustion that now constituted her life, on Henrietta alone. Henrietta knew she had been her father's favorite, which perhaps made it worse, while Elsie was her mother's.

Poor Elsie, Henrietta mused, as she poured a dash of boiling water into the cracked brown mug. Pa had always teased that Hen had been born with all the looks and Elsie with all the brains. Both girls had resented that, but secretly Hen much preferred her lot, if her father's words were to be taken seriously. Who needed brains? And anyway, she had often reflected, she wasn't in such short supply of those, either, no matter what her father had teased. Elsie, on the other hand, while not ugly necessarily, had nothing about her that set her off. She was extremely plain, with pale skin, straight dishwater hair and grayish eyes. Everything about her, in fact, seemed gray and washed-out. Henrietta had tried on several occasions to smarten Elsie up, but she simply wasn't that interested. When she wasn't sewing, the younger of the Von Harmon girls preferred to spend her time reading.

"You're never going to get a man that way!" Henrietta would warn her, but to no avail. Elsie seemed completely uninterested in men, except, that is, when Stanley happened to come around, and then her otherwise-dull eyes would strangely light up.

Henrietta let out a deep breath as she plopped a teaspoon's worth of sugar into her mug. The bowl was almost empty, which meant that Ma would soon send her down to the armory. As she absently stirred her tea, thinking oddly of her father, she heard a noise and stiffened, listening, before she realized it was only Jimmy, shuffling down the hall toward her. There were only two bedrooms for all of them. Ma, Hen, and Elsie slept in one bed, with the twins on a pallet near the bed, while Jimmy, Herbert, Eddie, and Eugene slept in the bed in the other room. Jimmy, just five, was Hen's favorite, she had to admit. He rubbed his eyes as he stumbled toward her.

"Is it morning 'ready, Hen?" he asked sleepily.

She held out her arms to him, and he crawled into her lap. She supposed he was a bit too old to be sitting in laps, but he was small for his age and still liked to cuddle. Even though Henrietta had been held by various men all night, it felt good to hold Jimmy and bury her face in his hair, breathing him in and squeezing him tight as he put his little arms around her neck and held his ragged scrap of a blanket up to his nose for comfort, wheezing slightly as he did so. Jimmy had always had a bit of a wheeze to him.

"It's still nighttime, Jim," she whispered. "Plenty of time yet to dream a little dream."

"But all I can think of is scary 'tuff," he whined.

"Tell you what, when you lie down, you go on and think of one happy thought and just keep thinking that, then there's no room for a bad one to crowd in."

"But I don't know what to think 'bout."

"Hmmm. Let's have a think. How about the carnival at St. Sylvester's? I'll take you this year . . . you and all the kids. And I promise to buy you a cotton candy. Each of you!"

Jimmy sat up excitedly. "Honest, Hen? Promise?"

Henrietta smiled at his bright face. "Shhh! Don't want to wake up Ma. Yes, I promise, but you'd better get back to bed now," she whispered. "The sun's almost up and that don't give you much time to lie there all delicious-like and think about the carnival." Eagerly he slid off her lap, then, and tiptoed back to the boys' room, which was anything but delicious, as they all huddled together in one small bed with just a thin blanket on top of them. In the winter, they often resorted to putting their coats on top of them in lieu of proper blankets. It was particularly bad for Eugene, who was almost sixteen, and was growing so quickly that his feet hung off the end of the bed.

Henrietta sighed as she stood up and quietly put her empty mug in the sink. They always needed more money. She already worked six nights a week at the Promenade, but maybe she could pick something else up besides. Maybe she should try another waitress job, she speculated, as she eased into bed next to Ma and Elsie, or maybe she should pick up the lunch shift at the Promenade on weekends as Mama Leone had hinted at. She had been eager to say yes, but was worried what Ma would say, so she had told Mama Leone she would think about it.

She lay tossing and turning, worrying for what seemed like hours before she finally drifted off just as the sun was making its way over the horizon.

It seemed to Henrietta that only a few moments had passed before she heard Ma's voice calling. She opened one eye a tiny bit and quickly shut it again when she saw light streaming through a rip in the curtain that hung listlessly at the one small window in the room. After a few minutes, however, of wishing for something that simply wasn't going to come, namely, a chance for more sleep, she swung her legs over the side of the bed. She tiredly wrapped her thin robe around her and stumbled out to the kitchen, immediately picking up Donny, who sat crying on the floor. Eugene, just finishing up his toast and coffee, didn't look up. Donny quieted enough as she held him for Henrietta to pour a cup of coffee from the pot on the stove.

"You're up then?" Ma said as she stood pressing wet clothes through the clothes wringer, lightly slapping Herbert's hand whenever it ventured too close.

"I work the night shift, Ma. Remember?" Henrietta put in irritably.

Ma merely sniffed. "Mrs. Jonkovic says her young Jacek thought he saw someone who looks just like you coming out of the Promenade last night in the wee hours. He swore it was you, and don't you know Ludmilla Jankovic was pleased as punch to tell me, the ol' witch. Of course, I said it couldn't be you as you're working the night shift at the electrics. Been named top solderer last month, too, I told her!"

Eugene snorted.

Top solderer? Whatever did she mean by that? Henrietta wondered, slightly mystified.

"You better not be playing me for a fool, missy!" Ma said, waving the laundry stick at her.

Something told Henrietta this had to do with Stanley somehow. What kind of nonsense was he feeding Ma? Despite her annoyance, she bit back a smile. "Well, if I'm not at the electrics, Ma, you'll be the first to know," she said with forced disinterest. "And anyway, you should have asked her what Jacek was doing out in the wee hours in the first place." She shifted Donny and lifted the sugar bowl lid.

"It's empty," Ma said bitterly. "You'll have to go down to the armory this morning. Ludmilla says there's a truck coming in. Make yourself useful for a change."

"Not this morning, Ma," Henrietta whined, "I'm supposed to go in early today!" She had decided in the night that she would try the lunch shift. They simply needed the cash. She would somehow have to come up with an excuse to leave the apartment early. "Can't Eugene go, seeing as he's got nothing else to do?"

"I'm going down to the ice factory today, see if they've got anything," Eugene said surlily, "if you must know." He stood up abruptly. "I best get going. I can see when I'm not wanted. Might even try the Pioneer, see if they need someone," he said, giving Henrietta a spiteful look as he slipped on his coat.

"Eugene!" Ma called after him as he banged out. "You promised no billiard halls!" she called after him. When the only response was the sound of him stomping down the stairwell, Ma turned angrily to Henrietta, who had sat down wearily at the table. "Hen! Why do you pester him so? I'm fed up with it!"

Henrietta sighed. "That was hardly pestering him, Ma. Asking him to go to the armory for a change when I've got a job and he doesn't? He should never have quit school. That's what he really likes, and he's been a real sourpuss since then."

Donny began squirming, and Henrietta gently set him down, whereupon he toddled off to presumably find his twin. Henrietta smiled as she watched him go.

The tension momentarily broken, Ma let out a deep breath and said in a rare confiding tone, "You're not the only one that thinks that. Father Finnegan was here again asking."

"Tell him to shove off," Henrietta said hotly.

"Easier said than done, Hen," she said, looking up from the wringer. "It's hard to say no to a man of the Church. Maybe Eugene really does have a vocation."

"Hardly, I would think," Henrietta stood up to pour the dregs of the pot in her mug. "Ever ask Eugene himself?"

"I tried, but he won't talk about it. Says it's none of my business and storms off."

Henrietta made a note that if she had ever spoke to Ma the way Eugene sometimes did, Ma wouldn't have hesitated to slap her across the face.

"I don't know what's to become of him. I really don't," Ma said, her voice wavering uncharacteristically.

"I'll have a word with him," Henrietta said.

"He won't listen to you."

"Sometimes he does, if I catch him in the right mood."

Ma did not respond, so Henrietta stood up and put her mug in the sink. She looked at the back of her mother, bent over the laundry, scrubbing. Henrietta longed to put her arms around her, but she knew from experience that Ma would shake her off, annoyed, so she didn't. "I'd better get going, then, if I've got to go to the armory," she said, walking into the bedroom to change. Ma didn't say anything to stop her but simply kept on scrubbing.

By the time she was on her way to the Promenade, it was already a bit past eleven, the time when the Promenade opened for the day. Mama Leone liked the girls to arrive about fifteen minutes early for their shifts, and Henrietta needed even a bit more time than that each day so that she could hurriedly change clothes. She was sure she would catch hell from Mama Leone, unless, of course, she had forgotten that she had suggested that Henrietta show up for the lunch shift. It had been late last night when she had pulled her aside, her breath more than usually heavy with whiskey.

Henrietta was the first in line to jump off the streetcar, where she had sat eagerly in the very first seat, irritated at its slowness and all the while practicing what she planned to say when she finally got to the Promenade. She headed down Sedgwick toward the gritty brick building on Lincoln Avenue near Armitage that was now a ballroom, though it had started out life humbly enough as a small shoe factory. It was nothing, of course, compared to the elegant Aragon Ballroom over on Lawrence Avenue. Whenever she had a chance, Henrietta listened to WGN's one-hour broadcast from the Aragon, where all the big bands played, but it was a rare treat because she was usually working during it. She had always wanted to see the inside of the Aragon, but tickets were expensive, and a strict dress code was maintained. Nothing she owned seemed fancy enough.

She stared at the back of the Promenade, having decided to exit the streetcar at the top of Sedgwick, near Dickens, and walk down, hoping to sneak in the back door in the alley before

Mama Leone could notice her. She hurriedly crossed the alley and slipped through the doorway, which oddly stood open. She lingered momentarily to let her eyes get adjusted to the dark interior and to listen for Mama's whereabouts. Not hearing her heavy footsteps or heavy breathing, she quickly headed for the little dressing rooms. So far so good, she encouraged herself, looking over her shoulder to see if anyone was behind her, but as she turned back around, she ran right into Polly, who seemed to have appeared out of nowhere.

"Ow!" Henrietta exclaimed, rubbing her head. "Oh, Polly! It's you!

Thank goodness!" Henrietta whispered.

Something in Polly's face, however, told Henrietta that all was not well. "What's wrong, Poll? Did she notice already? I'm just a little bit late, but I'm sure no one's even here yet, anyway. Hey!" she paused, listening, "Why's it so quiet? Why isn't the band playing?"

"Oh, Hen," Polly said, her voice oddly emotional. "She's dead!"

"Who?" Henrietta asked, startled.

"Mama Leone!" Polly whispered. "Someone stabbed her!"

"No! Are you sure?" Henrietta asked, leaning against the wall, her mind racing. "What . . . what happened? Did someone call the cops?"

"Of course someone called the cops!" Polly sounded almost hysterical. "Didn't you see the squad cars in front?"

"No . . . I came in the back so Mama . . ." Her voice trailed off. Mama Leone dead! It couldn't be! She was obviously not Henrietta's favorite person in the world, but still—murder! But why would anyone want to murder a fat old dance hall matron? Actually, Henrietta speculated to herself, she could think of several reasons.

"What happened?" she asked, incredulous.

"No one really knows, I guess. Oh, Hen," she whispered, looking around nervously, "I've got to tell you something."

"And what would that be, ladies?" came a voice behind them, and a uniformed man appeared out of the shadows of the darkened hallway. It was one of the cops! Henrietta and Polly stared at him, frozen.

"Tell you what, why don't you two come along with me. You can tell the boss all about it."

"Why? What have we done?" Polly asked nervously.

"I didn't say you did anything. Just follow me," he said as he pushed past them. "Please," he added with exaggerated politeness. "The inspector wants to talk to all the girls."

Henrietta looked nervously at Polly, who gave her a grim look and turned to follow the cop down the hallway toward what had been Mama Leone's little office. Henrietta had always hated going into the cramped room where Mama Leone had sat in her throne behind a grimy little desk that looked surprisingly like a plant stand to dole out the evening's earnings. The room was dingy and always had a stale odor about it. Henrietta always tried to hold her breath during the whole exchange, but she would inevitably have to breathe at some point, expelling air as she did so. Out of habit, she held her breath but loudly sputtered it out when she saw that it was none other than Clive Howard who sat behind the "desk," calmly looking through stacks of papers scattered everywhere.

"I was wondering when you would turn up," he said matter-of-factly. There was no trace of a smile now, however, as he continued looking over Mama's disorganized mess.

"It's you!" Henrietta said incredulously. "You *are* a cop! You lied to me!"

Slowly he looked up from what he was doing. "Well, if we're being precise, I'm not a cop, I'm a detective inspector. And anyway," he said, standing up and coming around to the front of the desk, "don't look so hurt. I'm sure you would have lied about your age if I'd pressed you hard enough to tell me." He casually leaned against the desk, his arms folded.

Henrietta looked away.

"Oddly, you look different than I remember," he said, his eyes travelling up and down her.

Henrietta looked down at her factory overalls and blushed, having caught the slightest hint of a smirk on his face. It irritated her beyond belief. She was about to speak but thought better of it.

"Sit down, ladies," he commanded them, nodding toward two chairs that the cop from the hallway had arranged. "Thank you, MacKenzie," the inspector said to him, as MacKenzie moved back into position by the door. The girls reluctantly sat down, Polly looking petrified.

"Now, then. Let's start at the beginning, shall we? Your names?"

"But we haven't done anything!" Polly said nervously.

Inspector Howard looked at her carefully. "I didn't say you did. Just a few routine questions, that is, unless you've something to tell me or something to hide, either one."

"That one was whispering she had something to tell her," MacKenzie interjected, pointing from Polly to Henrietta.

"Did she, now? Well, we'll get to that in a moment," the inspector said, putting his finger up to his lips, as if running the possibilities through his mind. "Name?"

Polly hesitated briefly and then said, "Polly. Polly Smith, for what it's worth."

"Got that, Jones?" the inspector said over his shoulder to the officer standing behind him, scribbling furiously on a notepad.

"And this one is Henrietta Von Harmon, if I remember correctly," he said, looking at her for confirmation, which she gave with a slow nod. She couldn't stop staring at him. She couldn't believe he was really a cop! But then again, she had suspected it, hadn't she? Somehow, she felt sad—betrayed—but that was silly, wasn't it? It had just been a dance. Get a hold of yourself, she told herself angrily.

"A little after one, I think . . .," Polly was saying. Henrietta hadn't been listening to the question.

"How about you?" Inspector Howard asked Henrietta. "What time did you leave last night?"

Henrietta struggled to concentrate on last night. "Yes, a little after one, I'd say. We left together," she said, inclining her head toward Polly. "Like we always do." Henrietta suddenly remembered, however, that last night Polly had excused herself and gone back in, saying she had forgotten something, while Henrietta had waited for her outside. She wasn't about to tell that to the cops, though! She glanced nervously at Polly.

"What is it, Miss Von Harmon?" the inspector asked astutely. "Something you remember?"

"No, I . . . nothing," she said, forcing herself to look into his eyes.

He stared at her for a few moments. "You do realize this is a murder investigation?"

"Yes, I . . . I do," she said, bravely managing to hold his gaze for a few more moments before she looked away.

The inspector leaned back and took a deep breath. "Listen, girls, we can do this here or we can do this down at the station, so I suggest you cooperate. Understand?"

Both girls nodded.

"Now, let's go back to the beginning. How long have you two been here?"

Henrietta spoke first. "About two months. Just like I told you last night. I didn't lie about that," she couldn't help add. She read the challenge in his eyes, but he didn't respond.

"And you? Miss Smith?" he said turning his attention to her.

"About two years, I suppose. On and off."

Officer Jones began scribbling again.

"Then you've been here long enough to know if this Leone woman might have had any enemies?" the inspector asked Polly.

Polly shook her head slowly, as if in a trance. "I couldn't really say."

Henrietta involuntarily let out a dry little cough, causing the inspector to direct his attention back to her. He raised an eyebrow for her to continue.

"Well, everyone hated Mama Leone!" she said, exasperated. "I know she's dead and all, but that's the truth, isn't Polly?" she said, looking over at her for confirmation.

Polly nodded. "It is, yes."

Why was Polly acting so strangely? wondered Henrietta. She would have to get to the bottom of this later. Obviously, something had gone on last night. Maybe she knew something. But why not tell the police, then?

"Yes, but enough to kill her?" the inspector asked. "Had she argued with anyone in particular last evening? Think. It could be important. A regular, maybe? One of the girls? A bartender?"

Polly drew in her breath.

"Go on," Inspector Howard urged.

"Well, she did argue with the band last night, with Artie and Al, that is."

"Polly!"

"Well, she did!"

"She has a run-in with them every night; you know that! Them and half the place!" Henrietta argued in defense of Artie. She glared at Polly, but Polly kept her gaze fixed on the edge of the desk in front of her.

"And who is this Artie and Al?"

"They're brothers. Karzan's their last name, but their band's called the Rhythm Section. They play here almost every night," Polly said, picking up speed, as if relieved to have something to say.

"What did they argue over?"

"Money, of course."

"What do you mean?

"They always argued over money. Mama Leone never wanted to pay them, see? She kept stringing them along, always saying she'd pay them the next week. Last night, I guess they'd had enough. Started screaming, they did. Said they weren't comin' back anymore if she didn't pay up. Said she'd be sorry then."

"Getting all this, Jones?" the inspector asked, not taking his eyes off Polly.

"Yes, sir," Jones answered, scribbling away.

"What happened then?" the inspector asked Polly.

"Mama Leone screamed back at them. Called them every name in the book, but then took both of them back here, said she'd pay them since they wouldn't stop their bawlin'."

"They both came back here with her?"

Polly nodded. "I think so."

"Then what?"

"I don't know. I left then."

"Anyone else around?"

Polly paused for a moment. "Just Henrietta, here. We walked out together like we always do. And Mickey, the bartender. He was countin' the till like he always does, then he and Mama usually lock up."

"What time was this?"

"About one, maybe one-thirty, right, Hen?"

Henrietta shrugged her acquiescence, though she was burning with anger at Polly and felt dangerously close to an outburst. "It wasn't Artie!" she said suddenly, no longer able to contain it.

The inspector turned his gaze to her. "And why do you say that?" he asked calmly.

"'Cause he just wouldn't. He's not like that. I . . . I don't think he could kill anyone."

"Oh, you'd be surprised what people are capable of, Miss Von Harmon. What time does the band usually get here?" he asked Polly.

"Usually about ten, I guess."

"They here now?"

"No," Polly said quietly. "They haven't turned up yet."

The inspector turned to Jones and nodded toward the door. "Go round up those two characters," he said. "And see if someone can find this Mickey. Seems he hasn't shown up, either."

"Yes, sir," said Jones, flipping his notepad shut and stepping toward the door.

"Oh, and see if Henderson has located Mr. Mercer yet. All we have so far is a Miami number." Henrietta vaguely recognized the name Mercer as being the owner of the Promenade, though she had never actually met him. She had always thought of this place as belonging to Mama Leone, but of course that was ridiculous.

"Yes, sir," Jones answered, and hurried out.

"You girls know where to find this Mr. Mercer?" the inspector asked, looking at them steadily. Henrietta shook her head and looked over at Polly, who was studying her fingernails in an obvious attempt at nonchalance. The inspector might be buying it, but Henrietta wasn't.

"Course I don't know where Mercer is. Never even met him. Can we go now?" Polly asked in a bored tone. She seemed to have recovered her presence of mind, finally. "I've a terrible headache."

The inspector studied her for a few moments before finally answering, "Yes, I suppose so, girls. We'll let you know if we need to speak with you again. Leave an address and telephone number with Officer Henderson out by the bar in case we need to ask you something else," he said, looking back at the stacks of paper in front of him.

"But I can't!" Henrietta said in a panic, causing him to look up at her again, this time in surprise. "You can't let my mother know I'm here! That I work here, that is. You won't tell her, will you?" she pleaded. "And anyway, we don't have a telephone."

MacKenzie, still in the room, suppressed a smile, and Henrietta expected the same from the inspector, but there was something kind in his eyes as he held her gaze. "No," he said finally, as if he had taken a moment to make a decision. "We won't tell her unless we have to. We'll do our best to keep your secret, won't we, MacKenzie?"

"Oh, aye," MacKenzie answered with a smirk.

"That would explain the overalls, though," the inspector added.

Henrietta blushed uncomfortably.

"What are we supposed to do now?" Polly asked. "Are we closed for the day?"

"I'm afraid so, Miss Smith. This is a crime scene. We have to comb through this place, and I have to speak to every single dancer. And until we can locate this Mr. Mercer, it'll have to remain closed. Don't go far—either of you," he warned.

Still dazed, Henrietta followed Polly through the maze of tiny hallways to the dance floor and spotted what must have been Officer Henderson taking information from some of the other girls who had lined up in front of the bar, busily whispering to each other as they waited. No one, Henrietta noticed, seemed particularly saddened by Mama Leone's death.

"What'd you do that for, Poll?" Henrietta asked angrily when she was sure she was out of earshot of the inspector.

"Do what?" she asked absently, peering impatiently down the line, seemingly eager to give her details so that she could leave. She appeared to be in a terrible hurry.

"You know! Why'd you say that about Artie and Al? You know they didn't do it!"

"I had to! We had to answer their questions, Hen. I'm sure neither of us would appreciate a trip downtown, now would we? Anyway, they did have an argument. That was the truth!"

"Yeah, but they have an argument every night! That doesn't mean they killed Mama Leone!"

"So? The cops'll figure that out eventually."

"But what if they don't!" Henrietta hissed as she and Polly moved a step forward in the line.

"Anyway, I don't know why you're so sweet on Artie. He's a chump, if you ask me. He's not what you think, doll."

"Hey! What's that supposed to mean? And, anyway, Mickey's not such a great catch!"

At the mention of Mickey's name, Polly's flippant mood changed instantly. She seemed nervous again. "Look, Hen," she said leaning closer to her, "I've got to tell you something," she whispered. "Something important . . ."

"What about?" Henrietta whispered back.

"Not here," she whispered as Officer Jones walked by, tipping his hat to the girls in line, causing some of them to giggle. "Come see me at my place when you can."

"Well, how about now? I can't stay here, and I can't go home, so . . ."

"Not just at the moment," Polly said nervously. "I've got to go see someone. But later, okay?"

"Yeah, sure. But what are we going to do until this place reopens? Think Mr. Sneebly's got any work?"

Polly shook her head. "I haven't thought that far."

The girls had reached the head of the line at this point, and after Polly quickly gave her name and address and telephone number, she hurried off, waving a brief goodbye to Henrietta before she pushed open the heavy front door and disappeared.

Henrietta hesitantly gave her information as well and, stepping to the side, mulled over what to do next. It was true what she had said to Polly about not being able to go home now or Ma would surely throw a fit. She was reluctant to leave her dresses and shoes here, however. Who knew how long it would be before the Promenade reopened, if at all? She didn't know much about the owner, Mr. Mercer, never having even seen him before. All she had once heard from Mama Leone was that he was very particular. It seemed unlikely that he would sell the place, seeing as it was always crowded, picking up the overflow from grander places like the Aragon. It seemed more likely that he would just find a new floor matron.

But how long would that take? The safest bet seemed to be to take her things with her, just in case. Looking around surreptitiously, then, to make sure none of the cops were watching, Henrietta made her way back to the dressing rooms to collect her things.

Miraculously, she reached the back room where she had stashed her little wardrobe without running into any of them, though they were scurrying all over the place. She decided not to switch on the lights so as to not draw any attention to herself, but it was difficult to see with what little light streamed in from a tiny, dusty window at the other end of the room. Of course, she had not brought any bag bigger than her handbag with her. So as she stood in front of her three dresses hanging in an old armoire, she wondered how she was going to transport them. They would simply have to be folded and re-ironed; she sighed and moved to slip them from their hangers. Just then, however, she heard the door behind her click softly shut.

She stiffened with fear as a deep, resonant voice said, "I'm glad to catch you alone, Miss Von Harmon."

CHAPTER 4

Henrietta stifled a scream as she turned, peering through the dim light to make out what she perceived to be none other than Inspector Howard standing by the door, his hands in his pockets.

"What are you doing here?" she asked, her voice wavering.

"I could ask you the same thing," he said quietly, raising his eyebrows. "Hiding something?" he asked, looking beyond her to the open armoire.

"No, I . . . it's just my clothes. They're mine! Honestly."

Henrietta imagined she saw a trace of a smile.

"I'm sure they are. Mind telling me what they're doing back here? Weren't you saying something last night about costumes, something on the shadier side?"

Henrietta was silent, nervous fear gripping her. How could she explain? Surely, he didn't think that she . . . ?

"Let me guess. Young girl, parents don't know she's working here. Not respectable, that sort of thing." He started walking toward her. "Let's see, they think you work in a factory, perhaps the 'electrics' I think you mentioned last night. I bet you told them you work the night shift, right? That explains the late hours. Change clothes here," he said casually, nodding toward the armoire. "No one's the wiser." He stopped just in front of her. "Am I close?" he said, grinning condescendingly.

"Just about," Henrietta said, with a subtle toss of her auburn hair, as she tried to control the rapid beating of her heart, unsure if it was caused from fear or from something else entirely. How could he have guessed so easily?

"Not part of this Mama Leone's backstage operation, then?"

"No! I'm not . . . I—" Henrietta stopped abruptly, not wanting to implicate herself and also growing slightly offended at his suggestion.

"What about this Miss Smith?"

"Polly? No, not her. At least I don't think so."

"You don't seem very sure."

Henrietta looked up at him defiantly, "Well, even if I did know, why should I snitch on my friend?"

"Because it might help us catch whoever did this. Mama Leone was murdered, remember? We need to find out who's responsible. The more pieces of the puzzle I have, the better. Please," he added in a slightly softer tone.

Henrietta searched his eyes and found nothing threatening. She let out the breath she had been holding. "Polly's the one who told me all about it. I asked her if she was in on it, but she said it wasn't for her. And anyway, she's sweet on Mickey, so I don't think she would have resorted to that."

"I see," said the inspector, thinking deeply.

"And while we're on the subject," Henrietta said earnestly, "it wasn't Artie and Al!"

"Well, that's a relief. Simply because you say so, I can scratch them off the suspect list."

"Suspects! Inspector, honestly, Artie doesn't have it in him!" She wanted to add that it was probably Al and his big mouth that had done most of the arguing with Mama Leone (Artie had complained about him often enough to her), but in the end she thought better of it and kept silent.

"My, my, Miss Von Harmon, you're quite knowledgeable," the inspector said, pushing his hat back to the crown of his head. "Lucky I stumbled upon you. Again, let me attempt a guess. Am I correct in assuming this Artie is the clarinet player I saw you eyeing last night? And based on the fact that he's probably bought you a couple of drinks here and there, you're convinced he's innocent."

Henrietta blushed. "Well, he is! I just know it! And anyway, they were just sodas!"

The inspector laughed outright.

Henrietta's eyebrows wrinkled. "What's so funny?"

"You are," he said, composing himself again. "You're a strange commodity."

"Gee, thanks," she said, her hands on her hips in an attempt to appear indifferent. "Bet you say that to all the girls."

"Not usually, no," he said smiling. "Listen, what are you going to do now?" he asked after a brief pause.

"What do you mean?" she asked suspiciously.

"I mean for work, until this place reopens?"

"After the cops are finished messing about, you mean?" she said, getting bolder.

"Yes, in a manner of words."

Henrietta shrugged. "Beats me. Haven't thought that far," she said, echoing Polly's words of just a few minutes ago. "Maybe go back to Poor Pete's, but now that you know I'm a twenty-six girl, you'd probably follow me and break it up. I couldn't do that to Mr. Hennessey."

"No, that's true. Too risky," he agreed facetiously.

Catching his amused tone, Henrietta looked him over for a moment before turning back toward the armoire, trying instead to concentrate on pulling the dresses off their hangers. He was obviously bent on teasing her.

"Why don't you do a little job for me?" he finally asked quietly.

Henrietta paused in her work, wondering what he could mean by a "little job." Purposefully, she did not turn around to face him but, swallowing hard, asked, "Such as?"

"Nothing too far off the mark," he explained languidly. "I want you to try to get in as an usherette at the Marlowe, downtown on Monroe. Ever hear of it?"

Henrietta let out deep breath, not even realizing that she had been holding it, and turned around to face him. "No," she said, shaking her head.

"That was quite a sigh," he commented, his eyebrow raised again. "What did you think I was going to say?"

"I don't know," she blushed.

"The Marlowe is a burlesque theater," he said, looking at her steadily.

"I see," she said, trying not to appear disturbed. So, he did think she was capable of more unsavory acts.

"It's not what you think."

"How can it not be?" she asked, with more misgiving in her voice than she would have wished.

"It's just short-term. You'd be undercover, as it were."

Henrietta didn't say anything, but just looked at him, trying to decide if she should feel flattered or insulted.

"Listen," he attempted to explain, "we've been trying to get a girl into the Marlowe for a long time, but no luck. Obviously, we can't rig it. The girl we put forward has to be good enough to get it on her own. And with a girl like you, now . . . well, we just might stand a chance."

"How do you mean?" Henrietta asked, leaning toward the supposition at the moment that she should feel insulted. He obviously believed her loose and cheap enough for the job.

"Just that you're well-versed in hiding things, playing a double role, that is. And you've got this rather perfect combination of innocence and flirtatiousness, shall we say. Quite charming—if you go for that sort of thing," he said somewhat hastily.

Henrietta wondered what he meant by that and felt the heat creeping up her face. It was humiliating to think she was so easily read, so easily found out, that her attempts to toy with him last night had probably been obvious to him and—worse (she was loath to admit to herself)—that they had clearly fallen short of sparking any interest.

The inspector cleared his throat. "That and more so because you are really quite lovely. Lovely enough indeed to perhaps catch even Neptune's eye."

Henrietta looked up quickly, trying to ignore the quickening of her pulse at him calling her "lovely." Attempting to sound aloof, she asked coolly, "Who's Neptune?"

"Neptune's the owner of the Marlowe, where we suspect many not-so-nice things happen behind closed doors. We need a girl inside to scout it out for us, see if you notice anything untoward."

"Untoward?"

"Anything unusual, suspicious."

"Do you always talk like that?" she asked. There was something definitely strange about him, Henrietta thought.

"Does it bother you?" he asked with what Henrietta perceived to be the slightest upturn at the corners of his mouth.

"No," she answered deliberately, "but you don't really sound like a cop."

The inspector paused, absorbing that. "Coming from you, I think I'll take that as a compliment," he said, taking his hands out of his pockets and folding his arms in front of him. "But you don't really sound like a taxi dancer, either."

"What do you mean by that?" she asked, slightly irritated. "And besides, how would you know? That is, if any of what you said last night was true about never coming to a place like this before."

"Oh, that was true, all right," he said with an annoying smile. "Just a guess, you might say."

Henrietta looked intently at him for a moment and then looked away. "What would I have to do exactly?"

"Not much more than you're doing now, I should think. Smile, flirt, show men to their seat, get them drinks, that sort of thing."

"So, I wouldn't have to . . . to dance . . . take things off?" she asked nervously.

"No, no. Certainly not," he laughed. "You'd just be an usherette."

"Is it dangerous? I mean, I've heard bad things about places like that . . ."

"Not too, I should hope. We'll have men outside all the time, watching, so I shouldn't worry."

Henrietta tried to think quickly. It was true she needed a job, but wasn't this taking it one step too far? Taxi dancing had been difficult enough for her to come to terms with.

"Why should I?" Henrietta finally asked.

"Because I suspect you need the money," the inspector answered, too smoothly for her liking. "We'll pay you double what you make here."

Henrietta bit her bottom lip. Double! It was very tempting...

"Listen," the inspector went on, trying a different tack, "you want to help prove this Artie, and Miss Smith, for that matter, are innocent, right?"

"Polly? You don't suspect her, too, do you?"

"Maybe. There's something she's not telling us," he said, looking at her again with those . . . those eyes.

Henrietta remembered then that Polly had gone back in last night alone and that she had told her that she had something important to tell her. Surely, she hadn't killed Mama Leone, though? Why would she have? Henrietta tried to keep her face a blank in front of the inspector, as he seemed to have an unsettling way of reading her mind.

"Well, what does Mama Leone's death have to do with the Marlowe, anyway? How would working there for you help prove their innocence? Which is ludicrous, by the way," she put in with what she hoped was the right amount of indignation. "You've got nothing on them!"

"Perhaps not. But Miss Smith is holding back; I'm sure of it, and this Artie and Al—and Mickey, while we're at it—have all flown the coop. Doesn't look so good, does it? And I've just got this hunch that Neptune may have had something to do with it."

"Neptune? But why?"

"It's not important," he said, putting his hands comfortably back in his pockets. He cocked his head to one side and looked at her intently. "So, will you do it?"

Henrietta thought quickly. Surely, he didn't really suspect Artie or poor Polly, did he? Was this merely a bluff to get her to do his dirty work—perhaps some other "job" he had in mind? Why should she help him? And yet, what choice did she have? Ma would kill her if she ever found out she was working in a risqué theater as even so much as a ticket girl, but on the other hand she couldn't go home like this. Not again.

She needed a job, and double the money sounded too good to be true. And she had to admit that it sounded rather exciting; she'd practically be a spy! But what about when it was all over, then what would she do? She would have to figure that out when the time came, she told herself and pushed that worry to the side just as another possibility dawned on her.

"Would I report back to you?" she tried to ask as innocently as possible.

"Why, yes," he grinned at her. "Of course you would."

Henrietta smiled to herself and turned back to the dresses. "Oh, all right," she said, attempting a bored voice. "I suppose I'll do it. I'll try, anyway. Maybe I won't even make the audition."

"Oh, something tells me you will," he said behind her. "The audition is in two days' time. Nine a.m. sharp. Monroe and Riverside, near Canal."

"Got it," she said, determined not to look back again, but she couldn't resist and turned to him, her dresses all in her arms.

"Do you need help getting those home?" he asked genuinely.

"No. I've got some things to do first."

"I see. Well, good luck, then, Miss Von Harmon. I'll be in touch. I presume you're on your way to warn Miss Smith, so say hello from me."

Henrietta blushed at the fact that he had seen through her again! She opened her mouth to deny that she was planning on heading over to Polly's, but he was already out the door, having left as silently as he had come in.

CHAPTER 5

Henrietta struggled under the weight of the dresses. She had managed to get most of her belongings into a dusty old carpetbag she had found in the dark recesses of the Promenade's back room, but she still carried two of the dresses draped over her arm, which had proved decidedly awkward on the motorbus over. Luckily, she was not in heels on top of it but was still in Eugene's boots, having come straight from the Promenade dressed as she was. When she had emerged from the backroom, balancing her load with not a little difficulty, she had looked around, hoping to catch another glimpse of Inspector Howard, but not seeing him, she had left and headed for Polly's.

Polly lived at Mildred and Wrightwood, on the upper floor of a three-flat in Lincoln Park, a decent enough neighborhood, mostly factory workers. Henrietta had only been over to Polly's a handful of times, usually after the curler demonstrations on

Saturdays if they had ever happened to get off early, having not attracted a large enough crowd to prolong the demonstration. It was a tiny apartment, just a few rooms, but Henrietta had envied the fact that she had the place, and especially a bed, to herself. Though Henrietta had asked from time to time, Polly did not often speak of her family, and Henrietta got the feeling they either did not exist or perhaps lived far away.

Henrietta stood outside Polly's back door, breathing heavily after climbing three flights under the weight of the carpetbag, and grateful that Polly hadn't opened the door immediately upon her knocking, as it gave her a chance to catch her breath. The back stairs, leading up from the alleyway, were not enclosed, and Henrietta relished the cold air that whipped past her. It had been a warm March so far, but the air was still frosty at times. Polly always used the back stairs, saying that the front door of the building often stuck and that, likewise, the lock on her own front door was loose and didn't always like to open. Once, she had told Henrietta, she had been trapped in the front stairwell for a couple of hours before her downstairs neighbor had arrived home and heard her calling for help. After that ordeal, she had resorted to using the back stairs no matter what the weather.

Henrietta knocked again, this time louder. "Polly!" she shouted and leaned her ear toward the door. Perhaps she wasn't home yet from her mysterious errand. Henrietta had just resigned herself to sitting down on the top step to wait for her when she thought she heard the click of Polly's heels on the other side.

"Who's there?" came Polly's voice, sounding almost shrill.

"It's me, Henrietta!" she shouted, moving back toward the door. "Open up, will you?"

The door opened a tiny bit, and Polly peered out. She looked as if she might have been crying. "Poll, what is it?" Henrietta asked anxiously.

"You alone?" Polly asked, looking out onto the tiny porch as if someone might be standing behind Henrietta.

"Course I'm alone," Henrietta said, puzzled, turning to look behind her as well.

"You better come in," Polly said, opening the door wider for her. "What's all this, then?" she said as she observed Henrietta's bundle. "Moving in?"

"Not quite. May I?" she said, nodding toward the little table in the kitchen. Not waiting for an answer, she deposited the bag on the table and draped the dresses over a chair. "God, that's better," she said as she looked over at Polly, who had her arms nervously crossed in front of her.

Polly's hand appeared to tremble a bit as she lifted her cigarette to her lips for a deep drag.

"You look terrible! Like you've seen a ghost or something," said Henrietta, dismayed that the normally cool, sarcastic Polly was in any way disturbed. "What's going on, Poll?"

Polly took another deep drag of her cigarette and shrugged. "Don't really know where to start, doll." She looked away then, as if she were about to cry again.

"Come on, let's sit down," Henrietta suggested, not knowing what else to do. "You need a drink. Got any whiskey or anything?"

Polly nodded. "Under the sink."

"You sit down. I'll get it," Henrietta said, gesturing toward the "front room," which Polly had cleverly created by hanging a thick curtain to divide the one long room into a kitchen and tiny dining area on one side and a parlor of sorts on the other. Usually, though, Polly had one of the panels tied back to make it easier to get in and out, and she ducked slightly under one of them as she went in and sat down stiffly in the worn armchair nearest the radio.

Henrietta meanwhile hurried over to the sink and pulled back the thin blue-and-white checked cloth that hung below and found a cheap bottle of whiskey hiding there. She took two glasses from the cupboard above and quickly went back to the front room, where she poured them each a glass and handed one to Polly, who seemed almost startled by it, so lost was she in her own thoughts.

Henrietta sat down opposite her and crossed her legs. Resting one elbow on her knee and cradling her chin in her hand, she studied Polly carefully. When she didn't speak, however, Henrietta finally broke the silence. "What's going on, then, Polly?" she asked.

Polly didn't respond but simply took a large drink of her whiskey, gasping at the burn as it went down.

"Poll, you don't know anything about . . . about Mama Leone's death, do you? You . . . you went back in last night. Did you see something?"

Polly looked at her and nodded slowly, seemingly relieved that Henrietta had somehow guessed the source of her woes. "I did go in. I wanted to ask Mama Leone something. Never mind what it was about. I . . . I waved to Mickey as I went past the bar," she said absently, trying to recall all of the details of the night. "He was alone, counting the money. I walked past to her office. I knew she was probably still there; she had just paid us all out. The light was on"—she stopped to take a drag of her cigarette—"and I . . . I heard voices. Threatening her, it sounded like—"

"Not Artie and Al?" Henrietta asked, hesitantly.

"For God sakes, no! It wasn't those two. It was someone else, two of them, I think. Never heard them before. Mama Leone was trying to tell them off. But I could tell her voice was scared. I ran to get Mickey, and we hurried back. Mickey listened at the door for a minute and then told me to beat it, that he'd take care of it. I didn't want to leave, but then I heard Mama Leone scream, and Mickey busted the door open and shouted for me to scram before someone got hurt. I . . . I ran, then, Henrietta. I just ran. And now he's gone!" she burst into sobs.

"You mean Mickey?"

"Of course I mean Mickey!"

Henrietta let her cry for a moment, more for lack of something to say than anything else. "It's okay, Poll. It's going to be okay. Don't worry; the cops will figure it out."

"No, it's not okay!" she said, lifting her head from her lap, her makeup smeared from her tears. "I've tried to find him. I went 'round to his place today after I left the Promenade, but he's gone. No sign of him."

Henrietta wondered how she happened to have a key to Mickey's apartment, but she didn't ask.

"Now the police will think it's him."

"Well, they suspect everyone at first, don't they?" she suggested, not wanting to tell Polly that she was apparently a suspect as well. "They'll eventually work out that it wasn't him," she said, though she did wonder why he would have disappeared if he really were innocent—but then again, so had the Rhythm Section.

"It's not so simple, Hen. If he does turn up, they're sure to figure out he was skimming the till."

"He was?" Henrietta asked, trying not to show her surprise.

"Just a little, like. Thought it was his due since Mama Leone was such a tight bitch. He could do time just for that!" Polly said agitatedly.

Henrietta didn't know what to say to that. She knew Mickey was a rough character; she supposed it fit. But why was Polly so attracted to him, anyway?

"Or what if those thugs last night did him in?" Polly continued anxiously. "I mean, you don't think they killed him, too, do you?" she asked, her hand trembling again as she brought the cigarette up to her lips.

Considering what had happened to Mama Leone, Henrietta believed it to be a distinct possibility, but she didn't say so. "Course not. He'll turn up, I'm sure. He's just laying low for a bit." Henrietta took a sip of her whiskey, studying her friend. "You should be careful yourself, though, Polly," she added, thinking of the inspector.

Polly stared ahead absently, deep in thought. "Yes . . . that's just it, Hen," she whispered. "I . . . I think they might have seen me."

"Who?"

"The thugs—you know, the ones who stabbed the bulldog."

"Oh, Polly!"

"I might be imagining things, but I . . . I thought I might have been followed on the way home today."

"In broad daylight?"

Polly shrugged. "Just a feeling . . . probably nothing."

"Why haven't you told any of this to the police? They think you're holding back, you know. Which you obviously are!"

"I can't tell the police that Mickey was involved!"

"Well, right now they think he's a suspect, when obviously he's a witness. And anyway, Mama Leone doesn't strike me as the sort who kept the books very clean, if the state of her office is any indication. Nobody will be able to tell he skimmed some out of the till. Believe me, I had plenty of chances to dip my hand in at Poor Pete's, and Mr. Hennessey, conscientious as he was, would never have known." She took another sip of whiskey. "You'd better go to the police, Polly. Tell them what you saw."

Polly's eyes narrowed, and she looked at Henrietta as if considering something. "How do you know they think I'm holding back, anyway?"

Henrietta looked down at her drink and swirled it before looking back up at Polly. "That Inspector Howard—or whatever his name was—" she fibbed, "he found me in the back while I was packing up my stuff." Henrietta gestured toward the pile of clothes in the kitchen. "He questioned me again. Trying to figure it all out, I guess." She put on a smile, then, and tossed back the rest of the whiskey in her glass. "Even offered me a job," she said, wincing at the burn as she glanced nervously at Polly for her reaction.

"Oh, yeah? Doing what?"

"An usherette, turns out. Sounds simple enough."

"Where?" Polly asked in a slow, even way.

"The Marlowe. Ever hear of it?" Henrietta answered, with a slight toss of her hair.

Polly's face went deathly pale. "No, Hen," she said in a voice barely above a whisper. "Not the Marlowe!" she said standing up anxiously. "You stay away from that place. You have no idea what that place is like!" She poured out more whiskey in both glasses.

"It's not what you think," Henrietta said, hastily trying to repeat Inspector Howard's own words to her. But not only were they eluding her, she was also momentarily having a hard time remembering why she had agreed to this in the first place.

"No, it's not what you think!" said Polly, taking a large pull from her glass. "It's a gangster's hangout, Hen. Real rough types. You think Casanova was bad," she said, "just you wait. He's a pussycat compared to the bruisers at this place."

"How would you know?"

Polly lit another cigarette, her hand trembling again. "My sister once worked there."

"Your sister? I didn't know you had a sister! Why didn't you say?"

"Because."

"Is she still there?" Henrietta asked, hoping for a friend at this apparently horrible place.

"No," she said, barely above a whisper. "She went missing about a year ago. Police never found her."

"Oh, God, Polly!" Henrietta said, standing up and putting her arms around Polly, who had begun crying again. "Oh, God. I didn't realize. Why didn't you ever tell me?"

"I don't know," Polly murmured, trying to wipe her smeared mascara. "It never seemed the right time. And anyway, I've been trying to keep a low profile."

"What happened?" Henrietta asked, not knowing what to say.

"I . . . Libby came up here a couple of years ago. From Missouri—that's where we're from. She's older than me; I was still at home with my grandmother. My parents are both gone, so that's who we lived with. Libby thought she could find work up north, but it turns out it's just as hard to find something here as it was in our little speck on the map. Well, almost, anyway. She . . . she finally found something at the

Promenade, though she didn't say doing what. Then she wrote one day and said she got a new job, a better one, but she didn't say where. Then the letters stopped coming altogether. My grandmother got worried then. We waited and waited, but no word ever came. Finally, we went to Levy's drugstore and worked up the courage to call the Chicago police, but they didn't take it seriously. Said girls go missing every day, that she'd turn up eventually. So, I followed her here. Got a job at the Promenade, just like her; wasn't too hard, as you know. I . . . I used a different name."

"You did?" Henrietta asked, surprised by the flood of information that the usually unemotional, chilly Polly was offering up.

"Yes, I'm really Polly Shoemacher."

"So, what happened?" Henrietta asked, not sure if she really wanted to hear the end of this.

"I . . . I couldn't find her, of course. A couple of the girls told me they thought she had got a job at the Marlowe," Polly said, looking intently at Henrietta, who consequently felt a wave of fear pass through her.

"I eventually went to the police myself. There was a search, if you can call it that. It went on for about a month, but nothing came of it. Just another nameless, faceless girl that went missing. I confronted Mama Leone about it, but she denied everything. Said she had no idea what happened to Libby. Here one day, gone the next. But I know she was lying. That's what I went back in for last night. I just had to ask her one last time. I knew she had been drinking more than usual. I thought maybe it would have loosened her tongue, but I never got the chance." She rubbed her brow as if in pain and took another drink of whiskey. "Henrietta, you can't go work there. There's something not right. I know it's linked to Libby's disappearance, but I can't quite figure it out. I even tried to audition for the usherette job, but I didn't get picked, of course."

"Well, maybe I won't either. You never know how these things will go. I'm not sure if my legs will pass," she said, looking down at her overalls.

"Who are you kidding? You're a shoe-in. Henrietta, please," she said, grasping her friend's arm. "Please don't."

"I need the money, Polly. The inspector said he'd pay me double what I made at the Promenade! I just can't pass that up."

"There are some things worth more than money, Hen," Polly said bitingly.

"Yes, I know," Henrietta said, thinking of her father.

"Who'd you say put you up to this?"

"That inspector that was nosing around. Inspector Howard, I think his name is," Henrietta fibbed again.

"Didn't he come in last night and dance with you? What was that all about?"

Henrietta bit her bottom lip. "I don't know. He seemed very interested in Mama Leone and the backstage stuff, come to think of it."

"Don't you think it's odd that Mama Leone turns up dead the next day? I wouldn't trust him, Hen. Something he's not saying."

"That's funny. That's what he said about you." Henrietta couldn't help but smile, despite the situation.

"This is serious, Henrietta!" Polly said fiercely. "Jesus, what are we going to do?" Polly began pacing the floor, her hand on her forehead as if to think.

"About what?" Henrietta asked, mystified. "Listen, Polly, it's just a short-term thing to help the cops. They think Mama Leone's death might have something to do with some guy there named Neptune. I'm just supposed to look for anything suspicious . . . you know."

"Suspicious? What does that mean, exactly? The whole thing's suspicious!"

"Look at it this way, Poll. If I make it in, then I can maybe find out about Libby," she said hopefully.

Polly looked at her, the slightest shard of hope lighting up her eyes before it disappeared again just as quickly. "I think it's too late for Libby," she said soberly, looking away.

"You never know, but even if it is . . . if it is too late, don't you want to find out what happened? Find out who's responsible?" Inspector Howard's words were finally finding their way back to her in fits and starts.

Polly sighed deeply. "All right. Suit yourself. But don't say I didn't warn you. You've no idea what you're getting yourself into."

"Will you help me, then?"

"Help you? How do you mean?"

"Will you lend me a dress for the audition? Maybe the green one?"

Polly was silent for a few moments before she spoke. "All right," she relented. "Let me go get it, and you can try it on."

"What will you do, Polly?" Henrietta asked, stopping her before she left the room. "For work, I mean."

"I've got a little saved up. I've got to find Mickey. He's got a cabin up north in Wisconsin somewhere. Always said he'd take me there someday," she said with a small smile. "He might be there."

"Maybe he doesn't want to be found," Henrietta said quietly. "By anyone at the moment."

"Maybe. But if that's the case, I won't stay long. I've just got to know if he's alive somewhere."

"But what about what Inspector Howard said, about not leaving?"

"He can go take a leap. Listen, Hen, if you're so chummy with him, you explain it. You tell him Mickey didn't have nothing to do with it, either."

"I'll try," she said, suspecting that the inspector would be terribly upset, and wondering if he might even put out a warrant for Polly's arrest. "You could get in loads of trouble, Polly. If you run, they might suspect you, too."

"I don't care, Hen," she said in a suddenly sad voice. "I don't care much about anything anymore. Not after Libby. Mickey's the first real thing I've had, don't you see?"

Henrietta didn't want to tell her about the other women she had seen Mickey frequently dallying with, so she merely nodded and took another sip of her whiskey. "Say, Polly," she said, an idea suddenly dawning on her. "Can I ask another favor? Can I leave my stuff here?" she called out, Polly already having gone back to the bedroom. Not waiting for her to answer, Henrietta continued, "While you're gone, I mean? I still have to worry about fooling Ma," she said, gesturing at her shabby outfit as Polly came back into the room. "Can you imagine if she saw me in an usherette's getup?" she said, smiling at the thought.

"For God's sake, Henrietta!" Polly snapped. "Why don't you just tell her? You're a grown woman! It's ridiculous that she thinks you work in a factory. She'll soon get over it; you'll see. She doesn't have a choice; she needs you, and she needs the money."

Henrietta was stunned by Polly's brutal honesty, and the smile quickly left her face. Polly could sometimes be so cruel.

When she saw Henrietta's hurt expression, Polly instantly regretted her words and put her arm around her shoulders. "Hey, don't mind me," she said in a softer tone. "Course you can leave your things here. It'll be good. You can look after the place for me. I'm sorry, doll. I'm—I'm not myself, I suppose."

"You're sure? It won't be for long—just until I get the lay of the land at the Marlowe. Find a place to stash my things there."

Polly slid her arm from around Henrietta's shoulder and stood facing her, taking both of her hands into her own. "Just be careful, Hen. Please."

"I will. I promise."

"And I'd watch out for that inspector if I were you. I don't trust him."

"I'll try," Henrietta said with a weak smile, wondering, however, if it was already too late.

CHAPTER 6

It was bitterly cold the morning of the audition. Henrietta stood shivering in the blustery March air, waiting in a line of women that stretched from the infamous Marlowe Theater all the way down Monroe and around the block onto Market Street. Henrietta had had no idea that so many women would turn up, though she supposed they were all in the same boat—hungry for work like the men she had passed on the corners holding out tin mugs as she hurried past. There seemed to be more and more vagrants the closer she got to the Loop. The saddest ones were the soldiers who had somehow maneuvered through the Great War but who now couldn't seem to find their way once returned. In some strange way, being in such a large company of women who saw nothing wrong with wanting a job at the Marlowe made her feel better about her decision, but nervous as well that the competition would be fierce.

She had been waiting over an hour already and was nearly frozen. She hadn't wanted to wear her bulky overcoat, so she had borrowed a light mackintosh from Polly. The two had parted company that night and had not seen each other since. Henrietta had not needed to stop by the apartment until this morning to get ready, but when she did, Polly was nowhere to be seen. Henrietta had rummaged through the closet and observed that most of her things were gone, so she assumed she had left on her quest up north to find Mickey. Likewise, she had not heard from Inspector Howard since he had first propositioned her. He had simply given her the time and address of the audition but nothing more, which had surprised her, though what she was expecting she couldn't rightly say.

She felt strangely detached as she stood in line, as if she were in the wrong place at the wrong time, not sure of why she was even there. She wondered if she were indeed making a big mistake, a feeling that was getting stronger the longer she stood in the cold. Her teeth were beginning to chatter. She tried to force her growing reservations from her mind as she stamped her feet against the dropping temperature and blew on her numb hands cupped in front of her mouth, wishing desperately that she were holding a hot mug of coffee instead. She tried thinking of home as a way to distract herself from both her nervousness and the actual pain she was beginning to feel in her extremities, especially her toes.

The day prior, she had pretended to be ill as a way of explaining why she was not going in to work at the electrics. She could have gone to Poor Pete's, but she didn't feel like explaining the whole thing to Mr. Hennessey, as she knew he would not approve of her new source of employment, and she didn't want to lie to him. She supposed she could have gone and stayed at Polly's, but somehow that didn't seem right, either.

At first Henrietta saw her "illness" as a chance to spend some extra time with Jimmy and Doris and Donny, but her mother, fearing she was contagious, had made her stay in bed. Initially, Ma had tried to force her to go in to work, despite not feeling well, sure that Henrietta would be fired for staying home, but Henrietta had stubbornly insisted, mustering up a nasty cough or two as she lay in bed. Ma had eventually given up, but as soon as she left to run down to the corner shop and the butcher's, the three little ones had made their way into the room and sat with her while she told them stories and tickled them. Any other time, she would have relished a chance to lie in bed all day, but the guilt she felt made it difficult to enjoy. In the end, she had gotten up and dressed, claiming to feel remarkably better, and had cleaned the house for Ma and done the ironing, though Ma, still disgruntled from before, had not expressed any gratitude.

At any rate, Henrietta was glad she had been there when Father Finnegan had unexpectedly shown up, Eugene angrily in tow, just as they were finishing up making supper.

"What's he done now, Father?" Ma had asked, alarmed, nervously wiping her hands on a dish towel.

"I'm afraid I found him down by the pool hall, Mrs. Von Harmon."

"I was looking for work!" Eugene said sulkily to the floor.

Ma swiftly clipped him on the ear. "You watch your mouth, boy! You apologize to Father."

Eugene paused for several dreadful moments before finally mumbling, "Sorry, Father."

Satisfied, Ma told him to get out and get washed up.

"You'll stay for supper, Father?" she asked, glancing at the lone pot on top of the stove.

Henrietta saw his eyes travel to it as well before he made his excuse that he had a Knights of Columbus meeting to attend. Henrietta had never really liked Father Finnegan. He was a big man, with graying hair and a deeply wrinkled face that always made it look as though he were frowning. He had been a chaplain in the war, and he had an odd, militaristic demeanor about him still, even on the altar, expecting the poor altar boys to be exact in their movements and to wear their lace cassocks perfectly.

"I'm sorry about Eugene, Father," Ma had said as he moved to the door to leave. "He's—he's not been the same since . . ."

"No need to explain, Mrs. Von Harmon," Father Finnegan condescended, holding up his hand to stop her. "I've seen this sort of thing many a time. No father. Difficult. He should be in school, that one should. He should contemplate a vocation in the church. Very promising, he is."

"He doesn't have any more of a calling to the church than I do!" Henrietta said, unable to keep still any longer.

Father Finnegan turned his gaze to her and kept it there. "We are all of us aware of your lack of vocation, Henrietta, but your brother might not yet be lost." Before anyone could respond, he had raised his hat in farewell and slipped out the door, saying a rote "God be with you" as he went, almost colliding with Elsie as she hurried up the stairs.

"Oh, Hen! Why on earth do you have to open your mouth all the time?" her mother moaned.

"What's happened?" asked Elsie quietly as she hung up her coat. "Feeling better, Hen?" she asked with her sweet smile.

The rest of the night had gone on uneventfully, dinner mostly consisting of Ma scolding both Henrietta and Eugene, who sat silently eating, refusing to respond to anything Ma said to him, except to say, "I'm not goin' into the church, Ma, and I ain't goin' back to school."

Later, Henrietta had tried to have a word with him as she had promised Ma, perhaps get him to confide in her like he did when they were little, but Eugene remained mostly silent as she implored him to either go back to school or to be the man of the house and find work. Eventually she had given up and left him to sulk while she went back to the kitchen to help with the dishes. If nothing else, the evening's events had only made Henrietta more determined than ever to secure this job at the Marlowe, though she had to admit that Father Finnegan's barbed comment had indeed stung her.

Henrietta strained her neck again to see if there was any movement at the front of the line. The last group had gone in what seemed like a long time ago, and she tried counting the women in front of her in an attempt to guess whether or not she would be in the next group admitted. She had been watching, and it seemed, as far as she could tell, that they were letting in groups of about twenty each time.

"Like I said, honey," said a woman in front of her, smoking and leaning confidentially toward the woman standing beside her. "Nothin' to it. Just get up there, lift your skirt, give 'em a bit of a smile. All there is to it," she said, taking a puff of her cigarette.

"Then what?" said her friend, stamping her feet in the cold.

"My cousin says they tell you 'right' or 'left'. The door to the right leads right out into the alley. You're done. Try again next time. The door to the left means ya got a chance. So I'm told, anyway. That's where we're headed, doll, I just know it."

"Oh, Ida, I don't know. Maybe we shouldn' be doin' this, anyway."

"That's no way to talk! Don't be nervous! Nothin' to it!"

"Next!" called out a thin man in a tweed cap who had just emerged from the Marlowe. "Next group," he said emotionlessly, his voice thick and raspy, presumably from cigarettes, as he stood hunched over against the cold. The women began hurrying in, the thin man eyeing them steadily and counting them as they passed him. Henrietta prayed she would make it in. She just wanted this to be over. She was almost there . . . she could hear him mumbling, "You, you, you, you . . ." She shuffled along behind the other women and thankfully made it in just before he abruptly announced, "That's it," and shut the door again, roughly turning the lock.

Henrietta stood huddled in the darkened lobby with the other women, the foyer not being much warmer than it had been outside except that they were at least sheltered from the wind. The women's excitement was palpable, though, as the thin man made his way to the front of the group. She could hear what sounded like low, seductive jazz with a slow, steady beat coming from somewhere deeper inside the theater.

"This way," said the man lazily as he began to lead the girls along a darkened hallway.

"Excuse me? Mister?" shouted out one girl near the front. "Where should we put our coats and things?"

"Coats? Coats go here or there or maybe nowhere," he muttered, cryptically. "Prob'ly gonna need 'em again in a few ticks," he said, grinning at them with gray, crooked teeth as if amused by himself. "Out you go to the alley in two shakes."

He turned then and continued down a hallway and up a few steps, apparently unconcerned as to whether they were following him or not because he never looked around again.

Sobered by his less than encouraging words, no one else said anything, though there was a slight hum of whispered conversation as they made their way through the maze of hallways behind the thin man. Henrietta was oddly reminded of the ancient Promenade with all of its little twists and turns and alcoves, but this was on a much grander scale. Despite her efforts to the contrary, she eventually lost all sense of direction, though the sound of the band had gotten steadily louder, so she presumed they were headed somewhere toward the heart of the theater.

Finally, they arrived at what appeared to be the backstage area, and the thin man turned to them, gesturing them to stop. "Line up right 'ere," he said, waving absently with his hand at the general area behind him as he peered out through a crack in the heavy, velvet curtain.

Henrietta found herself toward the end of the line. She slipped out of her mackintosh and brushed out the skirt of the emerald-green dress she had borrowed from Polly. It fit her perfectly, hugging her curves tightly, and exposing more than she had ever dared to do while at the Promenade. Polly's matching shoes had been a bit too big, but Henrietta had remedied that by stuffing cotton wool in the toes, hoping it would do. She had had to admit as she had stood in front of the mirror this morning alone at Polly's that she looked rather ravishing. The deep green of the dress accented her auburn hair, which she fluffed with her small hands, letting some of it slip over her right eye, a look she knew to be alluring.

She placed a hand on her hip, hoping to appear confident, though her heart was beating wildly in her chest. She observed the women in front of her with a sinking feeling, as it was quickly becoming apparent to her that most of them seemed to have done this sort of thing before. They were all extremely attractive in their own way, but in addition to that, they also seemed to possess a self-assuredness that she seemed to lack. She felt horribly out of place as she awkwardly tried to listen to what was happening on the stage.

The music had just stopped, and Henrietta was surprised to hear what was a woman's voice calling out, "Left, right, right, left, right, right, left, right . . ." doling out the sentences for the girls currently on stage. The fact that it was a woman conducting the auditions rather than a man made her even more nervous, as she instinctively felt it might be easier to perform for a man. No matter, she told herself, and took a deep breath, trying madly to calm her nerves. She tried to think about how nervous she had been at the interview with Mama Leone and how absurd it had turned out to be, and almost laughed out loud at the memory, despite, or maybe because of, her current state of anxiety. Her attention was redirected, however, when she heard the women on stage shuffling off and then a shout, "Next group!"

Henrietta felt a sudden sense of panic and momentarily contemplated not going on at all and running away instead. She closed her eyes, trying to steady herself, and forced herself to remember why she was doing this. She tried to tell herself that she was overreacting, that this was no different than taxi dancing, for God's sake, probably even better, if she were honest. This way she wouldn't have to be held by different men night after night. Unfortunately, she kept hearing Polly's warning in her head, but she tried to block it out, remembering that she was here to prove Polly and Artie's innocence and maybe even find out what had happened to Libby. Plus, there was the money. And the inspector. Oddly, she didn't want to let him down, a feeling that simultaneously puzzled and irritated her.

The thin man, still at the head of the line, turned to them and grinned. "This is it, leddies. Do or die, as they say," he mumbled, holding open the curtain for them to file past. Henrietta could feel his eyes on her, a cigarette dangling from his thin, almost non-existent lips, as she made her way through and quickly found a chair upon which to toss her coat. No going back now, she said, forcing herself to smile and walking toward the front of the stage.

"That's right, ladies. Line up. Right in front," a woman's voice very sternly called out.

Henrietta peered into the darkness of the seats beyond the stage, but the footlights temporarily blinded her. She put her hand up to her eyes, shading them, and was able to make out a tall, severe-looking woman sitting a few rows from the front. Beside her sat a stocky man with a receding hairline and thick, bushy eyebrows. He pressed the tips of his thick fingers together, holding his hands just under his nose as if in prayer, but it seemed to Henrietta that his mood was not one of peaceful repose, but rather of mild irritation or perhaps boredom. His eyes never seemed to blink, and Henrietta couldn't help but think he looked cruel. She wondered if this could possibly be the infamous Neptune that the inspector had mentioned. She tried to look away, but she could feel him staring at her as she brushed down her skirt again.

"Hit it, Tony," shouted the woman, and the slow, steady jazz began. "All right, ladies, lift your skirts; let's see what you've got."

Out of the corner of her eye, Henrietta saw the other women seductively sashay forward in rhythm with the band as they lifted their skirts, smiling as they did so. Henrietta had practiced this in her mind, but still she found it hard to do now that the moment was upon her, though she had learned long ago, even as a young girl, what men liked, what they wanted. Deep down she knew what to do and stepped forward instinctively. Slowly, with what she hoped wasn't a nervous smile, she lifted her skirt all the way up to her panty line, giving her legs a little kick as she did so, and arching her body just enough to accentuate her bosom.

"Turn around!" shouted the woman from the seats. "Let's see your bottoms!"

Some of the girls giggled as they twirled around and dutifully flipped up their skirts to reveal their panties. Henrietta faltered. The inspector had said she would only have to show her legs, which wasn't so bad, really, considering it wasn't much different than appearing in a bathing suit on North Avenue Beach. But showing her bottom and her panties . . .?

In the end, she hesitated for only a few seconds, closing her eyes and pushing down the images of her mother and, oddly, of Mr. Hennessey before she found herself twirling around, lifting her skirt, giving her bottom a shake and turning back around, breathless from the adrenaline rushing through her.

And just like that, it was over. The woman in the seats leaned her head toward the man next to her, who hadn't changed position or attitude in the slightest, and listened while he whispered something to her and then gave a slight nod. Henrietta thought she saw the thin man down there as well, standing slack-jawed and staring at them.

"All right, girls," the woman said straightening up. "Left, right, right, right, right, left . . .," she said, going down the line, pointing at each girl and indicating which door she should exit from. Henrietta held her breath as the woman got closer to her. "Right, right, left . . .," she said to her, and Henrietta gave a squeal of delight. "Don't get too excited, ladies," the woman said, her eyes resting momentarily on Henrietta. "You'll do it all again later. Next group!" she called out loudly, and the next line of girls began to make their way onto the stage. Suppressing a smile, Henrietta took a deep breath and hurried off, though she uncomfortably felt Neptune's eyes on her as she went.

The door to the left led to a little room with no ventilation and no window. It had a haphazard row of wooden folding chairs along one of the walls, and a door at the back that stood half open, which Henrietta presumed was the way to the toilet. On the other wall was a cracked mirror, which several girls hovered in front of, applying lipstick or tucking up stray locks of hair. Most of the women, however, sat nervously smoking or chatting to pass the time until the whole line still outside on the street had shuffled through. Henrietta gingerly took a seat at the end of the row of chairs, next to a woman who was languidly filing her nails. She looked up briefly at Henrietta, giving her a quick, false smile before turning her attention back to her nails.

"Smoke?" said a girl across from her, holding out a package of cigarettes to Henrietta. She looked to be no more than fifteen. Certainly younger than Elsie.

"No, thanks," Henrietta tried to say in a friendly way.

"First time?" asked the woman beside her, not looking up.

"Here, you mean?" asked Henrietta cautiously.

"No, as an usherette," the woman said with a roll of her eyes, as she looked Henrietta over from head to toe as if really seeing her for the first time.

"Yes, it is, I'm afraid."

The woman gave a little snort. "Good luck."

"I was a taxi dancer, though . . . at the Promenade," she tried to explain.

"Don't make no difference. Entirely different thing altogether."

Just then the door opened again, and two new girls came in hesitantly, looking for a place to sit.

"How long do you think this will take?" Henrietta asked the young girl opposite her, deciding to ignore the woman beside her.

"Why?" asked the woman next to her. "Got somewhere to go?"

"No, I just . . . just curious is all."

"I've never been, either," said the girl across from her encouragingly. "Saw the ad in the paper and thought I'd give it a try. Why not, as my ma always says. Right now, I'm a waitress at the Bridge. On Clark? Ever hear of it?"

Henrietta was about to answer but the girl didn't wait for one. Having begun talking, she was unwilling or possibly unable, due to what seemed like a bad case of nerves, to stop, and so continued on rapidly. "No? Well, I've worked there for almost a year. Tips are okay, but better I'd say than the last place I worked. Now that was . . ."

Henrietta at first tried to follow what the girl was saying but found it hard to concentrate as she droned on. Each time the door opened to let in the latest "winners" of the initial lineups, she looked up hopefully, hoping they were the last.

The door always disappointingly closed behind them, however. As the room became more crowded, the air grew more thick and stale, and Henrietta found herself feeling rather claustrophobic. "Excuse me," she said finally, standing up and interrupting the girl across from her midsentence. "I need to stretch my legs."

The girl, having been stopped, looked up at her in surprise and shrugged, and then looked back toward the nail-filing woman for any sign of encouragement to continue her chatter.

Henrietta felt that they had already been there for hours as she walked slowly around the room, thinking about Ma, home alone every day with the three little ones, and wondering if she ever felt this claustrophobic. They had clashed over another argument just this morning before she had come out. Henrietta hated always lying to her, but she had had to tell her she was going out shopping before her shift at the electrics so that she could dash to Polly's and get ready. Ma had tried to convince her to stay in bed, saying she would catch her death if she went out in the cold while still under the weather. Henrietta found this advice inconsistent at best, as just yesterday, Ma had tried to urge her to go to work, despite Henrietta's being confined, albeit falsely, to bed, worrying that she would be let go otherwise.

Henrietta often found herself wondering if Ma was somehow uncontrollably contrary, almost like an addiction, and how she could stand being trapped in such a perpetually negative state. Obviously, Henrietta surmised, it was its own vicious cycle, which, to add to the frustration, Ma did not even seem remotely conscious of.

The door opened again, and this time it was the thin man who appeared, yet another cigarette dangling precariously from his lips. "All right, leddies," he said holding the door open. "One more time," he said, nodding his head back toward the stage. Henrietta was somehow last again.

"Thanks," she said to him as she passed, and she thought she saw a flicker in his otherwise dull eyes.

"That's right," said the severe woman with Neptune—if it was Neptune—still sitting next to her, immobile. "Move along. Hurry up!"

This time on stage, Henrietta was able to notice that the woman's eyelids were powdered with a very bright shade of blue, accentuated by the fact that they seemed to be permanently half closed. Despite the lazy attitude that this would at first glance suggest, she somehow managed despite it, perhaps with the aid of her perpetual frown and scowl, to exhibit an aura of severity. "Line up, girls. Hurry up! We haven't got all day! Profiles! I said profile! Turn to the right!" she said in an exasperated tone, as some of the girls nervously turned the wrong way, bumping into each other as they did so.

Henrietta turned the correct way, however, keeping her hand on her hip and holding up a bit of her skirt as she did so to reveal her slim legs. "Turn back!" said the woman to the group, and the girls nervously spun facing forward. After just a few seconds of observing them, she shouted out, "You!" pointing to one of the girls mid-way down the line. "You!" pointing to another girl, "you, you, you, and you," she said, pointing to Henrietta, "in the green dress. That's it. The rest of you, better luck next time. Out! Larry, show the new girls where to go."

Amidst several groans of disappointment from the crowd of women dejectedly gathering up their things, Larry, the now familiar thin man, materialized near the six chosen girls who were standing in a huddle whispering congratulations to each other, including an astonished Henrietta. "This way, leddies. This way," he said, leading them back behind the curtain and down a series of hallways.

Only six girls! Henrietta mused as she walked along. All this fuss to only choose a few! It seemed hard to believe that she had made it, and she wished Inspector Howard were there so that she could tell him. She was in! She was excited, of course, but not a little unsure, a feeling magnified when they eventually reached what she assumed was a dressing room of sorts. It was dark and chilly.

"Wait 'ere," said the thin man, gesturing with his thumb. "Mrs. Jenkins and Esther'll be along in a bit." He didn't bother to turn the lights on for them, and Henrietta, standing nearest the door, felt chilled as he passed by, grinning to himself as if he alone were aware of some secret joke.

Henrietta stood near the other girls who were whispering excitedly together and peered into the dark corners of the room. It was difficult to make anything out. There were again no windows, and she had no idea where they were inside the theater and hence no idea of how to get out if she needed to. It suddenly occurred to her that if she wasn't able to find her way out, how could the men the inspector supposedly had watching the place see or ever find her, especially with no windows? Surely the inspector had known that ahead of time, hadn't he? Then how could he ensure her safety? Perhaps he had men inside? she wondered, peering again into the dark corners as if they would suddenly materialize there. But that didn't make sense, she reasoned. Isn't that why they needed a girl inside? Had he lied about it not being all that dangerous? Perhaps Polly had been right about him after all. Henrietta wrapped her arms around herself and waited, hoping it wouldn't take too much longer before they could go home.

She jumped when the door finally banged open about ten minutes later. The blue eye-shadowed woman, whom Henrietta assumed was the Mrs. Jenkins that Larry had been referring to, burst into the room followed by a plump woman in a grayish housedress, her greasy hair pulled up on top of her head and a large brown mole on the side of her face. A permanent sort of frown was etched on her face as she peered at them, distinctly annoyed as she held her arms rigidly across her body.

"Why the hell aren't the lights on?" Mrs. Jenkins said loudly, looking around as if to find someone to blame. "Esther, get the goddamn lights on. Didn't any one of you ninnies think to turn them on?" she asked, looking accusatorily at the huddled group of girls.

Esther moved heavily toward the wall behind the door and switched on the lights. Henrietta resisted the urge to look away from Mrs. Jenkins, fighting down the fear that she would surely recognize her as a fraud, and instead tried her best to maintain eye contact. Mrs. Jenkins's eye did seem to rest on her longer than on any of the others before she pulled her attention away and addressed the group as a whole.

"All right, all right, girls," she barked out. "So, you made it. Congratulations. This is a tough place and a tough job, and if you don't think you can hack it, the door's right there," she said warningly, though her eyes remained half closed. "There's two types of girls here—the dancers and the usherettes. Don't forget which one you are. This dressing room's for the usherettes, the dancers' is next door." She paused dramatically, looking at each of them in turn.

"None of you looks too stupid," she went on, "so you should catch on pretty quick. The job isn't that difficult. You escort men to their seats, get them a drink and try to keep 'em drinking while the show's on. You keep any tips you get, so a smile and a wink goes a long way, but nothin' else. Got it? No fondling, no touching of any kind. As I say, this is a tough crowd. Men get drinking, the show gets more and more lively, should we say, and before you know it, they think they can reach out for a little feel or pull girls into their laps. The owner wants none of that, and I'm to enforce it. You saw how many girls were lined up today. You don't play by the rules, there's a hundred other girls would take your spot in a minute. Don't forget that." She paused again, staring at them. Henrietta caught her eye for a moment but then looked away quickly.

"There's four male ushers, or 'bouncers' as we like to call them," Mrs. Jenkins continued. "They're on duty each night to watch and make sure there's no funny business going on. As far as you girls go, you work for us, and we don't want any damaged property. Any violation of the rules, and you're out. Got it? You stay on the floor at all times. Just remember—the bouncers can bounce any one of you out as quick as one of the paying gentlemen," she finished, gesturing toward the door for emphasis.

"But, Mrs. Jenkins," one of the girls asked, raising her hand nervously, "what about going to the little girls' room?"

Henrietta thought she heard Esther mutter "Jesus, Mary, and Joseph!" under her breath with an accompanying roll of her eyes.

"If you must leave the floor to use the lavatory, you must take a partner," Mrs. Jenkins went on, loudly. "Never go alone! This is for your own protection, girls. We've had some terrible accidents in the past, and we don't want any more trouble. You new girls will be matched up with one of the older girls the first couple of nights. Any trouble, call for one of the bouncers. Any questions?"

No one dared say anything. Henrietta wondered if they really took the "no touching" policy as seriously as Mama Leone had.

"Right," Mrs. Jenkins continued. "Let's move on. You get one costume and one set of fishnets. You rip those or snag 'em, and a new pair comes out of your pay, understand? This is Esther," she said, gesturing behind her toward the thick woman who was still scowling. "She's normally an assistant of sorts—a maid, really, aren't you, Esther?—for the dancers, but today she's going to help you find a costume that fits. Soon as you find one, you can get a cubby and scram. You start tomorrow night. Be back here by three. Good luck," she said at the door. "You'll need it."

As soon as she was gone, the girls broke into excited conversation, one girl issuing a low whistle.

"Shut yer gobs," Esther muttered as she hobbled to the back of the room. "There ain't many to pick from, so get yerselves over here."

The girls followed her over to a large wardrobe, which she unlocked with a key on a frayed piece of string that she drew up from between her hefty bosom. After fumbling a few times, she eventually opened the wardrobe door, revealing a row of brilliant scarlet dresses and a variety of red heels set along the bottom.

"Right then, let's get the dresses sorted first, and then I'll be givin' ye the stockings."

There was a general scramble to grab a dress, the girls automatically stripping down to try them on. They were bright-red satin cocktail dresses, which flounced out just below the panty line due to the crinoline underneath. They were trimmed with white satin and were extremely low cut, the top being held in place by thin shoulder straps of delicate white lace. In addition, each of them came with a little red satin cap to pin on, one pair of fishnet stockings, spiked red heels, and white kid gloves.

The atmosphere in the changing room was one of excited competition of sorts as the girls searched for the right dress, laughing and teasing each other as they tried them on, tossing them back and forth trying to find just the right size. Henrietta finally ended up with one that fit pretty well, though it was a bit torn near the top of the bodice, just in front, which was a strange place for a random tear, she thought. She fingered it carefully and wondered if she could properly mend it. She knew Elsie could, she thought with a sigh, but she wasn't so sure of her own skill. She slipped it off and made her way back to Esther. Most of the girls had found one that fit and were hurriedly trying on the heels, anxious to get a good pair.

Henrietta approached Esther, who was waddling amongst the girls. "Miss Esther?" she asked tentatively.

Esther turned slowly around to face her. "It's just Esther," she said angrily. "Don't be puttin' on airs with me."

"Sorry. Esther. I . . . this one fits, but it's a bit ripped, I'm afraid."

Esther took the dress in her hand and turned it over. "Oh, aye. I forgot about this one. Aren't there any others ye could use?" she asked, twisting her head toward the empty wardrobe. Henrietta could see her faded brassiere through a gap between her buttons, the fabric of her pale housedress being pulled too tightly across her chest by her bulk. Not seeing any more available dresses, Esther gave out what sounded like a growl. "I'll work on it tonight then. One more thing for me to be doin'," she said, her eyes moving to the large sewing basket sitting askew on a table off to the side.

"I can do it, Esther," Henrietta's eyes following hers to the sewing basket. "I just wanted you to see it . . . so that I wouldn't be blamed for it. Honest. It's no trouble."

Esther eyed her carefully, considering. "Right so. But don't think ye'll be getting' on me good side," she said as she turned away, hobbling back to the wardrobe to hand out the stockings and gloves. "Find yerselves an empty spot and put yer things there if ye like," Esther said loudly to the group. "That or take them home with ye, makes no difference to me. Best get on with it then; things'll be getting' busy soon enough around here."

With the ripped dress hung over her arm, Henrietta hurried to find a pair of shoes that fit. She hesitated to pick out a cubby space, as she wasn't sure if she should leave her things at Polly's instead. In the end, she decided she would wait. She would stop at Polly's and mend the dress before going home. Ma wouldn't be expecting her until late anyway.

"Come on, come on!" she heard Esther shout. "I've got to get ye lot out of here. I've work to be doin' before the gentlemen arrive. Waste of me time, this is."

As they left the room and filed down the hallway behind Esther, Henrietta turned her attention back to the rip and started planning out how she would tackle it when she realized she had no red silk thread. She was pretty sure Polly wouldn't either, assuming she could find her sewing basket in the apartment. Not really wanting to go out and purchase a whole new spool, especially one that would be so costly, she tried to think of an alternative and realized that there was probably some in the sewing basket she had seen back in the dressing room. She stopped walking, the other girls pushing past her, and quickly calculated that she could probably make it back to the dressing room and still catch up with the group before they reached the front doors. She hurriedly turned around and ran back.

The door was ajar as she slipped back inside. Esther had turned off the lights, and Henrietta decided against turning them on again. Gingerly she made her way toward the table where she had seen the sewing basket. She froze, though, when she heard a soft scraping noise coming from the back of the room.

"Hello?" she called out hesitantly.

"What you doing back 'ere?" came what sounded like Larry's raspy voice. Henrietta peered into the darkness and indeed made out the bent figure of Larry, pushing a broom at the back of the room. He must be the custodian as well as Mrs. Jenkins's stooge, Henrietta surmised. Had he been there the whole time they were changing? If he had, why hadn't they noticed him?

Larry stopped sweeping and came toward her.

"I . . . I just came back to see if I could borrow some red thread," Henrietta said, holding up the dress. "There's a rip, you see, so I thought I'd just mend it, but I don't have any thread this fine at home."

Larry just stared at her and then at the dress as if not comprehending. A long line of ash from his cigarette broke off just then, spilling down the front of his dirty vest. Slowly he turned his attention to it and raised his hand half-heartedly to brush it off, not really succeeding, however. He looked back at her.

"Where'd you get that?" he asked, glancing back at the dress. Henrietta began to wonder if he were a simpleton.

"From Esther," she said slowly in case her theory was correct. "I'm just going to fix it."

"You're not supposed to have that dress. That belonged to her," he said without emotion.

"Well, this is the one Esther gave me," she said deliberately, becoming more convinced of his mental handicap. "I don't think there were any more left. I'll just get the thread and be on my way, then. I must hurry before . . ." She was going to say 'before Esther notices I'm gone,' but thought better of it and instead simply said, "I should hurry." She gave him a wary smile as she moved to pass him.

"It's in the basket. The thread."

"Yes, thank you, Larry," she said slowly and politely, though she was beginning to feel uncomfortable to be alone with him in the dressing room.

"I best get on," he said, grinning, picking up the broom he had been leaning on. "Musn't keep you. Mrs. Jenkins wouldn't like that. No, she wouldn't." He made his way out the door, pausing long enough to add, "That dress ain't a lucky one, though. It ain't no good," as he shuffled out.

Henrietta felt a chill run down her spine at this unwelcome observation but made herself open the basket and examine the contents. The interior was a disorganized mess, which Henrietta put down to perhaps so many women using it at once. She rummaged through bits of fabric, buttons, half-empty cards of needles and spools of thread before finding one of red silk. There wasn't much left on it, she observed, as she held it up to the light weakly coming in from the hallway, but she thought it would do. Just as she slipped the spool into her pocket, however, she heard footsteps coming down the hall. She hoped it wasn't already Esther back from escorting the other girls. She was sure she'd be annoyed at having to make the journey to the front of the theater all over again. Perhaps whoever it was would pass by . . .

Henrietta waited, listening, her stomach sinking when she thought she detected another set of footsteps that sounded surprisingly like Mrs. Jenkins's heels clipping along toward what Henrietta felt convinced was Esther's slow waddle.

"There you are, Esther! I've been looking everywhere for you," said the unmistakable voice of Mrs. Jenkins. She sounded irritated.

"I can't be everywhere at once, ye know," grumbled Esther. "Just getting' the new girls settled. Not very promisin', I'd say," she said, more to herself than to anyone.

Henrietta strained to hear better and silently crept toward the slightly open door, hoping to hear what else they had to say about the "new girls," if anything.

"Never mind that!" hissed Mrs. Jenkins. "He wants Iris tonight. You know what to do," she said just above a whisper.

"Aye. What room?"

"The usual, of course! My God, you're dense. Someday, I swear . . ."

"Right, right! No need to get all high and mighty with me, missus. I'll get it ready. Ye sure it's Iris he wants? She's fierce young, if ye ask me."

"Just do as you're told!"

"Right, right," she said, starting to shuffle closer to the dressing room. "It'll be ready. Blood's devil to clean, though."

"Be quiet!" Mrs. Jenkins hissed again, but there was no answer from Esther. Henrietta felt beads of perspiration on the back of her neck as she sensed Mrs. Jenkins was hovering just outside the dressing room door. It was too late to creep back to the table that held the sewing basket, so she froze there, holding her breath, hoping Mrs. Jenkins would go away. If only she could control the beating of her heart, which she was sure they could hear even on the other side of the door.

Finally, after what seemed an eternity, Mrs. Jenkins clipped away, and Henrietta breathed a sigh of relief just as Esther made her way into the room. When she saw Henrietta standing there, she cried out. "Jesus, Mary, and Joseph! What in the name of all that's holy d'ye think ye're doin' creepin' around in the dark like that? Nearly gave me a heart attack, ye did."

"I'm sorry . . .," Henrietta began.

Esther's eyes narrowed. "What are ye doin' back here anyway?"

"I . . . I just came to borrow some thread," she said holding it up shakily. "You know . . . to mend the dress? I didn't think anyone would mind. Larry thought it'd be all right," she added hastily.

"Larry?" she asked, disconcerted. "What's he got to do with anythin'?"

"He saw me take it. He didn't say not to, anyway."

Esther looked at her carefully. "Ye didn't hear anythin' in the hall then, did ye?" she asked suspiciously.

"No! . . . No," she tried to say calmly. "I was just getting my things together is all."

Esther continued to stare at her for a moment more and then let out what sounded like a grunt. "Come on then. I'll show ye the way out. As if I haven't got better things to be doin' than runnin' around like some trained dog." She was mumbling to herself, waddling back down the hall.

"Oh, no! I can find my way, Esther. It's no trouble, really," Henrietta urged, elated that the woman had accepted her fib.

"And risk ye snoopin' about? Think I'm a fool, do ye?" she grumbled. "Ye seem the snoopin' type, ye do. No, I'll take ye down meself. But don't be makin' a habit of getting' left behind, hear me?"

"Yes, of course. I'll try," Henrietta said, dutifully following Esther to the front. She was eager to get out of the maze, almost frantic, and once deposited outside the front door, which Esther then locked from the inside, Henrietta felt inexplicably relieved, gulping in huge breaths of the cold, frigid air as she began her walk home.

CHAPTER 7

It was only four in the afternoon when Henrietta descended from the streetcar, having ridden it north from downtown to Polly's Lincoln Park neighborhood. It was only a few blocks' walk, and Henrietta looked forward to a hot cup of tea while she mended the dress, currently folded and lying in the bottom of the old carpetbag she had "borrowed" from the Promenade. She was famished as well, but she wasn't quite sure what she was going to do about that. She was trying to remember whether she had seen a tin of biscuits on the counter that Polly had left behind or whether she had just imagined them.

She was trying to keep her mind on the biscuits or the tea, or anything besides the conversation she had overheard at the Marlowe. It had plagued her all the way home. What did "he wants Iris" mean exactly? She hoped it wasn't what she imagined it might be, but then again, what about Esther's comment about the blood?

She shuddered as she thought about it. And who was he? Neptune? Was it the man in the seats next to Mrs. Jenkins at the auditions, the one whose eyes never left her?

She pulled her coat about her tightly and glanced behind her. It was as if she could still feel his eyes on her, and she wondered, with a tightening in her stomach, if she were being followed. Instinctively she quickened her steps, hoping to reach the corner where several people were standing, waiting for a motorbus, feeling she would be safe standing amongst them.

She got up the courage to look behind her, but she didn't see Neptune, or anyone menacing, for that matter, but she still felt uneasy. She walked faster, keeping her gaze locked on the people at the bus stop. She was almost there! But before she could reach the little group, however, she suddenly felt a hand on her shoulder and couldn't help but let out a little scream as she dropped her bag and turned to face her assailant . . .

There stood Stanley, breathless, bent over with his hands on his knees.

"Stan!" she cried. "You gave me a shock!"

"Didn't you hear me callin' you?" he panted.

"Obviously not," she said, annoyed, her heart still racing.

"You okay, miss?" asked a gentleman passing by. Henrietta saw that several people had come over, having heard her scream.

"Yes, I'm sorry," she said to no one in particular. "I was just startled. I'm fine, really. Thank you." The crowd's attention was taken up then by the approaching motorbus, and the man who had asked after her gave Henrietta a last look before he, too, made his way over to the bus, reluctantly abandoning her to Stanley.

"What on earth do you think you're doing?" Henrietta asked, addressing Stan once they were left to themselves.

"Oh, Hen, what are you doing? All the way downtown, you've been."

"You haven't been following me all day, have you?" she asked, exasperated.

"Well, Hen, I had to! When I heard what happened at the Promenade, well I was worried sick!"

Wearily, Henrietta bent to pick up her bag to continue on her way, knowing that nothing good could come of the conversation Stan currently meant to have.

"Here! I'll get that," Stan said, reaching down quickly and grabbing the handle of the carpetbag before Henrietta could get to it.

Henrietta sighed and kept walking. "Suit yourself."

"Hen! The Marlowe ain't no place for a girl like you!" he whined, hurrying to keep up.

"Stan, I'm not a girl; I'm a grown woman. You don't need to follow me about. I can take care of myself, thanks very much."

"What were you doing down there, anyway? That's a bad part of town, Hen."

"It's not a bad part of town, Stan. And anyway, if you must know, I've got a new job."

"Doin' what?" he asked suspiciously.

"Never you mind!" she said, trying to put him off.

"You know I'll find out, so you might as well tell me."

Henrietta realized this was probably true. "All right, I'll tell you, but don't make a scene." She cleared her throat. "I got a job as an usherette at the Marlowe," she said with a toss of her hair.

"Henrietta Von Harmon!" he squeaked. "You've gone too far this time! This really is the limit! That's a gangster's hideout and all that! Oh, Hen! I'm beggin' ya this time."

"Oh, don't be so melodramatic, Stan. Anyway, you're just a kid. What would you know of gangsters? Why don't you go hang about Elsie? She's sweet on you, you know."

"Elsie?" he said, befuddled. "Aw, don't try to confuse me! We've got to get you out of this mess before it's too late!"

Henrietta couldn't help but smile at Stanley's pleading eyes and nervous habit of biting his lip as if the world were about to explode at any minute.

"This isn't a laughing matter, Henrietta!" he said, thoroughly annoyed. "Why can't you just go back to the Promenade? It's back open, you know. I'm sure you could get your job back!"

"Is it?" Henrietta was surprised that they had reopened so quickly. They must have located the owner, Mr. Mercer. She wondered if the inspector was any closer to finding Mama Leone's killer. Why hadn't he contacted her? she fretted. And anyway, how was she supposed to find him to tell him she had made it through the audition and had gotten the job? She had reached Polly's building, and she was eager to be rid of Stan. She needed time to think and to mend the dress.

"This is my stop, Stan," she said, reaching out and taking the carpetbag from him.

"Here?" he said, looking at the building, distracted. "I wondered why you got off in this neighborhood. Who lives here?"

"My friend Polly, if you must know. From the Promenade. You remember her, don't you?"

"Oh, your pal? The short hair?"

"Yes, that's her. This is her place. I'm keeping some things here for a while. You know, 'cause of Ma. Anyway, Polly had to leave town for a bit, so I'm keeping an eye on the place for a bit. Until things get settled at the Marlowe, anyway."

Stanley looked carefully up and down the street as if assessing its degree of safety. An old woman sat on the front steps of a building halfway down the block, and down the other way, two boys were attempting to fit a box onto a set of wheels to make a sort of scooter, while a girl with a dirty pinafore and what looked like her younger sister looked on. "Looks like a nice enough neighborhood," he said hesitantly. "It's getting dark, though. I'll just make sure you get in safe," he said, taking back the carpetbag.

Henrietta sighed, knowing it wasn't worth arguing with him. "Come on, then," she said, making her way toward the alley and the back stairs. A cat scurried under the fence that ran along the back of the alley.

"Why we goin' up the back?" he asked, closely following her.

"The front door sticks," Henrietta said, slowly climbing the steps to the third floor. At the top, she bent down and reached under the coal bucket, scooping up a key.

"You didn't go and put the key there, did you?" Stan asked incredulously. "Anyone could find it there!"

Henrietta turned back to face him. "Well, that's where Polly keeps it," she shrugged. "Do you always worry this much? How do you sleep at night? And anyway, shouldn't you be skipping off home?"

"All I'm saying, Hen, is that you should keep the key . . .," he broke off suddenly, watching as the door in front of Henrietta creaked open at her touch before she even had a chance to place the key in the lock.

"That's odd," Henrietta said, pushing it open further and stepping into the apartment. "I could have sworn I locked it this morning."

"Henrietta, no!" hissed Stan, following her and trying to grab her arm, but it was too late.

Before she knew what was happening, a hand reached out and grabbed her, pinning her, while another hand pressed itself over her mouth, making it impossible to scream. Panicking, Henrietta tried to bend and twist away from her capturer, but the man held her tight. She looked back desperately at Stan, only to find that the same had happened to him.

"Listen, sister," came a rough voice very close to her ear, his breath smelling of beef or maybe cigars. "I'm gonna take my hand away from your mouth, but if you scream, your friend gets it, understand?" he said calmly, cocking a pistol and waving it in front of her. Same goes for you, pipsqueak," he said, looking at Stanley. "You got it?" the voice asked her again. Terrified, Henrietta nodded. The man released her, then, and she gasped for breath as he pushed her into the middle of the room, pointing the gun at her.

"What about him?" said the other man, who still held Stan roughly, one hand over his mouth and one hand twisting Stan's arm behind his back.

"See what he's got on him."

The man let go of Stan with a little shove.

"You keep quiet, or she gets it," snarled the first man as the second man searched Stanley's pockets, removing only a thin wallet.

"Just this," he said holding it up.

"Keep it for the boss."

"Hey, you can't keep that!" said Stan indignantly.

The second man hit him in the head. "Shut up, kid!"

Stanley bent over in pain, trying not to cry.

"Leave him alone!" cried Henrietta.

"So, you decided to come back, eh? We thought you would. Just a matter of time, just like the boss said."

"I . . . I think there's been some mistake," pleaded Henrietta. "I don't live here; I just stopped by."

"Sure, sister."

"Hey, look at this," said the second man, who had decided to pick through Stanley's wallet. He held up the little calendar Stanley kept hidden there. "Look at all these dates circled in red. What's this mean, Mickey?"

"Mickey? I'm not Mickey!" Stan squeaked.

"Look at this, Charlie. Even got the date circled that that fat broad at the Promenade got done in. What's these dates mean? Payouts? Knock-offs?"

"I . . . I don't have to tell you anything," said Stanley, still rubbing his head. The man stepped toward him, and Stan gave out a little cry, backing away. "I don't know what you're talking about!" he insisted.

"Sounds like bullshit, I'd say," said the second man as he drew back his hand to strike him again.

"Kelly! We'd better leave the questioning to the boss. You know what he's like. Don't want 'em too roughed up."

"Yeah, all right. But a couple of good punches'll get this canary singin', I reckon."

"You're making a terrible mistake!" Henrietta whined. "I'm not Polly!"

"Tell it to the boss," said Kelly, glancing out the little side window. "He's on his way up."

"Honestly!" Henrietta said, panicking. She could hear footsteps on the back stairs. Desperate fear filled her, her heart fluttering and her breathing coming in rapid, short bursts. "No matter what you think, I'm not Polly! I'm . . ."

"Miss Von Harmon!" a voice finished for her. "What are you doing here?"

"Inspector Howard?" she asked, incredulous.

The two men looked at the inspector, puzzled, lowering their guns slightly. "What's going on here?" he asked, looking rapidly from Charlie to Kelly. The inspector rubbed his forehead wearily and sighed. "You've got the wrong girl. How many times?" he said almost to himself, exasperated.

"You sure, boss?" said the first man.

"Yes, yes. Obviously, there's been some mix-up. This is the plant." The plant? thought Henrietta, flustered. Suddenly her knees felt weak, and she felt she might faint. "May I sit down?" she asked weakly.

"Yes, of course!" said the inspector, coming over to her and putting his arm around her. "Here, let me help you," he said, guiding her to a chair by the kitchen table. He crouched in front of her and studied her face.

"Hey!" Stanley said, suddenly finding his voice. "What's the big idea?"

"Where'd you pick him up at?" the inspector asked, slowly standing up with his hands on his hips.

"Came in with the dame," Charlie answered, putting his pistol back in the holster inside his jacket.

"Found this on him," Kelly said, tossing the little calendar toward the inspector, who deftly caught it midair.

"Hmmm," Inspector Howard said, flipping through it. "What do these red circles mean, kid?"

"Inspector, let me explain—" Henrietta tried to intervene.

"I'd rather hear his explanation right about now, Miss Von Harmon, if you don't mind."

"What do you want with Henrietta?" Stanley said, ignoring the question. Kelly shoved him toward Clive. "Just answer the question, pipsqueak."

"Inspector!" shouted Henrietta, but he ignored her.

"They don't mean anything!" Stanley mumbled. "It's just nights that I got to dance with Henrietta is all. I like to keep track," he said, his face flushed as he stared at the floor, avoiding looking at Henrietta.

"It seems you have a number of admirers, Miss Von Harmon," the inspector commented, his eyebrow arched.

"Inspector, really. Stanley's just a pal. He . . . he thinks of himself as my protector, I suppose. He follows me home sometimes is all. It doesn't mean anything." She had seen Stanley look back up at her as she spoke, but he looked away again, sullen.

"That's right," Inspector Howard said, recognition registering on his face as he looked at Stan. "I remember you. I thought you looked familiar. You were dancing with Miss Von Harmon that evening just before I came up." The inspector looked him over. "What's your name, kid?"

"Stanley," he answered sulkily. "Stanley Dubowski."

"Notice anything funny that day at the Promenade?"

"Not that I can remember," he said, shrugging his shoulders.

The inspector leaned back against the table, thinking, his arms crossed in front of him. "So you follow Miss Von Harmon home, do you?" he asked, looking at him shrewdly.

"Sometimes. What's it to you?"

Kelly reached out and gave him a rap on the back of the head, but the inspector shook his head ever so slightly at him in mild disapproval.

"Just that you might have noticed something unusual at closing time. Who's the last to leave at night?"

"Usually the bartender. He locks up from what I can tell," Stan answered, scowling at Kelly and rubbing his head.

"Front door or back?"

"Front."

"What about Mama Leone?"

"She lives up above, I think. I never see her leave."

"Anything different about the night she was killed?"

"No. Polly and Henrietta came out as usual . . ." He paused for a moment. "Wait—there was something else, I think."

Henrietta felt herself tense and willed Stanley to be silent.

"Actually, now that I think about it, Polly went back in. I remember because it made me mad that she just left Henrietta standin' out there alone in the dark. I was about to go over to her, break my cover—but then, before I could make up my mind, she finally came back out."

"Then what?" the inspector asked, leaning forward slightly with interest.

"That's all. They just walked to the streetcar stop together like usual."

"It wasn't her!" Henrietta interrupted.

The inspector looked at her coolly. "Again with your powers of deduction, Miss Von Harmon. But we'll get to that later. For now, perhaps you would leave the questioning to me."

"Sorry," Henrietta said meekly. "It's just that I know it's not her. There are some things you should know —"

"Yes, I rather guessed that." He turned his attention back to Stanley.

"Did you see this Mickey come out?"

"Nah, not that night. I was off after the girls soon as Polly came back out."

"I see." The inspector seemed to be thinking something over. Finally, he spoke. "All right, kid," he said, tossing him his wallet back. "You can scram. Let me know if you think of anything else."

"I'll wait for Henrietta; thanks just the same," he said sulkily.

The inspector tipped his hat back to sit on the crown of his head. "As it happens, I'm not quite finished with Miss Von Harmon. I have a few more questions for her. Don't worry. I'll make sure she gets home all right, sonny. I'm sure you can show yourself out, or do you need Kelly to help you?"

Kelly grinned at him.

Stanley seemed to hesitate and looked apprehensively at Henrietta, who merely rolled her eyes. "I'll be okay, Stan. I'll see you round the neighborhood. Look in on Elsie, why don't you?"

"Aw, shucks!" Stan murmured after pausing a moment more and then stomped down the back stairs.

The inspector turned his attention back to Henrietta. "Nice kid," he said. "Does he know about Artie?"

Henrietta blushed. "That's none of your business! And, anyway, Stan means well," Henrietta said. "He just gets carried away sometimes. At least he doesn't jump out and try to strangle me," she said, giving Charlie and Kelly each a dirty look. "What are you doing here, anyway?" Henrietta asked the inspector indignantly.

"Seems I could ask you the same thing," the inspector said, stroking his chin as he observed her. "Funny, I'm having déjà vu. What are you doing here?"

"I asked you first!"

He eyed her carefully. "All right. We're staking the joint. We came 'round yesterday to find Miss Shoemacher"—he halted, watching her face. Henrietta tried not to reveal anything, but she apparently failed, as he added, "Yes, we know all about her alias. But judging from the state of the place, she seems to have gone. Might you know where she is? All the suspects in this case seem to be conveniently disappearing. Do you not find that odd, Miss Von Harmon?"

"Look, Inspector, I . . . I know it looks bad," she said, twisting her hands. "But I . . . I came here to see Polly that day—the day Mama Leone's body was discovered. Remember? You had somehow guessed I was headed here before I even left the Promenade."

The inspector remained cool. "Yes. And?"

"She was in a terrible state. And she did go back in that night. But she didn't kill her. Honest! She told me that she went back toward Mama Leone's office and she . . . she heard voices. Threatening ones."

"This Artie and Al, presumably?"

"No! Honest! Two different men. Ones she didn't recognize. She went to get Mickey, but when they got back, they heard Mama Leone scream. Mickey bust open the door and told Polly to run."

"Then what?" the inspector asked, his eagerness unmistakable.

"Polly came out, and we . . . we left. I didn't know anything had happened. She seemed a bit upset, but I thought she was just tired, just the usual. But now she's mad with worry about what happened to Mickey. That's where she went, you see. She says she went round to his place the next day—you know, the day the body was found—after we left the Promenade, but he wasn't there. She's a nervous wreck, said she had to go find Mickey to make sure . . . to make sure he . . . isn't dead, I suppose."

"Did she get a look at the two men in the room with Mama Leone?"

"Not really, I don't think. She didn't say, except that she was afraid they saw her, which was another reason she wanted to leave town. She's terribly frightened. I've never seen her this way. Truly, Inspector. You have to believe me."

"Did she say where she was going?" he asked, ignoring her plea. Henrietta thought for a moment. "Somewhere up north. Something about a cabin Mickey has in Wisconsin."

"Did she mention a town?"

Henrietta considered again and shook her head. "I don't think so. But there's something else." She glanced over at Kelly and Charlie, who still stood near the doorway. "This might be important. Polly had a sister . . ."

"Libby Shoemacher?"

Henrietta exhaled a deep breath, deflated that he already seemed to know about her important discovery. "Yes," she disappointedly. "You know about her?"

"Yes, I did a little digging and found that one Polly Shoemacher, a.k.a. Smith, reported that her sister had gone missing some time ago. According to the flimsy report filed at the time, Libby had worked at the Promenade for a brief time and then the Marlowe, so I started wondering if perhaps Polly was attempting to follow in her big sister's footsteps, maybe even get revenge on the woman she thought might be responsible for her disappearance," he said, looking steadily at her as if to gauge her reaction. "Seemed a workable theory, that is until I heard this version, if it's to be believed, of course."

"Of course you can believe it!" Henrietta said hotly. "Why would Polly make up a story that could potentially implicate Mickey?"

"You have a point," the inspector mused. "But why run then? That or he's dead."

"Oh, I hope not, for Polly's sake! Maybe . . . maybe he thought the cops would think it was him?" she asked hopefully.

"Perhaps." His eyes flashed at her. "Or maybe he was afraid to get mixed up with the police for a different reason," he said suggestively. Henrietta remembered how Polly had told her he had been skimming the till, but she kept her eyes on the floor.

"Let me guess, dipping his hand in, right?" the inspector said with an arched eyebrow.

Henrietta could only stare at him. "How did you—?"

"Not hard to figure out," he said dryly, "not after you've been doing this as many years as I have." He crossed the room and looked out the window. "The real question is where is he now? He's a prime witness." He looked back at Henrietta. "We need to find Miss Shoemacher."

"But why? If you don't think she did it, why do you have to find her?"

"Because she'll lead us to Mickey. And because she's in very great danger, I suspect."

Henrietta felt her stomach knot up and put her hand up to her forehead. She suddenly felt weak and very tired. Inspector Howard's hard expression suddenly gave way to one of concern.

"Kelly, Charlie—you two get back to the station, tell Jones to get on this cabin business. See if he can start digging something up. I'll take it from here," he said, looking back at Henrietta.

"Sure thing, boss," Kelly grinned, giving the inspector a knowing wink, that, Henrietta noticed, he had the decency to at least pretend to ignore. Kelly disappeared out the back, then, with Charlie following closely.

"You look pale. Are you hungry?" the inspector asked in a softer tone now that they had gone.

"Desperately. But then again, I'm always hungry," she said with a faint smile.

"Come on, then. Let's get you something to eat," he said matter-of-factly, nodding toward the back door.

"That sounds awfully like a date, Inspector Howard . . .," Henrietta ventured.

"I'd hardly call it that," he said brusquely.

"What would you call it, then?"

"I'd call it police business," he said, his eyes revealing nothing more. "You're no good to me if you pass out from hunger before you've told me what happened at the Marlowe."

"But after that I'm allowed? To pass out, that is?"

"Are you always this flippant, Miss Von Harmon?" he asked coolly.

"That depends."

"On what? Pray, do tell," his eyebrow slightly arched again.

"On how hungry I am," she said casually.

"Not one of those opportunistic types, then."

Henrietta stifled a laugh. "I would have been happy to tell you what happened at the Marlowe had you arranged for a more civilized interview, Inspector, but as it was, your overzealous sidekicks got in the way of it," she retorted, and she thought she saw him bite back a grin.

"All right. Kelly and Charlie can sometimes be a bit enthusiastic, I admit. But they are very effective; they've saved me on more than one occasion. Anyway, it couldn't be helped, or sort of couldn't be helped. How were we to know you'd be creeping around Miss Shoemacher's apartment?"

"And for your information," Henrietta continued, ignoring his question, "The 'audition' wasn't exactly as you described. I had to show . . ." she stopped short, suddenly not wanting to say "panties" or "bottom" in front of him, "things that I wasn't prepared to, if you must know. That isn't what I agreed to. Maybe you're not exactly on the level," she said, narrowing her eyes at him. "Polly said I shouldn't trust you, and maybe this proves it," she said, crossing her arms in front of her.

This time the inspector let out a little laugh. "I can assure you, Miss Von Harmon, that I'm very much 'on the level,' as you put it. I apologize that you were asked to do things that made you uncomfortable, shall we say. It is not what I was led to believe. Honest," he said with what looked like a flicker in his eye.

Henrietta paused, confused, and wondered if he were indeed teasing, even flirting with her. What did he mean by 'not what I was led to believe'? Was he referring to the audition or to her willingness to participate in risqué behavior? He put his hand out to her to help her up, and she took it.

"Well, I'll forgive you just this once," she said with a smile, her dimples showing. When she stood up, she found herself very close to him, and when she looked up at him, she thought she saw something in his eyes, but he stepped back, then, looking away. Oddly, she felt disappointed, unable to decipher him. One moment she was convinced she felt his attraction to her; the next he was as cold and aloof as ever.

"Why did you come here, anyway?" he asked, adjusting his hat and placing his hands on his hips as he studied her.

"To Polly's, you mean? Because I can't go home yet; Ma can't know about this. And anyway, I have to fix my dress, or my costume, I should say."

"You made the audition, then," he said, his eyes lighting up briefly.

"Yes, thanks for asking."

"I knew you would."

"Listen, are we going to get something to eat or not? Otherwise, I've got to get sewing. I've got a long night ahead of me here, and don't you have other people to terrorize?"

The corners of the inspector's mouth twitched. "You're not getting off that easily, Miss Von Harmon. I expect a more detailed report than that."

"All right, then, what do you suggest?"

"I know of a particularly good sausage wagon on Wrightwood. I'll pop down and get a couple while you start sewing. It'll save time."

"Expensive taste."

The inspector gave a wry smile. "You might say that. But for now, duty calls." He paused before going out the door. "Anything to drink in this joint?"

"Some whiskey, I think," Henrietta offered, wondering if Polly had drunk any more of it. She quickly looked under the sink and held up the half-empty bottle for the inspector to see.

"I suppose that will do. Lock the door behind me," he said seriously. "Don't let anybody in but me. Nobody. Understand?"

"You mean in case Kelly or Charlie turn up and confuse me again for Polly?" she offered sarcastically.

"I'm serious, Miss Von Harmon. I'll explain later."

Henrietta wasn't sure what to make of his cryptic warning as she searched for Polly's sewing kit in her bedroom and, upon finally finding it, sat down in the armchair in the front room to begin her evening's project, the events of the day floating back to her, filling her once again with a sense of unease.

Thankfully, the inspector was only gone for about a half hour or so before he returned with two sausages for each of them and two large bottles of beer. Henrietta tried not to devour hers too quickly, but she hadn't eaten since early morning and only a bit of toast at that. She hadn't realized how hungry she really was.

She looked over at the inspector, trying to understand his odd aloofness one minute and his seeming flirtatiousness the next. More than likely, it was a game to him. Perhaps all cops acted like this, she reasoned. They were probably used to getting their way and expecting certain privileges. He was extremely handsome; she would give him that. He had a strong jaw, which was usually stubbled, she had noticed, and a charming smile, when he did smile, which wasn't often. His eyes were perhaps his best feature, though always a trifle sad. Why hadn't she noticed before how devastating he was? She wondered why he wasn't married and looked again at his hands. He wore no ring, but she noticed that his hands were long and graceful and that he ate with perfect manners, which is not what she would have expected in a cop. He seemed different somehow. He reminded her of someone, but she just couldn't place it. She was tempted to ask him outright if he was married, but she could not work up enough courage, and, anyway, what did it matter?

"Suppose you tell me now what happened?" he asked, taking another drink of his beer, having finished his sausages. He was sitting on the divan opposite her, his legs casually crossed. He had taken off his overcoat and his suit jacket and had loosened his tie.

Henrietta looked away from him and took up the costume again. "I'm not sure where to start."

"What is it like inside?" he prompted her. "What's the layout?"

"It's very creepy. Very dim, hard to find your way around, lots of twisty hallways. It would be easy to get lost, or to hide, I suppose. It reminds me of a maze."

"How many girls?" he asked, draining his bottle.

"Tried out, you mean? I couldn't say. Hundreds, I'd imagine."

"How many made it?" he clarified.

"Six of us."

"Six? You're sure? That seems a lot."

"Funny, I was thinking the opposite."

"Once they're in, not many quit, so there's usually not that many openings. It means that . . . well, never mind," he said, standing up. "Where'd you say that whiskey was?"

"Under the sink," she replied, and bent over her work again as he went to get it. He returned with the bottle and two glasses, holding one out to her. She accepted it, though she was not yet finished with the beer he had given her. She took a large drink of it before setting it down and coughed slightly as a result.

"Who're the ringleaders?" he asked, taking his seat on the divan again.

"Probably Mrs. Jenkins," Henrietta replied. "She seems to be the person in charge, and she was mostly running the auditions."

"Not a man?"

"No. I thought that strange, too. But there was a man sitting next to her, watching everything. Mrs. Jenkins kept bending over and whispering with him, like he was telling her what to say. But he never moved. He just sat there staring. It gave me the creeps." Henrietta shuddered, remembering it all again.

"Hmmm," the inspector said, deep in thought, holding his glass near his mouth but not taking a drink.

"Do you think it could have been Neptune?" she asked.

"What did he look like?"

"Stocky. Thick eyebrows, small black eyes."

"That's him," he said, taking the drink. "Anyone else?"

"Just her assistant, Esther, and the custodian, or whatever he is. Bit of a simpleton. Esther's okay, I suppose, but she was put out having to help us find costumes. Mostly works for the dancers and wasn't too happy about having to help us."

"What's this Mrs. Jenkins like?"

"No nonsense. Says we can't go anywhere alone. We always have to have a partner, even going to the bathroom."

"Why's that?"

"She says it's a rough crowd, I think is how she put it. She says there's been some accidents lately."

"Accidents?" the inspector asked, his brow furrowed. "What sort?"

"She didn't say exactly, but I overheard something strange. It was quite horrible, actually," she said faintly, taking another drink of the whiskey.

"Go on," the inspector encouraged, though his face was drawn tight.

"I overheard Mrs. Jenkins and Esther in one of the hallways when I went back to get some thread for this," she said, momentarily holding up the dress. "Mrs. Jenkins told Esther that he—whoever that is—maybe Neptune?—wants Iris tonight. Then Esther said she seems young and that blood is hard to clean." Henrietta added this last bit barely above a whisper.

If the inspector felt any alarm at this revelation, he didn't show it, but kept his face very still, moving only to take another sip of his whiskey. His eyes looked apprehensive, however. "Anything else?" he asked carefully.

Henrietta thought for a moment. "Just that it's odd that this dress has a rip in the bodice, of all places," she said, holding it up for him to see, "and that the custodian—Larry, I think his name is—told me that this was her dress and that it was unlucky."

"Who's her?" he asked as his eyes traveled across the bosom of the dress.

"No idea. Libby Shoemacher maybe?"

"That seems a stretch."

"I suppose you're right. But what do you think it all means?" she asked, her eyes narrowed as she threaded a needle.

"Something not good, I imagine," he said quietly as he stood up. He began to pace slowly in front of the window, and after watching him for a moment to see if any more information would be forthcoming, Henrietta went back to sewing. A comfortable silence settled upon them, broken only when the inspector shook himself from his reverie and asked her if she minded him smoking a pipe.

"Course I don't mind! You don't have to ask. My own dad used to smoke one from time to time."

The inspector stood up and rifled through his suit coat pocket, deftly locating a small rosewood pipe. He methodically filled and then lit it, a spicy cloud slowly rising toward the ceiling after a few moments. Eventually he sat back down across from her, leaning his head casually against his fist, his arm propped up along the back of the divan. Despite his assumed informality, Henrietta was acutely aware of his eyes upon her.

"Sorry this is taking so long," Henrietta finally said apologetically. "I'm nearly done. My sister, Elsie, would have been much quicker than me, I'm ashamed to say. But I naturally couldn't take this home, now could I?" Henrietta said, holding it up in front of her.

The inspector looked at the dress again. "That's certainly not a Dutch girl costume," he said with a slight smile, his eyebrow arched again. An unexpected look of concern then rippled across his face. "You can't stay here, Miss Von Harmon," he said seriously. "It's much too dangerous. They'll be watching. I'm sure of it."

"Who exactly?"

"If I'm guessing correctly, the two thugs who bumped off Mama Leone. And if they didn't get a real good look at Polly, they might think you're her. It's already happened once today with Kelly and Charlie, and it's very likely it could happen again."

Henrietta felt dangerously close to tears. "But, Inspector, I can't go home each night. Not like this," she said, giving the costume a little shake.

"Who's at home, then, that you're so worried about?" he asked gently, his head tilted and his eyes holding hers.

Henrietta hesitated a few moments before answering. "My mother, I suppose. There's eight of us. Eight kids, that is."

"Eight?" he seemed surprised.

Henrietta tried to smile and shrugged.

"And your father?" he asked quietly.

Henrietta looked away. "He died. A few years ago."

The inspector looked as though he were about to ask something else but then seemed to change his mind. "I see," he said, standing up and walking back toward the window. "Well, regardless of your precarious position at home, you can't come back here any time soon, even to change clothes." His aloofness had returned. "You'll just have to change at the Marlowe. It'll look more natural, anyway."

"Well, that's easy for you to say," Henrietta said, her face burning as she pulled the thread through the last stitch and balled it into a knot, hating the old feelings of shame that crept out of a place she had believed safely hidden away. She bit the thread with her teeth and held up the dress to survey her handiwork. Not perfect, she assessed, but she supposed it would have to do. "I guess I'm finished," she said to his back as she began slowly packing up the sewing kit.

"Right, then, I'll see you home," he said, turning and moving toward the divan where he had left his suit coat. As he slipped it on, she stood up and realized then that she was still wearing Polly's emerald dress. "You'll have to wait just a minute while I get out of this," she said uncomfortably. He was standing very near her now, and he was looking at her with a tender, sad sort of look she didn't recognize. Was it compassion? she wondered and hoped to God it wasn't pity. Whatever it was, there was an awkwardness between them. He seemed about to say something, by stopped himself. "Yes, of course," he said instead, looking away and sitting back down on the divan to wait, puffing deeply at his pipe.

Henrietta made her way to Polly's bedroom and softly shut the door, one hand reaching for her buttons as she did so. She quickly undid them and let the dress drop to the floor. As she gingerly stepped out of it, she looked behind her and felt her stomach flutter, knowing that only a thin door separated her from the inspector beyond. For one breathless moment she allowed herself to imagine him coming in unawares, seeing her in her underthings... Would he still have the same look of pity, or would it be replaced by something else? she wondered briefly. She felt herself flush and scolded herself for such thoughts. No, she decided, this was not the way to attract such a man as the inspector, if one were wont to do so, which, of course, she wasn't, she muttered as she hurriedly put on Eugene's clothes.

No, the inspector seemed a different sort altogether—respectable, honorable—one which Henrietta had rarely come upon. They were, after all, alone together in this apartment. He could easily overpower her. But she hadn't been afraid once, nor had he once overstepped the mark, though she thought she might have read desire in his eyes. But perhaps she was mistaken, though; he could be decidedly chilly, and what did it matter, anyway?

She shook herself from her thoughts and paused for a quick second in front of Polly's little mirror to check her hair, hating the fact that she had to appear in front of him yet again in the baggy overalls and boots, but there was nothing for it. With a sigh, she opened the bedroom door and returned to the front room where he stood waiting for her, his extinguished pipe in hand.

At the sight of her in Eugene's clothes, his eyes lit up in amusement once again, and his mouth twitched as he surveyed her. "Why, Miss Von Harmon, you look simply ravishing," he said, smugly. "Ready?"

"Yes, I think so," she said, avoiding his eyes, and looking instead around the room to make sure she hadn't left anything. "I think you might be overreacting, though, Inspector, about staying here, that is," she said, slightly irritated, as she made her way to the door. "It seems to me that the real danger lies inside the Marlowe, not here," she said, gesturing round the apartment. "And anyway, how do I contact you if I do get into trouble? You said you'd have men watching, but I didn't see anyone!"

"Well, if you saw us, that would defeat the purpose, wouldn't it?" he said patronizingly. He picked up the carpetbag for her and opened the door. "If you're ever in real danger," he said more seriously, "call the station at 124; they'll know how to reach me. Don't worry, though. I'll have men on the lookout. Some even in the audience at times, if we're lucky, but we've got to be very careful not to blow our cover. We've been after Neptune for a long time."

"What exactly am I supposed to be looking for?" she asked as they descended the back stairs, the inspector still at the top, locking the door behind them.

"Anything suspicious. Keep an eye on Neptune if you can, and this Jenkins. Try to get to know some of the girls. Get them to trust you; they might open up then."

"Oh, is that all?"

She had reached the bottom of the stairs and walked around to the front of the building, which sat on Mildred Street. She looked forlornly toward Wrightwood as the inspector came up behind her. "I've probably missed the last streetcar down to Armitage," she sighed.

The inspector laughed. "You didn't really think I was going to put you on the streetcar, did you?" He stepped toward the curb, raising his hand to hail a cab.

It took Henrietta a few moments to realize what he was doing, but when she did, she hurriedly stepped forward, putting her hand on his arm. "No, don't get a taxi!" she said. "I . . . I don't want to spend the money. I'll just walk; I've done it often enough before. It'll do me good," she tried to say cheerfully. "It'll give me time to think."

His brow creased as a cab pulled to a stop in front of him. "Don't be ridiculous. Get in!" he said sternly.

Obediently, Henrietta climbed in, the driver taking her carpetbag and setting it beside him on the front seat while the inspector got in beside her.

"Where do you live?" he asked.

"Twenty-nine ten West Armitage," she said somewhat sullenly. She wasn't sure why she was irritated with him.

"Got that, driver?" the inspector asked, leaning forward. The driver merely nodded, and the inspector sat back in the seat next to Henrietta.

"This isn't necessary, you know," she said, looking out the window.

"Perhaps not. But if someone is watching, they won't be able to follow you this way," he said quietly.

"Oh," was all Henrietta could think to say. Their arrangement was beginning to be more than she had bargained for.

The silence between them continued, Henrietta not wanting to look over at him. The emotion and stress of the day, plus the late-night whiskey and now the rocking of the car, were all taking their toll on her. She was feeling very tired suddenly and tried to stifle a yawn.

"Well, thanks, I suppose," she mumbled finally, watching the buildings on Lincoln Avenue and then Fullerton speed by, no traffic to hinder their progress west.

"Don't mention it," the inspector said thinly, not looking over at her either, but continuing to gaze out the window on his own side.

Henrietta remembered very little of the rest of the ride home, waking up with a start when the cab came to an abrupt stop in front of her building. She opened her eyes, trying to ascertain where she was, and suddenly realized she had been asleep on the inspector's shoulder. "Oh, I'm terribly sorry!" she said, looking quickly up at him and then away.

His eyes held that strangely tender, sad look again, which she couldn't readily decipher. She busied herself collecting her handbag and brushing her hair into place with her hands while the inspector got out of the car and came around to open the door for her. She didn't look at him as he walked her to the door, carrying her carpetbag, the cab idling as it waited for him to return.

"Be careful, Miss Von Harmon," the inspector said grimly, handing her the bag.

"Yes. I will," she said, looking up at him finally. He was standing so very close to her that she could almost feel his breath in the night air. Her legs felt weak, but perhaps it was merely the cold.

"There was just one other thing I forgot to tell you . . ."

"Yes?" she asked hopefully.

"Just that your man, Artie, has been cleared. Seems he has an airtight alibi."

"Artie?" she asked, distracted.

"In all night with his mother. Jones spoke with her himself. So you needn't worry that you're stepping out with a murderer," he said with a sad smile.

Henrietta was in turmoil as she shuffled through the emotions that ripped through her. Artie had told her a while ago that his mother was dead. Who had Jones talked with, then? And she resented Artie being called 'her man,' especially by the inspector. "I . . . I think you've got it all wrong, Inspector. Artie—"

"I'd best be going, Miss Von Harmon. That's your affair," he interrupted, turning to walk back to the cab. "Just thought I'd let you know."

"But, Inspector, you've got it all wrong!"

"I don't think so, Miss Von Harmon. Jones was quite clear," he said, still not turning around.

"Aren't you even going to wish me luck?" she called out almost desperately, not knowing what else to say and suddenly not wanting him to leave.

"Good luck, then, Miss Von Harmon," he said, turning back momentarily and politely tipping his hat to her. "I'll be in touch," he said, as he turned around and climbed into the cab without looking back again.

Henrietta sighed as she watched him go and pushed heavily on the door to go in, not knowing why she felt so low as the cab pulled away. How could she be falling for a cop, anyway? she wondered, realizing it fully. Had she totally taken leave of her senses? Besides, even if she was falling for him, he was clearly not interested in a girl like her.

Meanwhile, as the inspector sat in the back seat of the cab travelling south, he removed his hat and ran his hand through his hair. Try as he might, he couldn't stop thinking about how very young she had looked, asleep on his shoulder. He swallowed hard and hoped to God he wasn't making a mistake.

CHAPTER 8

Henrietta smiled nervously as she pulled on her white kid gloves and adjusted her red satin cap again. She wasn't sure if it looked better perched on the crown of her head or a bit off-center in a possibly more alluring position.

It had been hard to tell as she had hurriedly gotten dressed, having to fight for time in front of the mirrors that lined one whole wall of the usherettes' dressing room at the Marlowe Theater. Below the mirrors were six makeup vanities and cushioned stools, stained over the years from spilled rouge and face powder, not at all as nice as the professional makeup stations in the dancers' dressing room next door. Theirs had high stools, lighted mirrors, and fully stocked vanities with rows and rows of pretty shades of lipstick and rouge. Esther was never far from the dancers, helping them to dress or touch up their makeup, and was even seen occasionally getting them drinks from the bar. The usherettes, on the other hand, were left to fend for themselves.

Mindful of Inspector Howard's warning to stay away from Polly's place, Henrietta had reluctantly taken her things to the Marlowe that afternoon and found an empty cubby to store them in. She had no choice but to show up in her factory clothes, though she had come early to try to avoid being seen. Only Esther had been around, hobbling between the dressing rooms, and if she had noticed, she didn't comment, barely even saying hello to Henrietta. Ma hadn't made any comment either when Henrietta left a bit earlier than usual, nor did she realize that she had come home before the usual time last night, having gone to bed early.

Henrietta felt herself blush again for the hundredth time, thinking about how she had fallen asleep on the inspector's shoulder. How ridiculously childish he must think her! And yet, when he had walked her to the door, his eyes had not held amusement or annoyance, but rather something else entirely, something difficult to read . . . something that had felt strangely like attraction. Surely, she was wrong there, though, she mused, thinking about how he had abruptly left, barely wishing her luck.

With a heavy heart she had climbed the stairs after he had said his quick goodbye, and she had been relieved to hear Ma's light snore as she silently came through the door. She'd absently slipped off her shoes, thinking about the long day's events, but had nearly screamed when she suddenly spotted a shape sitting on one of the kitchen chairs. She put her hand over her mouth to keep quiet and leaned forward, peering into the darkness, and realized with relief that it was only Jimmy.

"What are you doing still awake?" she had whispered, her heart in her throat as he ran up to her. "Did you wet the bed again?"

He shook his head. "Oh, Hen! I saw you get out of a motorcar! Can I go next time?" he said, speaking all in a rush and climbing up into her lap after she had quietly eased into one of the kitchen chairs.

"Shhh!" Henrietta whispered again. "Maybe someday. But it's a secret, okay?"

Jimmy nodded, his blanket by his nose, staring off as he visualized this prospect. "You haven't forgotten your promise, have you, Hen?" he asked earnestly, looking up at her.

"What promise was that, Jimbo?" she asked patiently, though she was so dreadfully tired.

"You know! The carnival! Eugene told me it's this Sunday. I told him you was going to take us, but he don't believe me. He says you're too busy, but you're not, are you, Hen? We're going, right, Hen?"

"Course we're going, silly thing!" she managed to say cheerfully.

Jimmy wriggled with delight in her arms.

"Best get back to bed now, though," she had said, letting him slide off her lap. She had stood up, then, to make a cup of tea, wondering how she was ever going to manage the carnival, and prayed they had Sundays off.

"Almost time, girls!" shouted Mrs. Jenkins from across the theater, causing Henrietta to jump, shaking herself from her reverie. She pushed all thoughts of home and Inspector Howard, for that matter, from her mind as she stood with all the other usherettes, waiting near the bar for Mrs. Jenkins to give them any last-minute instructions. She felt her pocket for her little notebook she had brought for good luck and patted her cap, making sure it was secure. In the end, she had decided to have it tilt to the side.

"First night, isn't it?" whispered a woman beside her. Henrietta had noticed her earlier from afar while the girls were putting on the last touches of makeup in the dressing room. She looked Swedish or Norwegian or something like that, Henrietta had surmised. She was taller than Henrietta, with large, plump breasts that looked as though they would spill out of her tight usherette costume at any moment; long, blond hair tied up loosely under her red cap; sky blue eyes; and flawless skin. She was exceptionally beautiful, even in Henrietta's eyes, like a model or a perhaps a film actress. Henrietta wondered why she wasn't one of the Marlowe's dancers instead of just an usherette.

"I'm Lucy," the blond woman said. "Don't worry. It's not so bad. Done this before?"

Henrietta shook her head. "I used to be a taxi dancer, though," she offered up meekly.

"You'll be fine, then. Used to men ogling you. No different, really. What's your name?"

"Henrietta," she said.

"Nice name," she said with a smile. "Goes both ways."

Henrietta wasn't sure what she meant by that, but her attention was diverted when she heard Mrs. Jenkins call out, "All right, girls!" as she bustled over to them. "New girls, remember to partner up. Hurry! We don't have all night."

Henrietta looked at Lucy imploringly, who smiled and nodded her agreement.

"Remember—no touching!" barked Mrs. Jenkins. "The bank's closed, if you know what I mean. Any trouble, call one of the boys over. Don't go anywhere alone. Stay with your partner! Smile! That's it! You're here to be friendly with them, but not too friendly. Sell the drinks, that's what we want!" She placed a sheet of paper on the bar. "Here's your stations for the night, so find your places. Let's go; come on! Larry!" she called out. "Why aren't you at the door by now! It's time to open up."

"I'm goin'; I'm goin'," Larry said absently as he dipped behind the curtains. "There's time enough," he mumbled, his perpetual cigarette spilling ash as he went.

The night began pretty well. Men, and even a few women, began filing in, the girls formally escorting them to their seats, though it seemed unnecessary, as most of the men appeared to know exactly where they were going. Henrietta found her station, disappointingly near the more sparsely populated back rows, and began taking drink orders as she observed what the other girls were doing. Pretty soon she was practically running back and forth between the rows of stained, dirty seats and the line of usherettes at the bar, mostly delivering beer but a few cocktails, too. It seemed only moments before the house lights dimmed, indicating that the show was about to start, though in truth it had already been a full half hour since the doors had opened. The orders slowed a bit now, the crowd intent on watching the show as the thick red velvet curtains opened and the dancers came onstage, the band playing loud, seductive jazz.

Curious, Henrietta dared to look, too, from time to time. The show began innocently enough, the usual showgirl routine, Henrietta initially observed, though as the evening progressed, the show became more risqué as the dancers began removing various articles of clothing. Henrietta tried to keep her mind on the task at hand, though she embarrassingly found herself staring a couple of times, shocked by what she was seeing. She had caught a glimpse of a burlesque show at the World's Fair, but this was more like striptease, the dancers stopping just short of full nudity. Once or twice, Lucy had to nudge her back into action, indicating with a nod of her head in the direction of Mrs. Jenkins, who seemed to have the uncanny ability to be watching everyone at once at any given time.

The mood of the crowd became more raucous as time wore on and as more clothing flew off. Men began shouting and cheering and became decidedly more friendly whenever Henrietta appeared with fresh drinks, their eyes bleary and red from the cigarette smoke hanging in thick clouds over the rows and rows of seats and the alcohol flowing freely. Once or twice a man tried to pull her onto his lap, but Henrietta managed to extract herself somewhat gracefully before any of the bouncers noticed.

One thin, wiry man in the back row had the audacity to put his hand under her skirt, and it was all Henrietta could do to not slap him. Instead, she smiled sweetly and made her way back to the bar, breathing deeply. She had learned long ago that the shy, quiet ones were sometimes the worst, their pent-up desires bubbling dangerously close to the surface and becoming quickly volatile given the right situation.

"How're you holding up? Been groped yet?" asked Lucy, who had suddenly appeared beside her at the bar.

Henrietta rolled her eyes and smiled. "A few times. You?"

Lucy waved her hand as if she had either lost count by now or no longer cared. "Hey, Ed, how about two vanilla sodas?" she said to the bartender. "You want one, don't you?" she asked Henrietta.

Henrietta hesitated, wondering if they were free. Lucy seemed to read her mind.

"Soda and coffee are complimentary for us, while you're working, that is."

"Am I that obvious?" Henrietta said, smiling shyly.

"Listen, love. We're all here for the money. A girl can't be too careful."

Henrietta took a sip of the soda that Ed deposited in front of them.

"Thanks," she said. Despite the fact that she had clearly been given one of the worst stations, as had all the other new girls, Henrietta had made a surprisingly large amount of tips so far. It wasn't such a bad job after all, she weighed up, though she hadn't really had a chance to observe anything out of the ordinary, anything "suspicious." Wasn't that what Inspector Howard had instructed her to do?

"You got your station covered?" Lucy suddenly asked. "Jenks is circling around."

"Yes, I just passed through. Everyone's enraptured just now," Henrietta said with a smile, allowing her eyes to stray toward the stage, where the dancers had only thin lace ribbons covering their breasts and string-like panties, though they hid behind large, white-feathered plumes made into a sort of fan. "In fact, this might be a good time to freshen up. Can you cover for me?" Henrietta asked.

"I'd better come with you," Lucy said, setting her shiny silver tray on the bar. "You know what Jenks said."

"But what about my station?" Henrietta asked, setting her tray down as well. "Jenks isn't really serious about all that, is she? I mean, honestly! I think I can go to the bathroom on my own!"

"They'll be okay for a few minutes," Lucy said indifferently waving her hand toward the audience. "And, yes, Jenks is always serious. Better not take any chances. You don't want to get on her bad side," Lucy advised as she led Henrietta toward the lavatories. "Anyway, it's probably for the best," she said, turning back toward her. "There's been some attacks on girls in the bathrooms in the past. Men are such swine!"

Nervous as to what they would find, Henrietta was relieved to see it was just an ordinary bathroom with several girls crowded round the mirror adjusting their makeup and adjusting themselves to reveal as much as possible.

"Better hurry up, girls!" Lucy said conspiratorially. "Jenks'll be looking for you!"

"Oh, all right, Lucy," said one of the women, looking Henrietta over as she snuffed out her cigarette in the sink. "We know what you're after."

Henrietta saw Lucy roll her eyes at them before they filed out, giggling and whispering, as Henrietta found an empty stall. When she emerged, she was glad to see that only Lucy remained, standing near the mirror, tucking up loose ends of her hair under her little cap.

"Friends of yours?" Henrietta asked, smiling as she patted her own hair into place.

"Oh, they're all right, really. Just a bit jealous at times. You'll soon discover who your friends are around here."

"Well, I can see why they'd be jealous of you! You're gorgeous! You should be one of the dancers. Or a model, maybe," Henrietta said, looking down to try to find a lipstick she had wedged into the tiny pocket of the dress. "Why are you just an usherette, anyway?" she asked as she pried the lipstick out and pursed her lips to apply the deep red color.

"Seems I could say the same for you," Lucy said from behind her. Henrietta was surprised to feel Lucy's fingers in her hair, pulling it gently aside so that she could rub her shoulders. Despite the strangeness of this action, Henrietta felt her muscles relax and closed her eyes briefly, allowing herself to savor it for just a moment before she forced herself to turn around, suddenly feeling a bit awkward. "Thanks," Henrietta said uneasily, attempting to smile.

Lucy smiled back, her startling blue eyes wide and excited. Henrietta couldn't help but stare at them; they were unlike any color she had ever seen, a powdery blue, almost like a slice of the sky. Before Henrietta could realize what was happening, however, Lucy leaned toward her and gently kissed her on the lips.

Henrietta pulled back, horrified. "Lucy! What are you doing?" she hissed, wiping her lips of any trace of Lucy's.

"Sorry," Lucy said casually with an arched eyebrow, disturbingly reminding Henrietta of Inspector Howard, which somehow made the whole thing worse. "I just thought that maybe . . . you know," she said with a slight shrug, "you might feel the same."

"Well, I don't!" Henrietta said, her heart racing.

"It couldn't have been all that bad. You did say I was gorgeous," Lucy said, attempting to smile.

"I'm not that way. . ." Henrietta insisted, both confused and mortified.

"You sure?" Lucy asked.

"Of course, I'm sure!"

"Got a man, then?"

"Well, sort of," Henrietta said hesitatingly and was perturbed when an image of the inspector came into her mind. Startled by it, she forced him out and instead tried to conjure up an image of Artie leaning close to her after a set with his mischievous smile, though it was a decidedly more fuzzy picture than the one presented by the inspector, his eyes intense and full of . . . of something.

Lucy laughed. "I see. Well, anyway, no hard feelings, right?" She smiled at Henrietta in such a genuine way, holding out her hand to her as a peace offering, that Henrietta couldn't help but smile back and took her hand, albeit hesitantly. "I like you, sweets," Lucy said to her, "so you'd better stick with us. You're more innocent than you let on, and there's lots of wolves prowling around here, and I don't just mean the men."

You can say that again, thought Henrietta, as they made their way out, wondering if Mrs. Jenkins realized that her partner system was inherently flawed. She was trying to act casual in Lucy's presence, but in point of fact, she was quite shaken. She had heard of men being "that way" and had even come across a few that she had suspected might be more effeminate than most, even, she had to reluctantly admit, her own brother Eugene—but a woman? Henrietta hadn't realized that women could feel that way, too. Oh, why was everything always so mixed up! Suddenly she felt rather distraught.

"Listen, Henry," Lucy whispered as they approached the bar. "Things can get a little shady around here," she said, looking around quickly, presumably for Jenks, as she put her hand on Henrietta's arm. "Stay after tonight. In the dressing room. We always have a few drinks after the show, usually some laughs. Why don't you stay, too?" she suggested. "Don't worry, no funny business," she said with a reassuring smile, correctly reading the indecision on Henrietta's face. "Look, you can meet some of the girls that way. You need friends to survive around here."

Henrietta wasn't sure what to say. She was very unsettled by what had happened in the bathroom, but Lucy seemed genuine now, and the inspector had told her to try to befriend the girls, to look for something suspicious. Was this what he had meant? Perhaps she should accept . . .

"Why not?" Henrietta found herself saying. "I can't stay late, though . . ."

"Meeting your fellow?" Lucy said, giving her a little wink.

"My fellow? Oh! No, not that. Just that my mother . . . she'll be expecting me."

Lucy laughed. "You're a gumdrop, you are! How'd you end up in a nasty place like this? Well, no matter. You stick by us."

They collected their silver trays, which were sitting haphazardly at the end of the bar, and quickly surveyed the room. Henrietta spotted Jenks talking to one of the bouncers and pointing toward the stage.

"What about Jenks?" Henrietta said quietly to Lucy. "Doesn't she mind you staying after?"

"Nah. She leaves us to ourselves. Let's just say she's got other things to worry about after the show. You know, behind the green door."

"Behind the green door?" Henrietta asked, mystified. "What does that mean? Outside?"

"Shhh!" Lucy whispered, glancing at the bartender at the far end of the bar. "Not here. I'll explain it all later."

Before Henrietta could respond, however, Jenks had spotted them and angrily signaled them to get back to work.

"Good luck!" Lucy whispered and hurried off.

Henrietta made her way back to her station to collect a fresh list of orders, her legs still a bit weak. She tried to block out any self-consciousness she was feeling about what had gone on in the bathroom, as well as Lucy's hints as to what Jenks might be up to after the shows, but it proved to be difficult. She wondered disconcertingly what she had gotten herself into and found herself quickly surveying the room in an attempt to locate any of the undercover men that the inspector assured her would periodically be there, but she couldn't detect a one. Perhaps they were outside in a car, she mused, though she wasn't sure how that would help her one bit. She didn't exactly relish the notion of going to this "party," but she saw no other way. Besides, she told herself, the inspector was counting on her, wasn't he?

The show ended at around midnight, and the last of the men stumbled out eventually, leaving Larry to finally be able to turn up the house lights and begin his long night of sweeping, Jenks stopping to talk to him and he merely nodding lazily to whatever she was saying to him. Henrietta, still a bit apprehensive, watched Jenks disappear behind the curtains and then turned to face Lucy, who had already undone her cap, letting her long, silky blond hair tumble down.

"Come on," she said to Henrietta, putting an arm through hers, "I need a drink!"

Henrietta smiled and took a deep breath, thinking that that wasn't such a bad idea. Lucy led her backstage through the maze of hallways until they somehow found themselves just outside the usherettes' room. Dancers were in the hallway as well, going in and out of their dressing room, and drinking, too. As Lucy had predicted, Jenks was nowhere to be seen, though Henrietta thought she caught a glimpse of Esther.

As they stepped into the usherettes' dressing room, Henrietta was surprised to see that it had been transformed from its normal, dreary state. A phonograph had appeared from somewhere and someone had put on Fred Astaire's "I Won't Dance." In one corner, there were bottles of gin and whiskey and some assorted small glasses and, of course, bottles of beer. Henrietta was surprised by the red glow that seemed to permeate the whole room and realized that someone had put make-shift shades made out of what looked like red tissue paper over the lightbulbs that hung down on cloth cords from the ceiling. Most of the girls had taken off their uniforms and slipped into their street clothes, while others wore only thin dressing gowns. Some were smoking and laughing in corners; others were counting their tips.

"Come on in!" Lucy said. "Fancy a drink?" she said, making her way toward the back where the booze was kept.

"All right," Henrietta said, uncomfortably following her and attempting to unpin her cap as she went.

"Gin?"

"Beer's good, if that's all right," she said, looking around as they squeezed their way between the women standing about, talking or dancing. Out of the corner of her eye, she saw a slight movement and, looking closer, saw that a couple was entwined on a couch partially hidden by a makeshift curtain. Henrietta could see that they were kissing passionately, and she quickly averted her eyes, wondering how they had snuck men in here. Perhaps it was one of the bouncers, she guessed, and shuddered to think what Jenks would say if she knew.

As she stood waiting for Lucy to pour the drinks, laughing and talking with someone near her, Henrietta couldn't help but steal another glance at the couple. They didn't seem to notice her staring, she observed, nor did anyone else seem to be paying any attention, so she dared to look a bit longer, watching the man gently caress the woman's breasts through her silky robe. Henrietta felt her breath come faster and herself grow warm and looked away accordingly. When she looked back, curiosity overcoming her again, the man had pulled back a little, and Henrietta, despite the dim light, was horrified to discover that it wasn't a man at all, but another woman! Just then, Lucy turned back to her with the drinks and, seeing Henrietta's shocked face, realized in an instant what was occurring.

"Right this way, gumdrop!" she said, handing her the beer and taking her by the elbow. "You shouldn't be seeing such things; you're much too innocent." As Lucy led her to the front of the room, Henrietta now noticed many such couples entwined in the shadows.

"Are . . . are you all—" she struggled to find the right words—"like that?" she finally settled with.

Lucy laughed. "Some, not all. You'd be surprised, though. Sure you're not?" she said, looking coyly at her over the rim of her glass.

"Oh, no! I'm . . . quite sure," Henrietta said, looking away.

"Well, you don't have to worry about us. We don't mind what way you are. Just friends, then," she said, holding up her glass of gin in salute.

Henrietta followed suit, but, not knowing what to say, looked distractedly around the room, searching for a diversion. The record had changed to Xavier Cugat's "Lady in Red," and several girls were swaying to the music. "How about you? Do you have any special . . . person?" Henrietta managed finally.

Lucy took a sip of her gin. "I'm between relationships, I guess you'd say, but I do like a special someone," she admitted, glancing toward the girl she had been laughing with back by the drinks. "You won't mention what happened before, will you? In the bathroom?" she asked nervously. "It's important we girls stick together, you know."

"Well," Henrietta said, seeing her opportunity and leaning forward slightly with a smile. "That depends. What can you tell me about Jenks and this green door business?" she tried to ask in an innocent tone.

"Oh, that? You sure you want to go into all that right now? You just got here, and it's not a very nice story. Not quite the thing, don't you know, dahling," she drawled, putting her hand on her hip and gesturing around the room with her other hand as if to pretend they were at a posh dinner party or an exquisite club.

Henrietta indulged her and smiled. "Please," she urged. "You've got me intrigued. Is it something dangerous? Shouldn't I know what to look out for?"

Lucy's eye fell to the mended patch on the bustline of Henrietta's dress and took another drink. "I suppose you're right," she said with a sigh, dropping the façade, and looked around furtively to make sure no one was listening. "Well, it's just that we think something funny's going on. We're not sure, but we think Jenks is hiding something behind the green door."

"What green door is that?" Henrietta asked, confused.

"You know—the one off to the right of the lobby? It looks like a closet?" she added, seeing Henrietta's blank expression. "When you come into the theater," Lucy used her hands to help explain, "the crowd goes to the left to find their seats and we go to the right toward the dressing rooms and the backstage area? Well, did you notice a couple of doors in a little alcove about halfway down the hallway before ours veers off? One of them is a broom closet and the other one is a little green door. Ever notice it?"

"I think so," Henrietta said, her brows furrowed as she tried to remember. "I thought that was a closet."

"Well, it's not. For one thing, Jenks is way too protective of it, and for another, it's always locked. Believe me, we keep trying it."

"Who's 'we'?" Henrietta asked, taking a sip of her beer.

"Rose, here," Lucy said, nodding at a graceful, long-legged woman standing with her back to them and talking to someone else. She reminded Henrietta of a greyhound. "And Gwen over there," Lucy said, her eyes lighting up as the woman by the drinks caught her glance and smiled. She was a bit shorter than Lucy, with short black hair that turned up at the ends, and dark, almost sad eyes. She was very serious for an usherette, observed Henrietta. She must be a good actress when on duty.

"Maybe it's something valuable she's hiding in there," Henrietta said, drawing Lucy's attention back.

"That's what we thought, till we saw people going in and out late one night."

"People? In a closet?"

"That's just it, it's not a closet. We think it leads to another hallway with rooms off of that."

"Why would you think that?"

"We—we went looking . . . after Libby went missing . . ."

At the mention of Libby, the hair on the back of Henrietta's neck stood up. "Go on," she said eagerly.

"Well, actually, just Gwen went. We thought that, being shorter, she would be less noticed if she wasn't on the floor for a bit. Rose and I covered her station. She hid in the lobby and watched. After one of the numbers, one of the dancers, Evelyn, appeared. She stood outside the green door by herself. Gwen almost called out to her, but just then Jenks appeared with a guy from the audience in tow. Just before they got to the door, Gwen saw the man slip Jenks something that Jenks put in her pocket. Cigarettes maybe, or cash, she thought it looked like."

Henrietta's mouth felt dry, and she drained her beer. "Then what?"

"Jenks unlocked the door and led the two of them inside, the man grabbing at Evelyn and laughing as they went in."

"Was Gwen able to see inside?"

Lucy shook her head. "Not really. Just that it was another hallway. Jenks closed it as soon as she came back out. Gwen could see she was headed back to the floor, so as soon as Jenks was out of sight, she went the long way 'round and got back to us before Jenks even knew she was gone."

"So, you think it's prostitution, then?" Henrietta asked slowly.

"Seems like it."

"But what about this . . . this Libby?"

"That was a while ago," Lucy said, frowning. "She was a good friend . . . if you know what I mean . . . of Rose's. She started out like us as an usherette, but Jenks moved her up to a dancer. Sometimes that happens, but not usually. One night she just disappeared. Jenks said she had quit, but that didn't add up."

"Why's that?"

"Because she left all her stuff behind."

"Do you still have it? Her stuff, I mean?" Henrietta tried not to let her voice sound too excited.

"Yeah, Rose's got it. Why?"

"Just wondering. I . . . did she ever talk about what was behind the green door?"

"That's just it. She only went the once. Well, that's what we think anyway. Told Rose that she had a chance to make a lot of money, but she wouldn't say how. That's the last we saw of her. Rose was crushed, poor thing. Jenks told us the next day that Libby had quit, and Rose had the sense to grab her things. Sure enough, ol' Larry appeared the next day looking for it, even asked us for it, but we lied and said she never kept anything here. Jenks must have sent him."

"What do you think happened?" Henrietta said, peering at Lucy through partially closed eyes, as the smoke floating above them was getting rather thick.

"I'm not sure," Lucy sighed. "We've been trying to figure it out. We've tried talking to the dancers, to Evelyn, but no one's talking. Evelyn told us to stay out of it, that it's not worth looking into and would only bring us trouble. She looked really frightened. Said if we knew what's good for us, we'd mind our own. Begged us not to ask her anymore or she'd get it."

"Hmmm," said Henrietta, trying to make sense of it.

"We can't be too snoopy because if Jenks suspects we know anything, I'm sure we'd be fired, or maybe worse," she said raising her eyebrows apprehensively. "We haven't been able to find out much else, but now Iris has gone missing, too."

Henrietta felt her throat slightly constrict. "Who's Iris?"

Lucy looked at her worriedly before answering. "Iris was—is—an usherette, too. Disappeared just like Libby." Lucy's gaze dropped to Henrietta's bosom, and, catching her attention, she peered at it closely. "I think that might be Libby's dress you're wearing," she said uneasily.

Henrietta's hand went to the mended patch. "So, no one knows where Iris is, either?" she asked quietly, ignoring Lucy's comment.

"She hasn't come in today, and no one's heard from her. I know it's only been a day, but it just seems oddly like what happened with Libby . . ."

Just then Gwen appeared with a bottle of beer, which she thrust at Henrietta, and a half-empty bottle of gin, which she waved in front of Lucy. Lucy smiled in response and held up her glass while Gwen poured. "I didn't think you'd ever come back for a refill, so I thought I'd help you out," she said, looking at Lucy a tad longer than was perhaps necessary. "Who's your friend?" she asked, looking Henrietta up and down.

"This is one of the new girls, Henrietta. She's a bit green, if you know what I mean," she said with a small smile. "She's straight as an arrow, though. So she says," Lucy said, looking playfully back at Henrietta.

"I was just asking about Iris," Henrietta said, not wanting the conversation to be sidetracked.

"Do you think that wise?" Gwen asked Lucy quietly, as if they were alone.

Lucy shrugged. "She's all right, Gwen."

"I—I heard something yesterday. I . . . about Iris, that is," Henrietta suggested. She wasn't sure how much she should share with them, but she needed them to trust her.

"What was it?" Gwen asked quickly, giving her full attention now to Henrietta.

"It was after the auditions. All of the other girls had left, but I went back to get some silk thread to mend this dress. It was the only one left . . ."

"I think that was Libby's—" Gwen began.

"Yes, I told her," put in Lucy.

"Anyway," Henrietta said, fingering the tear again, "I came back here, and then I heard Jenks and Esther in the hallway. Jenks told Esther that 'he' wanted Iris that night, and Esther said that she was young and something about blood being hard to clean up."

"Jesus," Gwen mumbled, looking away. "Who's he?" she asked sourly.

"I guess I was hoping you could tell me," Henrietta said, surprised.

"I have no idea," Gwen answered. "You, Lucy?"

Lucy shook her head slowly.

"Who owns the Marlowe?" Henrietta asked, fresh from her experience at the Promenade and doing her best to imitate the inspector.

"I think it's some guy by the name of Neptune," Lucy responded absently.

Henrietta's stomach lurched. "Is he . . . is he ever around?" she asked hesitantly.

"Not much. He gives me the creeps when he is, though. He's a swine, like most men. Always staring," Gwen said disgustedly.

"Oh, Gwen, do you think it could have been Neptune with Iris, do you?" asked Lucy.

Gwen shrugged her shoulders.

"I think I might have seen him at the audition," Henrietta put in. "Bushy eyebrows?"

"That would be him. He's always whispering with Jenks at the auditions. Has the final say, of course."

"What are we going to do? About Iris, I mean?" Lucy asked, looking at Gwen. "Libby might have gone of her own accord, but not Iris. She was afraid of her own shadow."

"Maybe go to the police?" Henrietta suggested tentatively.

"No!" Gwen said with a force that took Henrietta aback. "They won't do anything. It'll just be like Libby all over again. We need real proof this time."

Not the time to tell them she was working with the police, then, Henrietta decided.

"There's a chance that she's all right, you know," put in Lucy pensively. "Maybe just home sick in bed."

"Yes, but don't you think it strange, come to think of it, that Jenks hasn't blown her top over Iris not coming in today?"

"Maybe she knows something we don't," Lucy suggested. "Like the fact that she's sick or something."

"Maybe," said Gwen disbelievingly. "But until we figure out what to do, everyone try to stick together. There's definitely something very wrong going on around here," she said gravely. "But mum's the word for now," she said, looking from Lucy to Henrietta, where her gaze remained. "Understood?"

Henrietta nodded her acquiescence and was about to speak when Rose came up with another girl, and after more introductions, the conversation turned to lighter subjects. While Rose and the other girl, whose name Henrietta had already forgotten, discussed the cheapest place to buy stockings, Gwen and Lucy managed to slip off to talk by themselves in a corner, Lucy giving Henrietta a little wink as she passed her. Henrietta made a guess as to why they were sequestering themselves and felt slightly sick to her stomach. Looking around uneasily, she realized that she wasn't going to get any more information tonight, so she decided she should look for an escape as well.

Knowing what she did about most of the women in the room being the "other way," Henrietta felt uncomfortable changing in front of them, but there was nothing for it. She tried her best to slip discreetly out of her costume behind the ratty screen by the old armoire, though she could feel eyes on her as she did so. When she was finally arrayed back in her factory clothes, she draped her coat over her arm, and after looking around once more for Lucy and Gwen, who seemed to have well and truly disappeared, she hurried out, anxious to get away.

The hallway was dimly lit, but welcome after the distorted red glow in the dressing room. While her eyes were trying to adjust, she managed to trip over poor Larry hovering just outside the door.

"Oh!" she called out as she felt herself falling, but Larry gripped her arm to help catch her. She was surprised that his grip was so strong.

"Sorry, miss," he said, his cigarette bobbing. Up close, Henrietta could see that his face was a mass of wrinkles, and his back was slightly bent. He looked as though he had had a hard life. He looked too old to have been in the war, but perhaps he had done manual labor. He stood sheepishly rubbing his head.

"Are you hurt?" she said, suddenly feeling sorry for him.

"Not much, miss, no."

"You startled me. I . . . I didn't see you there." Her eyes looked at him suspiciously. "You weren't eavesdropping, were you, Larry?" She gave him a small smile to encourage the truth.

"No, miss! I wasn't. Just that you can never be too careful round here," he said, beginning to slightly move the broom back and forth in front of him as if it were a comforting habit to do so. He looked over his shoulder. "Can't be too careful, that's what I always say. Accidents have been known to happen."

If he was trying to warn her of something, it wasn't having the slightest effect, as all Henrietta felt as she listened to him was a deep sense of pity. She observed his rumpled, unwashed state and tried not to breathe in the peculiarly strong odor that surrounded him. She wondered where he lived.

"Don't you ever go home, Larry?" she asked.

Larry swung his head to and fro like the broom.

"Do you sleep here somewhere?"

"Sometimes. That I do, miss. Mrs. Jenkins says it's okay if I do. It's better that way, I say, 'cause then I can keep an eye on things better."

"Yes, I suppose you're right," Henrietta said kindly. An idea suddenly occurred to her, then. "Say, Larry," she said, using her dimpled smile on him, "you don't happen to know what's behind that green door, do you? You know? The one over by the hallway off the lobby—by the broom closet?"

She thought she saw a flicker of recognition in his eyes, but it disappeared just as quickly and his face remained a blank. "Don't know nothin' bout it," he said quickly. "I don't hafta clean over there. That's Mrs. Jenkins's special closet, that is."

"Hmmm," Henrietta said to herself, thinking it all over.

"Why you want to know?" he said, squinting up at her.

"Oh, just some of the girls were talking about it," she said, inclining her head toward the door she had just come through. "No matter!" she tried to say lightly. "Forget I mentioned it. Well, I've got to be going. Hope you get some sleep."

"Haf to lock up. That's what I haf to do," he called after her as she walked down the hallway, causing her to wonder again if he were simple. Jenks probably gets him for next to nothing, the old cow, she mused, as she pushed open the main doors and slipped out into the night.

She half expected the inspector to be there, but there was no one nearby at all. She surveyed the nearly deserted street in front of the Marlowe, hoping to see a squad car with perhaps Charlie or Kelly inside, unwelcome though they might be, but there was nothing. So, bundling her coat around her, she made her way alone to the train stop, having survived her first night at the Marlowe, but feeling oddly disappointed as she left.

CHAPTER 9

"Oh, Hen, isn't this wonderful?" Elsie said as they wound their way through the maze of booths precariously perched in St. Sylvester's side parking lot, transformed now into the annual spring carnival. Bright booths and colorful pennants had been strung up, zigzagging their way across the lot, creating a contagious air of festivity in what was normally a dull, soggy lot sprouting weeds and collecting bits of trash along the broken fence that surrounded it.

The carnival spilled out beyond the lot as well, running almost all the way up to the grassy area and the tiny cemetery that lay immediately behind the church, a carryover from the old days before people began to use the larger St. Boniface Cemetery on Clark. As Henrietta and all of the rest of the Von Harmons, excepting Ma, of course, weaved through the crowds of people milling about, trying their luck at the games or sampling the wares at the food tents, an excitement usually reserved only for Christmas was upon them.

Henrietta had had only a few hours' sleep before being woken that morning by her mother, who'd gruffly reminded her that she had promised to take the children to the carnival after Mass. She herself refused to go, saying that she wanted a day to herself to put her feet up, which Henrietta suspected was only part of the truth. The rest of it, Henrietta knew, was Ma's usual avoidance of social situations since her father's suicide. Each year, Henrietta observed, it seemed to get a little worse, making Ma ever more insular and out of sorts as time wore on. She couldn't avoid going to the shops and to Mass, of course, but other than that Ma kept herself to herself. An event such as the carnival would have been out of the question for her.

She had not always been like this, Henrietta had brooded, as she'd rolled over onto her thin pillow, listening to the warbling of the early morning birds outside. As a little girl, Henrietta remembered her mother being happier, though it was true that she had never been overly affectionate. There had always been a bit of a distance between her and her mother, but these days, it seemed utterly hopeless. Nothing she did could ever make Ma happy.

She sighed, lying there thinking about it all until Jimmy appeared by her bedside and shook the mattress, imploring her to get up. Reluctantly, then, she dragged herself out of bed and sluggishly got dressed. At least it was sunny for the carnival, she observed, as she pulled back the curtain a tiny bit and resolved not to think about the Marlowe at all this day if she could help it.

Martha Von Harmon had begrudgingly poured Henrietta a cup of coffee from the pot on the stove as she listened to

Henrietta and Jimmy talking and laughing in the bedroom. The Lord only knew what was going to happen with that one, she thought, woefully wiping her hands on her dirty apron. Henrietta was just too beautiful for her own good, and she knew it; that was the problem, Martha mused. If Henrietta were completely innocent as to her charms, it would be one thing, but she had seen how Henrietta looked at men and how they looked back. She knew what she was doing, all right!

It had been just the opposite for her. Being raised in her family's upper-class home, she had known very little of men or what went on behind closed bedroom doors. Her own mother had been very strict, observing closely and exactly all the rules of the higher society in which they moved, her father being a rather wealthy banker. Martha was the only daughter in a house of boys and as such could not help feeling that she had let everyone down by not being the slim, petite example of girlish beauty that the family would undoubtedly have preferred. Regretfully, she had always been a bit big and rather plain and had a very bad habit of slouching, having to frequently be told to "sit straight, Martha!" There was a dearth of suitors around her, except for those arranged to come for dinners by the special effort of her parents, young men whose families, despite their very genteel breeding, were decidedly in want of the very large dowry Martha would bring with her to the altar.

Martha had always hated those dinners, feeling like a prize pig on display, and much preferred the company of Leslie Von Harmon, the handsome butcher's delivery boy, who had neither money nor position despite his aristocratic-sounding surname. Martha came to live for a smile from him whenever he dropped off the weekly order, feeling almost pretty when he indulged her this way.

She had eventually begun to smile back, and then one day, when the cook had gone out on an errand, she had invited him in and had even daringly offered him a cup of tea. He had indeed come in, and, well, one thing had led to another in the butler's pantry. She had been confused by what he wanted to do to her, with her, and she had shockingly found herself pregnant not long after. Les just laughed when she subsequently told him about her condition and simply responded that he supposed they should get married. Her parents, of course, were furious and refused to permit the marriage. They wanted her to "visit" an aunt in New York for the duration of her confinement and quietly deposit the baby in a local orphanage. Martha refused to be parted from Les, however, and with threats of disownment ringing in her ears, she ran off with Les one night and was married.

The romantic dream had burned away quicker than even she could have ever fathomed, however, and her descent into poverty and misery began almost immediately with barely a whisper of true love. Martha found herself overwhelmed by her new life and even more befuddled when Henrietta had come out of her, followed by nine more, two of which had subsequently died of the flu.

Henrietta had always seemed more Les's girl than hers. She had his flirtatious personality, his long eyelashes, and his dimples, that was for sure. Of course, Martha loved her daughter, but as Henrietta grew older, she at times found it hard to like her, not knowing what to do with this beautiful creature that had somehow come out of her big, awkward body. Consequently, she usually held her at arm's length, never letting her true emotions show, just as her parents had always done with her. Surely that was the right way, was it not? What was the good of spoiling a child, especially one like Henrietta, who obviously didn't need one bit of extra attention?

And yet, Henrietta was the antithesis of her, always lavishing her younger siblings with hugs and kisses, something Martha longed to do herself but just couldn't. Surely this was a bad sign for what lay ahead for Henrietta, she guessed, as the girl seemed to crave physical attention. Not only that, but everything seemed to come easy for Henrietta; she never seemed to have a day's worry in her life. Already Martha could see that Henrietta's dimpled smile and a toss of her thick auburn hair opened all manner of doors for her, whether it was an extra pound of sugar at the armory hastily handed to her by some puppy-eyed sop in the back of the truck, or even her seemingly endless supply of jobs. She just prayed it never went beyond that; she didn't think she could bear another incident of shame, not after Les. Most days she refused to allow herself to think of him, of what had happened, but in her heart, she didn't really blame him; that was the worst of it. Deep down she knew she had been cruel to him, but she hadn't been able to stop herself. And now he was gone.

She was determined not to let anything else happen, trying her best to keep tabs on Henrietta, but it was useless trying to contain the beauty and the energy that emanated from her daughter. She had to admit that she simply did not know what to do with Henrietta. If only she would settle down, then she wouldn't have to worry about it anymore. But for all of Henrietta's flirtations, there never seemed to be anyone steady, no one who hung about, except for Stanley, that is. Now *there* was a perfectly good candidate, Martha thought to herself. But Henrietta, headstrong as always, did not seem the faintest bit interested. True, she could probably get any man,

Martha recognized with a touch of bitterness, but you could do worse than Stanley. He was a bit younger, but what did that matter? In fact, that might be better, Martha had mused more than once. He was steady, dependable, decent. But Henrietta seemed determined to foist him off onto Elsie, who was so much more like Martha herself. Bigger, unassuming, shy . . .

"Hen! Can we have a go, do you think?" Eddie begged.

"Yeah, Hen! Let him have a go! Please!" they all asked in various voices. "If he wins the vase, we can bring it back to Ma—then she might not be in such a bad mood," said Herbert hopefully as they all crowded around the ring toss game.

Henrietta grinned. "Oh, all right. Here," she said, opening her coin purse. "Here's a nickel for each of you," she said, putting a coin into each of their outstretched hands. "You can each play one game, but that's all!"

"Does it have to be the ring toss, Hen? Or can I do the balloon pop one?" Eugene asked.

"Any one you choose," Henrietta said benevolently. "But just one, so choose carefully," she added.

With squeals of delight, they ran off in separate directions, leaving just herself and Elsie, each one holding one of the twins by the hand, and Stanley, who had showed up, rather conveniently, at the apartment just as they were leaving that morning. Henrietta suspected her mother had had a hand in his appearance, and he had begged to be allowed to come along, offering to help with all the kids. Knowing it was useless to protest, Henrietta had begrudgingly agreed. She had not seen him since that night at Polly's apartment, and she could guess why he had kept his distance. Obviously, he was still upset by the whole thing, though he had managed to be convincingly cheerful around her mother. For once, Henrietta was grateful to have all of the kids around, preventing conversation between them. Now that they had scattered, however, Henrietta could sense he was about to speak.

Sure enough, unable to contain himself any longer, he finally asked, "How's things?" as they weaved their way through the crowd, glancing nervously at Elsie to see if she were listening.

"Fine, Stan, thanks."

"Yes, fine, Stanley," Elsie said, looking dreamily at him. Elsie never shortened his name, as if by elongating it she could savor him for even an extra moment.

"How's . . . how's work?" he asked eagerly.

Henrietta shot him an annoyed look, giving a slight nod in Elsie's direction. "Fine, Stan! We work at the same place, remember?"

"Yes, I know," he said, becoming flustered as he tried to mend his mistake. "But, you know, since we work different shifts—you working so late, that is . . ."

"Oh, that's true, Stanley! She doesn't get home until ever so late. Sometimes not until almost dawn!" Elsie added innocently.

"Dawn!"

Henrietta expertly picked up Donny, who was dragging his feet in the dust to create little clouds around his already worn shoes, forming a human shield between herself and Stan. "Elsie stays up quite late at night, too, reading . . . don't you, Els?" she said, taking her free hand and gently putting Elsie's hair back behind her shoulder in a more attractive fashion.

"Yes, but I'm sure Stanley doesn't want to hear about that!" Elsie said anxiously.

"Oh, you never know with Stan; he's full of surprises," Henrietta said wryly. "What did you say the name of your book was, Elsie? *The Boy Who Worried Too Much?*"

"Don't be silly, Henrietta!" Elsie laughed nervously.

"Hey!" said Stan, trying to walk a little faster so that he could see around Donny.

"Oh, now I remember," Henrietta continued as if neither of them had spoken. "It's called *The Woman Who Knew What She Was Doing.*"

"Hen!" said an embarrassed Elsie. "You're making fun of me. What will Stanley think?" she asked, glancing shyly at Stan, who was still determinedly looking at Henrietta. "There is no such book, and you know it," Elsie continued. "I'm actually reading *Great Expectations*. I got it from the library. It's quite good. Have you . . . have you read it, Stanley?"

It pained Henrietta to see how hard Elsie was trying to get his attention.

"What?" he asked, looking at Elsie distractedly. "*Great Expectations*? Well, I have, as a matter of fact. I've read all of Dickens's work," he said proudly.

"My! A warehouse boy who reads! What will we have next?" Henrietta couldn't help but put in, though she regretted it as soon as she had said it.

"Well, some of us are trying to better ourselves," Stan said defensively, bracing his thumbs behind his suspenders. "In the right way," he put in and turned his attention to Elsie, which Henrietta perceived was an attempt at a slight toward herself. "What do you think of it?" he asked Elsie.

"It's quite good," Elsie said, unable to contain the huge, telltale smile spreading across her face.

"Miss Havisham is a strange old bird, isn't she?"

"Oh, yes! I hope I don't end up like her!" Elsie said, biting her lip through another big smile. Her eyes were electrified as she looked at him. Henrietta had to look away, embarrassed by her obviousness. If only she would listen to Henrietta about how to flirt, how to be subtle.

Stan grinned at Elsie. "Impossible! A girl like you? Never."

Henrietta perceived that she might have just seen a spark, perhaps, of interest on Stan's part. It was so maddening! They were perfect for each other, if only she could get Stan to see beyond his irritating obsession with herself. If only she could get them alone together somehow . . .

Before she could finish that thought, however, she felt a tug at the bottom of her dress and looked down to see Herbert, holding Jimmy's hand. "Aw, Hen, he's got to go to the bathroom. Can't you take him? I was watching Eugene. He's just about to throw the darts at the balloons, but he said he'd wait for me if I ran him back to you. Will you take him?" Herb pleaded.

"I'll take him," Stan volunteered. Henrietta saw her opportunity.

"No, thanks anyway, Stan. I've got to freshen up a bit myself. Here," she said, depositing Donny in his arms. She opened her coin purse and put more coins in Elsie's front dress pocket. "There you are. I promised everyone cotton candy, so you two go get some for everyone. We'll catch up," she said, taking Jimmy's hand and giving Elsie a little wink as she inclined her head toward Stanley, who was awkwardly trying to balance a squirming Donny. Elsie blushed and smiled her thanks and then led the way further into the carnival, Stan trailing behind.

"Come on, then," Henrietta said to Jimmy as she led him back toward the church, which she knew had a crude sort of bathroom in the cellar, rather than taking him to use one of the outhouses built for the occasion. She decided to take a shortcut through the cemetery rather than have to go all the way around the large carousel that had been set up beside it. As they walked among the crumbling gravestones, Jimmy happily swinging her arm as they went, Henrietta pondered Stan and Elsie and wondered how she could get the two of them together.

"Henrietta!" came a whisper from behind her.

Not again! despaired Henrietta. If this was Stan, she would kill him! Why didn't he ever listen to her!

"Stan, I asked you to stay with Elsie and the kids," she said, turning around, but Stan was nowhere to be seen. "Stan?"

There was a rustling of leaves coming from a large viburnum bush they had just passed, new buds already covering it, and Henrietta was shocked to see Polly emerge.

"Polly!" she cried, hurrying back and embracing her. "What are you doing here? I've been so worried! I've so much to tell you! Did you find Mickey?" she asked, her questions tumbling out as fast as she could say them.

Polly pulled back from her embrace but held onto Henrietta's hands. She shook her head sadly. "He wasn't there. Looks like it's been empty for months."

"You look terrible!" Henrietta said, noticing her disheveled hair and the deep circles under her eyes. "You haven't been back to your apartment, have you?" she asked worriedly.

"Course I have. I slipped in late last night. Why?"

Henrietta refrained from saying anything more in front of Jimmy. She looked down at him, squirming, desperate for the toilet. "Listen, Jim. You go on ahead. It's just in there," she said pointing toward the church. "Down the back stairs."

"But it's dark down there!"

"Be brave! I'll be right here. Give me a shout if you need me. Go on!"

Jimmy stared at the church as if deliberating the proposition, and after hesitating a few moments, sprinted off, desperation having won out. Henrietta watched him go before giving her attention back to Polly. "Oh, Polly! The police are looking for you! They think you're in danger."

"It's Mickey they want; I just know it," she said, staring strangely at Henrietta.

"Yes, they want to find Mickey, too! They don't suspect him—truly, Poll! They want him to help identify the two killers, you know—the ones you heard."

"I'll bet," she said absently again, and Henrietta began to wonder if she was quite lucid.

"Polly, are you alright? How did you know how to find me here?"

"I went to your apartment to find you . . ." she said, absently. "Your mother told me you'd come to the carnival. Don't worry," she added in response to Henrietta's anxious look, "I didn't let the cat out of the bag. Just said we worked together. Seemed nice enough. Don't know what you're always going on about—"

"Polly!" Henrietta interrupted. "You've got to come to the police with me. Inspector Howard is on the level, honestly."

"No, Hen. Not just yet. I'm going back to the Promenade to see if anyone's seen him or knows where he went. Sometimes he used to talk to Jack."

"Yes, I'd heard it reopened. But, Polly! You can't go back there! Stay here with me and then come back to Ma's with me. I have a lot to tell you about the Marlowe—about Libby. I—"

"No, Hen," Polly interrupted, distractedly waving her hand as if that were all over long ago. "I've got to find Mickey."

"There you are!" came a shout, and Henrietta turned to see Stanley striding purposefully around the carousel with Elsie and all the kids following. Herbert was still finishing his cotton candy, and Eugene held out two others, presumably for her and Jimmy. "Where's Jimmy?" Stan asked.

Henrietta looked back toward the church just as he emerged, running as fast as he could, shouting, "I saw a big spider! I saw a big spider!" Henrietta couldn't help but smile and turned to catch Polly's reaction, but she was gone.

"Polly?" she said, twirling around, but she was nowhere in sight. "Polly!" she shouted, but she couldn't see her anywhere in the mingling crowd.

"Polly?" said Stan, bewildered. "Did you see Polly?" he asked, distractedly looking out into the crowd.

"Yes . . . she was right here just a moment ago!"

"Who's Polly?" asked Elsie, intrigued.

"She's someone I used to work with," Henrietta said, trying to outwardly brush it off despite her inner alarm and realizing, as she carefully looked out over the crowd, that Polly was truly gone. A feeling of unease crept over her.

"Right!" she attempted to say cheerfully. "Ma will be wanting us back soon. Let's go see the juggler, and then we need to get back."

"Aww!" came a universal moan.

"I've got to go out later anyway, it turns out, so there's no use crying about it. Come on! Let's see this juggler!" she said as she ushered them back toward the crowd.

"Oh, but Henrietta!" whined Eddie. "Tonight's your night off! How come you hafta go out again?"

"Yeah! Hen! Don't go out again!" begged Jimmy.

"It will just be for a little bit, you'll see! Come on, hurry. Or we'll miss this juggler!" Henrietta pushed in front of them, then, and led them through the cemetery back into the carnival proper.

"Wait, Henrietta! Could I . . . could I talk to you for a minute? Alone?" Stan asked anxiously. Henrietta could feel Elsie's nervous eyes on them.

"Now's not the greatest time, Stan," Henrietta said, trying to put him off. "Maybe later. Can't it wait?"

"No, it can't," he said, hurriedly foisting Donny off onto a nearby Eugene.

"Oh, don't split off, Stanley," Elsie said, almost despairingly, obviously worried about what Stan might have say to her sister.

Henrietta rubbed her forehead. She knew there was no way of getting rid of Stan at this point. If she didn't speak to him now, he would simply follow her, and she needed to be alone tonight for the plan that was beginning to formulate in her mind to work. Why does he have to be involved at all! She fumed. If he hadn't followed her to Polly's apartment, he would be none the wiser. An idea suddenly occurred to her, however, on how she might take advantage of the situation. "Okay, Stan, I'll give you a few minutes alone, but then you have to do something for me in return. Agreed?"

"Well, that depends on what it is, I suppose," he said cautiously.

"Come on, Hen!" whined Herbert. "We're going to miss it!"

"Suit yourself!" Henrietta said to Stan, bluffing, and began to walk across the lawn with the kids following eagerly.

"Oh, all right. You win," Stan called out. "Come back!"

Henrietta smiled to herself and, leaving the rest of them to wait, returned to where Stan had remained standing, shifting anxiously from foot to foot, Elsie looking on with a frown as she bent down to pick up Doris.

As soon as Henrietta got close enough, Stan lost no time in beginning. "Henrietta," he pleaded. "I'm begging you to give up this murder business. Can't you see how dangerous it is? And now that Polly's back in town, I've got a very bad feeling. And I can't always be there, you know, to look after you. God knows I wish I could, but I have to work, too!"

Henrietta sighed. "Stan, I appreciate your concern, but I'm fine. There's nothing to worry about! Honest. And anyway, I'm not in any real danger. Inspector Howard has men inside the Marlowe, watching, just in case."

"Well, if that's true, then why do you have to be there at all?"

"Because they need a woman to snoop around backstage. The cops can't find much out just sitting in the audience."

"Snooping around for what, exactly? What is it that they're looking for, anyway? Gambling ring?"

Henrietta weighed up lying, but she didn't have the energy. "A missing girl—Polly's sister. And there might be another. But I really shouldn't say more than that, Stan."

"Jeez Louise, Hen! This is serious! You're going to get yourself killed—or worse!" Stanley's voice grew increasingly more elevated and high-pitched. Henrietta saw Elsie glance over at them.

"Shhhh," she whispered. "Nothing's going to happen to me," she said, trying to convince herself of this as well.

"Henrietta, please. Say you won't go back there anymore. I . . . I've got money I can lend you if you need it. You've got to see sense."

"Listen, Stan. There are young girls there who might be in danger. I'm trying to help them."

"You're a young girl in danger! Don't you see that?" he said hysterically.

"Don't be so melodramatic. And, anyway, I'm not a young girl. I'll be okay."

"Henrietta! Please!" shouted Elsie. "People are lining up!"

"Be right there!" she shouted back. "Speaking of young girls," she said turning her attention back to him. "It's time to explain the favor you agreed to," she said, smiling at him.

"Aww, what is it?" he moaned, convinced he wouldn't like it.

"Take Elsie out," she smiled mischievously.

"Aww, Hen. She's just a kid," he said, looking back at Elsie with the children huddled round her. She had been staring over at them, but now, embarrassed that he had caught her looking, she quickly looked away.

"She's not a kid! She's seventeen. Anyway, she's perfect for you."

"But I . . . I mean . . . it's just that . . . I don't think I like Elsie that way. I—"

"Stan," she said, resting her hand on his arm, which caused, in turn, a bright pink hue to quickly spread up his neck to his cheeks, "it's no use with me. I'm not the girl for you. I'm too old for you, and, to be truthful, I see you as another kid brother, not a sweetheart."

Stan closed his eyes momentarily to absorb the blow. "Is there . . . is there someone else?" he asked dramatically, finally finding the courage to open his eyes again and look at her.

Henrietta tried her hardest not to smile.

"It's that inspector, isn't it?" he asked, looking at the ground before she could say anything. "You're in love with him, aren't you?" Henrietta drew in a breath in shocked surprise. Why would Stan ever suppose that? Was she that obvious, or had it just been a lucky guess? Either way, it disturbed her, particularly as she had not yet even allowed herself to fully contemplate her feelings for Inspector Howard. Thus far, she was only aware of a curious unease that had crept into her heart regarding him, a vague suspicion that she might be indeed falling for him, but what would Stan know of it? She was obviously not in love with the inspector, she argued with herself, and yet there was something about him that she just couldn't quite put her finger on, something that comforted and unsettled her at the same time. But in love? Surely not!

Stop it! she said inwardly, willing herself to gather up her runaway thoughts. This had just been a silly, erroneous suggestion on Stan's part, and she was taking it too seriously! But she saw that she could use it as an opportunity to perhaps squash Stanley's relentless pursuit of her in hopes that he might slacken his pace and perhaps change course for Elsie. Instead of adamantly refuting his absurd suggestion, then, as it had been on the tip of her tongue to do, she decided instead to play along with it.

"Yes," she said hesitantly. "Yes, you've found me out, Stan. It is the inspector! I am in love with him," she said indifferently. She forced her tone to be cold and callous, but she was surprised that merely uttering those words out loud had caused her face to feel hot. She gripped his arm tighter. "I'm sorry, Stan, but my heart belongs to another," she managed to say with a straight face. "You might do worse than Elsie, you know. She really cares for you . . ."

"Aw, Hen, I just couldn't."

"Well, you promised to take her out."

"I didn't really. You tricked me."

"Come on, Stan. For me?" she couldn't resist flashing him her dimpled smile. "Why don't you go to the library together? You and Elsie? Then get a cup of coffee or something after. You could discuss the books you're reading."

"Oh, all right," he said, kicking the dirt beneath them. "But I'm not gonna give up on you, though. Inspector or no!"

"Henrietta! Please!" shouted Jimmy. "I can see him down there!"

"I'm coming!" she called to them. "Go on, and I'll catch up!" She looked back at Stan. "Promise?"

"Only if you promise to be careful." He wore a worried frown. "I don't like this one bit, Hen. That inspector better watch over you."

"He will," she said quietly as she started back toward the lot where the rest of them had dispersed, hoping as she went that this was true.

CHAPTER 10

By the time Henrietta had deposited everyone back home, it was nearly suppertime. The walk home had been peppered with comments about the carnival and small arguments about what the best part had been, though for herself, Henrietta could only think about Polly and what to do, having forced the other matter regarding Stan's ludicrous suggestion about the inspector aside, at least for the time being. She would worry about that later; it was Polly she needed to concern herself with.

Unfortunately, though, regarding Polly, she saw no choice but to seek out Inspector Howard, hopefully before it was too late, and could not help but feel disappointed that he had not turned up to find out how her first night at the Marlowe had gone, or if she was even still alive, for that matter, so dangerous had he led her to believe it was. She was embarrassed to admit to herself that she had half expected him to step out from behind some random booth at the carnival or to spot him watching her from the beer tent, his pipe in hand; but that, of course, was silly.

Stanley had said little on the walk home and had gone ahead with Eugene until they had reached their building, at which point he began biting his nails. Henrietta smiled blandly at him as she pushed open the big front door. She handed a squirming Donny to Eugene to carry up and ushered the rest of them in, saying, "Up you go! Go tell Ma all about it, but don't shout in case she's got one of her headaches!"

As Elsie moved to go past her, Henrietta stopped her and gently took the now-sleeping Doris from her arms. "I'll take her," she whispered. "You say goodbye to Stan; see if he wants to come up for coffee." Elsie nodded, unsure, and looked panicked to be alone with Stan without a child as a shield.

"Bye, Stan!" Henrietta said cheerfully, giving him a meaningful look as she slipped inside. When she got to the first landing, she peered out of the little window there and saw that they were talking, albeit awkwardly, Stan shifting nervously from foot to foot.

Eddie had unfortunately not been able to win the vase for Ma, but on the walk home, Herbert had managed to pick a few dandelions growing in the cracks of the pavement to give to her. She had smiled sadly when he handed her the somewhat wilted bouquet, which had been crushed for too long in his chubby hand. She set the flowers on the tiny counter, not even bothering to put them in water, as she served up the hash she had made for their supper, asking them how they had enjoyed the carnival, each of them vying for her tired attention.

Henrietta helped get the twins settled in their chairs before slipping back to the bedroom to change. She had decided upon a plan, and now all she needed was the courage to carry it out. She put on one of her better dresses that she had usually worn at the Promenade and was just slipping into her heels when she heard Elsie finally come in from outside. Above the chatter coming from the next room, she heard Elsie say, "I won't be a minute, Ma!" and was surprised when she appeared in the bedroom, her face flushed. Elsie was not usually one to pass up meals.

"Oh, Hen!" she said breathlessly, coming over to her as Henrietta stood peering into the little mirror. "You'll never guess! Stanley asked me to go to the library with him!"

"Really, Els?" she said, turning toward her with a big smile. So, Stanley had done it! "I always knew he was sweet on you! You'll have to borrow something of mine to wear. Maybe my blue dress," Henrietta suggested, turning back toward the mirror.

Elsie plopped down on the bed, causing the thin mattress and the worn-out springs to sag depressingly close to the floor as she aimlessly fingered the loose threads of the quilt folded at the end of the bed. "I always thought he was sweet on you," she said, perplexed. "Say!" she said after a few moments of contemplation. "You didn't force him to ask me, did you, Hen? I'd die of embarrassment if you did!"

"Course I didn't!" Henrietta lied easily, not looking back.

"Then why were the two of you talking alone?" she asked nervously.

"Because he was asking me if I thought it'd be all right to ask you," she said, turning toward her with a smile.

Elsie's eyes lit up. "Really? He . . . he was nervous to ask me?" she asked, as if this fact somehow endeared him to her all the more. "But what was all the talk about this Polly?" she asked, after brooding for a moment.

Henrietta tried to remain nonchalant. "Oh, just a girl from the electrics. In a bit of trouble is all. Now, we'd better get going before Ma yells."

Elsie stood up and spontaneously hugged Henrietta. Together they went out to the kitchen where Ma was complaining about no one respecting her enough to come to dinner on time, as if this were the Ritz and people could come and go as they pleased. Disgruntled, she roughly set a plate in front of Elsie and had taken up the spoon to fill a plate for Henrietta when Henrietta spoke up.

"No, Ma. I don't want any, if that's all right," Henrietta said gingerly.

"Why not?" Ma said plainly, clearly irritated.

"I . . . it's just that I'm going out."

"Going out? Tonight's your night off," she said, spoon still suspended in midair. A tiny bit of grease dropped onto the cracked linoleum.

"Yes, I know. But I . . . I've got a date," Henrietta said, relieved that inspiration had come upon her at last.

"A date? With who? Stan?"

Elsie bit her lip.

"No, Ma. Not Stan," Henrietta said, shooting Elsie a comforting glance. "Just someone I work with."

"What's his name?"

"Clive," Henrietta said, scrambling for an answer. Why hadn't she said Artie? she wondered, annoyed with herself.

"Clive?" Ma said unbelievingly. "That sounds posh."

"Maybe he's a foreman! Is he, Hen?" Elsie asked excitedly.

"Sort of," Henrietta said, not being able to help smiling at her.

"Why haven't you told us about him?" Elsie asked eagerly.

Ma, however, was not to be appeased so easily. "It isn't enough, is it, that you're gone every night? But on your one night off you can't be content to sit home with us, you have to gallivant off!"

"Ma, you're the one that says I should settle down and get married! How do you think that's going to come about, then?"

"And where'd you get that dress?" Ma asked, ignoring Henrietta's rebuttal.

"I bought it with some of my wages," Henrietta said nervously. "It was on sale!"

"Buying clothes when the rest of us are eating charity food from the armory!" Ma was incredulous.

"I've got to go," Henrietta said angrily. "It's no use trying to explain anything to you!"

With that, Henrietta made her way around the table where all of them had stopped eating to watch the argument and gathered up her hat and the black shawl hanging by the door. She banged out the door, not giving Ma another look.

"Oh, sure!" Ma called out after her. "Go on and leave then! Just like your father! Try not to make a mess of it at least!"

Henrietta was still fuming, repeating Ma's parting words over and over in her head as she made her way downtown to Station 124. What was particularly infuriating was that it wasn't even a date at all, but just a flimsy excuse to get out of the house to find the inspector. What would happen if she ever should court anyone? She closed her eyes at the notion and tried instead to think about what she would say to Inspector Howard when she saw him, but her thoughts there were jumbled, too.

The sun was just beginning to set as she alighted from the streetcar and made her way along Canal to the station on

Jackson. Though she'd been hungry when Ma was dishing up their meager dinner, she had gone without so that she could get to the station faster, fearing that the inspector might already be on his way home.

Hurriedly, she dashed up the shallow steps of the imposing stone structure in which the words "POLICE STATION, No. 124" were chiseled into the thick gray stone above the door.

Inside, there were several officers loitering about and a dirty, bundled-up woman sitting on a stone bench, apparently waiting for something. Two thin, dirty children huddled near her, and the baby she held in her arms cried sporadically, causing her to rock it slightly as she hushed it in a foreign language, maybe Italian; Henrietta wasn't sure. She approached the long counter, globe lamps perched at either end, which gave off a dull, sleepy glow, behind which an officer stood looking through a stack of paperwork. Her eyes darted around the station hoping for a glimpse of the inspector or maybe even Charlie or Kelly.

"Can I help you, miss?" asked the officer behind the counter, almost knocking over his mug of coffee as he took in Henrietta's radiant beauty, her auburn hair hanging down around her shoulders. "I'm looking for Inspector Howard. Is he in?" she asked nervously, trying to see around him to the offices beyond.

"Inspector Howard? No, not him. Detective inspectors don't have to work Sundays, see? 'Cept if there's an emergency, like. Something I can help you with?" he said, his eyes roaming over her.

Henrietta sighed. Now what? "No," she said absently. "Thanks just the same. I . . . perhaps you could give him a message for me?"

"Sure thing," the officer said, taking up a pen from the inkwell. "Go on, then," he said, waiting for her to begin.

"Just tell him that I . . . that I wanted to speak to him. I've heard from Polly."

"Polly. Got it," the officer said, concentrating on his work. "Name?"

"Name?"

"Yeah, name. What's your name?"

"Oh. Henrietta. Henrietta Von Harmon."

"Telephone number?"

"I . . . I don't have one."

The officer arched his eyebrow. "Well, how's he supposed to contact you?"

Henrietta shrugged.

"Look. Maybe I'd better ring him; I recognize the name," he said, rubbing his chin. "You're the one he's got down at the Marlowe, ain't you?" he said, sizing her up and reaching for the telephone.

"No! Please! Don't disturb him at home—with his . . . family," Henrietta suggested, hoping the officer would inadvertently shed some light on the inspector's private life.

"Family? He ain't got no family!" he guffawed, balancing the receiver on his shoulder."

"Just his girl, Katie, in his bed at night," snickered one of the officers standing nearby, obviously eavesdropping. The other officer with him laughed, too.

"Hey, Murphy!" the officer behind the counter said, shaking the telephone receiver at them. "There'll be no more of that!" he said sternly. "Show some respect for your superiors, or you two'll be on traffic duty on LaSalle."

"Yes, sir. Sorry, sir," they said, though they were still smiling. "It's true, though, ain't it?" Murphy muttered.

"That's none of your business how the inspector spends his time. Now beat it!" he shouted. The two offending officers accordingly disappeared deeper into the station, laughing as they went. "Now, Miss Von Harmon, where were we?" he said, peering back at her and resting the receiver back on his shoulder.

Henrietta barely heard what he said, so stunned was she. As she had stood listening to the quick banter between the officers, she had felt like a rock had been dropped in her stomach. Her thoughts were whirling, but she had to put them aside for the moment and stop him from making the call. She would be mortified to disturb him at home while he was with another woman. "No, please! Honestly! I'll catch up with him later," she said, taking a few steps backward.

The officer looked unconvinced. "You sure? Where you going?"

"I'm . . . I'm not sure . . ."

"Well, if he rings the station, he'll want to know where to find you. At home, then?"

"No! Not at home! I . . . I'll be at the Promenade, I think," she found herself saying. She would have to look for Polly herself. "Thank you," she said again, stepping further away from the desk.

"Well, if you're sure, then. I'll give him the message," he called after her as she quickly slipped out the door.

Henrietta hurriedly walked back down Jackson. She was pretty sure she could catch the 151 back uptown toward the Promenade, swallowing hard as a wave of disappointment washed over her. So, he had someone.

But that made sense, didn't it? Henrietta reasoned. A man such as the inspector was hard to find; surely he would have been snatched up long ago. But why, then, had the officer said that he had no family? He must not be married to this woman, this girl, as they had called her. This surprised her more than anything else. He had seemed like a decent man, good, not like all the rest, but she had obviously been wrong. It made her want to cry, though she couldn't exactly say why.

The streetcar pulled up, then, and she numbly climbed on board, finding an empty seat in the back. Almost immediately, it lurched forward again, not many people having gotten on. Tears formed in the corner of her eye as she sat watching the buildings pass by, dark with shadows, and she found herself thinking again about her father. She hadn't thought of him in a long while, but she had discovered long ago that those painful memories were more than willing to come out and be remembered at even the slightest suggestion. They were part of a stale, ancient ache that never really went away.

She could understand why her father had done what he had done. Maybe it was a sin to even think that, but she supposed he just hadn't been able to take it anymore, the job being the last straw. Ma crabbing at him constantly. She nearly hated Ma for how she had treated him. Shamed him, ground him down until he just couldn't see his way clear anymore. Well! She had got what she deserved, Henrietta fumed. But the worst was that Henrietta hadn't even gotten to say goodbye to him. Not really. No one else knew that he had stopped by the apartment that afternoon, just briefly, after his pilgrimage to Mr. Schwinn's lawn and before he had stumbled off to Poor Pete's. Henrietta had seen him coming down the street from the front room window and had gone down to meet him. She had somehow sensed something was not right with him. She had tried to help him up the stairs, but he had refused, saying that he had to go out again. A little job he had to do.

"No, Pa, don't go out tonight!" she had begged him.

"I've got to, Hen," he had said, his eyes sad and weary. "It's for the best. You'll see."

"Please," she whispered.

Henrietta was surprised to see tears in his eyes as he came back toward her and hugged her. "I love you, Hen. Most of all. I always have. You take care of them, hear? I'll be back later."

"Pa, please!" Henrietta begged, tears blurring her vision. Her father had pulled her hands off his sleeves, trying to smile as he did so.

"Go on. I'll be back. Go in! A grown girl like you shouldn't be cryin' like this," he said sternly. He gave her a last look and then walked off down the street. Henrietta had been in two minds whether or not she should go after him, but she hadn't, not wanting to upset him more. She cursed herself now for not following him. Instead, she had just stood there on Humboldt Avenue, crying, watching him until he turned the corner and was gone. In her darker moments, she sometimes wondered if the terrible thing that had happened had somehow been her fault, though she barely dared to ask the question, even to herself.

Well, she speculated, as she watched an old woman gather up her bags a few seats ahead of her, at least she now knew why her flirtations with the inspector had not sparked an interest, and though she tried to use this explanation to make herself feel better, it oddly wasn't working.

She could see the Promenade, all lit up, looming ahead. Roughly she pulled the bell for her stop, wiping her tears as she did so. She needed to put all that behind her, she scolded herself. She had more important things to worry about. And if the inspector was too busy with certain others to check in with her regarding the case, she would just have to take things into her own hands. She wondered, too, if she might see Artie, and found herself hoping. She hadn't thought about him in what seemed like a long time—so much had happened!—and she felt she owed him some attention, some effort toward their budding relationship.

She approached the ticket booth and saw that it was Edith on duty tonight. She was listlessly flipping through a copy of Look! magazine, smoking in the little lit-up booth.

"One, please!" Henrietta said, walking up quietly.

"Oh, God!" Edith jumped. "You scared me to death!" She broke into a big smile. "I wondered when you would turn up. Didn't ya know we reopened?"

"Well, I'd heard, but I've been busy with a few other things."

"Well, ya haven't missed much," Edith explained eagerly. "The cops still don't know who stabbed Mama. The place was crawlin' with 'em for a while. Gave up now, I guess," she shrugged.

"Who's the floor matron now?" Henrietta asked, shivering a bit in the night air.

"Some dame called Mrs. Katz," Edith shrugged. "She's all right. Runs a tighter ship than Mama, so if you're looking for your job back, better mind your p's and q's."

"I'll remember that. Thanks," Henrietta smiled. "Mind if I go in for a minute? I'm looking for someone."

"Oh, yeah? Who?"

"Polly? Or maybe Mickey?"

"Funny you should ask about Polly. She showed up outta the blue today, too. Sure it ain't somethin' you two planned?"

"She did? Is she still here?" Henrietta asked eagerly, glancing toward the big glass doors as if to see who might be inside.

"Don' know. She came in earlier . . . didn't see her leave, but then again, I mighta missed her when I was busy with tickets."

"How about Mickey?"

"Haven't seen hide nor hair of him since the whole thing happened. He shuffled outta here mighty quick."

"Can I?" Henrietta asked, nodding her head toward the big doors.

"Sure, doll. Just don't tell anyone, you know?"

"Thanks, Edith."

As she approached the entrance, one of the doormen opened the door for her and the sound of Tommy Dorsey's "On Treasure Island" came belting out. Henrietta thought she recognized the band, but she wasn't sure. "Who's on tonight, Reggie?" she asked as she stepped inside.

"Why, hello, Miss Henrietta! I wondren when you gonna come back. Don' you recognize da Rhythm Section?" Reggie asked with a big smile, his white teeth almost glowing against his dark skin. "You haven' ben gone all dat long, miss!" he said, laughing.

Henrietta smiled at him and felt a buzz of excitement as she stepped in further and saw that it was Artie up on stage after all. She felt a surge of warmth watching him and wondered why she had been so silly on the bus over. Who cared what the inspector did with his time and with whom? He was too old for her, anyway.

She couldn't help smiling as she watched Artie with his slicked-back hair and his big blue eyes, swaying with his clarinet on stage as he sang into the big silver microphone. She had missed this place, she realized, looking around. It was strange that just a short time ago, a place she perceived as being so risqué now seemed quaintly innocent compared to what went on at the Marlowe, and Henrietta found herself longing for the simpler days before any of this had happened.

She glanced over to the corner where Mama Leone used to sit, obviously empty now, and felt a strange sort of sadness, though admittedly she hadn't really liked the woman. Still, it seemed business as usual at the Promenade, as if Mama Leone had never even existed. Was that the way it was for everyone? Did no one's life make a difference? She mused glumly.

Henrietta shook herself from such depressing thoughts and made her way over to the bar. Jack, Mickey's friend, was working, as well as some other bartender she didn't recognize. He must be new. She smiled at Jack when he finally looked up at her.

"Hello, there," he said, winking at her with a mischievous grin. "Must of missed the reunion invite. First Polly, now you. What's a pretty dame like you doin' in a place like this?" he teased.

"That depends," she said batting her lashes and smiling back at him. It felt so easy, so natural to be flirtatious here, whereas at the Marlowe (and with the inspector, truth be told), she still felt nervous and second-guessed herself constantly. "Is Polly still here?" she asked casually.

"Nah," Jack said, wiping the glass in his hand. "She was lookin' for Mickey. Can't find him, she says. Seemed upset."

"Have you seen him?" she asked.

"Not since that day Mama Leone turned up dead. Scooted out of town would be my guess. Mickey has a record, you know."

"Did Polly say where she was going?"

Jack thought for a moment. "Don't think so."

"What time did she leave?"

"Oh . . ." Jack looked up at the clock behind the bar. "Few hours ago, I think. Can't be sure, though."

Henrietta bit her lip and looked around, as if she would suddenly spot her in the crowd of couples out on the floor.

"You want a drink?" Jack asked. "On the house?" he said, smiling suggestively.

"Not just yet," she said, returning his smile. She could hear the band winding down, and she didn't want to miss Artie on his break. "Catch you later, okay, Jack?" she said giving him a little wink.

"I hope so," he said, watching her walk seductively away.

"We'll be right back, ladies and gents! Just a short break!" announced Al's high tenor voice. Henrietta gave a little wave to Artie as he set his instrument down, but he didn't see her. She had been up on that stage before, once even sitting on Artie's lap when Mama Leone had been distracted backstage, and she knew how hard it was to see very much from up there because of the lights. Never mind, she assured herself happily, she would slip around back and surprise him!

Henrietta had known the brash crooner from the South Side for almost six months, and his boyish grin had always melted her heart. He always had a way of making Henrietta laugh. She played it cool with him, not wanting him to get the wrong idea, but as she hurried through the maze of hallways to the backstage area, she felt her resolve crumbling a little. She felt as though she needed to be held in someone's arms after all that had happened. She needed something normal and safe, thinking again about Lucy and her gang of usherettes fondling each other, not to mention the inspector and his girl.

Henrietta quickened her step, finally turning the corner to where the performers sat amongst a hodgepodge of makeshift furniture backstage, usually drinking between sets. She stopped suddenly, though, when she came upon a couple entwined in the shadows. Her first thought was to back away, but as she began to do so, she looked twice and realized with a gasp that it was Artie! She was mortified, unable to move. He had his hand inside the woman's blouse while he arduously kissed her neck. He stood between her slightly parted legs, though she was still mostly clothed as she sat on a crate.

The woman was the first to notice her, but rather than stop Artie from continuing, she attempted to shoo Henrietta away with a wave of her hand indicating that they didn't wish to be disturbed.

Henrietta wasn't sure whom to be more shocked by. "Artie!" she said loudly and turned away so that she would not see him adjust his trousers, which seemed to be loosened.

"Henrietta!" he said, turning toward her, pulling his jacket back down into place and smoothing his hair. "What you doin' here, doll? Thought you flew the coop with dizzy Polly."

Henrietta just stared at him, dumbfounded.

The woman, smiling at her like a cat that had caught the canary, ran her hand through Artie's hair and said to him, loud enough for Henrietta to hear, "I'll let you handle this one, Artie Tartie." She eased herself off the crate, then, and slowly sauntered away. Henrietta watched her go as if in a daze. She didn't recognize her.

"What do you mean 'what am I doing here'?" she finally asked, looking back at Artie, her face burning. "What are you doing with her?"

Artie had recovered his composure and grinned at her sheepishly. "Men have urges, Henrietta. They gotta be answered. All I can say," he shrugged. "'Sides, I didn't think you was that interested, if you know what I mean . . ." he stopped to light a cigarette.

Henrietta looked away. Oh, yes, she knew all about men's urges, all right! "Women who give in to men's urges aren't the ones they end up marrying, Henrietta," Ma's voice rang in her ears. What would she know about it, though! Henrietta had testily speculated more than once.

"I see," she said, humiliated. Grasping for something to say, she suddenly remembered what the inspector had told her. "Why did you tell the police you were with your mother? You know, the night Mama Leone was stabbed?"

"What does that have to do with anything?" he sputtered.

"Just that you lied, and I defended you!"

Before he could answer, however, she had figured it out.

"Oh, I see," she said glancing in the direction in which the woman had disappeared, "you were with her. But why didn't you just tell the cops that?"

Artie shrugged. "Don't sound as good, does it?"

"It will sound even worse when they figure out you lied!" she said, disgusted. "Oh, what does it matter?" Suddenly she wanted nothing more than to get away. She felt like such a fool. "Goodbye, then, Artie. Good luck."

"Hey, no hard feelings, eh?" he asked hesitantly, as if unsure which woman to pursue at this point. Henrietta weakly waved a hand at him and turned away.

"Hey, Henrietta!" he called after her. "We had some good times, didn't we? You were swell, doll! Come back some time!"

Henrietta barely heard him, though, as she hurried back to the main floor, her cheeks burning with shame. Polly had been right about him all along! How could she have been so stupid! She made her way along the edge of the dance floor, avoiding the bar. She had no desire to talk to anyone; she needed to get out of here. She managed to make it back to the main doors without anyone stopping her.

"Dat was fast!" Reggie said smiling at her as he held the door open for her.

Henrietta gave him a false smile. "Thanks, Reggie." She approached the ticket booth for just a moment where Edith was still perusing Look! magazine.

"Hey, you weren't kidding!" Edith said, looking up in surprise. "Couldn't find 'em?"

Henrietta shook her head miserably. "If Polly turns up again, will you tell her to come by my place?"

"Sure thing, doll."

"Thanks." Henrietta was about to leave, but could not resist the temptation to turn back to Edith to ask her something. "Say, Edith . . . did you know Artie was a snake?"

Edith looked at her quizzically. "Artie from the band? Him? Course he's a snake. He's a musician! What'd ya expect?" At Henrietta's crestfallen expression, she quickly added, "Hey! Don't worry, doll; you'll find someone else! A girl like you," Edith arched her eyebrows, "you've got your pick, and don't you know it!" she smiled at her.

Henrietta smiled back. "Thanks, Edith. I should go." The same thing could be said of cops as well as musicians, she thought bitterly. They couldn't be trusted, either.

"Be careful!" Edith called after her.

"Thanks, I will!" Henrietta said, walking to the curb and waiting for a couple of lone cars to pass before crossing Lincoln Avenue. It was still relatively early, though she supposed it was safe enough to return home from her "date" without arousing Ma's suspicions. But what about her quest to find Polly? Perhaps she should go to her apartment and look for her? The inspector had warned her to stay away, but someone needed to warn Polly. And anyway, she felt an overwhelming urge to do something.

She made up her mind, then, that she would go herself, despite what the inspector had said. She changed direction accordingly and started walking toward Clark where she could pick up the 151 streetcar north rather than the 47 west to Logan Square, her thoughts all a jumble as she walked. Two disappointments in one night; it was almost too much to bear! And yet, she tried to convince herself as she hurried along, surely she was being melodramatic. The inspector had never for a moment been interested in her, and if she were truthful, she hadn't really cared for Artie all that much. And what did any of it matter, anyway? She knew Ma wanted her to settle down and get married, but what would Ma do then? They couldn't live on the meager wages that she and Elsie brought in, though Eugene was bound to find something eventually.

She let out a discouraged breath as she approached the streetcar stop, several people already there waiting. She had started out so badly wanting, needing, in fact, to speak with the inspector, but now she hardly cared.

"Are you in the habit of taking the wrong streetcar home, Miss Von Harmon, or are you by chance heading for Miss Shoemacher's apartment—against my wishes, I might add?" said a deep voice behind her.

Henrietta spun around. It was the inspector, casually standing with his hands in his pockets, his hat perched at the back of his head.

"Inspector Howard! What are you doing here?" she asked in shock. She immediately felt a knot in her stomach, unsure of how to act around him now or even how to control her emotions, presuming that that was even a possibility.

"Didn't I just ask you that, in a manner of words? Is this to be our opening conversation every time we meet?"

Henrietta could not help but smile. "How did you know I was headed to Polly's?" she asked, still unsettled, feeling her way.

The inspector's eyes darted to the number on the bus stop sign and then back to her. "Well, the 151 heads up Clark to Lincoln Park, where Polly lives, and you would have no other reason to go that way, not unless there's someone new in your life, but given the very little amount of free time afforded you, I very much doubt it. Polly's being your destination is therefore the only logical conclusion."

"Oh. I see. Well, you've found me out, then," she said trying to smile. "Wait a minute!" she said suddenly. "How did you know I was here? At the Promenade?"

"I pegged you as being a better detective than that, Miss Von Harmon," he said, tilting his head slightly to the side, his eyebrow arched.

Henrietta pondered. "The sergeant, of course! I told him not to call you, not to disturb you and . . .," she looked away.

"He had his orders. If you were ever to turn up, he was to ring me straight away."

"Well, I'm sorry if I took you from something. Or got you out of bed . . ." She couldn't help looking him over, but he didn't look as though he had just thrown on his clothes. A bit rumpled maybe, but still all present and accounted for.

He looked at her, puzzled. "Of course I wasn't in bed! Look, Miss Von Harmon. What is it you wanted to tell me? I'm assuming it was somewhat urgent. Wasn't that the whole purpose in coming to find me? And now that I'm here, I'm rather eager to hear this bit of information. Perhaps we might walk a bit," he said nodding back in the direction of the 47, which would take her back to Logan Square.

"Yes, but that's just it," she said, stubbornly remaining where she was. "I . . . I was off to Polly's. I wanted to warn her. I saw her today, you see, and she doesn't realize the danger she's in. She said—"

"You've seen Miss Shoemacher?" he interrupted. "Where?"

The sternness of his question caught her attention. "Didn't the sergeant mention that?"

The inspector closed his eyes briefly in irritation.

"I saw her at the St. Sylvester's carnival," she went on. "I was with my . . ." she didn't finish. "Anyway, she went round to our place, and my mother told her where to find me. She looked terrible!"

"What did she say?" he asked evenly.

"Just that Mickey wasn't at the cabin. She's frantic to find him. I'm not sure why. She seemed a bit crazed, to tell you the truth. I tried to tell her what I had heard about Libby, but she didn't seem to care—"

"Libby? You have information on Libby, too?"

"Well, a little."

The inspector let out a low whistle. "You work fast, Miss Von Harmon. Pretty soon you'll be a regular dick," he said with a rare grin.

Henrietta couldn't help but flush with pleasure.

"Did Polly say where she was going?" he asked.

"Just that she was going to try the Promenade to see if Mickey had come back or if anyone knew where he was."

"I take it she's not in there."

"No," Henrietta answered, impressed that he had already figured that out, "I went myself, but neither of them are there. Apparently, Polly did turn up asking for him earlier today, but she left. No one's seen Mickey."

"Well, that saves a trip there—for now, anyway. Good work, Miss Von Harmon."

"I'm worried she'll go back to her place and that someone might . . . you know . . . be waiting there for her, like you said. I tried to tell her that she wasn't safe, but she wouldn't listen."

The inspector remained silent, thinking. "You're right; she's in a considerable amount of danger. I need to telephone the station and get a squad car over there. Come on," he said, taking a step back toward the lit-up Promenade. "I'll use the telephone in there."

Henrietta pulled back. "No . . . it's . . . it's awfully noisy in there," she said quickly, desperate to avoid Artie, or anyone else, for that matter, in the inspector's company. "We could try the Lodge—it's just down here," she said, pointing down Sedgwick.

"Yes, I suppose that would work," he reluctantly agreed, coming back toward her. They walked along in silence for a few moments before he spoke again. "Too bad, though," he said, without looking at her. "You could have introduced me to your man, Artie."

Henrietta looked at him to catch his expression. She thought she saw a wisp of amusement in his eye, but his face belied only polite interest as he turned to look at her.

"He's not my man," she said sorely.

"Do I detect trouble in paradise?"

Humiliated, she tried holding his gaze but failed. Instead, she looked away and shrugged.

"I see. Like that, is it? Well, never mind; these things happen." Whether he meant it sincerely or was merely being sarcastic, she wasn't sure, but the fact that it vaguely sounded like something the protective Mr. Hennessey would say irritated her to no end.

Having reached the Lodge, the inspector made a beeline to the telephone booth in the back, Henrietta waiting awkwardly for him by the bar, observing and assessing the clientele as she did so. A dark, grotty old man's bar was her easy conclusion. The walls were of dark paneling, stained even darker by the perpetual haze of smoke that hung in the air. There was no light at all except four stringy bulbs with flimsy shades, one of which was ripped, hanging down over the bar.

The inspector finally emerged from the booth. "They're on their way," he confided grimly. "Let's hope it's not too late. They're going to call me back at this number, so I'm stuck waiting here." His eyes darted around the bar and then back to Henrietta. "How about a drink? You can fill me in on the rest of the details."

Henrietta felt an excitement that she knew wasn't warranted. "Why not?" she answered with a smile. "Should you really be drinking on duty, though?" she asked, not being able to help teasing him.

"Well, I'm not really on duty, am I?" he said, looking into her eyes briefly before returning to his efforts to get the bartender's attention. Henrietta wasn't sure what to say to that, so she just said, "All right, then, I'll have a Tom Collins."

The inspector grinned. "A Tom Collins? That's quite vogue. You're coming up in the world, it would seem."

"I take exception to that, Inspector," she said in a serious tone, though her dimples had mischievously appeared.

"Whiskey, neat, and one Tom Collins," he said to the bartender who had finally made his way over to them.

The bartender vacillated for just a moment as if he hadn't heard right, obviously unused to anyone ordering anything but beer or shots in his place, but then said tiredly, "Okay, bub," and shuffled off to find the Tom Collins ingredients.

"Well, you shouldn't. I only meant it in the nicest possible way," he said, his mouth twitching, nonetheless. "Anyway, suppose you get talking. What happened tonight?"

Henrietta sighed disappointedly, as she was rather enjoying the direction the conversation was going. "I don't know where to start, really."

"Was Neptune there?" he asked, helping her along.

"Not that I could see."

The bartender plopped the drinks down in front of them and took up the money the inspector had laid down. The inspector handed Henrietta her drink and removed his hat, a gesture of respect for her that touched her very much but somehow made her feel all the more sad.

"Cheers, then," he said, gently clinking her glass with his own.

"Cheers," she responded, and took a sip of her Tom Collins and then another. Artie had introduced her to it and she had thought it marvelous. She could hardly taste the alcohol.

"How did you hear about Libby?"

"There was a party afterwards."

"A party? At the Marlowe?"

"Well, a sort-of party. Just in the dressing room. Some of the girls stay after."

"And you got invited your first night?" his brows narrowed. "Seems a trusting lot."

"Well . . .," Henrietta faltered, unsure of how much to reveal, "there's this girl—woman," she corrected herself. "She's my partner, like I told you we have to have. Her name's Lucy. We . . . she . . . had to follow me to the restroom, so that Mrs. Jenkins wouldn't get angry, and, well, you know . . . she thought I might be . . . well, the other way," she said, raising her eyebrows awkwardly as she took a sip of her drink, in hopes that this would communicate what she meant, trying not to blush as she did so. "You understand, right?"

The inspector's eyes remained crystal cool as he looked at her steadily. "Yes, I think I get the picture," he said, slowly knocking back his whiskey. "Want to tell me about it?" he asked evenly.

"I . . . she . . . tried to, well, kiss me." She quickly glanced up at him to catch his reaction, but he remained curiously still, just watching her. "But I told her it wasn't . . . that I'm not like that . . . and she was awfully sorry. Said I should stay afterwards for a drink to get to know some of the girls . . . that I needed friends to survive there."

"Hmmm," he said, looking at her intently before finally dropping his gaze. "I see. And so you stayed."

"Well, I remembered what you said, that I should look for anything suspicious—"

"Another!" the inspector called out to the bartender. He seemed disturbed, but by what Henrietta couldn't fathom.

Henrietta took a sip of her Tom Collins.

"Go on."

"Well, it was an interesting party, I guess," she said, trying to act as if she saw women lovers all the time. She didn't want the inspector to think she wasn't up to the job. "I'm sure you see that sort of thing all the time," she said to him with a toss of her hair, the auburn in it looking almost golden in the light of the nearly naked bulb that hung near her. The inspector did not say anything in response but took another drink of whiskey.

"And Libby was a part of this group, you think?"

"Yes!" she said, excited by his quick understanding. "I think she was the lover"—she said the word discreetly—"of one of Lucy's friends. One night she disappeared behind the green door, and no one's seen her since. When they asked her, Jenks said she had quit, but the girls didn't buy it 'cause Libby had left all of her belongings behind."

"The green door?"

"There's this little green door tucked away near a broom closet. It's locked day and night apparently, but Lucy and her friends went spying one night during the show and saw one of the dancers go in with a man from the audience. He handed Jenks some money or cigarettes, they weren't sure which, and Jenks unlocked the door for them."

"Did they see anything else?"

"Just looked like a long hallway with more doors."

"What about this dancer? Did she come out?"

"Yes, the girls tried to question her later, but she told them not to get involved, that it didn't concern them and if they kept asking questions, it'd be her that would suffer for it."

The inspector was silent, thinking. He knocked back his whiskey again. "Did they?"

"What?"

"Lay off?"

"I think so, but now Iris has gone missing, too. Remember? Esther the maid's comment about the blood?"

"Jesus."

"The girls think that maybe . . . maybe she was forced."

Just then the telephone rang in the booth at the back near where they were sitting. Henrietta jumped at the sound, and the inspector stood up quickly to answer it. He didn't take the time to shut the door, so Henrietta could hear part of what he was saying, which, in fact, wasn't much.

"You're sure?" he was saying. "Got it. Keep a lookout, then. Thanks, Clancy. Yes, I found her," he said glancing over at Henrietta. "I'll see you back at the station."

He came back and leaned against the barstool as if not wanting to take the time to sit back down. "That was Clancy. No sign of Polly at the apartment, though it looks as though she might have been there earlier. Seems to have disappeared again." He eyed her only half-empty drink. "We need to leave, I'm afraid."

"Well, I can't leave this! You've paid for it!" Henrietta said, aghast.

He shrugged and put his hat back on. "It doesn't matter."

Stubbornly, however, Henrietta drank back the whole thing at once and gathered up her handbag. "Can't waste that!" she said and noticed that the corners of his mouth twitched again as they made their way out.

It had started to rain a bit. She had of course not taken an umbrella with her as she hurriedly left the apartment earlier tonight, so she tilted her hat against the rain and cocked her shoulder as she began walking toward the streetcar stop, assuming the inspector was following her. She felt a gentle tug on her shawl from behind, though, as he pulled her back under the awning of the bar. "What are you doing? I'll call a cab."

"Oh, no, not again," Henrietta pleaded.

"Why? Was it so very terrible last time?" he asked quietly. They were standing so close that Henrietta could smell the wet wool of his overcoat.

"Oh, no," she said, looking up at him. "It's just that my mother thinks I'm . . . that I'm on a date, if you must know."

"A date?" he asked, his eyes darting back toward the Promenade. "And were you?"

"No! I . . . I just said that so I could get out of the house," she smiled uneasily.

"Who did you say you were going with?"

"Clive," she said, before she could stop herself, and instantly felt a flush of hotness shoot over her, either from embarrassment or from the alcohol she had drunk so quickly. "I . . .," she fumbled quickly, "I couldn't think what else to say!" She attempted a little laugh, but it was painfully unconvincing. "They think you're . . . that my date is a foreman at the electrics," she hurried on. "So, you see, they can't see me get out of a cab. A line foreman wouldn't be able to afford that. That's all."

Henrietta stopped talking then, still mortified, but tried to appear as though nothing was wrong. When she looked up at him again, his brows were furrowed, but he didn't seem angry, rather a bit distracted, or possibly confused. Maybe he didn't know what a line foreman was, she surmised.

"Funny you didn't say Artie," he said, pulling his gaze from her finally and raising his arm at a passing cab. "Taxi!" he shouted. "Oh! That reminds me!" she said as a taxicab slowed down and pulled over to the curb. "I should tell you—Artie wasn't with his mother that night. She's been dead for years!"

"I see," he said, unaffected.

"He was with a taxi dancer! He just told me."

"Still an alibi, isn't it?"

"But, he lied!" she said, wanting Artie to be punished. She felt a complete fool that she had spent so much time defending him.

"That type usually do, I'm afraid. Best be careful there," he said as he took her arm and gently guided her toward the cab, depositing her and shutting the door before walking around to pay the driver. "Twenty-nine ten West Armitage," he told him.

Henrietta, confused as to why he wasn't getting in, too, rolled down the window. "But I—wait a minute . . . aren't you coming?" she asked.

"No, I've got a few things to take care of," he said, bending down closer to the open window, his outstretched arms braced against it.

"But you haven't told me what I'm supposed to do next. At the Marlowe, I mean."

"Just do what you have been doing. Keep a lookout and listen. Don't do anything foolish. This is bigger than I first imagined. And very dangerous."

"And how do I know you're not dangerous?" she teased, feeling slightly woozy. It had somehow come out before she could stop it.

The inspector just stared at her, incredulous. "I'm a detective inspector of the Chicago Police!"

"How do I know? I've never seen a badge or anything."

He stared at her as if trying to determine whether she was serious or not. He seemed to be fighting back the urge to smile, though he kept his eyes cool. Deftly he reached inside his jacket with one hand, his other still braced against the car, and pulled out his badge, holding it up in front of her before slowly lowering it. "Satisfied?"

"At the moment," she smiled.

He was staring at her lips now, and she felt a terrible yearning inside of her for him to kiss her. She knew it was wrong in so many ways, but she couldn't help it. Her breath was labored, her chest heaving involuntarily as he began to lean in closer to her.

"Listen, bub!" the cab driver called from the front seat. "I don't got all night, ya know."

Abruptly, the inspector turned his head, then, swallowing hard and scowling at the back of the driver's head. Reluctantly he stood up. "The time for games is over, Miss Von Harmon. You must be very careful. Don't do anything foolish," he said seriously.

"Nothing I can't handle, you know, Inspector," she said, disappointed.

"I'll be in touch," he said, lifting his hat to her. "Remember what I said."

The cab pulled out into the street then, heading west. Henrietta leaned forward and said to the driver, "Just drop me off a couple of blocks before the address he gave you."

"Whatever you say, lady."

"Thanks." Henrietta leaned back against the greasy seat, then, and wondered what he had meant by "the time for games is over." She felt guilty that she had tried to tempt him, even if it hadn't been premeditated. She had only been half conscious of it as it was playing out; it had happened so naturally. At least he was faithful, she owned, as she tried to push thoughts of him hurrying home to Katie out of her mind. It was now painfully clear to Henrietta that he wasn't interested in her in that way and that she would simply have to accept it, but she longed to mean something to him just the same.

As the cab sped along, an idea began to form in her mind of just how she could manage that. If she could only help him crack this case, she reasoned, she could prove herself to him, could somehow still be important to him. A girl like her, she realized sadly, could never win the heart of that type of a man, even if he were free, she owned. That was obvious. But having found him, she longed to somehow remain a part of his world, and right now the likeliest way to do that, she speculated fearfully, was to somehow get beyond the green door.

CHAPTER 11

The next few weeks passed rather uneventfully at the Marlowe, though Henrietta tried her hardest to figure out the mystery of the green door, passing by it as often as she dared, even trying the knob a few times, but it was always locked. Once when she knew Jenks had conveniently left the theater on an errand before showtime, Henrietta had headed straight for the green door, only to disappointedly see Esther coming directly out. Henrietta had barely enough time to slow down before she nearly ran into her. Esther scowled when she saw her.

"What d'ye want?" she asked, turning to lock the door, though Henrietta was sure she heard something or someone from beyond.

"I was . . . I was just looking for Mrs. Jenkins," Henrietta stuttered, flustered at having been caught.

"Well, she ain't here. Snoopin' around, are ye? This ain't the place to go snoopin' if ye know what's good for ye," she said, looking Henrietta over carefully.

"I wasn't snooping! I just wanted to find Mrs. Jenkins is all."

"Right then, I'll tell her ye were lookin' for her when she gets back."

"Thanks," Henrietta tried to say cheerfully and scurried back to the main floor of the theater to find her station, which was still always an inferior one, something that Lucy tried to tell her happened to all the new girls, though Henrietta had noticed that some of them had already been given better ones. The more lowly stations were fine with Henrietta, however, as they gave her more time to look around.

So far, she had observed a few odd things but nothing concrete. She noticed, for example, that Jenks usually perched herself near the heavy red curtains that covered an exit doorway to the right of the stage, just before the few wooden stairs that led up to the stage itself. Jenks mostly concerned herself with looking out over the crowd, as well as giving the usherettes the evil eye if she noticed they were slacking or allowing themselves to be touched by the men in the audience, sending one of the bouncers over if she noticed things getting out of hand. Henrietta also noticed that there was definitely a hierarchy amongst the usherettes, Lucy and her gang not being near the top despite their physical allure.

It was in fact a woman named Ruby, and her sidekick, Agnes, who seemed to Henrietta to be Jenks's current favorites. They were given the best stations and could be found whispering from time to time with Jenks throughout the night. Henrietta had asked Lucy about them while they were both waiting for Sam, the bartender, to fill their orders.

"Oh, those two? Forget about them, gumdrop! They're Jenks's little spies," Lucy had confided.

"Spies? For what?"

"Who knows exactly, but I think they watch to see if there's anything going on between the usherettes and the saps in this joint or even the bouncers."

"Why's it so forbidden? Don't you think that's odd?" Henrietta had whispered.

"I think it's because they want men to pay for any action they get. You know—behind the door . . ."

"Do you think Ruby and Agnes are in on it?" Henrietta asked as she looked across the room at Ruby smiling at Jenks as she passed her by.

"I'm sure of it. They're part of the 'White Feather Club' now."

"'White Feather Club'?"

"Don't you see the white feather in their hair, just by their caps?"

Henrietta peered at Ruby, but it was hard to see from that distance and in the darkened room.

"Hey! Move aside!" shouted another usherette beside them. "You two deviants wanna make out, do it after the show! Some of us 'ave got customers, ya know!"

"Simmer down!" said Lucy, sticking her tongue out at the woman as she lifted her full tray of drinks and stood off to the side, Henrietta following with her own tray so that the next usherettes could get to the bar.

"Ew!" said another woman, a blond with small eyes who uncannily resembled a ferret. "Who knows where that tongue's been!"

Several girls in line tittered.

"Wouldn't you like to know, Mable!" Lucy retorted. "Come on," she said to Henrietta, "Jenks'll be over here in a minute if we're not careful. We'll talk later," she said, nodding her head in the direction of backstage.

As soon as Larry put on the house lights, Henrietta made her way hurriedly to the dressing room, hoping to catch Ruby or Agnes before they left for the night, but they disappointingly did not turn up. In fact, as Henrietta thought about it, she realized she had never seen them back there after a show. She recalled having seen them sometimes beforehand, getting dressed, but she had never had any reason to speak to them except to politely say hello, which they had practically ignored.

She was just buttoning her overalls when the others began trickling in. When the girls had first seen her change into them after a show, they had laughed and joked, causing Henrietta to have to tell a modified version of her secret from Ma. It was unfortunate, however, to be dressed essentially as a man at this type of party, making her all the more attractive to certain people.

"Hello, Henry!" Gwen said, gliding in from the main floor, wired from the long night of work. "Looking dashing as ever," she drawled.

Henrietta smiled, amused. She liked Gwen. She had a naughty streak to her, but she could be sweet as well. It was clear that she was crazy about Lucy. Who wouldn't be, Henrietta thought, considering how beautiful Lucy was and how kind. "Lucy's coming, right? I was hoping to catch her."

"'Fraid I'm already caught, gumdrop," Lucy said just then, entering the room and putting her arm around Gwen.

They laughed, and Henrietta poured the drinks while they changed. "Don't Ruby and Agnes ever stay behind?" Henrietta asked as she handed out glasses of gin.

"With us? I think not," said Gwen. "They've got better things to do, it would appear."

"They used to weasel their way into the dancers' room after the show, that or go out with the bouncers, but I haven't seen them do that in a long while," said Rose, who had joined them, a drink in hand, her crossed arms in front of her.

"The bouncers?" Henrietta asked. "Does Jenks know?"

"What do you think?" Gwen asked, as if the answer was obvious. "She'd kill them."

"What did you mean before, Lucy, by the 'White Feather Club'?" Henrietta asked quietly, looking around as she did so. The other girls were dancing or smoking; Glen Miller's "Blue Moon" was playing on the phonograph. A few had already made their way to the corners.

Henrietta saw Gwen raise her eyebrow at Lucy as a warning, but Lucy ignored it. "Oh, Gwen, no one's listening," she whispered, "we should tell her."

Gwen shrugged her acquiescence as she attempted to look around disinterestedly.

"So?" Henrietta asked eagerly.

"Well," Lucy began mysteriously, "we've been watching more carefully these last few weeks, and we've got a theory."

"So to speak," added Rose.

"About the green door?" Henrietta asked, trying to guess.

"Yes, we've made up a name for Jenks's little operation. We call it the 'White Feather Club'," Lucy explained. "We think it's Jenks's way of 'marking' who's available—you know, for the green door. We think that's how the men know who to choose. If you look closely, some of the dancers have a small white feather just above their ear. Have you seen it?" Lucy asked eagerly.

"I guess I never noticed," Henrietta said slowly.

"We didn't make the connection either until recently. We just thought some of the dancers wore them for accent," added Gwen.

"But if it's mostly dancers, then how can they be in the show and behind the green door at the same time?"

"Good question," Lucy said, seemingly impressed with Henrietta's astuteness. "We're not sure, but we think some go during the show and some after. That would explain Jenks's absence from this part of the theater after the show."

"And did you notice that as the evening goes on, the dance numbers have fewer and fewer girls? I think they arrange the routines that way on purpose," Rose added.

"No," Henrietta pondered, "I didn't realize."

"Did you see that Ruby and Agnes have a feather now?" Lucy asked Gwen.

"I'm not surprised," Gwen said, draining her glass.

"Libby had one, too," Rose said crisply. "I didn't realize at the time what it meant."

"And Iris?" Henrietta asked.

"No, that's the strange thing. None of us remember her with a feather, but she disappeared just the same."

Henrietta's mind was whirling. Perhaps there hadn't been time for Iris to have been given the feather? Maybe Neptune's girls were separate? "How do you think Jenks decides who to choose? I mean, for the white feather? I mean, has she ever approached any of you?" Henrietta assumed they would be a shoo-in for this sort of thing, knowing how attractive they would be to men.

The three of them exchanged glances as if deciding whether to explain. Finally Rose spoke up. "We think Jenks is . . . you know . . . like us, that's why she never approaches us. Turns a blind eye, as it were."

"She certainly looks blind!" twittered Gwen, and Lucy laughed.

"But . . . but I thought Libby was—"

"Yes, it doesn't make sense to us, either. She wanted to make extra money, though, and she must have kept pestering Jenks until she let her in. Something must have convinced Jenks to go along with it."

"Say, why are you so curious about what goes on back there? You aren't thinking of doing anything stupid, are you?" Lucy asked, her eyes narrowed.

"Well . . . maybe," Henrietta shrugged. When they all gasped, she hurriedly added, "Just to find out what happened to Libby—and to Iris."

"Excuse me for saying this, sweets, but why do you care so much?" Rose asked.

"Libby's sister, Polly, was—*is*—my good friend. She came up here from Missouri looking for Libby, but now she's in a mess of trouble, too. I told her I'd keep an eye out for Libby."

"Well, you should tell your friend you couldn't find anything!" Gwen insisted. "You don't want to get messed up in that, Henry."

Lucy put her hand on Henrietta's arm. "Henry, please, don't. We've heard screams sometimes. We've confronted Jenks about it, but she told us someone saw a rat. How dumb does she think we are? Hardly a rat, I'm sure, but we're convinced something dangerous is going on. Libby and Iris weren't the only ones to go missing over the years, you know."

A wave of fear passed over Henrietta, but she pushed it aside as she looked at their anxious faces. She couldn't possibly explain everything to them, so she decided to drop it, at least for the time being. "Perhaps you're right, girls," she smiled weakly. "Let's just forget it. Whose round is it, then?" she asked, holding up her empty glass, successfully breaking the tension, though she caught Lucy looking at her in a strange way several times during the night as if she didn't quite believe her.

That had been over a week ago, and since then, Henrietta had taken note of all of the women who had white feathers, mostly dancers. She made it a point to loiter outside their dressing room, hoping to find out any information that might help her get included in the club, as she was determined now to do. Whenever she peered in, however, she did not observe anything unusual, except that their setup was much more lavish than the usherettes', but she had already known that. Usually when she passed the dancers' dressing room, some of them could be seen sitting in their high vanity chairs, drinking cocktails and laughing. They did not in the least seem frightened or coerced, but rather very gay and stylish. Perhaps it was an act, speculated Henrietta, or perhaps these particular dancers were not involved. They couldn't all be in on it, could they?

She kept a more watchful eye on Jenks during the shows as well, whom she now realized was periodically escorting various men throughout the evening through the red curtains and down the narrow hallways to the green door. Several times she had gone out of her way to pass by Jenks and smile, but Jenks always seemed to be able to detect her falseness and would merely stare back with her blue, half-closed lids or tell her to get back to her station. Henrietta wondered if Jenks was herself part of the ring, having to perform later, after the show, like the other girls in the White Feather Club. Henrietta shuddered at the thought. It seemed unlikely, but having come home late at night for years, she had seen her share of wretched women, not in the least attractive, plying their trade on darkened corners. Beauty seemed to have less to do with it than the willingness, or rather, the desperateness, to lie down in a squalid hovel or even a darkened doorway with whichever man approached.

She had also tried befriending Ruby, who was having none of it, seeming to suspect her immediately of an ulterior motive. Henrietta had sidled up to her one night after Jenks had passed by in the process of yelling at various girls before the start of the show.

"Places, girls!" Jenks had barked out. "Stop the chatter! Remember! No touching! Partners only! Show more cleavage, Dorothy!" she said, exasperated, to one of the girls. "This isn't the convent, you know. Plenty of other girls on the streets who'd be happy to flash their tits for some dough."

An embarrassed Dorothy had set her tray down and tried to adjust herself to be more provocative. Henrietta looked down at her own bosom and shifted her bodice as much as she dared, glancing over at Ruby as she did so. "I sure could use some extra money," she said quietly without looking at Ruby.

Ruby didn't say anything. Henrietta wasn't sure what to say next. "You wouldn't know how a girl could make a few extra bucks around here, do you?"

Ruby finally turned her head to look at her disdainfully. "I'm sure I don't know what you're talking about. But if you're suggesting what I think you're suggesting, I'd forget about it."

Another person warning her off! But before she could respond, Ruby went on, "I'm guessing you wouldn't have what it takes. This is the big time, see, and you're a bit wet behind the ears, shall we say."

"Ha. Well, I'm not!" Henrietta said unconvincingly. "I've done this plenty of times."

"I doubt it," Ruby said coolly. "And anyway, it's a moot point, considering it's all hypothetical. Better run along before Mrs. Jenkins spots you. You're not supposed to be down in this section."

Henrietta tried to think of something witty to say in return, but nothing came out. She seemed to have no choice but to reluctantly go back to her station near the bar and wait, thinking as she did so. It was strange to her that in Ma's world, she was little more than a floozy, taking on risqué jobs and getting ahead in the world by her looks and supposedly allowing certain liberties, but in this world, she was seen as little more than an innocent child, a "gumdrop," as Lucy called her. She couldn't seem to win either way.

After her years at Poor Pete's and her brief time as a taxi dancer, there wasn't much she hadn't seen. She was definitely no innocent, and yet, she had admittedly not been prepared for what she witnessed on stage or in the usherettes' dressing room at the after-show parties. Lucy had become her protector of sorts, fending off advances from other girls at the parties and attempting to playfully shield Henrietta's eyes when any couple became too engrossed in a dark corner. Henrietta usually laughed and told Lucy she wasn't so naive, but what she saw out of the corner of her eye undoubtably shocked her. Women touching each other in places she hadn't realized were part of sex, both of them seeming to find so much pleasure from it.

She had never told anyone, even Elsie, but as a child back in their old apartment, she had often heard her parents late in the night when they still had one of the bedrooms to themselves and all the kids had been packed into the other two or scattered about on the floor. There had been a lot of grunting coming from her father as the thin mattress springs squeaked, but she had never heard any moans of pleasure coming from her mother as she did now at these after-show parties. She had always known that men enjoyed sex, but not women, and the sight of them stirred something in her, piqued an interest she didn't have before. Dozens of men had ogled and even touched her, but she had never felt anything in return. She didn't know she should feel anything or that it was even possible.

But now, however, something was being awoken within her, though she was in part ashamed of it. She couldn't at times help thinking about the inspector—Clive, as she secretly sometimes called him in her mind. But she knew that was wrong, too. Not only was he involved—possibly in love—with someone else, but he was much too old for her. Hadn't she herself rejected Stan because of a few years' difference in their ages? How hypocritical she was being! But was she really? she countered. Was it really age that made her reject Stan? No, it wasn't just years, she knew, it was the fact that he seemed so young and immature, so hovering, so blindly devoted. Somehow, it didn't appeal to her.

He had definitely slacked off in his sleuth maneuvers (that or he was becoming better at not being detected) since the church festival, after she had lied about being in love (was it a lie?) with the inspector and foisted Stan off onto Elsie, who seemed delighted by his new attentions. He had kept his word and taken Elsie to the library, but he hadn't come around as much lately, at least according to Ma and Elsie. Well, what did she expect? She had told him she didn't care for him in that way, but she had hoped he would have transferred his affections onto Elsie. She realized now that that had been merely wishful thinking. People couldn't just turn their emotions on and off. Of course, Stan wasn't going to love Elsie!

Elsie did not see it that way, however, and had related their library date to Henrietta in the greatest detail. Stanley, she said, had been most attentive, and they had thoroughly enjoyed discussing *Great Expectations*, though they had to reluctantly stop at a certain breathless point, of course, because Elsie had not yet gotten to the end. She wondered if Stan had come away from their "date" with the same rapturous opinion of it as Elsie had.

Henrietta's musings drifted back to the inspector. He was different from most men—certainly Stan, anyway—strong and commanding, but gentle, too. His eyes were kind. She still remembered how it had felt to be held by him as they danced for the first time at the Promenade, before she had found out that he was a cop and a phony, she added bitterly. For a little while, it had been real, though. She tried to imagine what type of girl—woman—he went for. Who was it that he invited into his bed at night? He was obviously not interested in a girl like her, not in that way, anyway, she told herself again.

Still, she couldn't bear the thought, now that she knew him, of not being near him, of not seeing him from time to time. She was afraid to lose him—in any capacity. A part of her realized that this was childish, but she couldn't help it. She had deduced that the only way to be a part of his life was to be what he needed her to be. After all, he had enlisted her help on the case because he assumed she was more experienced than she was, so she needed to continue to play that part, no matter how scared she really was by the knowledge of a prostitution ring just on the other side of the theater, not to mention talk of screams and blood. She had become good at pretending to be something she wasn't over the years, and if she didn't want the inspector to lose interest—as she suspected he might already have, as she had strangely not seen him in several weeks—she would have to continue to try to play her part well.

"Miss? Oh, miss!"

Henrietta snapped out of her ponderings and turned to see Larry standing beside her. That was odd. Larry, or Lazy Larry, as most of the girls called him, usually did not appear on the floor to begin his perpetual sweeping until after the house lights were turned up at the end of the night. Occasionally he could be seen behind the bar wiping glasses if the bartenders were falling behind. He looked at her, his yellowing, watery eyes peering at her. She gasped when he held up a tiny white feather in front of her face, grinning to show his gray, crooked teeth as he did so. "This yours, miss?"

Henrietta searched his face for any deeper meaning but she found none. "No, it's not mine," she said finally, taken aback by what he held in front of her. "But I wouldn't mind having one . . . if you—" She waited for him to pick up the hint, but his face remained blank.

"Musta come off somethin' is all," he said, putting it into his tiny vest pocket and shuffling away. "Mrs. Jenkins'll know what to do with it, I reckon," he mumbled as he went.

Henrietta breathed out slowly. What an odd coincidence, she mused, as she hurried to get more drink orders, unaware of how long she had been standing there thinking. Perhaps it was a sign, she thought hopefully, as she squeezed down the rows of men, more determined than ever to find a way beyond the green door.

As it happened, she got her chance rather unexpectedly a few days later. She had arrived at the Marlowe early, having stopped off at Keirschbaum's bakery to get a couple of day-old rolls for Larry, whom she had become increasingly sorry for. She didn't dare stop at Lutz's in their neighborhood in case it somehow got back to Ma, who would surely disapprove of her spending wages on charity cases. "Charity begins at home," she had said often enough, though to Henrietta this had always seemed horribly hypocritical, as Ma seemed anything but charitable in any given way. No, she had to stop at a place closer to the theater.

The line at Keirschbaum's was unexpectedly short this morning, however, and she made it to the Marlowe faster than she had expected. Conveniently, Larry was there, outside, tacking up posters near the marquee, listing which band was playing that night—as if the choice of band had the slightest influence on whether men came in or not. He seemed genuinely stunned when she handed him the bag of rolls.

"Ta, miss," he said slowly, after opening the bag and examining the contents.

Henrietta winced as a long ash from his dangling cigarette dropped off onto his battered jacket. Though Larry repulsed her, she couldn't help but feel sorry for this poor, dim-witted man who seemed broken beyond repair. At one point she imagined Larry might be an avenue into Jenks's inner circle, but after watching how Jenks bullied and shouted at him, she gave up this idea altogether and was kind to him because no one else seemed to be. He was like a stray dog that everyone got enjoyment from kicking. She had given him a brief smile and gone in, then, leaving him wordlessly standing there, staring after her.

No one seemed to be around yet as she wandered down the crooked hallways toward the dressing rooms. She slowed as she approached the dancers' dressing room, however, as she always did now, and was surprised to find that it was closed. She wondered if perhaps Esther was inside; it was difficult to know when and where she would somehow pop up. She waited, listening, but she didn't hear anything. This might be her chance!

Looking up and down the hallway, she gently pushed open the door and stepped gingerly inside, hoping to find some clue regarding the White Feather Club, though she couldn't imagine what that would be. She lingered for a moment, letting her eyes adjust to the dimness, her breath sounding loud in her ears. She suddenly held it, though, when she heard what sounded like a moan coming from the back of the room.

"Esther?" she called out, tiptoeing forward, her heart fluttering. "Is that you?"

The moaning had stopped as she made her way toward the back of the room, which had been sectioned off with large screens with oriental scenes painted on them.

"Who's there?" came a man's voice that Henrietta thought she recognized but couldn't quite place. She heard a shuffling and then the man's voice again, this time directed to whomever he was with behind the screen. "I thought you said we wouldn't be bothered!" he said angrily.

"Sorry!" called Henrietta, realizing that she had walked into a romantic tryst. She tried to quickly retreat, but as she did so, she backed right into one of the chairs sitting by the dressing table, causing it to make a loud scraping noise across the floor. "Don't mind me! I'm just leaving!" she called out again.

She could hear the angry zip of trousers, then, and before she could get away, Carlo, one of the bouncers, stepped from behind the screen. "Who is it?" he demanded, peering into the darkness while he fastened his belt.

Henrietta stared at his bare chest for a few seconds before she managed to turn her eyes away. "I'm terribly sorry," she said. "I was just looking for . . . Esther," she fibbed.

"Well, she obviously ain't here."

"Who is it, Carlo?" came a woman's voice from behind the screen.

"It's one of the new girls," he said, irritated, as he pulled on his shirt.

Henrietta thought she recognized the woman's voice, too, but was still surprised when she saw Agnes come from around the screen, buttoning her dress.

"Oh, Agnes! I'm sorry! I just . . ." Henrietta said, averting her eyes and stepping back, wanting horribly to get away from there.

Carlo strode past her, giving her a scowl as he did so. "Nosy bitch," he said under his breath.

"Carlo, you don't have to go!" called out Agnes with a hint of desperation. He ignored her, however, and hurried from the room, banging the door closed as he went.

"Now look what you've done!" Agnes said, furiously, turning to her as she finished buttoning.

"Agnes, I . . . I didn't mean to—"

"I suppose you'll go and tell Jenks, won't you?" Agnes said, her irritated tone belying a hint of anxiety.

"Well, I . . ." Henrietta waivered, realizing that she might be able to use this opportunity, though she hated doing it this way. "I'm not sure," she said deliberately. She tried to appear as if she had the upper hand, but her chest was tight with nervousness. "It is against the rules, you know."

"All right, be that way. What do you want?" Agnes asked, assuming she was defeated and reaching for a cigarette from an open box on the nearby dressing table. Henrietta watched as she lit it and took a long drag on it as if to steady her nerves. She indicated with a nod of her head that Henrietta could take one, too, but Henrietta declined.

"I want to get a white feather. You know, from Jenks," she tried to say with confidence.

Agnes's eyes fluttered a bit before she recovered her smooth exterior. "What would you know about that?" she asked, nervously blowing out a tower of smoke from the corner of her mouth.

"Let me just say I need some extra money."

"No chance."

"All right, then. I'll have to ask Mrs. Jenkins myself. I hope I don't forget to keep your little secret."

"Listen, kid," Agnes said eagerly, "the green door's not for you. It's pretty hard-core."

"I can handle myself!"

Agnes let out a snort.

"I've done this before, you know," Henrietta said, trying not to sound false. "Lots of times."

Agnes studied her for a few moments before she shrugged and blew out another cloud of smoke. "Whatever you say, kid." She stood up and looked in the mirror, brushing her hair back into place. "Fine. I'll put in a good word with Jenks for you. But no promises."

"When?"

"When, what?"

"When will you talk to Jenks?"

"Tonight, if I can. It's not always up to her, though. Neptune's got the final say, though I daresay he'd like you," she said, turning from the mirror to look Henrietta up and down. "Funny he hasn't picked you already."

At the mention of Neptune, goose bumps broke out on Henrietta's neck and arms, and she was grateful for the dim light to hide them. "I've... I've heard of him," Henrietta said, clearing her throat. "That's Jenks's boss, right? The owner?"

"That's right," Agnes said, looking at her with new admiration. "You don't miss much, do you, kid?"

"But I never see him around," Henrietta went on, ignoring the offhand compliment. "How does he know which girls to pick?"

"Oh, he's around all right," she said with a grin. "Unlike Jenks, he prefers them young, virginal. So, you might stand a chance," she said, applying lipstick. "God help you, though." She stood up straight and extinguished her cigarette in one of the ashtrays on the dressing table. "He likes to take a ride first, you see, before putting girls in the stable." A dark shadow passed briefly across her face. "And he's a very rough rider." She put the lipstick in her handbag and snapped it shut.

Henrietta swallowed hard, trying to control her rapid breathing.

"Anyway, I've got to go. See you 'round," Agnes said, giving her a false smile and waving briefly to her as she made her way past Henrietta toward the door.

"Thanks, Agnes. Sorry about Carlo," she called after her.

"Oh, he'll come around," she said, pausing before going out. "And don't say I didn't warn you," she added solemnly.

And with that she disappeared, leaving Henrietta to think back through the conversation as she stood alone in the dark, her heart pounding.

CHAPTER 12

All that evening, Henrietta was on edge. She was watching for some sort of signal or acknowledgement from Jenks, and several times attempted, unsuccessfully, to make eye contact with her.

Despite Henrietta's increased watchfulness, however, Jenks ignored her as much as usual, preoccupied, it would seem, with the evening's activities. Henrietta also tried to single out Agnes, who also proved to be very deft at avoiding her, and shortly after the show began, disappeared with what appeared to be a client. It was almost as if the whole episode between her and Agnes had never happened, except that Henrietta was a bundle of nerves now, waiting for some sort of intimation regarding her admission into the White Feather Club.

Even Lucy and the gang noticed her restlessness and questioned her about it, Henrietta replying that she was simply tired. This was not too far from the truth, actually, as she had been awake half the night with Ma and a crying Jimmy, who had had a toothache.

Lucy's remedy for tiredness, or nerves, for that matter, was whiskey, which she urged Henrietta to drink down after the show. Henrietta obeyed, attempting to calm herself while she waited for a chance to slip out of the party once everyone became preoccupied. When the moment finally came, she aimlessly wandered the hallways, hoping Jenks, or someone, would approach her, but to no avail. Perhaps Agnes hadn't had a chance to talk to Jenks? Henrietta wondered. Or had Agnes just lied to get rid of her earlier that day? That did not seem likely, however, since Henrietta could still tell Jenks at any moment what she had witnessed between Agnes and Carlo.

In the end she decided to go home, though she was in two minds about whether or not she should stop by the station to tell the inspector everything that had been happening. She had not seen him since that night at the Lodge when he had warned her not to do anything foolish. She was pretty sure that trying to get into the White Feather Club would count as foolish in his opinion, so in the end, she thought better of stopping to confer with him. She reassured herself that he would be happy with the results she hoped to eventually be able to deliver, though he would probably not approve of the means.

It was odd, though, that he had not been in touch. Had something happened? she worried anxiously. She considered stopping somewhere to use the telephone, but she was reluctant to speak to Clancy or to leave a message with him, as, like last time, he was sure to call the inspector and disturb him. No, Henrietta sighed, she would simply go home and give Ma some relief if Jimmy was still acting up. She had so many thoughts running through her head, she wouldn't be able to sleep for a long time, anyway, she reasoned.

The next day at the Marlowe proved to be just as uneventful as the previous one—at first. Henrietta wasn't as skittish tonight and spent most of the evening trying to attract Jenks's attention, but again with little success. After weighing it all up endlessly, she decided that if nothing happened by the end of the night, she would approach Jenks to report Agnes. She wasn't sure what that would gain her and considered it might even put her in a decidedly more negative light with Jenks, but she felt she had to call Agnes's bluff. She had seen Ruby coldly staring at her at various points in the night and felt sure Agnes had confided in her. Well, if Agnes wasn't around to witness her reporting to Jenks, Ruby would be, and Henrietta thought she saw a glimmer of anxiety in Ruby's otherwise calculating eyes.

Henrietta recognized the band's final set of the night and disappointedly made her way to the bar to count her tips thus far, a favorite pastime among the usherettes when not busy or when bored. Henrietta did not own a wristwatch, but she guessed there was probably less than a half hour left of the show. Lucy passed by in a hurry, saying, "See you in a bit, right?"

Henrietta nodded, still counting.

"I don' think so, not just yet," came a voice uncomfortably close to her ear, accompanied by hot breath on her neck. Henrietta hunched her shoulders in response and jerked away, turning as she did so to see Larry standing beside her, wringing his hands. His repugnant odor was overwhelming at such close quarters.

"Larry! Don't scare me like that!" she said, exasperated, scooping her coins and even some bills off the bar and slipping them into her pocket. She had lost count and would have to start over later. She wiped the back of her neck to be rid of any traces of Larry's breath, his eyes closely following her movements.

"Mrs. Jenkins wan's to see you," he said, grinning. "I'm to fetch you."

At first Henrietta was inclined to dismiss him, but then she suddenly wondered if this could be the summons she had been waiting for. "Mrs. Jenkins wants to see me?" she asked, looking around the crowded theater as if to locate her, but she was not in her usual spot by the curtains, stage right.

"This way, miss," Larry mumbled, not really answering her question. "Hafta go to her office, like," he said almost to himself as he shuffled behind the bar to where a dilapidated little door was located along the back wall. Henrietta had not necessarily noticed it before, and if she had, she would have guessed that it was merely a liquor cabinet of sorts. She was utterly surprised, then, when she saw Larry pull it open and then bend and creep through. It was some type of doorway, not a cabinet! Mystified, Henrietta watched as he turned and gestured with his hand that she should follow, further confusing her. She glanced at Sam to gauge his reaction, but he had his back coincidentally turned to them.

"Larry!" she called to him as she reluctantly followed him behind the bar. "Wait! Why are we going this way? Surely this isn't the way to Mrs. Jenkins's office!" she said, wondering if he was even more backward than she first suspected. She peered in after him, having reached the open door. Larry was already halfway down a set of stone stairs that led into what looked like a cellar.

"Short cut!" he called up. "Come on! She's waitin'. Not much time till the end of the show! Too busy then."

Henrietta looked around again, but there was no one anywhere near the bar just at the moment. She tried to see if she could spot Lucy or any of the gang, but they were not in sight. Sam, too, was busy at the other end of the bar. She glanced down the dark stairs again to where Larry stood, urging her with his hands to follow. She inherently sensed that she should not follow him, but what choice did she have? She had wanted to be in the White Feather Club, and now she had to go through with it. Perhaps this was some kind of initiation?

Shuddering, she stepped across the threshold and was surprised by the cold air emanating from below. She felt her way with her hand on the damp stone wall beside her. As she got closer to where Larry stood at the bottom of the stairs, the dank smell of the cellar combined with Larry's stale, smoky body odor nearly took her breath away. At the bottom, Larry was waiting with an old flashlight that looked like a remnant from the war. All she could make out was a long, low, narrow stone hallway that stretched out indefinitely before them.

"Where are we?" she asked nervously, her voice echoing slightly against the stone. "Is this some kind of a joke, Larry?" she asked, trying to make her voice sound commanding, though in actuality, it shook with fear.

"Don' know any jokes," Larry said, leading the way down the hallway.

Henrietta followed as closely as she dared, not wanting to be far from the tiny stream of light coming from the flashlight that regrettably only illuminated the immediate patch in front of them. "Do you think there's any spiders?" Henrietta asked nervously, peering at the wall but unable to see in the blackness.

"Ain't no spiders. Snakes eat 'em all."

Upon hearing this Henrietta almost screamed but clamped her hand over her mouth to prevent it and hurried closer to Larry despite his foul odor.

"Where . . . where are we going?" Henrietta asked nervously as the hallway arched to the left. She could still see nothing but darkness ahead. Every so often they passed large, closed, warehouse-style doorways, as if this had once been some sort of storage facility or receiving dock.

"Told you. Mrs. Jenkins wan's to see you in her office."

"Her office?"

Larry didn't answer.

"Surely her office isn't down here!" she pressed.

"Short cut. Lots o' short cuts aroun' here." He let out a strange little cough that Henrietta perceived to be a sort of laugh. "Lots of tunnels under the city, lots of tunnels above ground, too," he mumbled to himself. He halted briefly outside one of the doors, looking back at her, hesitating, as if he were going to enter but then seemed to change his mind before he continued on down the passageway.

Henrietta, terrified, could think of nothing else to say. Her teeth were chattering either from the cold or from fear, and they continued on in silence until the hallway abruptly ended with a wooden staircase. Henrietta wondered if they had walked under the entire theater and where they would eventually surface. She followed Larry up the creaking stairs and waited as he gave the door at the top a shove. Noiselessly it opened, and they stepped into another long, low hallway, painted a dull rose color and dimly lit with sconces along the wall. Henrietta peered down it and noticed many doors coming off of it, all of them closed, though she was pretty sure she could hear voices behind them.

"This way, miss," Larry said, gesturing with his hand to the left. This part of the hallway ended with a small green door and just before it was a partially open door from which a crooked rectangle of light spilled out. "This's Mrs. Jenkins's office. This one here," he said quietly, grinning. "Gotta be quiet, like," he said, nodding his head toward the other end of the hallway. "Can't disturb anyone, see? Betcha don' know where you are, do you?"

Admittedly, Henrietta had lost all sense of direction. She had never been to this part of the Marlowe, never even knew it existed. As they walked toward the green door at the end of the hallway, however, it suddenly dawned on her that they must in fact be on the other side of the green door. She had done it! She had breached the inner sanctum, but now what? she worried as she looked quickly around, trying to take it all in. What if Jenks wanted her to start tonight before she had even gotten a feather? Could that be what had happened with Iris? she speculated frantically. Suddenly she felt a wave of nausea. She should have told someone where she was going, but how could she have? She wondered if perhaps Sam had at least seen her leave.

"Go on!" Larry said, not waiting for an answer to his previous question and giving her a little push forward. It was so uncharacteristic of him that Henrietta turned to look back at him. He just stood, there, however, grinning slightly with his crooked gray teeth. "Can't keep Mrs. Jenkins waitin'," he whispered.

"Larry!" Jenks hissed from inside the room. "Is that you? Did you get her?"

"Yes, ma'am!" he answered, urging Henrietta with a frantic bobbing of his head and shooing motions with his hands to go in. "Comin', ma'am."

Henrietta took a deep breath and stepped into the room, Larry following her, suddenly becoming obsequious in front of his master and rubbing his hands nervously. "Here she is, Mrs. Jenkins. I brought 'er, just like you wanted. All ready for work, she is," he said, as if proudly turning over a captive and waiting for the expected praise.

"I can see that, Larry," she drawled, not looking at him. "Come in, come in," she said to Henrietta, slightly piqued.

Henrietta stepped further in, taking in the contents of the room as she did so, though she tried not to make it obvious. She couldn't have been more surprised. Whereas Mama Leone's tiny closet fitted her gruff personality in its spartan, slipshod décor, Jenks's office was decorated in a particularly soft, feminine style, the very opposite of how Henrietta perceived Jenks. There was an ornately carved cherry desk, upon which various ledgers and account books were stacked, as well as a somewhat worn, paisley armchair and loveseat nearby in what seemed to be a makeshift sitting room with a fringed floor lamp and doilies neatly placed. In the back was a tiny sink, above which were several shelves that held, among other things, a chintz teapot and cups as well as canisters of what were presumably sweet treats.

Henrietta was also surprised to see a window against the back wall, framed in lace curtains, out of which Henrietta could see the lights of several boats flickering on what must be the Chicago River beyond, though it was impossible to see at this time of night. It was the only window she had ever seen in the Marlowe, and she realized by the view that they must be at the back of the building. Henrietta finally gathered up the courage to look directly at Jenks, though she needn't have worried, as Jenks and Larry were staring at each other in an odd way. Henrietta couldn't read what was in Jenks's face at that moment. Perhaps disgust at having to rely on such an imbecilic creature?

Jenks, seated behind the desk, nodded at him ever so slightly, then, as if they understood one another, before she barked out, "That's all, Larry. Get back to work!"

"Yes, ma'am," he said, raising his shoulders in what seemed a strange sort of bow and rubbing his hands together nervously. "I'll leave you to it then, Mrs. Jenkins," he said with a grin, and left the room. Henrietta listened to him make his way down the hallway and back down into the cellar passageway. She was glad to be rid of him but terrified to be alone with Jenks. Henrietta stood uncomfortably in front of Jenks, hoping she wouldn't notice her trembling as she surveyed her through her half-closed lids.

"There's something about you I don't like," Jenks said finally.

"Something doesn't sit right with me. I can't figure it out, though."

"I . . . what do you mean?" Henrietta tried to ask innocently. "I . . . I just heard a girl could make some extra money. Let's just say I'm interested," she faltered, feeling her face redden as she did so.

"Shut your trap," Jenks said. "I can tell a phony from a mile away. Agnes tells me you're on the level, but Agnes will say anything if she's cornered."

Henrietta opened her mouth to speak but then thought better of it.

"Still, it seems you've caught Neptune's fancy, so I'm overruled, as usual. He's wanted you in from the very beginning." Henrietta shuddered at the remembrance of him from the audition, the way he stared at her with his beady eyes.

"Agnes says you've done this type of work before, but I doubt it. Still, what should I care? It'll just be more mess for Esther to clean up. I just don't want no tears and no hysterics, got it? You want in, then you do as you're told."

"Of course," Henrietta tried to say smoothly, wondering why her lack of "experience" was so obvious to everyone. She had always managed to bluff her way any other time. She had even convinced Inspector Howard, and he was a detective with the police! "You shouldn't worry about me," she said with a toss of her hair. "I've worked in other places, you know."

"Something tells me you're lying," Jenks said, looking her up and down again.

Henrietta tried hard to control her breathing. "Well, I'm not!" she said, putting her hand on her hip, but feeling foolish as she did so. "Anyway, as you said, what do you care? Am I in or not?"

Jenks surveyed her coolly. "All right. You can start tomorrow night, though I'm sure it's a mistake. Neptune's eager to get you in the stable, though."

Henrietta swallowed. "How will I know who's mine for the night?" she tried to ask casually.

Jenks laughed. "Oh, there'll be more than one, my little chick, don't you worry."

"Yes, obviously," Henrietta said quickly. "It wouldn't be worth it otherwise, would it?" Henrietta met her eyes, reading the distrust there but trying to evade it. "How's it work, then?" she asked steadily.

Jenks studied her for a moment and then explained, "I'll put you in a front section. Interested customers slip me cash as they walk in. First come, first dibs. It's mostly the dancers they get a choice of, but there's a few of you, as you know by now. Sometimes the bouncers help spot interested 'patrons,' should we say, and point them out to me."

"I see. Simple enough. I just wait for a signal from you, then?"

"That's right. On my signal, you come down to the front side curtain. I'll show you where to go from there. You can't both leave together, or it would look suspicious. One at a time. Nice and easy, like."

"Got it. Want me to wear anything special? I mean, once I'm back here?"

Jenks laughed. "Chick, you ain't gonna be wearin' anything, unless they want something kinky. You'll figure it out. There's clothes in the room. You do what you're told and there won't be any trouble, understand?"

"Yeah, sure. Easy enough."

Mrs. Jenkins surveyed her again before shaking her head slightly as if trying to accept what she knew to be a careless decision. She reached down and opened the bottom drawer of the desk and drew out a tiny wooden box, which she set roughly on the top of the desk, almost spilling what appeared to be a glass of wine sitting there. Carefully opening it, she reached in and unceremoniously pulled out a white feather and handed it to Henrietta. "I'm assuming you know what to do with this."

"Yes. Thanks, Mrs. Jenkins," she said, thinking she should exhibit some sort of gratitude as she took it from her.

"You won't be thanking me later when this is all over, I dare say, but there it is." She got up from behind the desk and walked out into the hallway toward the green door. "Out you go. This way. I've got customers waiting, I'm sure." She grasped at a gold chain around her neck until she found an attached key and then bent to unlock the green door. Henrietta, standing behind her, glanced over her shoulder down the long hallway.

"Which room will I be in?" she asked, hoping she could give the information to the inspector.

"What difference does it make?" Jenks asked, annoyed, standing in the doorway, nearly filling it, her hand on the knob behind her. "You'll go where you're told."

She made no attempt to get out of the way, however, so Henrietta had to squeeze past her. As she did so, Jenks deftly reached out her free hand and held Henrietta's cheeks between her thumb and fingers, squeezing them as she did so. "Not a word of this gets out, hear, my little chick?"

Henrietta tried to nod.

"Not a word to those lesbos." She smiled when she saw a flicker of fear in Henrietta's eye, telling her that her barb had hit its mark. "Oh, yes. I've got my eye on them, don't you worry. Nothing gets past me. I've got eyes everywhere. And don't forget, I can take what I want whenever I want it," she said and kissed Henrietta roughly on the mouth. She let her go then, and, utterly stunned, Henrietta had to use all of her effort not to wipe it off. "Get out, now! No funny business!" she hissed and gave Henrietta a little shove through the green door, closing it behind her. She heard the scrape of the lock, and, shaking, Henrietta took several minutes to collect herself, looking desperately around as if to solicit help, but the hallway leading from the lobby was deserted.

Tightly she gripped the little white feather, no longer than the width of her hand, and hurriedly put it in her pocket, her mind racing as she tried to take in what had just happened. She had done it, finally gotten beyond the green door, and she felt both elated and terrified at the same time. She was in the White Feather Club, but now what?

She was afraid to tell Lucy and the gang, sure that they would be upset, angry even, but they were sure to notice the feather tomorrow regardless. She wanted awfully to leave, feeling as though she would die if she didn't get some fresh air, but, looking down at her flounced red satin dress, she knew she couldn't walk out just yet. She knew she had to make an appearance in the usherettes' room to at least get changed. She would have to pretend to be ill, which wasn't so far from the truth, as she walked with shaking legs toward the other side of the theater.

CHAPTER 13

Clive sat at the bar of the Lodge nursing his scotch. He couldn't help looking up at the doorway every so often to see if she were coming. He had sent Kelly undercover to wait outside the Marlowe with a message for Henrietta that she should meet him here. He had important news for her. Mickey had turned up dead, and he was pulling her from the operation. He knew the chief would be upset if they didn't come away with a conviction soon, but his conscience would no longer allow him to endanger Miss Von Harmon—Henrietta—any farther. He would have to think up something convincing to tell the chief later.

He ran his hand through his hair as he went over the facts of the case one more time in his mind, trying to figure out what he had missed. He had been working on busting Neptune's ring for almost a year, convinced that he was somehow connected to the mob. Various characters had come within their grasp, little players like Mickey or even Sneebly, though Henrietta didn't know that. They had always melted away, though, or provided little enough information if they were briefly held, even when pressed in what some might call an illegal way. Someone had screwed up, though, with Mama Leone's death, and it had left a tiny crack for Clive to wriggle through.

His men had been casing the Promenade on and off for a long time, convinced that Mama Leone was a supplier of girls for Neptune's prostitution ring. Finally, Clive had decided to go in himself to sniff around, and he had most certainly not expected to meet the likes of Henrietta. She was perhaps the most beautiful girl—woman—he had ever seen, even, he had to admit, more so than Catherine.

He had been intrigued with Henrietta as they had danced; she was both innocent and beguiling at the same time, as if she weren't fully aware of all of her charms and was still experimenting with the unusual box of gifts she had been born with. He had gotten the information he wanted from her easily enough, but he had not been prepared for Mama Leone's death the next day and wondered if his presence had been noticed and Mama Leone killed before they could move in. Or was it merely a coincidence? Just in case, he had been careful not to get too close to the Marlowe from that point on. If he were recognized, the whole operation might go up in smoke. Keeping a safe distance seemed to be working, but it made it difficult to communicate with Henrietta, who, he was pretty sure, no doubt imagined herself abandoned by him.

When he had been called to the crime scene at the Promenade that day, he had to admit that he had looked forward to having to cross-examine her. Not only did he guiltily wish to gaze upon her once more, but he was intrigued to see what her reaction to his being a cop would be. He had been impressed the night before when she had guessed it. It had amused him to listen to her accuse him of lying and to hotly defend the clarinet player, as if he even remotely suspected him. As the interview had proceeded, however, an idea had come to him and he realized that perhaps he could use her, having sized her up pretty accurately, or so he believed. They had tried before to get girls into the Marlowe, but they had always failed to get past the "audition." As he had looked her over yet again in the back room of the Promenade, he realized she might be exactly what he was looking for. He had been a bit surprised, though, and saddened, really, at how little it had taken to convince her to go undercover for him.

She had made it through the audition, just as he had guessed she would, and was proving to be a most excellent informer in her own naive way, but Clive was getting a bit worried that she might be in over her head. He had to admit that he had thought her more experienced when he first met her, but now he realized that she was a lot younger than he had first supposed and clearly more innocent . . .

Clive tried to steer his ruminations back to the case. The large amount of cash they had found in Mama Leone's office would seem to prove that not only was her death not the result of a robbery gone wrong but instead lent itself to the theory that Mama Leone was getting kickbacks from Neptune for goods supplied. How else would she have amassed that much cash? But why kill her, then? Was she getting greedy? Was someone blackmailing her? Mickey was obviously an accidental witness and therefore killed, but why wasn't this Polly coming forward? Was she part of the ring? He took another sip of his scotch. If they could only find her, she might be able to give them more information about what Mama Leone had been up to, who her contacts were, not to mention more information about her missing sister.

That had been a bungled affair—the missing sister. His predecessor who had handled the case had not gone deep enough, he was sure. Neptune had been picked up at the time and questioned. Clive had merely been a junior detective then, but he had witnessed the various "interviews" the police had conducted while they held him temporarily at the station. Neptune had merely glared at them through his bushy eyebrows, grinning maniacally at the time, and insisting that he be allowed to talk with his lawyer, as if he had one. In the end, they had been forced to release him, very much worse for wear, thanks to the officers on duty that night, not having anything concrete on which to hold him.

Something just didn't add up, though, Clive told himself again. He was missing something; he just knew it. For one thing, if Neptune was really running a prostitution ring, why would two girls have gone missing? Weren't they more valuable to him alive than dead? Had something gone wrong? Had they threatened to squeal? One thing was clear, however. If Neptune had killed two girls already and now Mickey, Henrietta was very probably in danger as well. He would pull her from the operation tonight. She had gotten him enough information to confirm his theory, and instead he would double his efforts to find this Polly. Surely, she held the key to the mystery.

Where was she? Henrietta, that was? he wondered as he again glanced at the door. He leaned back and took out his pocket watch again. The frown on his face softened momentarily as he lingered to look at the photograph wedged inside the cover. It was Catherine on their wedding day. He snapped the watch shut and took a large gulp of his whiskey, trying to block the memories that always lingered just below the surface.

He had been born into a wealthy, upper-class family, just he and his older sister, Julia. His father had wanted him to go to law school, but the war had intervened. His father insisted that he could get him a deferment, but Clive had refused and had joined up the first chance he got. He was not usually the rebellious type, and he knew the sorrow he would cause his parents and his childhood sweetheart, Catherine, if he went away, but his sense of duty and honor could not be quelled no matter how much his mother cried or how tender Catherine's kisses were. Given the imminent situation, both sets of parents had agreed to let them marry hurriedly before Clive shipped out. They had had very little time together, but it was enough for Catherine to be with child as she waved goodbye to him as he leaned out the window of the train departing Union Station bound for New York, where a ship lay waiting to carry him to France.

When he had returned just eleven months later, his right shoulder in tatters, he discovered that Catherine and the baby, a little girl, had both died in childbirth. No letter had ever reached him, informing him of his great loss. He lay in bed for months, recuperating, until finally his shoulder had healed, though the war was over then, and no one was sure anymore why it had even begun. It took much longer, however, for his broken heart to heal, and he buried it very deeply, not caring what happened to it anymore and accepting that the world for him would always be a little bit darker now. He had lost count of the nights he had lain awake asking himself why he had lived. Why had he made it through only to come home to an empty house, an empty life?

Almost immediately, he had given up any idea of becoming a lawyer, though he was still interested in a different aspect of the law—upholding it. He could no longer stomach the idea of sitting in an office, pouring over corporate policies for his father's firm or worse, standing in a courtroom persuading a group of men as to the innocence or not of a fellow man. Law, order, justice was all that made sense to him now, but he was determined to do something concrete to stop the tide of hurt and sorrow he had seen inflicted on innocent people at the hands of a few. It was his own small way of correcting the injustice that had been dealt to him, and so he had joined the police force, quickly rising to the rank of detective inspector, one of the youngest ever to do so, and meanwhile quietly closing that particular chapter in his life in which could be read his short affair with love.

As the years passed, he had been successful in keeping himself aloof from women, sharing his small apartment with only his dog, Katie—his girl, as he liked to affectionately call her—though his parents had begged him to meet someone else. They had held elaborate dinner parties at their home on the exclusive North Shore and had introduced him to several eligible women, many widowed by the war, but he just couldn't seem to make himself be interested in any of them, preferring instead to nurse his wounds privately, usually with a bottle of scotch. His sorrow was made worse by the knowledge that not only did it pain his parents to see him alone, but that they were doubly despondent that the family name—and fortune—would not be handed down. It could not be helped, however. He just couldn't forget—forgive—what had happened, not only with his own fledgling family, but at the front itself.

That is until now. He had met this silly, no not silly, divine, girl—woman—Henrietta, and, if truth be told, he was a bit frightened, unnerved, by the response she had elicited in him. The part of him that he believed comfortably buried was coming alive again almost against his will, and he could not stop the guilt that washed over him. He had no wish to betray Catherine nor to rob the cradle he saw before him, but he found it difficult, almost impossible, to stop thinking about Henrietta. She haunted his dreams in a way Catherine never had. He had practically grown up with Catherine; it had made sense for them to marry, but Henrietta . . . she was something different altogether. But who was he fooling? She was young and, dear God, so beautiful; she could have any man she chose to flash that lovely smile of hers at. Why would a girl like her have any interest in a broken-down old man like himself? Now, in his mid-thirties, he felt like he had already lived a whole lifetime. How could she ever give her heart to someone like himself? And yet, though it scared him to admit it, he suspected he had already lost his heart to her, wanting to protect her, keep her safe, love her.

It had taken every ounce of his self-possession to stop himself from striding down the hallway that night at Polly's apartment and busting open the thin door behind which he knew she stood undressing, or from simply wrapping his arms around her as she had sat sewing across from him when she had told him of her large, impoverished family. Something about the scene had uncomfortably reminded him of the few blessed evenings he had had at home with Catherine before he had shipped off, how they had sat in quiet contentment before he had led her to the bedroom . . .

But while Catherine had been very quiet and demure and while he had once loved her for that, he oddly found himself attracted to Henrietta's fresh enthusiasm, her spunk, as it were, and he longed to drink from that fountain of youth, to refresh his weary soul after so many years of mourning, and yet he knew this was wrong. He was too old for her; she deserved someone young like herself, someone like that pipsqueak his men kept picking up. What his name? Stanley?

His men had repeatedly spotted him following Henrietta on her way home from the Marlowe and had picked him up before he could blow the whole operation. He was obviously moonstruck with Henrietta, and who could blame him? Perhaps it would be better to leave Henrietta to the likes of him, someone her own age; after all, he seemed keen enough to watch over her. But then again, Henrietta did not seem to appreciate Stanley's efforts, if he read the situation correctly, and he smiled to himself at how annoyed she seemed to be with him, but protective, too. Or what about that numbskull, Artie? Though he sensed that that situation was on the rocks, if it had ever been anything real to begin with.

Had he imagined that there was something in her eyes when she sometimes looked up into his own face—a longing perhaps? Desire? His heart skipped a beat whenever he caught her looking surreptitiously at him, but he tried to dismiss it as useless fancy on his part. Let's face it, he admitted as he tossed back the last of his scotch, she was very charming, and he had seen her flash her blue eyes at other men as well. She was a slippery fish, and he wasn't sure she was all that keen to be caught. And, anyway, he had lost his love of the sport, or had he? Too often, he had found himself imagining what it might be like to kiss her soft lips, to feel her body close to his . . .

Stop it! he told himself. This is madness! A thoroughly useless pursuit. He had never been so distracted on a case in his life, and he worried it was clouding his understanding of the facts. The sooner she was off the case, the better.

He looked up, then, from the empty glass he was staring at to signal the bartender for another when he saw with a start that she was standing right beside him.

"Where'd you come from?" he asked, surprised, and felt a warmth inside at the sight of her face lighting up in a smile. "I've been watching for you. Bartender!" he called loudly. "Another! And for you," he said, standing, making room for her at the bar next to him. "Tom Collins, wasn't it?"

He saw her blush slightly. "Well, if you don't mind."

"Tom Collins," he said to the bartender, who had just plopped down another scotch in front of him.

"I got your note," she whispered irresistibly. "Very mysterious. How did you know?"

"Know what?"

"That I needed to talk to you," she continued, whispering. "So much has happened."

He looked worriedly at her face, trying to ascertain if what had happened was good or bad. "Such as?"

She looked around her and then back at him. "Maybe we should sit at a table," she suggested, nodding toward one over in the corner.

"Not a bad idea," he said, laying down some cash and taking up the drinks.

Clive watched as she removed her coat and sat opposite him. Even in her faded overalls, she looked exquisite.

"Let's have it then. What's this big news?"

She leaned dangerously close to him over her absurd Tom Collins. "I've been beyond the green door!" she whispered excitedly. "I got a white feather! But I had to endure a kiss from Jenks, if you can believe it. Perfectly wretched, it was," she said making a face of disgust.

Clive felt a pain of fear in the pit of his stomach. "Slow down. What do you mean?"

"Just what I said. You told me to look for anything suspicious. Obviously, that would be the green door and what goes on beyond it. Lucy and her friends told me that the girls that are part of it wear white feathers in their hair. That's how the men know who's available." She was talking very fast. "It's mostly dancers, but Ruby and Agnes have one, too, which is unusual, you see, 'cause they're usherettes. I tried to get friendly with them, but they weren't interested. That is until I caught Agnes doing the business with one of the bouncers. I hated doing it, honestly, Inspector, but I had to . . ."

Clive's stomach knotted. "Do what?"

"Well, blackmail her, I guess you'd call it."

Clive found himself wanting to laugh, despite the severity of the situation, at the thought of her attempting to blackmail anybody, but he manfully held it in as Henrietta continued her tale.

"She told Jenks I wanted in . . . to the White Feather Club—that's what Lucy and the gang call it. I think Jenks was annoyed by the whole thing. She doesn't like me; she even said so, right to my face, if you can believe it. She thinks I'm up to something . . . but then, why would she kiss me? Maybe she knew I'd find it horrible?" she mumbled to herself, mulling it over as she paused to take a drink.

"Wait a minute. Wait a minute," Clive said, motioning with his hand for her to stop. "Agnes got Jenks to approach you about this white feather club?" He asked the question awkwardly, trying to understand it. "Is that right?"

"Well, yes, but it was Larry who brought me to Jenks's office. Through some tunnels under the theater."

"Tunnels? What sort of tunnels?"

"You know, the usual sort of tunnels. Dark, narrow, creepy."

"Hmmm," he said, running his hand through his hair. He did not like the sound of this, but it might explain a few things. "Where do they lead?"

"I told you! To Jenks's office," she whispered.

"From where? Where did you enter?"

"That's the strangest thing. From this little door behind the bar. It looks like a cabinet, but it leads down some steps to these tunnels. Cold and damp, stone walls, no light. Larry had a flashlight, but it didn't help much."

"Larry's the custodian?"

"Sort of. He does Jenks's bidding; he's completely in her power, poor thing, however disgusting he might be."

"Were there other passageways down there?"

Henrietta thought for a moment. "I don't think so, but it was hard to tell. There were big doors, like warehouse doors. Didn't look like they'd been used in a long time, though."

Clive wondered if would have been easy access to the river in the past. Perhaps it really had been a warehouse. If so, it would be a convenient way to get rid of the bodies of the two missing girls—or any others. He took a drink. "Then what?"

"We went up some steps, and then we were in another hallway! At one end there was a green door with Mrs. Jenkins's office right next to it. It took me a few minutes before I realized that I was on the other side of the green door, that we had come up from below to a place behind it!"

"It was a hallway, you say? Any windows?" he asked, trying to imagine how a raid might go.

"No, the only window I saw was in Jenks's office itself. I could see the river beyond."

So, this hidden hallway must be in the back of the building, he surmised. "Anyone else around?" He thought he saw Henrietta blush. She took a sip of her Tom Collins.

"No one I saw, but I think I heard people. Behind the doors as we walked back to Mrs. Jenkins. Lots of moans, bed squeaks," she said quietly, not looking at him at first but then resolutely lifting her head and making eye contact, the slightest toss of her hair, as if to prove she was unaffected. "You know. I'm sure that's where the business is being transacted."

It pained him to see how she was pretending. How had he not noticed this before? He was rarely wrong when it came to sizing people up, especially when interrogating a suspect, but she had completely thrown him for a loop. That night at the Promenade when they had danced, she had seemed so much older than she really was, like she had been around the block a few times. Well, she *had* been around the block, but not in that way, it was clear to him now; she had somehow retained her virtue on the way. But how could that be? he mused. She had seen a lot; worn low-cut, sleazy dresses; drank shots of whiskey when necessary, and yet she still blushed at the mention of beds squeaking in the night.

He looked away from her and took another drink, not sure how much longer he could trust himself alone with her. "What did Jenks say?" he managed.

"Just that she doesn't trust me, but that Agnes vouched for me. Oh, yes—I forgot this part. She said she was being overruled by Neptune. That he—" Her fingers tapped the table nervously. "That he . . . has wanted me from the beginning. So she was forced to give me a feather." He thought he perceived a slight timorousness in her voice as she said it, making his stomach churn.

"And what's this about the kiss?" he asked steadily, nervously storing the detail about Neptune wanting her. This was sounding worse and worse.

"Oh," she said, screwing up her face in what looked like disgust. "Seems Lucy and the girls are right. Jenks is . . . you know, the other way, too. Apparently, that's why she leaves them alone. But as I was leaving, I . . . Jenks grabbed my face and kissed me and said something like she could take what she wants." Henrietta visibly shuddered. "Then she pushed me through the green door and I . . . I left as soon as I could get away and then—well, you know the rest. Kelly followed me down Canal and handed me your message. And here we are. So," she paused, finally. "What do you think? Haven't I done well?"

Again, it was distressing to see how badly she wanted to please him, but his mind was whirling. He had to admit that this was just the situation he had been hoping for. He was so close to nailing Neptune he could taste it, but how could he jeopardize Henrietta this way? It would be dangerous enough if he were sending in an experienced woman of the streets, but Henrietta was a complete innocent. Somehow, she had faked her way through to this point, though, or had she? Had Neptune all along seen through her where he himself had not? Was this what Neptune was after all along? Young girls for himself while supplying experienced prostitutes for the crowd? Had Henrietta walked right into a trap? God, it would be a beautiful sting, though; this chance might never come again! But could Henrietta actually pull it off? What if something went wrong? No, he just couldn't risk it. He held up two fingers to the bartender, signaling two more drinks. He could feel Henrietta looking at him expectantly, wanting him to praise her.

He cleared his throat. "Yes, it's excellent work, Miss Von Harmon. First rate. But I'm afraid I'm pulling the plug on this operation. It's getting far more dangerous than I thought."

"Inspector! You can't do that! Not after all I went through to find out about the door and get the feather and all that. I'm supposed to, well, you know, start tomorrow night. We're so close! Surely you can think of a plan?"

He could think of several plans, but unfortunately all of them were risky.

"Please! I want to do this. I want to help."

"You *have* helped," he insisted. "Plenty."

"But I want to finish this. See it through."

"But why?" he asked, looking at her steadily. "Why do you want to do this so badly? We'll pay you for the work you've done so far, if that's what you're worried about." He knew this wasn't it, and the look of anger on her face confirmed it.

"It has nothing to do with the money! I—"

The bartender arrived then with two new drinks and clinked together their empty glasses between his thumb and forefinger, lifting them neatly off the table and silently retreating.

"Honest, Inspector. I . . . I want to help find out what happened to Polly's sister."

He arched his eyebrow at her, disbelieving.

"I have a sister, too, you know. Please just let me try."

There was something she wasn't telling him about her motivation. Surely, she couldn't be all that concerned for Polly and her long-gone sister. A bit maybe, but enough to risk her life? There was something else, but he just couldn't put his finger on it. Why was she so eager to help him? He went through the details once more in his mind. He had to admit it was the perfect setup, but he could not in all likelihood ensure her safety. Not a hundred percent, anyway. Something just wasn't sitting right.

"You don't think I can do it, do you?" she asked him, a hurt look on her face. "That's why you're hesitating, aren't you?"

"I'm quite sure of your many talents, Miss Von Harmon, but it's your safety I'm rather thinking of."

"Seems you should have thought of that before now," she said heatedly.

He winced at the jab and admitted to himself that she was right. He had been foolish.

"You could send someone in, you know. To be my client—undercover, like." The toss of the hair again.

"Perhaps," he said grudgingly. She's very clever, he reflected with a grin. He had been thinking along the same lines. "I suppose I could send in Charlie to . . . solicit you."

"It wouldn't be you?"

He could hear the disappointment in her voice. And there was that look again. Was it desire he read in her eyes? He swallowed hard. "They might recognize me from the night at the Promenade. I'm not entirely sure Mama Leone wasn't stabbed because they spotted me and were afraid she'd talk."

Her brows furrowed. "Yes, of course. I see," she nodded absently. "So, it would be Charlie." She sipped her drink carefully.

"Believe me, Charlie's a good one to have in a pinch. You'd be okay with him."

She seemed to think this over. "So, Charlie chooses me," she said as if checking items off a list. "Then what?" she asked, taking a drink.

Clive's mind began to consider the situation more closely. The plan was oddly sounding plausible, and he couldn't help but follow the line of speculation. "Once Charlie got back behind this green door with you," he suggested, almost to himself, "he would get the lay of the land, hopefully sniff out Neptune red-handed and then wait for the raid, if it even came to that. Shouldn't be too hard for Charlie and the boys to nab him," he said snapping his fingers. "Meanwhile, I'd be waiting outside in the back with my men just in case Neptune tries to give them the slip that way." Or if Charlie signals for help should things get out of hand, he speculated to himself, not wanting to share this possibility with Henrietta. Why was this plan sounding so logical? He had to admit he was excited about the prospect of finally closing this case. Perhaps he would get a citation for it. Besides, with Charlie behind the scenes, would Henrietta really be in any danger?

"So, it's a plan then? We're actually going to do it?" she asked excitedly.

"You're really not afraid, Miss Von Harmon?" he asked gently.

"Afraid? Not a bit!" He perceived that she shook her head a little too quickly. "And don't you think you should call me Henrietta?" she asked coyly. "After all, we're sort of partners, aren't we? And we have danced together, remember?"

He did indeed remember, but he pushed this thought aside. He could swear she was flirting with him, but he reasoned that it must be the excitement of the case that was making her giddy. "Yes, but that wasn't the real thing, was it?" He had meant it in jest, but he could see by the look on her face that he had injured her. He tried to think of something to say to counter this, but she beat him to it.

"Well, yes. I suppose that's true, isn't it? Just part of the job," she said somewhat stiffly. "I don't know what I was thinking. Suppose we go over the details, then, about the plan before I need to leave. Ma will be wondering if I've disappeared off the face of the earth." She tried a little smile but failed miserably.

"Yes, I suppose we should."

There was nothing for it. If he were going to allow this scheme to go forward, he had to retain his professional distance, or he would not be able to watch it happen. As it was, it was going to be difficult enough to sit in a squad car in the back alley, knowing what was supposed to be happening to her inside the theater and hoping Charlie could stop it in time. But if she were brave enough to go ahead with it, surely he could, too, couldn't he?

Later that night, after he had gotten home and fed an exuberant Katie, he had a final scotch and lay down in his big empty bed, his shoulder aching. Try as he might, he could not stop thinking about Henrietta, how they had parted very cordially, despite his desire to hold her, kiss her, love her— somehow hang on to her as she slipped into her building. His thoughts drifted against his will to imagine what it would be like to undress her, to have her lying here next to him.

He groaned and turned over to the other side, beating the pillow as he did so, causing Katie to move to the end of the bed and resume her sleepy position. He needed to let this go, needed to stop it, or how was he any different from Neptune in his lust for young girls? He tossed and turned through the night and then finally lay curled up in a sweat, a prisoner to a deep, troubled sleep in which he cried for the first time in a long, long while.

When he woke the next morning, he tried to hold onto the foggy strands of his dreams, not sure if he had been crying for Catherine or for something else altogether, and hoped, regardless, that it wasn't a bad omen.

CHAPTER 14

"Oh, Henrietta! What have you done!" said Lucy as the two of them stood in the dressing room.

Lucy had grasped hold of Henrietta's hands but then let one of them go to reach up in an attempt to pluck out the white feather she saw artfully arranged in Henrietta's auburn hair. Henrietta pulled back so that she couldn't reach it, though, smiling nervously despite the struggle. There was only about thirty minutes before the show opened, and most of the other usherettes had gone out already. The band's warm-up notes could be heard floating back from the stage.

Henrietta had tried hiding in the bathroom until everyone had gone, pausing only momentarily in the dressing room to pull out the tiny feather from her pocket and place it in her hair, her hands shaking a bit as she did so. She took a deep breath to steady herself, having been discovered by Lucy, who had stayed behind as well, searching for her. Lucy looked as though she was on the brink of tears as she stared, horrified, at the feather in Henrietta's hair. "Is this your idea of a joke?" she asked her.

"Lucy, don't worry! I'll be fine!" Henrietta said, trying to sound reassuring, if not for Lucy than for herself.

"Who put you up to this? Was it Ruby? I'll get her!" Lucy said vehemently, squeezing Henrietta's hands as she did so.

"No! No one put me up to it. I—"

"Is it the money? You'd only have to say. I know you got it hard at home, gumdrop, but we could've all scraped together to lend you some to get by."

Henrietta smiled and felt in danger of crying, touched by her new friend's generosity and her strained emotions. "No, it's not the money. I just . . . I just have to find out what happened to Iris—and to Libby."

"For your friend, you mean?"

"Yes. For my friend, Polly. We were taxi dancers together. Then the dance matron was murdered, and, well, maybe it's all connected."

"But Libby disappeared a long time ago! And how would it be connected?" she asked disbelievingly. "And anyway, isn't that a thing for the police to figure out, not that they're much good at it," Lucy said, wryly.

Henrietta vacillated. Should she tell Lucy to whole truth? She supposed it wouldn't hurt since it was unlikely that after tonight she would be working here any longer. The realization oddly saddened her. "Listen, Lucy—"

"There you two are!" said Gwen urgently, suddenly appearing at the doorway. "Jenks's been asking for you, especially Henry—" She stopped when she saw Lucy's face. "What's wrong?" she asked, stepping into the room, Rose close on her heels.

"Better hurry, girls; Esther's been dispatched to find you two!" Rose said breathlessly, popping into the room as well.

Lucy merely pointed to Henrietta's white feather, eliciting the expected murmurs of shock from Gwen and Rose.

"Henrietta, is this some sort of joke?" Gwen echoed Lucy, looking nervously down the hallway. "If it is, you'd better not let Esther see you," she said stepping into the room further.

"No, it's not a joke!' said Henrietta. "I spoke with Jenks and she . . . she agreed I could be 'in the club,' as it were."

"You can't be serious!" said Gwen.

"That's what I told her," said Lucy dejectedly, as if already giving up hope.

"Listen! It's not . . . it's not what you think, girls. I'm just trying to find out what happened to those missing girls. I won't let it get out of hand."

"Good luck!" said Gwen, derisively. "How do you think your dress got torn in the first place? And what about all the screams?" Henrietta felt sick to her stomach. She had hoped to avoid all this fuss; it was lowering her resolve by the minute.

"Forget it," said Rose, finally speaking. She looked into Henrietta's eyes briefly and then said resignedly, "It's just like Libby all over again. She didn't listen to us, either. It's her funeral. Come on, girls, let's go."

Gwen took one of Henrietta's hands and squeezed it. "Good luck, sweets," she said with a sad smile, and then dropped her hand and hurried after Rose.

"I guess we'd better go, too," Lucy said, keeping her voice even as she started to turn away.

"Lucy—listen—it's not what you think," Henrietta whispered. "I'm . . . I'm working with the police—it's a setup," she said, searching her eyes to see if she understood.

"A setup?"

"Shhh!" Henrietta said looking toward the open doorway. "Yes, I'm undercover! I'm . . . they're trying to find out what's going on around this place. With Neptune and all that."

"Really?" Lucy asked disbelievingly. "All this time you've been—"

"Yes, sort of. I'll explain it all later."

"Are you a cop?" Lucy asked, drawing back a little.

"No! I'm . . . I'm just a girl like you. I just . . . the police want me to help them."

"Holy mackerel, Henry! Why didn't you say?"

"I couldn't! But now do you see why I need this white feather? It's the only way to find out what's going on behind the green door," she said, whispering still, but stopped suddenly when they both heard Esther's distinctive waddle in the hallway.

"Where are ye?" Esther shouted. "Mrs. Jenkins is fit to be tied!"

"We'd better get going," Lucy whispered agitatedly. "Come on."

"I'll tell you the rest later," Henrietta whispered back. "But don't tell anyone—even Rose or Gwen—promise?"

"Yes, yes, I promise."

They were nearly at the door when Esther's big form filled it. "There ye are! Mrs. Jenkins'll have the hide off ye both if ye don't get out there right now. Here I am, runnin' all over creation lookin' for ye, and all the while ye're back here carryin' on with yer nonsense. Don't think I don't know what goes on around here. Shameful, that's what it is."

It was impossible to know how long Esther's tirade would have gone on, but Henrietta and Lucy did not stick around long enough to hear it and instead ran through the hallways to the main show floor. They pushed through a set of thick curtains stage left and hurried onto the floor and back up toward the bar to find the list of assigned stations for the night. Lucy gave her a quick hug and a smile, whispering "good luck" as she held her momentarily, then picked up her silver tray and hurried to her station before Jenks could find any further fault with her.

Henrietta picked up her tray as well, studying the station list and finding that she was now in a premium station, of course, down in front, center. Larry stood hanging about the bar, waiting for his signal from Jenks to go open the doors. Nervously she arranged the cigarettes for sale on her tray, trying to catch her breath as she did so, not ready yet to go to her station. She could feel Larry's eyes on her, so she finally looked up at him, giving him a false smile.

"Nervous, is ya?" he grinned, looking deliberately at the white feather.

"Maybe a bit," she smiled, relieved that she didn't have to keep up the façade of experience around him and surprised that he seemed to know about the "club."

"I'll be seein' ya later then," he grinned. "Always has to be a first time, doesn't there, miss?"

Unnerved, Henrietta wasn't sure what to make of his comments but felt a strange desire to confide in someone, and Larry, in his unworldly, imbecilic state, seemed the perfect person with which to do that at the moment. "Yes, you're right, Larry, there does have to be a first time," she answered, feeing herself blush, or was it just unbearably warm? It suddenly dawned on her that he must have a more integral part than she would have supposed. "Ah, you're the escort, aren't you, Larry?"

He grinned idiotically.

"Well, then, you'll be able to keep an eye on me," she suggested with a weak smile.

"Oh, aye, miss. I'll look after ya."

"Larry!" shouted Mrs. Jenkins from across the room. "What the hell are you doing! Get out there and open the doors, you fool!"

"Be seein' ya later, then, miss!" he repeated, and after his writhing bow, he hurried away to the lobby where the first of the crowd was waiting.

Alone now, Henrietta took a deep breath and tried to slow her heartbeat. As the men began filing in, she eagerly began searching their faces, anxious to find Charlie. The inspector had said he would be wearing a brown suit.

She flushed warm again when she thought back to last night, when she had suggested he call her Henrietta and he had rebuffed her. It had cut her to the quick, especially when he had said that their dance at the Promenade hadn't really been real. Of course it wasn't, she scolded herself. She was just a dancer for hire, little better than a prostitute one might say, she thought with a wince.

When she had gotten her summons from him through Kelly, she had resolved on the way to the Lodge that once there she would only talk about the case. It had been difficult, though, to keep her mind only on the facts and the evolving plan and not his warm, hazel eyes that made her stomach clench each time he looked at her. He was so confident, so distinguishably handsome, she couldn't help it. And though he tried to be the aloof inspector most of the time, she had seen that he could be attentive as well. She longed to brush her hand along his cheek and ask him what troubled him, as she might do to one of her siblings if they were ill or sad.

But she couldn't trust herself to leave it at that. Just the scent of him if he were standing too close to her made her melt with desire to be held by him, to bury her head against his chest. She didn't care that he was so much older than her; it made her feel safe in a way she hadn't since her father had died. And anyway, hadn't Ma told her that "age doesn't come into it"?

Oddly, she had thought again of her father as she had climbed the steps to the apartment last night, the inspector barely saying goodbye as he had hurried off down the street, eager, she assumed, to get back to Katie waiting for him at home. Would her father have approved of what she had made of her life so far? He had told her to "take care of them," and hadn't she done that? Still, she had to admit to herself that she had lost her way a bit.

If she were honest, she knew that a part of what Ma was always going on about was true. She was unnaturally attracted to risqué situations, relying on her looks to get along or not get along, as the case had been with certain restaurant owners with wandering hands. And now she had agreed to this green door operation; in fact, it had been her idea! She had mostly done it to impress the inspector, but it hadn't seemed to have worked and it was too late now to get out of it. She gripped her tray tighter as more men poured in, joking and shouting to each other, many already drunk, as they found their seats.

She promised God there and then, in silent desperation, that if she made it through this night, she would change her life. That she would look for some sort of decent, respectable job that Ma, that she, would be proud of. She looked down at her bare chest, her breasts barely covered by the lace trim running across the bosom of the dress, and promised that there would be no more disguises, no more lying after tonight. She said a final silent prayer and touched the feather one last time as she saw that Jenks was signaling her to get in position in her station.

As she walked slowly down the aisle, she searched the crowd for Charlie and tried not to panic when she didn't spot him. Naturally, he needed to be a bit late, she supposed. He wouldn't want to appear too eager. Still, she speculated, she would feel better once he arrived. Ruby caught her eye from the nearby station and scowled at her. Not knowing what else to do, Henrietta busied herself with taking orders and hurried back up the aisle toward the bar. As she looked up, however, she gasped to see none other than Neptune staring at her from behind the bar!

He was dressed all in black and stood near the little escape door she had gone through with Larry. He had his arms folded casually across his chest and leaned against the doorway in a relaxed attitude, a small, cruel smile on his face as he watched her, his black eyes following her wherever she went.

She averted her eyes from his, panic nearly paralyzing her, though she forced herself to assume a position of casual indifference as she waited behind the other girls crowding at the bar to get their orders as soon as possible. As it turned out, Ruby was standing in front of her. "Think you're something don't you?" she sneered under her breath. "We all know you're a fake," she continued in a low voice. Without thinking, Henrietta glanced up to see if Neptune had heard her, but he had vanished. He was nowhere near the vicinity of the bar, though Henrietta noticed that the door to the tunnels was slightly ajar. She hadn't noticed if it had been that way just a few moments ago or not. "You won't last long!" Ruby was saying.

"Yes, yes, Ruby, I daresay you're right," she said irritably, pushing past her, eager to get back to the front rows.

As she delivered her first round of drinks, a wave of relief filled her when she finally spotted Charlie in the third row near the end. He winked at her once but otherwise did not look at her. Still, it made her feel so much better now that he was here.

Within minutes the house lights dimmed, and the band began its opening number, the stage curtains being pulled aside to reveal the dancers in their first act. Henrietta was surprised by how different the show looked from such close range and how much louder it was. She nervously looked over at Jenks, who had told her she would give her a signal when she wanted her, but hadn't said exactly what that would be. She noticed several men give a nod and a look to Jenks, and by the second number she saw several girls leave the floor through the side curtain near Jenks. She looked at Charlie for some direction, but he was only looking at the stage. Jenks had reappeared from behind the curtains but did not catch her eye. Perhaps she was misreading the signal?

Stan sat nervously in the back row of the Marlowe, watching Henrietta's every move. He had had to dip into his savings that he kept in a coffee can under his bed to afford even this cheap seat. He nervously patted the mustache he had made by cutting his own hair and gluing it to a piece of old canvas, which he had in turn glued to his lip with model airplane glue. He tried not to touch it too often, as he wasn't sure how secure it really was. He had made it in secret in his bedroom at the little desk he had once used for his schoolwork but had since outgrown.

He had had to make several before he was satisfied with the result. He had carefully glued it to his upper lip earlier tonight, his own facial hair too thin yet to be convincing. He wasn't sure how he was going to get it off, but he would worry about that later. He had taken his father's fedora as well and found a big overcoat. So far so good.

He had been able to make it past the ticket booth with no trouble at all. They hadn't asked him for any identification to prove that he was eighteen. Either his disguise was very convincing, or they didn't really care how old he was so long as he paid. Stanley hoped it was the former.

He could see Henrietta down near the front, close to the stage. She was skillfully weaving down the aisles, quickly hurrying between the seats and the bar. It made him sick to see how the men stared at her, shifting themselves in their seats and sometimes elbowing each other as they pointed to some part of her body. He had to admit, however, that when he saw Henrietta dressed in such a low-cut, short dress, with fishnet stockings and high heels, he had had to swallow hard himself.

Out of respect for her, he wanted to avert his eyes, but he couldn't help letting them stray every once in awhile and felt his breath grow shallow when he did. Oh, Hen! he despaired. Why had she gotten caught up in all this? She had said she was in love with that inspector, but he never saw her with him. Despite what he had told her, he had still tried to follow her, but he was usually stopped by those pesky undercover police. Still, he seemed to have evaded them tonight, he reflected proudly.

Somehow it didn't add up, though. Was Henrietta really in love with the inspector or had she just told him that to put him off following her? If so, it had worked—at least initially.

He had begun to see Elsie, at first just to appease Henrietta, but he had found over time that he genuinely enjoyed Elsie's company. She was nothing like Henrietta, of course, but he liked the fact that she looked up to him instead of treating him like a little boy the way Hen did. His feelings were all discombobulated. He felt a true warmth, a true friendship with Elsie, but unfortunately, he found his blood still stirred whenever he was around Henrietta.

Still, he was beginning to value Elsie's tried-and-true domesticity over Henrietta's vivaciousness. After all, he concluded, what good would that do in making a home? No, Stan definitely had an eye on the future, and he couldn't see Henrietta making a good wife and mother. That's what he needed. At least that's what his mother always told him.

"Beauty fades," she always chided him, not being particularly fond of Henrietta Von Harmon herself. "Marriage is more than what happens in the bedroom, you know," she would say, shaking a wooden spoon at Stanley as he felt his face redden. "The lights is usually off anyway!"

"Ma!" he would say in reply, hoping to end the conversation there, but it had in actuality given him something to think about.

So, after the obligatory library date, he had asked Elsie out again and found her to be more than willing to accept. They had fallen into a routine of taking a walk in the beautiful Victorian Humboldt Park after mass each Sunday, sometimes stopping for a cup of coffee afterward at the boathouse. Stanley had once surreptitiously asked Elsie if Henrietta seemed to mind their stepping out, but Elsie had exclaimed, "Oh, no! She's quite happy when we walk out together!"—a comment which had oddly reassured him. Sometimes they spent part of the afternoon discussing Henrietta's strange lifestyle, among other things, until Elsie would eventually change the subject.

Strangely, he had just this morning been contemplating a way of asking Elsie out on a "real" date, wondering where he should take her, possibly the Aragon, when she had shown up, crying, at his house. His mother, with a very disapproving look, had shown her into the parlor and had shockingly left them alone (no doubt listening on the other side of the door) while Elsie had hurriedly told him what had happened between her and Henrietta just this morning.

Stan had had a bit of trouble piecing together all of Elsie's bursts of information between her bouts of crying but had finally gotten what he perceived to be an accurate picture of the distressing situation. Something about Henrietta waking this morning desperate to find something, though at first she wouldn't tell Elsie what it was. Not dreaming at first that it was the little white feather she had found on the pillow between them in the morning, Elsie had finally dug it out of her pocket and held it out to Henrietta, asking if this was the thing she was missing. Elsie had been shocked by how quickly Henrietta had grabbed it up, saying she mustn't play around with her things, as if Elsie were a child and was in the habit of playing with things, especially feathers! Elsie had guessed, judging from Henrietta's strange reaction, that the feather must be a token from her date with Clive.

Stan had listened astutely to this part, especially when Henrietta had said that yes, that was what it was. But then later, just before Hen had left for work, she had pulled Elsie aside, and—after another bout of crying—Elsie related to Stan how Henrietta had confided that it wasn't really a love token, that it was part of a . . . a costume of sorts. Then Hen had told her the horrible truth—"Oh, Stanley!"—of how Hen was indeed an usherette at the Marlowe and that she was posing tonight as a . . . a lady of the night—the fact that she could not even bring herself to say the word prostitute endeared her all the more to Stan—to help the police catch some criminal. She had told Elsie, she said, so that in case anything went wrong, then at least they would know what had happened.

Elsie had fully broken down then and had thrown herself at him, and not noticing at first, Stan had almost missed catching her. When he did so, however, he was surprised by the electricity he felt coursing through him to have Elsie in his arms, and further resolved, if not for any love of Henrietta, then for his deepening feelings for Elsie and her current state of distress, to stop Henrietta in this mad scheme before she got hurt, or worse. It was bad enough when she had insisted on traipsing around the World's Fair in a Dutch girl costume or working as a twenty-six girl or even a taxi dancer, but this—this was going too far! Hadn't he said so at the very beginning?

He had promised Elsie then that he would get to the bottom of it, taking her back home and daring to kiss her on the cheek as a way of comforting her, which had caused her instead to blush profusely, notwithstanding any comfort she may indeed have garnered from it. Immediately he had dashed back home and had begun to fashion his disguise, the whole time cursing Inspector Howard for taking advantage where Stan knew he knew better. He should never have trusted him! Not only was he not protecting Henrietta, but he was positively putting her in harm's way!

He sat in the back row, tilting his fedora toward Henrietta so that she wouldn't notice him. He sat watching, nervously jiggling his leg, waiting for exactly what he wasn't sure. He tried to assume an air of indifference or to focus on the rather shocking dance routine on stage, in which he saw more of a woman's body than he ever had before. He hated the fact that he was aroused by what he saw and tried instead to think of Elsie. He forced himself to look away and to locate Henrietta again.

For one wretched moment he was afraid he was too late as he couldn't see her anywhere. He almost stood up in fear to get a better look—why was it so darned dark in here?—when he spotted her. She was standing by a tall, stout woman that he assumed was this Mrs. Jenkins Elsie had mentioned. The woman was looking pointedly at Henrietta and indicated with a nod down the aisle at a man in a tight brown suit, standing, his hands in his pockets, grinning at her.

Stanley saw Henrietta nervously set her silver tray down, leaning it carefully against the wall, and smooth down her skirt. She was looking at the floor. God, she must be frightened! Stanley despaired, and he had to fight the adrenaline surging through his body. This must be her first customer, the bastard!

He watched as Henrietta disappeared through the curtain and the man advanced to stand beside Mrs. Jenkins, discreetly handing her something, probably cash, from his pocket as he did so, the annoying grin never leaving his face. The woman motioned for him to wait and disappeared behind the curtain as well. Stan looked around anxiously for the police, but no one appeared. Where were they? Desperate, he realized that it was up to him now. This was his chance! He had come here tonight not knowing exactly what he was going to do, but getting rid of Henrietta's first "customer" seemed like the logical thing at the moment.

He quickly stood up and made his way across the row, having to squeeze past the other men sitting alongside him, annoyed by his interruption as they twisted around him trying to still watch what was happening on stage and telling him to sit down. Ignoring them, Stan made his way across the back of the theater and started down the aisle toward the man in the brown suit, his anger rising and his pace quickening as he did so. When he finally reached him, he wasn't sure what to do next, but in the end settled for roughly poking him on the shoulder.

The man, for his part, turned around quickly, obviously annoyed at having been poked, but Stanley was ready for him with a solid punch to the jaw, noticing as he hit him that up close he somehow looked familiar.

Charlie, taken aback for a moment, grabbed Stanley by the lapels of his big overcoat and was about to punch him back, when he suddenly recognized Stanley. "What are you doin' here?" he asked Stanley, mystified.

Stanley still could not place him. "I . . ." was all he got to say before both of them were grabbed from behind by two bouncers. "Hey!" Stanley tried to protest, "I—"

"Shut up, kid," Charlie said to him as the bouncers hauled them out of the theater. "Don't blow it."

"But I—hey!" he said trying to twist from the tight grasp of the bouncer, who merely shook him in response. "I'm just here to save—ow!" he shouted as Charlie kicked him in the shin, despite being held by a bouncer himself.

"You two wanna fight?" said one of the bouncers. "Then fight outside!" The doorman held the door for the bouncers, who shoved Charlie and Stan out, both of them falling roughly to the ground. "Stay out, or we'll call the cops!" shouted one of the bouncers before they disappeared back inside the theater.

"Nice goin', idiot!" Charlie said as he wiped the blood dripping from his split lip with the back of his hand.

"Well, at least I stopped you from . . . from being with her," Stan said, picking himself up, still not recognizing how he knew him.

"I'm from the fucking police, you idiot! You've just blown the sting!"

"The sting?"

"Yeah, it was a setup. Now she's in there by herself. I was supposed to protect her."

"Oh, God!" Stanley almost cried.

"Come on," Charlie grunted as he slowly stood up. "Let's go tell the boss. He ain't gonna be happy, I can tell you that."

CHAPTER 15

Henrietta stood waiting for Jenks on the other side of the curtain for what seemed like an eternity. She tried again and again to calm herself down. Nothing was going to happen, she told herself for the hundredth time.

She had seen Charlie in the audience, and he had annoyingly winked at her. The inspector had instructed her to go with Charlie to whatever room they would be led to and wait for the raid, if it came to that. She reassured herself that she could handle those easy instructions, though she hoped Charlie wouldn't try anything in the meantime. There was something about the way Charlie always looked at her that she decidedly didn't like.

She tensed when she saw Jenks come through the curtain and looked behind her to catch what she hoped would be an ironically comforting glimpse of Charlie, but he was nowhere to be seen. Jenks's brow was creased, and she seemed to frown more than usual. "Come with me," she said curtly, moving past Henrietta toward the labyrinth of hallways that led to the green door.

"Is there . . . is there something wrong?" Henrietta asked nervously as she hurried to keep up.

"There's been a change of plan. Neptune's decided he wants you tonight. I knew that was going to happen. I shoulda put money on it," she said as they clipped along. "Anyway, I'm to take you to him.

It's quite an honor really, but don't say I didn't warn you." They had reached the green door, and Jenks bent to unlock it, saying, "Now we'll find out what you're really made of."

"But . . . but what about my first customer? The one with the brown suit?"

"Him? He got in a fight and got himself thrown out. Not my problem he's lost the money he paid for you. Anyway, it doesn't matter; there'll be others. But we'll see what shape you're in when Neptune's through with you."

"But I—" Henrietta said, trying to keep the hysteria from her voice.

Jenks opened the door and gestured her through. "I tried to tell you. Don't worry, though," she said with a grin. "You'll get used to it. Just remember, the nicer you are to me," she said, rubbing Henrietta's breast as she passed her in the doorway, "the nicer the clients you get. Tit for tat, as it were," she said, amused by her own attempt at a joke.

Henrietta had no choice but to follow Jenks down the long corridor where she could hear other people already being entertained. Her heart caught in her throat, though, when she saw Jenks slow near the little door that led down to the tunnels. "Where—where are we going?"

Jenks did not reply; she was busy groping for the flashlight that hung on a hook just inside the door she had stiffly pulled open.

"I . . . I thought I was to be in one of these rooms close to you, you said," Henrietta continued, trying not to panic. How would anyone ever find her down in the tunnels?

"Get going!" Jenks said, giving her a little shove. "This hallway's for regular costumers. Neptune's den is down below. He doesn't like to be disturbed, let's just say," she laughed grimly. For a brief second, Henrietta contemplated running back down the hall and escaping, but she then realized this was not really an option. As if Jenks could read her mind, she said, "Don't think about changing your mind now, my little chick," she said overly sweetly. Carlo will be just outside the door, making sure no one gets in or out without my approval. Go on! I don't have all night!"

Henrietta felt her way down the steps and waited as Mrs. Jenkins descended with the flashlight. They walked in silence, though Henrietta was sure Mrs. Jenkins could hear the roaring of her heart beating nearly out of her chest despite the sound of their heels clicking on the stone floor. Henrietta was desperately trying to devise a possible escape plan when Mrs. Jenkins stopped all too soon in front of one of the warehouse doors, which contained a smaller door cut out from the bigger one for easier access in and out. It seemed like the one Larry had wavered in front of the other day, but she couldn't be sure; everything looked alike down here in the dark. Mrs. Jenkins fumbled for the key on the chain around her neck, opening the door finally and waiting for Henrietta to go in first.

It was a large, dingy, cavernous room, most of which was in shadow except the large bed in the middle. It was fitted with red satin sheets and was illuminated by lights hanging down from the ceiling, almost as if it were an operating table. The glow from the lights was further reflected by many large mirrors surrounding all sides of the bed. Henrietta felt chilled as she looked around, oddly reminded of the fun house she had seen at the World's Fair. At one end of the room there was a screen, behind which appeared to be drawers and racks of clothing. Nothing could prepare her, though, for the whole wall that held various whips, spikes, and what seemed to be menacing instruments of sorts. Henrietta swallowed hard and tried to keep from shaking. She was frozen with fear and felt she would vomit at any moment.

"Mrs. Jenkins," Henrietta begged. "I . . . I've changed my mind. You're right, I haven't got the nerve. I don't want the feather anymore," she said, ripping it out of her hair, causing some of her locks to come loose. She held the feather out to Mrs. Jenkins with a trembling hand.

"Too late, my little chick!" she said laughing. "You've made your bed and now you have to lie in it—literally. Neptune's on his way. Here," she said, moving behind the screen and rummaging among the clothes. "Put this on." She held out a short, pink silk nightgown. "He wants you in this."

Henrietta remained frozen, staring at Jenks with wide eyes.

Jenks became angry. "Listen, chick," she hissed. "There ain't no way out of this now. Put this on and save us all a lot of trouble. The sooner it's over the better. And for God sakes, don't cry! He hates that!" She looked her up and down. "I was right, wasn't I? You ain't never done the business, much less turned a trick, have you?"

Henrietta shook her head, fear paralyzing her and preventing her from speaking.

"Here . . .," Jenks said, going over to a cabinet by the bed. She pulled out a brown bottle and poured some of the contents into a glass. She handed it to Henrietta. "Drink this. It'll help relax you."

Henrietta nervously took it, her hand visibly shaking, and looked at it dubiously. "What is it?" she asked, sniffing it.

"It doesn't matter. Just drink it! It's for your own good!"

Henrietta decided she needed something to calm her down or she might pass out, her legs were trembling so badly. She took a small drink. It tasted bitter and burned all the way down.

Jenks laughed at her look of disgust. "Better in than out," she said with a grimace and moved toward the door. "I've got to get back to the floor. You put that on and get ready. He'll be here any minute, I suspect." Jenks opened the door to leave. "And don't get any ideas in your head about escaping. Carlo'll be right outside, making sure no one disturbs your night with Neptune." She looked her over one last time, letting out a low whistle as she did so. "I can see why he wants you. He's been looking forward to you. Has been for a long time; his favorite is virgins." And with that she stepped into the hallway and shut the door.

Hot tears filled Henrietta's eyes as she frantically considered what to do. Perhaps she could escape before Carlo got here? She ran to the corners of the room, feeling in the shadows for a door or maybe even a cabinet in which to hide, but she could find nothing. In desperation, she decided to try the door and after quietly turning the knob, was surprised to find it unlocked. She opened it just a tiny crack and peeped out, jumping when she saw Carlo standing there, his arms folded across his chest. He pointed back toward the room. "In you go," he said with a grin. "He's coming. I'd get changed if I were you. He doesn't like to be kept waiting."

"What if . . . what if I refuse to change?" Henrietta ventured to ask, barely above a whisper.

"Then he'll rip it off, and you won't like that. Happened about a month ago, some other dumb bitch thought she could defy him," he said, grinning despite the threat.

Henrietta quickly closed the door. He must be referring to Iris, she presumed, and sickeningly remembered Esther's concern about the blood. Surely whatever had happened, had happened right here in this room, on that bed. She willed herself to step behind the screen and started to mechanically undo her buttons, though her fingers were shaking so much she could barely manage it. Her mind was racing, and she thought hopelessly of the inspector. Where was he? Where was Charlie, for that matter? How would they ever find her down here if they did manage to get into the theater? The inspector had told her last night when they parted not to worry, but it was all going wrong somehow.

Her thoughts were interrupted then when she heard the door quietly open and close. He was here! Breathing rapidly, she hurried to finish pulling the nightgown over her head, blushing at how revealing it was. "I'm—I'm almost finished!" she called out, her voice cracking with fear. Trying to calm herself, she ran her fingers through her long hair, unpinned and hanging about her fair, white shoulders. She took a deep breath and stepped from behind the screen, recognizing a familiarly repugnant odor as she did so. It was almost as if—

She hurriedly looked up and felt a wave of relief to see none other than Larry in the room.

"Larry!" she said excitedly, never having imagined that she would be so glad to see him. Awkwardly she held her arms across her chest in an attempt to shield herself from his view and turned back to grab the pink silk robe, if it could be called that, which accompanied the nightgown. She had not thought it worth the time to put it on before. There was only a pencil-thin sash that she furtively attempted to tie around her, though it did not manage to obscure much. Still, it was better than being completely exposed. "Oh, Larry!" she said, rushing over to him. "Thank God you're here!"

Larry merely grinned at her. For once he did not have a cigarette dangling from his lips. Henrietta put her hand on his arm, which Larry studied carefully. He did not seem to be aware of the urgency of the situation. "Larry, I'm in great danger! There's . . . there's been some mistake. I'm supposed to spend the night with Neptune, but I've changed my mind. I'm so very frightened!"

Larry just stared at her with his stupid grin. "Are ya now?"

"Larry, you've got to help me get out of here! Please! Do you understand? He'll be here any second! Do you know any other way out?" she asked, looking frantically around the room again.

Infuriatingly, Larry continued to just stare at her, slack jawed.

"Larry!" she almost screamed. "We don't have much time! You've got to help me. I . . . I know you're probably loyal to Mrs. Jenkins, but, honestly, Larry, I'll make it worth your while. I . . . I'm working with the police. They're going to raid the place, but they'll never find me down here. I'm sort of friends with the inspector in charge, so I'll make sure no harm comes to you. Can you take me to Mrs. Jenkins's office?

I think they're coming through that window. That or go find them and bring them here. Can you do that?" she asked hysterically, searching his face for any sort of comprehension.

There was a faint flicker of understanding in his eyes as all of this information seemed to seep in, and the expression on his face finally changed to one of, if not alarm, then at least concern. "Seems we don't have a lot of time, then, miss," he said matter-of-factly. "You wait here," he said, turning back toward the door. He opened it, stepped outside and whispered something to Carlo and came back in, deliberately closing the door gently behind him and locking it with a key he took from his pocket.

"You have a key!" exclaimed Henrietta. "Good thinking! Lock ourselves in! Yes, it's probably too late to get past Neptune if he's on his way," Henrietta said, speaking very quickly. "But how will we alert the police? How will they know we're trapped down . . ." she stopped speaking, perplexed by Larry's studied attention to the wall of instruments. "Larry? Larry, what are you doing?" she asked, wondering if he was in fact deranged. She watched as he took down a sizable length of rope. "What are you going to do with that? Is it to tie up Carlo?" she asked, altogether baffled. She knew he had a strong grip, but she doubted he could overpower the likes of Carlo.

Her pulse began to quicken, though, when she heard the rope snap in his hands as he looked at her, grinning. "We'll have to forgo certain pleasures," he said evenly, "since we're unavoidably rushed. We need to get right down to business, it would seem."

Henrietta stared at him, unable to process his actions, and wondered why he was no longer speaking like a backward imbecile.

No! she protested to herself as the impossible dawned on her. It couldn't be! She shuddered violently and felt nauseous, struggling to keep the swirling contents of her stomach down. It was simply too much to take in.

"You're—" she started to say in disbelief.

"Yes," he said, snapping the rope again, "I'm the notorious Neptune, not the bumbling idiot everyone assumes I am. It's the perfect disguise, don't you agree? I'm just Lazy Larry, shuffling along with my broom. No one pays the slightest bit of attention to me. As I say, it's perfect; I go everywhere, anywhere, always listening, always watching. And no one knows the truth, of course, except my pretty little fillies."

Henrietta felt in danger of fainting; the strange liquid she had drunk was beginning to take effect, and she felt light-headed and dizzy. "But . . . but I *saw* Neptune! The real Neptune!" she said, trying to prevent herself from becoming hysterical.

Larry grinned. "Him? That's Vic, my bodyguard, you might say. He's my front man. Leads attention away from me, see? He's even taken the rap for me a couple of times with the cops."

"But what about Mrs. Jenkins? And Esther? They . . . how could they?"

"Oh, yes, of course they know. They work for me and play along with my disguise. It's amazing how a bit of information can be held over someone's head. That or money. Either one works well," he said with an evil grin. Within seconds, however, his face transformed into one of determined seriousness, and with force he commanded, "Enough small talk. We don't have much time, and I won't be denied. Now get the robe off and lie on the bed!"

"You can't be serious!" she said looking in disgust at his greasy hair and broken teeth.

His grin disappeared then and, catlike, he made a quick move toward her, and though she tried to back away, he succeeded in grabbing her. "Oh, I'm very serious," he hissed. "I said lie down! I don't like girls that defy me, and I especially don't like ones that run to the police, so you'll have to be punished."

Henrietta screamed. "Help! Help! Someone, please!"

Neptune slapped her, hard, causing her to cry out in pain, tears coming unbidden to her eyes. "There's no one out there who's gonna help you now, so you can scream 'til you're hoarse, but I don't particularly like it, so shut up!" he said, his face close to hers. He grabbed her arms then and moved to tie them to the bedposts when there was a knock on the door.

"What?" Neptune shouted over his shoulder as he suspended his work, breathing heavily, his greasy hair hanging in his face.

"Boss? We've got a problem . . ." said a muffled voice through the door.

Neptune slackened for a moment, hesitating, looking at Henrietta. Finally, he seemed to reach a decision and gave her a little shove. "Don't get any ideas!" he snarled as he rose up from the bed and went to the door.

Henrietta lay frozen, listening, her heart pounding and a thin layer of sweat covering her body. Her breathing labored and painful, she quietly tried pulling on the arm he had already managed to tie to one of the bedposts, but to no avail. Uselessly, she reached over with her free hand, but the knot proved impossible to untie.

"Better be a good reason," she heard Larry say as he unlocked the door and opened it a crack, but it was suddenly kicked open further by someone on the other side, though Larry managed to escape being hit by it.

"Miss Von Harmon?" shouted a familiar voice.

"Inspector?" Henrietta called out shakily. "I'm here! Help me!" she cried, straining anew at her bonds. Relief surged through her, and she felt hot, fresh tears come to her eyes, but then she quickly realized with horror that the inspector was a prisoner as well, his face bloodied and his hands tied behind his back, though he struggled anew at the sight of her.

The man accompanying him punched him in the gut, causing Clive to double over in pain. "I told you! No funny business! That includes kicking in doors and shouting. Now shuddup!" said the man, who was none other than the "false" Neptune, Vic. "He was comin' in through Jenks's window, just like you said, boss. Found this on 'im," he said, brandishing a pistol.

Henrietta looked hopefully at the inspector, but he had sunk to his knees, his head slumped forward as if unconscious.

"How many more?" Larry asked, irritated.

"Two came in the window with him, but they won't be talking any time soon."

Larry looked at him questioningly, as if urging him to go on. "And?"

"We nabbed 'em as soon as they came through. Carlo got a little carried away with one of 'em. They's tied up in Jenkins's office. Out cold."

"Why'd you bring him down here?" he asked, nodding at Clive. "You know I hate to be interrupted, especially with such a ripe one," he said, glancing back at Henrietta. She could see Vic's wolfish eyes on her as well, taking his time looking her over. "Can I have a turn with her, boss? I mean . . . you know, after you?"

Larry smacked him on the head. "Shut up, you ass. We've got to get out of this mess first. Why's he down here and not up with the others?" he asked again.

"Says he's an inspector with the police, says the place is surrounded and that they're gonna bust in in five minutes if he don't give the signal out the window."

Henrietta felt a spark of hope and tried to wriggle free, but she was tied tight.

"God damn it! Can't you idiots do anything right?" Larry demanded angrily.

"We tried gettin' the signal from 'im, boss, but he ain't talkin', and we was afraid we might knock him out cold if we kept bashin' him in the head anymore."

"Fuck!" Larry said, grabbing a large dagger off the wall. "Do I have to do everything around here?" He stalked over to the inspector and held the dagger to his throat.

"No!" Henrietta screamed.

"What's the signal?" Larry demanded, pulling his head back by the hair.

Clive peered up at him with half-open slits, but rather than answer, he spit in Larry's face. Enraged, Larry wiped the spit from his face and punctured Clive's neck with the tip of the knife, causing him to cry out.

"What's the signal?" Larry asked again, almost hysterical.

"Why should I give you the signal?" Clive said thickly, though the blood was trickling down his neck. "My men will be here any minute."

"All right, then. You want to play hardball?" he said, striding quickly over to where Henrietta lay struggling on the bed, her arm still awkwardly tied to the post. He held the dagger to her throat. "Tell me the signal or I cut her."

"Inspector!" Henrietta screamed.

"Stop it!" Clive said, struggling with his bonds, still on his knees. "Stop! All right, you win. It's in my pocket," he said, his head drooping. "The whistle. Two short blasts and one long out the window. It means all's well, and we've got it handled."

Vic reached his hand into Clive's front pocket and extracted a police whistle. "Got it!" he said proudly, tossing it to Larry.

"Let's hope you're telling the truth," Larry said to the inspector with surprising calm, "or she'll really be sorry. You won't recognize her when I'm through. Now, if you'll excuse me, I've a few things to attend to." He turned to Vic. "Lock 'em up somewhere. Not in here—there's too many weapons. Wouldn't want the copper to get any funny ideas. We'll get rid of them later when the heat is off."

He was untying Henrietta as he spoke and hauled her up beside him. He looked at her and grinned, reaching out to stroke the side of her face, red where he had slapped her. "Oh, I ain't finished with you yet, filly. We've some unfinished business before I dispose of you," he said, licking his lips.

Henrietta stood shaking, terrified and utterly paralyzed. She wanted to run or to scream, but all she could do was stare at his gray, crooked teeth. She had become fixated on them. He gripped her face, and she felt panic as he held the back of her head and put his mouth on hers, biting her lip as he did so. She let out a gurgled cry, the violation she felt worse than the physical pain. Small tears sprang to her eyes, and she wasn't sure how much longer she could stand upright, the stench of his unwashed, greasy body and her abject terror threatening to overpower her. She felt her legs going, but he gripped her by the arm and forced her over to where the inspector knelt. "Oh, no you don't, filly. No time for faintin' just yet. Time enough for that later."

He kicked the inspector in the stomach again, causing him to groan and double over so that he was almost prostrate. "Get up, copper," he said, nodding to Vic to hoist him to his feet. "I'll deal with you later, too. Now you'll see what it's like to be on the other side of the interrogation table. You know what to do," he said to Vic, before hurrying out, whistle in hand. "Don't take too long; I'm gonna need you upstairs."

Vic left the inspector swaying on his feet and strode over to Henrietta, who was trying to back away from him. Roughly he grabbed her and wrenched her hands behind her back and tied them with a rough piece of rope he produced from his pocket.

"Ow!" she cried, but he just gave her a little shove.

"Shut up! No funny business!" he snarled, his black pebbly eyes glistening below his bushy eyebrows. He pointed the pistol at them and picked up the dagger where Larry had dropped it on the bed. He waved the pistol at them, directing them to the door. Clive staggered through it. "Nice and easy now. Nice and quiet. One word and she gets it," Vic said, stabbing the tip into the side of Henrietta's arm as if to prove a point.

"Stop it!" she said, stumbling in front of him as she made her way through the door.

"Leave her alone!" Clive said, attempting to turn and face Vic in the narrow passageway.

"Shuddup!" he said, giving Henrietta a shove, though it was Clive who had spoken. "Just keep going and hurry up!"

"I can't see anything!" Clive mumbled from the front.

"Just keep movin'," Vic said, "till I tell you to stop."

They shuffled further down the tunnel, Henrietta trying to control her erratic breathing. She was pretty sure they were headed back toward the bar where Larry had first descended into the tunnels that day with her. God! She knew there was a reason she had always felt uneasy around him! She burned with fury at the memory of how she had once felt sorry for him, even bought food for him! She considered screaming for help, but she knew with the noise of the band up above them, no one would hear her, and she didn't dare risk being cut by the dagger. Her two earlier pokes were trickling blood, though she wondered why she could barely feel them.

"Stop right there!" said Vic. "This'll do." They had stopped midway down the tunnel outside a small door that resembled a closet or a storeroom. Vic pushed past them, Henrietta falling back against the damp wall as he pulled hard on the door to open it, the bottom scraping against the rough stone floor. "Get in," Vic said with a nod of his head. Henrietta hesitated as she peered in at the utter blackness. "I said, get in!" Vic said, giving her a shove. Clive tried to kick him, but Vic merely punched him in the face again and threw him into the darkness.

Henrietta fought her panic in the dark, claustrophobic space, made worse by the fact that her hands were bound, as the door closed and she heard the lock turn and then Vic's heavy footsteps as he moved away and up the stone steps. She had been right; they were near the bar, and this must be some sort of storage closet. Maybe it held supplies for the bar? she guessed, trying to calculate what it might contain, if anything, that could help them. She could see nothing in this darkness, though, not even a hand in front of her face should she have been able to hold it up.

"Inspector?" she said quietly as she struggled to stand up, wondering why he didn't speak, and bumping her head on a dangling light bulb as she did so. "Inspector?" she said louder, but there was still no answer.

Fear gripped her anew at the possibility that he had been knocked out—or worse—and that she was alone. Panicking, she hurriedly shuffled toward the door, feeling with her arm for a light switch in hopes that it might still work. She leaned against the wall, feeling the rough stones near the door with her upper arm and shoulder until she felt a hard nub. It took several tries before she managed to put enough pressure on it with her shoulder bone to switch it on.

She immediately turned her head away from the bulb, temporarily blinded by the dull light, but quickly looked around to find that they were indeed in some sort of forgotten, mildewed supply closet with shelves running along one wall holding ancient tins of what looked like cleaning fluid, boxes of straws and napkins, and old rags. Nothing very promising to help them escape. In the corner were a broom and a mop covered with a fine layer of cobwebs. Henrietta's eye eventually fell on the inspector, lying in a heap on the stone floor, blood oozing from a gash above his eye.

"Oh, God!" Henrietta cried, sinking to her knees beside him. "Inspector! Inspector Howard!" She tried rousing him with her knee, and eventually she saw his eyes flutter open, though he immediately squinted them closed again due to the brightness of the bulb swinging overhead. Finally, he struggled to sit up, breathing heavily from the exertion.

"Inspector! Are you okay? You look terrible!"

Despite the situation, his face relaxed when he saw her. "Thanks," he managed to say, looking around the tiny closet, trying to assess the situation. "Where are we? Still in the tunnel?"

"Yes, but we're near the end of it, just below the bar, I think." She looked him over carefully. "Your eye looks pretty bad," she said, wishing she could touch his face and dab away the blood.

"I'll survive," he grunted. "Maybe a cracked rib or two. God knows I've had worse. Are you hurt?" he asked anxiously, looking at her and then averting his eyes from the sight of her body in the short nightgown and robe. "Did he . . . did he do anything to you?" He held his breath, waiting for her to answer.

"No, I . . . he was about to . . .. He bit me," she said quietly, tears welling up in her eyes. "I feel so ashamed, so stupid."

Clive felt a surge of anger pulse through him, and he struggled to stand up. "I'm the one who's been stupid! We've got to get out of here." He stood and hit his head on the light bulb, causing it to swing wildly, bouncing the light all over the small room. He crouched over to avoid hitting it again as he looked for something sharp on the shelves. Unfortunately, he could find nothing, and resorted to trying to kick the door open, but it was difficult with his hands tied and the injuries he had sustained, the pain nearly knocking him out again each time he tried. The door refused to budge, and after a few more feeble attempts, he gave up.

"This is all my fault," he said, finally sliding down beside her again, exhausted, trying not to look at her body in the process. "I'm so terribly sorry to have put you in such danger," he said, scooting his body so that his back was almost to hers, just one set of shoulders touching so that he couldn't see her exposed. "I should never have agreed to this," he said thickly. "How could I have missed that the man I assumed was Neptune was just a front man? He's obviously been playing the entire police force for a very long time. What a mug I've been," he said disgustedly.

"You? I should have figured it out," Henrietta countered. "A lot of things make sense now, but it makes my skin crawl to think how Larry was always slinking around behind the scenes. Sometimes even in the dressing rooms! And all the time he was probably picking out his next victim." Henrietta suddenly felt in danger of being sick.

"I should have pulled the plug before it got to this," Clive said angrily. He was kicking himself for not following his intuition.

"Don't say that," Henrietta quietly urged. "It's not your fault. It's mine. I'm the one who insisted. I . . . I thought I could—" She broke off here, not wanting to reveal her true motives. They sounded silly now, anyway. How had she imagined that she could impress the inspector with this foolhardy scheme of pretending to be a prostitute? It seemed stupidly naive and ridiculous, as if it would have made her in any way more desirable to him, she realized, as she looked down shamefully at her flimsy nightgown. She had obviously failed in more ways than one.

Angrily, she pushed those thoughts away. What did it matter at this point, anyway? Right now, they had to figure out a way out of here. "When do you think your men will turn up?" she asked, looking hopefully at the door.

Clive closed his eyes in pain and then forced himself to open them. Time to tell her they weren't getting out of this alive. "That's not going to happen, I'm afraid."

There was silence between them as Clive merely studied the floor.

"What do you mean?" she said after a few seconds. "You do have a plan to get us out of here, don't you?" she asked nervously, panic beginning to creep back in, making her chest feel tight. "What about . . . what about Charlie?" she asked desperately.

"Your pipsqueak blew Charlie's cover and got them both thrown out for fighting," Clive said wryly. He turned to look at her, but the sight of the curve of her breasts through the nightgown caused him to look away again, swallowing hard.

"Pipsqueak? I don't know what you're talking about."

"You know, the one that we picked up with you at Polly's apartment."

"You mean Stan? He was here?"

"Yes, with an absurdly false mustache, I might add. Can't understand how he got in in the first place."

"Oh, God. Elsie."

"What do you mean?"

"I told Elsie—my sister. I didn't mean to, but she found the feather, and I just thought someone should know—just in case . . ." her voice trailed off as she realized that she might never see Elsie again. "I'm sorry," she said hopelessly and felt tears well up, "she must have told Stan."

"Well, he's locked up in the squad car where he can't do any more harm. After I threw him in the car, I took Charlie back in with me. We went through the window with Kelly, but they knocked both of them out. They must have been tipped off."

The inspector's brow furrowed, and Henrietta again felt her stomach knot as she realized it had been her that had inadvertently led Larry to stake the window.

"Kelly looks pretty bad; I think he might have bought it," he said grimly.

"Surely you have more men than that, though?" Henrietta asked despairingly. "What about the signal—the whistle?"

"There is no signal," he said bitterly. "I just made that up to buy some time."

"You mean there's no backup?" she asked incredulously, her throat dry.

"No. Not like that anyway. I've men posted at all the entrances, but something tells me Neptune's already set his dogs on them. I'm not too hopeful that they'll get in. And if they do, it's unlikely they'll find us down here before Neptune puts us in a car headed for the river.

I'm sorry, Miss Von Harmon. The game's up, I believe. I really am most sorry. More than you know."

"Oh, Inspector!" Henrietta cried. She was trembling, and the drink Jenks had given her earlier was making her feel clouded and fuzzy. That or she was in shock, or both. She wasn't sure what was real and what was not anymore. "But surely you'll think of something!" she said, breaking down in tears, unable to keep up the pretense any longer. "I'm so very frightened."

Without thinking, she leaned her head against the inspector's shoulder, and she felt him tremble, or was it a shudder? He was probably repulsed by her, she realized, and she could see why. She felt dirty and cheap, used and altogether ashamed, and so with a supreme effort, Henrietta made herself lift her head from his shoulder though she was so dreadfully tired. She wouldn't burden him any longer. She suddenly thought of her mother and wished she had taken time to say goodbye to her earlier today as she had hurried from the apartment . . .

"You can rest your head there . . . if you want," Clive said gently, his voice catching a little.

Surprised, Henrietta shifted her body and looked up at him. She no longer cared if he saw her in the nightgown. His eyes looked so very sad.

As Clive looked at her now, too, he could no longer contain what was in his heart for her. It would all be over soon enough, anyway. He realized with utter despair that it made no difference; that love was slipping from his grasp just as he was beginning to realize that it had existed at all.

"Miss Von Harmon—Henrietta," he began.

Henrietta started slightly as he finally called her by her Christian name. But that made sense, didn't it? That they might as well dispense with the formalities, knowing as they both did that Vic or Larry would be back any moment.

"Henrietta," he said again, turning a bit to be able to better look into her eyes. "There's something you should know. Something I have to tell you," he said softly.

Despite her fuzzy brain, Henrietta realized that he wanted to tell her about his girl, about his love. Maybe he wanted her to give Katie a message? But that didn't make sense, neither of them was getting out of this, were they? She shook her head slightly; she couldn't think straight. She was touched by his need to confess, however, but out of love for him—yes, love, she knew now—she decided to spare him this pain. "Oh, Clive," she said his name hesitantly, tenderly. "Stop, please. I know what you're going to say, and there's no need for you to go on. You don't have to say it," she said looking up at him eagerly, her face flushed. She felt so very warm, so sleepy, as if she would not be able to stay awake much longer.

"You do?" he asked, drawing in his breath. Had she guessed his feelings and sought to silence him before he even had a chance to utter them? Was he too old for her as he had suspected? Still, soon it wouldn't matter. He was determined to get this off his chest, to say the words aloud despite what her answer would be.

"Yes, of course, I do," she smiled knowingly. "I know that you're in love with a certain someone."

In love with a certain someone? His mind raced despite the sharp pain behind his left eye. What could she mean?

"I . . . I know you must love and care for her very much," Henrietta went on, "and I . . . well, I admire you for that," she added in a low voice. "Deeply. I only wish I could have someday met someone like you." She could not believe she was saying such things. Part of her brain seemed stuck in molasses while this other part could not stop speaking. It somehow seemed like the obvious thing to do. She looked up into his eyes again. "I know it doesn't matter now, but for what it's worth, I just want you to know you're someone I could have fallen in love with. Very easily."

Clive felt his heart explode as she put her head on his shoulder again, an electric shock running through him, but she had it all wrong! "Who do you suppose I'm in love with?" he asked, confused, his heart beating unnaturally fast. What had he ever said or done to give any indication of his affections for another woman?

"The woman you live with, of course," she said not lifting her head. "I suppose she won't mind, will she? If I rest my head here? It's very improper, I know," she said, drowsily, "but—"

"The woman I live with? How on earth did you ever get an idea like that in your head?" he asked, mystified.

"One of the officers at the station told me. Murphy, I think his name was. The night I stopped in? He said you were at home with your girl, but the sergeant—Clancy, is it?—said you had no family, so I figured she must be your . . . your lover . . . not your wife. Katie is her name, right? But still . . ." her voice trailed off as she closed her eyes.

"I'm going to kill Murphy and Clancy," he muttered. Agitated, he tried to turn until he faced her completely, causing her to lift her head from his shoulder and stare up at him again. "Is that what you really think of me?" he asked incredulously. "That I'd take a woman to my bed who's not my wife?"

"I don't know," she said, baffled as much by his urgency as the nature of his strange question. He uttered a sigh of disgust and looked away. "I—"

"Would you have taken me?" she interrupted quietly. "If I had asked? If you were free?" She was barely able to brace herself for his answer.

"No! Of course I wouldn't."

Henrietta winced and felt hot tears come to her eyes again. *Of course I wouldn't!* he had said. Well, of course. The pain of these words struck her harder than Larry's slap had earlier. She could no longer control the pent-up emotion that she was struggling to contain and, turning away from him again, began to silently weep. She tried terribly to hide it from him, but she couldn't help the rasping noises as her breath caught in her throat. *Of course I wouldn't!* Oh, how could she have been so stupid?

"Henrietta?" he asked, surprised by the muffled sounds coming from her. Though she had tried to turn her head away, he saw her tears, and his heart melted entirely. "Oh, Henrietta, please don't cry. I—what a fool I've been!" he pleaded, suddenly realizing how his answer must have sounded in her ears. "That isn't what I meant at all . . . it's . . . please don't cry! Can't you see? My God, I'm bungling this. Henrietta, I'm . . . I'm in love with you," he said softly. "I thought you knew."

Henrietta checked her tears, not quite sure she had heard correctly. "You are?"

"Desperately," he whispered, looking down into her eyes. "It's madness, I know." He couldn't help himself any longer and bent forward and softly brushed his lips against hers.

A current of electricity pulsed through her as he tenderly kissed her, but she made herself pull back. "Yes, it is madness," she said, a bit dazed, peering up at him. More than anything she yearned to feel the touch of his lips again, and yet she knew it was impossible. "Yes, we . . . we must think of Katie."

"Katie?" he asked incredulously. "My God, back to this! Katie is my dog, you silly girl," he said, agitated. "That's what the boys at the station meant by 'my girl,' idiots that they are. They obviously didn't think about how someone might interpret that. If I do get out of here, every one of them will live to regret it," he said grimly.

"So . . . so you don't live with a woman?" she asked, a smile creeping across her face.

"No, I live alone, if you must know," he said, ruefully.

Henrietta found herself laughing, almost giddy, despite their terrible situation, not able to believe what she was hearing. It all made so much sense now. How foolish she had been. She looked up into his face then and saw the longing in his eyes. "Oh, Clive . . . I've been so stupid."

"No, it's me who's been the stupid one. I should have spoken earlier. And now look at us."

"Yes, a bit of rotten luck, I suppose."

"You once told me that luck doesn't come into it."

Henrietta smiled that he still remembered the details of their first meeting. "I suppose you're right—" she began to say but stopped abruptly, her breath catching at the sound of the little door behind the bar creaking open.

"They're back," Clive muttered as they both struggled to stand up. Henrietta instinctively moved behind Clive who braced himself, afraid of what might be coming next. He wasn't about to give up Henrietta without fighting for her with every ounce of what he had left. He heard her whimper, huddled behind him, and he strained again against his bonds.

"Clive, I'm so frightened!" she said, her voice cracking. "I have . . . I have a confession of my own."

Clive winced, guessing what was coming next.

"I . . . I've never . . . done this—done *it*—before," she said, barely above a whisper. "I know I pretended to, but I haven't actually." They could hear footsteps and Clive turned to face her, gazing down into her deep blue eyes and long lashes, so innocent, so trusting. "Before they—he—takes me away, I just want you to know . . . I . . .I would have wanted it to have been you." She paused. "You know what I mean, don't you?" she asked tentatively.

He nodded slowly, his heart in his throat, unable to speak. Not since Catherine had he had so much emotion flowing over him. He could hear that their captors were almost upon them, and he bent to softly kiss her one last time, just as they heard the key twisting in the lock and the door pulled stiffly open. As it scraped across the stones, Clive whipped around and shielded Henrietta, momentarily blinded as he did so by the beam of a flashlight in his face.

"Don't you dare touch her!" he shouted, twisting his head around the light, trying to see.

The beam lowered then, and Henrietta was surprised to hear Lucy's voice shout out joyfully into the hall, "We found them!" before she fainted in a heap at the inspector's feet.

CHAPTER 16

Henrietta was not sure how long she had been out. As she slowly opened her eyes, she realized that the rocking motion she was experiencing was due to being in the backseat of a car. Her head was pounding. "Clive?" she asked hopefully, lifting her head from the shoulder beside her. She heard a sigh.

"No, it's Stan, actually."

Henrietta sat up straight, her head pounding, surprised to see none other than Stan beside her in what appeared to be a taxicab.

"Where are we?" she asked, looking out the windows at the dark, abandoned streets passing by.

"I'm taking you home. You've had a nasty shock. Don't you remember? A bit too much if you ask me, but then again you don't, so I guess it's not my business," he mumbled to himself.

She groaned as she put her hands to her head. It was all coming back—the failed plan, the dark tunnel, being locked up . . . Clive . . . the nightgown . . . his kisses . . . She looked down in a panic and was relieved to see that she was somehow dressed in her flannel shirt and overalls. "What happened?"

"You don't remember it?"

She peered at him closely. "Why do you have a mustache?"

Stan rubbed it irritably. "It was part of my disguise. But now I can't get it off."

"Disguise?" she said, puzzled, trying to remember. Something Clive had said about the pipsqueak getting in the way . . . locked in the squad car. "How . . . how did you get out of the squad car?" But where was Clive? She seemed to remember seeing Lucy . . . she had come to briefly in the dressing room . . . Lucy had been there, helping her to change . . . Larry! "Wait a minute!" she said, panicking, looking out the car windows again to get her bearings. "Why aren't we at the Marlowe? I need to see Clive!"

"Clive, is it?" Stan said biting his lip. "Not Inspector Howard?"

"Is he okay?"

"Of course he's okay. He told me to take you home."

"He did?"

"Boy, you really don't remember, do you?"

"I think I was drugged, if you must know," she said groggily.

Stan urgently bit his nails. "My God, Hen, see what I mean? How could you ever get involved in something like this? We've been worried sick, you know!"

"Who's we?" she asked nervously, afraid it might mean her mother.

"Me and Elsie, of course! She's the reason I was there tonight, in case you idiotically go thinking it was for you. I promised her I'd follow you, like I—well, like I used to."

Henrietta smiled in the darkness despite the pain in her head.

"Worried sick, she is," he kept on. "And who can blame her? You telling her your harebrained scheme of posing as a prostitute to catch some crime lord. Course she was worried! She'll be up now, waiting," he said, peering out the window as if urging the cab along faster. "Worried sick, she is," he said, relapsing into anguish. "You could have been killed—or worse!"

"Yes, I'm aware of that, Stan," she muttered. "You're not my father, you know."

"Thank God I'm not!" he said animatedly. "I'd probably send you off to a convent."

"Really, Stan, calm down. You're being ridiculous."

"Elsie wanted to tell your mother, but I said I'd handle it."

"And you did such a brilliant job, didn't you? If I remember correctly," she said, rubbing her temples, "you're the reason the whole thing got bungled in the first place!"

"Well how was I to know you weren't going to be *ravaged* by that creep," he said, his knee jittering up and down.

"He was an undercover cop! You don't think Clive knew what he was doing?"

"Well, not particularly, since it seems in the end you were rescued by a gang of women."

Yes, she remembered now. Lucy and Gwen had turned up. "Are you going to tell me what happened or not?"

Stanley sighed. "I don't know all the details, but something like some dame named Lucy and her friends got worried and called the cops."

"But the cops were already there."

"Yeah, but obviously not enough of 'em to do the job, 'specially since the inspector and his two sidekicks got themselves knocked out or tied up within the first five minutes."

"Because of you."

Stan ignored her and went on. "Lucky they called. Backup came, raided the joint. While they were rounding up the main suspects, it seems this Lucy found the keys behind the bar and went looking for you. Apparently you fainted just as they found you."

"Then what happened?"

Stan shrugged. "I don't know everything. I was locked up by his highness, remember? When he finally let me out of the squad car, he asked me to take you home. He's obviously busy filling out forms or whatever he does all day. He seemed a bit preoccupied. Cops were swarming everywhere getting statements, hauling people off to jail. I think that the only reason they remembered me is that they needed the car," he said moodily.

"Did they catch Neptune?" she asked anxiously.

"Who's Neptune?"

Henrietta groaned. "Doesn't matter."

The cab stopped, and when Henrietta looked out she saw that they had pulled up in front of her dark apartment building. Stan rustled in his pocket for the fare. "I'll get it, Stan," Henrietta said, looking on the floor to where someone had put her handbag for her, probably Lucy.

"Naw, the inspector gave me the money. I told him to get lost, but he insisted."

Stan plopped the money into the cabbie's outstretched hand, and the two of them wearily climbed out.

"Did he have any message for me?" she asked, trying to make her voice sound disinterested as they approached the building. Traces of what they said to each other were floating back to her. Had he really told her he loved her, or had it been she who had said it? Or maybe she had dreamed it? She felt so confused, so tired.

"He said to lay low and that he'll come round when he gets a chance."

"That's it?" she asked, disappointed. But then again, did she really think he would pass on some further declaration of his feelings through Stan?

Stan shrugged. "Did you expect something else? He's a copper. I did try to warn you, you know."

The front door of the building creaked open, then, and Elsie peeked out. When she saw that it was Stan and Henrietta, she gave a cry of delight and threw her arms around Henrietta while she flashed a grateful smile across to Stan. Holding tight to Elsie, the weight of the night suddenly washed over her, and Henrietta let the tears finally come in earnest.

"Hey! Cheer up!" whispered Mr. Hennessey, giving her a little nudge with his elbow. "Looks as though you've got the weight of the world on your shoulders." Henrietta looked up at him from the bar she was leaning against and smiled sadly. She had missed him more than she had realized. It seemed like an age since she had quit Poor Pete's to become a taxi dancer at the Promenade.

"You don't have to do this, you know," he added. "Why don't you take it easy for a bit?"

Henrietta stood up straight and methodically resumed wiping the bar, though no matter how many times her rag passed over it, it still seemed dirty to her. "Yes, I know," she answered, trying to be cheerful, "but I want to. I like to keep busy."

"If you need money," he said gently, "all you have to do is ask, you know. A loan!" he added quickly, not wanting to embarrass her by offering her a handout. "Pay it back when you can."

"Thanks, Mr. Hennessey. I'll remember that, if I need it."

In point of fact, she was okay for money just at the moment. She had been receiving a meager paycheck from Mrs. Jenkins for the short time she had been at the Marlowe, and the tips, despite her less-than-full stations each night, were better than any she had received from any other job. The "double" salary, however, that the inspector had promised her when he first propositioned her had not yet materialized, and Henrietta suspected it never would.

It had been just over a week since her ordeal at the Marlowe, and she was still trying to figure it all out. There had been nothing in the papers the next day when Henrietta had slipped out of the apartment early in the morning to buy a paper at the corner stand.

She had considered telling Ma that morning that she was ill again, but she knew Ma wouldn't buy it so soon after the last time. Besides, Ma would tell her to go in to work anyway, as she was always going on about how people like them didn't get to be off sick. "You'll be the first to be let go, and then where would we be? No, better not risk it, Henrietta," was what she would have said, so instead, Henrietta, still a bit woozy, left the apartment the next day at the usual time and walked in Palmer Square Park for a while, collecting her thoughts, before making her way over to Poor Pete's, where a jubilant Mr. Hennessey had greeted her back with open arms.

He had readily agreed to give her job back when she had asked and had not pushed her for any explanations. This somehow made her all the more eager to eventually tell him, however, about what had happened at both the Promenade and the Marlowe, at first holding some of it back but then spewing it all forth, except, of course, the last part of the whole story, the part about Clive.

She wasn't sure why she hadn't wanted to share this part, perhaps because she wasn't sure yet what to think herself. As the days had gone on, she had tried to remember exactly what had happened that night, but most of it still remained in a fog, only bits and pieces becoming clear as the days wore on. She was fairly sure Clive had indeed told her that he loved her, and the way he had looked at her had been so intense, almost violent, yet his kisses had been surprisingly tender and soft, the memory of which caused her breathing to speed up, even now. And she was pretty sure that she had not told him, in so many words, that she loved him back, had she?

But why, then, had she thought it necessary to reveal to him that she was a virgin? And what about Clancy's revelation to her the other day in the park? She was still so confused and unsure about it all. And why hadn't Clive appeared as Clancy said he would?

Roughly two days after the ordeal, she had been surprised when she was approached by none other than Clancy as she walked in Palmer Square, waiting for Poor Pete's to open up for the day. She had been startled at first to see him as he blustered across the park toward her and was immediately disappointed when she saw that Clive did not accompany him.

"There you are!" Clancy said, breathing heavily when he finally reached her.

"How did you know I was here?" she asked nervously, praying he hadn't stopped at the apartment.

"Oh, don't you worry," he said in response to the look on her face. "Inspector told me not to knock at your place. We've got other ways a knowin'," he said, smiling and tapping the side of his nose. "Now, then . . ." he said, fishing in his pocket for a pencil. He already had out his small notebook.

"Such as?" Henrietta asked.

Ignoring her question, Clancy licked the tip of his pencil. "Officially, Miss Von Harmon, I'm here to take your statement, but off the record," he said, leaning toward her confidentially, "I'm to tell you that the inspector will meet up with you very soon."

"Oh," Henrietta said, a bit deflated. "Well, perhaps you could tell me more about what happened that night. I'm afraid I fainted," she said, blushing.

"I'd heard that," Clancy said, and grinned. "Well, you know most of it, I should imagine. Couple of dames called for help; me and the boys jumped in the paddy wagon and off we went! Got the rats really scramblin' this time. Managed to catch a few in the net, though, so not a bad night all in all."

"A few? Which ones?"

Clancy screwed up his face as if to remember. "A Mrs. Jenkins, she's one of the ringleaders, I believe. Couple of the bouncers. They're still in the clink, trying to get them to squeal a bit more, as they say," he said, giving her a conspiratorial wink.

"What about Neptune?"

"Which Neptune you talkin' about? The little one or the big one?"

"The little one." Henrietta shuddered.

"Nope. 'Fraid not. Your girlfriends was fooled, too. Seems they still thought he was Larry the custodian and let him slip out the back. They helped nab big Neptune, a.k.a. one Vic "Snake Eyes" Martelli. Didn't realize till later they got the wrong guy. Still, they tried. Pretty good work for some dames, deviants at that, the inspector tells me. Shame, that is," he said, rubbing the corners of his mouth with his thumb and index finger.

"How did they manage to catch Vic?" Henrietta asked, ignoring his comments. She could hardly believe that Lucy and the gang had had a hand in his capture.

"Seems one of 'em, one Rose Whitman, kept a pistol, little one, like, in the dressing room. Inspector's been back and forwards with her about it all. Seems they got a gun between them after one of 'em went missing 'bout a month ago."

Henrietta shifted to absorb all of this. Why hadn't they told her they had a gun? But what reason would they have had to tell her this? Either way, she realized, she owed her life to them. She would have to find them when this was all finished.

"So, Larry got away?" she asked, suddenly feeling chilled.

"'Fraid so, miss. We'll catch him, though. Don't you worry."

"What about Polly? Have they found her yet?"

"Miss Shoemacher? Can't rightly say, but funny you should ask. Inspector's got a lead on her. They think she's been hidin' out in Arkansas with an aunt. Inspector himself went to check it out. Him and Charlie. Poor Kelly's in the hospital. Still touch and go, poor kid."

Henrietta did not think of the beefy Kelly as a "kid," but she did feel sorry for him, especially considering it was probably her fault that he had been clobbered so badly. She wondered if it would be appropriate for her to visit him.

"I'm keeping Katie for him while he's gone, see," Clancy went on. Henrietta shook herself from her revelry. "Oh, yes, his girl. You had me confused with that."

Clancy suddenly scowled. "Yeah, the boss smacked me a good one for that. Told me to stop shootin' my mouth off, 'specially in front of a lady," he said, still scowling. "Beg your pardon, miss, but I didn't mean nothin' by it. Don't know what I said wrong; I don't."

Henrietta smiled, especially at Clive's designation of her as a lady. Didn't that mean something? she hoped, but the thought was fleeting. "Don't mention it," she said, giving Clancy a little smile. "So, you've got Katie for a few days?"

Clancy nodded. "I do indeed," he said, his smile returning. "Beautiful girl."

"Has he had her for long?"

"Hmmm," Clancy said, screwing up his face again to remember and rubbing the side of his head with the stub of his pencil. "Must be goin' on about six, maybe seven years now. Says he found Katie in the streets. Brought her home. That was just after his wife died, I think, just before he joined the force. It was a blessing, really. Having Katie, that is, not his wife dyin', you understand," he added quickly. "Helped him no end, we all thought down at the station. Mind you, he's always kept himself to himself, but in the early days, sometimes he'd talk after a few whiskeys."

"He had a—? His wife died?" Henrietta asked hesitantly. A wife? She could hardly believe it! What else did she not know about this man?

Clancy looked at her fearfully, shocked he had again revealed too much information. "Oh, good Lord! Now I've done it again! Please don't let on I told you, miss. He's threatened to put me on permanent traffic duty if I open my mouth again!"

A part of her wanted to smile at his reaction, but she was too stunned. "What did she die of?" was all she could think to ask, though her mind was racing. "I won't tell. Promise!" she said when Clancy did not immediately respond but merely stood looking at her uneasily.

"Oh, all right," he said after a few more moments of consideration. "But you didn't hear it from me. It's common enough knowledge, I suppose." He took a deep breath. "She died in childbirth. He was away. France, I think it was. The war, you know. Took it hard, as you can imagine."

"And the baby?" she whispered.

"Died, too. Stillborn. Put 'em in the same grave, they did."

"Oh, that poor man," Henrietta said, sinking down on a nearby bench, her heart filling with pity for Clive and seeing him in a whole different light. He, too, was no stranger to sadness, then.

"Well, I must be goin', miss," Clancy said, still uneasy, flipping his notebook shut, though he had failed to actually write anything down. "Need a lift somewhere?"

"No . . ." she said absently, standing up again. "I should be going, too. I have to get to work. But I'll just walk," she added hastily. "I . . . I need to think."

"Sure? Poor Pete's, ain't it?"

"Yes, how did you know that?" she looked up in surprise.

Clancy shrugged. "'Spose it don't matter now if I tell you. Inspector's got a guy tailin' you."

"He does?" she said, looking around her nervously.

"Yeah, well. Can't be too careful, like, he says. Neptune, the real Neptune, that is, is still out there, ain't he? And the inspector doesn't want nothin' happenin' to you, if you get my drift."

"I see," she mused.

"Says you're a key witness, but, me, I think it's more than that," he said, giving her a little wink.

"I'm sure I don't know what you're talking about, Officer Clancy," Henrietta said with a faint smile.

"Well, for what it's worth, I'm rootin' for you," he said tipping his hat and striding off back across the park, leaving Henrietta alone with her jumbled thoughts.

Since then, Henrietta had kept on at Poor Pete's, biding her time until Clive reappeared, but she had no idea what she would say to him when—or if—he ever did. Poor Pete's with Mr. Hennessey was a sort of refuge for her, the only place she really felt safe. Clancy's news that Neptune was still at large had left her feeling nervous and anxious most of the time, despite the fact that someone was supposedly following her to protect her.

She often imagined she heard someone behind her at night on her way home from the tavern, but it was having the opposite effect she presumed it was supposed to have, making her feel jittery and even afraid, rather than more secure. What if Neptune had somehow gotten rid of her police bodyguard and was now the one actually following her home each night?

She had taken to walking quickly, looking behind her frequently when she left Poor Pete's each night. She had contemplated asking Stan to walk with her, or perhaps Mr. Hennessey, but Mr. Hennessey stayed even later than she did and she didn't want him to have to walk so far out of his way, not when he had been so kind already. Plus, he was getting older, she had noticed since she had come back. Likewise, she was hesitant to ask Stan, as she was afraid it might rekindle old feelings, which she was averse to do, especially as he and Elsie seemed to be getting on so well lately.

Henrietta was relieved and pleased to observe Stan's seemingly genuine concern and feelings for Elsie, and Elsie, too, had confided to her one night this past week that she secretly hoped wedding bells might be on the horizon. Privately, Henrietta judged this to be a bit premature, but she had listened attentively and not without a weary smile just the night before as Elsie eagerly related all of Stan's many attributes over the cups of cocoa she had stayed up making, patiently waiting in the dreary kitchen with its cracked and buckled linoleum for Henrietta to get home from her shift at Poor Pete's.

When they had finally crawled into bed next to Ma, Henrietta prayed that Stan would not disappoint Elsie, who was soon snoring away beside her. She herself was finding it difficult to sleep these nights, haunted by nightmares, knowing that Neptune was still out there. She still couldn't believe it had been Larry all along, creeping around the Marlowe, pretending to be an imbecile, all the while spying and plotting who his next victim would be, his next "filly" for his "stable." It made her skin prickle, and some nights when she thought of his filthy mouth on hers, she was afraid she might vomit, but she managed to keep it down, not wanting to attract Ma's attention.

She had rolled over on her side, then, and tried to think of other things, but her mind drifted to Clive, and that was just as unsettling. Where was he? Why did he stay away? Surely he would have been back from Arkansas by now, or had something gone wrong? Her stomach clenched in fear that perhaps Neptune had gotten him instead of her. Or was it simply because he regretted what he had said to her in the closet in what was obviously a desperate situation? She seemed to remember him saying that it was madness and tried to guess what that meant as she lay there.

Maybe he felt too much guilt toward his deceased wife, she mused. As the days had ticked on, she continued to convince herself that perhaps she had imagined most of what had occurred between them, that all along he had been fighting any feelings of attraction he might have for her because of his devotion to his wife—a theory which she could hardly fault him for. And this must surely be the source of his secret sadness, she reasoned, eventually coming to the conclusion that she could never replace that sacred bond he had once had with his wife, that he still had, it would seem. She needed to face the reality that he could never really be hers and that he wasn't coming back, though she would have liked to say goodbye to him and to wish him well.

Fitfully, she turned on her other side. She must figure out what to do next on her own. Perhaps, she contemplated with a smile, she really should apply at the electrics for lack of anything better.

She had received a short letter from Lucy in the meantime, which she had been relieved to get but likewise nervous to read, not knowing what details it would reveal. She needn't have worried, however, as in it, Lucy simply hoped she was well and getting over that terrible night and said that maybe Henrietta would be interested in meeting up with her and the gang some night? Apparently, she and Rose and Gwen were all working at a place called the Melody Mill, and they could probably get her in if she needed a job. Henrietta had smiled as she read it.

Afterward she was tempted to throw it into the fire but had instead folded it up carefully and placed it in her shoebox under the bed, the only private thing she had in which to collect scraps of newspaper or dried flowers or odd little mementos over the years. Though she wasn't the least bit interested in a job at the Melody Mill or in meeting up just then with Lucy and the girls, she had been glad of the letter, as if it proved that the whole thing had really happened. She would write to Lucy soon, she told herself. In the meantime, she would have to find something, something decent as she had promised God and herself that horrible night that she would do. Though she loved Mr. Hennessey like a father, she couldn't foresee working as a twenty-six girl forever, nor did working at the Melody Mill seem to be the respectable position she was searching for.

It was Sunday, the only day that Poor Pete's and, conveniently, the electrics, were closed, and Henrietta stood in the kitchen drying dishes with Elsie, who had nervously asked Stan over for their family supper, scant though it was. He had accepted immediately, Elsie had told her delightedly, and Henrietta hoped it wasn't simply because he wanted to be near her instead of Elsie. She had been relieved, then, when, despite his jittery leg when he sat next to her at dinner, he had been quite steadfast in his attentions to Elsie.

Later, as she and Elsie stood in the kitchen together doing the dishes, they tried to stack them quietly in an attempt to listen to what Stan was talking about in the other room with Ma and Eugene. Something about the battery factory on Damen Avenue. Stan was always trying to help Eugene find work, but Eugene's interest in school had oddly resurrected, which Ma blamed on Father Finnegan, whom she said was always badgering him.

"He thinks he's the world's expert!" Elsie said, referring to Stan, as she put the big roasting pan of lard carefully back in the stove, and Henrietta laughed. They were interrupted, though, by the faint ringing of the building's doorbell. "Oh, that'll be Mr. Dubala," groaned Elsie. "I'll go see what he wants," she said, going into the front room.

Stanley, Ma, and Eugene looked up quizzically as she came through from the kitchen, but she waved them back to their chairs, despite the fact that they hadn't actually stood up. "Mr.

Dubala said he'd drop off a bit of mending that needs doing by tomorrow. I'll just pop down," she said, opening the door with a short tug and descending the steps. Mr. Dubala was the tailor for whom Elsie worked, a widower who seemed oddly disappointed of late by Elsie's increased descriptions of the particularly fine qualities of one Stanley Dubowski.

Shy Mr. Dubala, never one to verbally press his suit, had perhaps become rather jealous of Elsie's newfound love and had taken to unexpectedly popping over to the Von Harmons' apartment from time to time with stray bits of mending that just couldn't seem to wait until the next day at the shop for Elsie's attentions. Only Elsie seemed unaware that his interest in her might go beyond wanting to simply be her employer, though he was more than old enough to be her father. Henrietta sighed at Elsie's naiveté as she hung her damp dishtowel on the worn knob of the cabinet.

"What did he want?" Henrietta asked, putting away the last of the plates when Elsie finally came back into the kitchen. "Let me guess, Mrs. So-and-So urgently needs a dress repaired by tomorrow lunchtime!" she said with a suggestive smile.

Normally this would have elicited a giggle from Elsie, but at the moment she merely said, "No, it was for you."

"Me?" Henrietta said, turning toward her. "Who is it?" she asked, reaching behind her to hurriedly untie her apron, trying to suppress a hope, even now, after weeks of his absence, that it might be Clive.

"He's not there now. Just said to give you this note," Elsie said handing it to her with a shrug.

Henrietta was surprised by how much her heart was racing as she took it and quickly opened the envelope. She pulled out the card, which said simply:

Meet me as soon as you can at the Viking monument in Humboldt Park. I'll be waiting.
— *Inspector Howard*

Henrietta blushed with pleasure. Finally, he had contacted her! She read it again and was impressed with his neat handwriting. She had so much to say to him, so much to ask. . ..

But why had he signed it Inspector Howard, rather than Clive? No matter, she mused dismissively; maybe he had done it this way in case Clancy read it on the way, assuming that it was indeed Clancy who had delivered it. Or maybe it was an indication that he wanted to revert to a more formal relationship, that he regretted everything after all. She looked up at Elsie, who was staring at her, waiting for an explanation.

"Well?" Elsie asked.

"It's . . . I've got to go out for a moment," Henrietta said, hurriedly pulling her fingers through her hair. It was a shame she was only wearing her faded blue paisley dress, but it couldn't be helped.

Knowing that Stan was coming over, she had purposefully chosen it to make herself look dull in comparison to Elsie. But if she changed now, she would arouse too many questions from Ma.

"Who delivered it?" Henrietta asked.

"I haven't the faintest. Never saw him before. What's all this about, Hen?"

"Was it a big guy, kind of stout?" she asked, trying to remember Clancy's body type.

"I guess so," Elsie shrugged. "I didn't pay much attention. This doesn't have to do with any of that wretched Marlowe business, does it, Hen?" Elsie pleaded. "Perhaps Stanley should go with you. Let me just ask him," she said moving to the door.

"No!" Henrietta said quickly. "Listen, Els, it's nothing bad, I promise. It's from Clive," she said his name softly.

"The foreman at the electrics?" she said brightening.

"He's an inspector, actually. With the police. I was working with him at the Marlowe, remember?"

"Oh! Him." She sounded disappointed. "Don't tell me you like him, Hen!" she said, the idea suddenly occurring to her. "Ma would probably kill you!"

"I don't see why; it's a perfectly respectable job," she said with a toss of her hair.

"Too dangerous is what she'll say. Not reliable."

"Well, good thing it's not up to her. Anyway, this is wasting time. I've got to go meet him at the monument. I think he has some information for me."

"Oh, Hen, I thought that was all over. You said it was!"

"It is! But this is . . . maybe something different," she whispered.

Elsie, reluctant to let her go, stared at her for a few moments. "You love him, don't you?"

Before she had time to answer, Ma called out from the front room, causing them to jump. "What's going on in there? It can't be taking you all this time to do a few dishes, surely. Stanley needs more coffee, Elsie!"

"Cover for me," Henrietta whispered, taking Elsie's hands.

Elsie sighed. "Oh, all right. But don't be gone long!"

Henrietta slipped out of the apartment a few minutes later, having convinced Ma that she needed a breath of fresh air and that she would be back before Texaco Town came on, after which Stanley had proposed they play a game of rummy. It was early June, her favorite time of the year, despite that it was also the month her father had died. She ignored the litter collecting along the curbs as she hurried along to Humboldt Park and concentrated instead on the intoxicating smell of fresh, wet dirt comingled with the heavenly scent of the lilacs and peonies planted at the North Gate, just down Humboldt Boulevard and across North Avenue. Sometimes her father had taken them here on Sunday afternoons to give Ma a rest, but Henrietta hadn't been back in years.

The light was just beginning to fade as she made her way toward the Viking monument, not completely sure where it was. She wondered why Clive had chosen such a remote meeting place. They wouldn't have much time before the gates were locked, as they were each night to prevent tramps from camping out, the residents of the wealthier part of the neighborhood having complained to the powers that be about the increased number of vagrants in the parks at night. Perhaps Clive would be able to circumvent the rules, she mused.

She continued on her way, pretty sure the monument was just past the pond, and was relieved when it finally came in view. She peered ahead but could not see anyone in the descending gloom and surmised that perhaps Clive was on the other side of it. She forced herself to slow down. It would look unseemly for her to be seen rushing to him; after all, she tried to tell herself, they were more than likely only meeting to say goodbye, or perhaps he had some new information on Polly.

She found a bench and sat down, surveying her surroundings. There was no one in sight, which she thought odd, considering the park was a popular place for a stroll on Sunday evenings. Granted, it was twilight, but shouldn't there still be some people about, making their way lazily toward the gates? It suddenly clicked in her mind, then, that something wasn't quite right about this situation, and she felt goose bumps form on her arms.

"Clive?" she called out nervously and hesitantly stood up from where she sat.

Just as she did so, she felt someone grab her from behind. Terrified, she tried to scream, but a large hand clamped her mouth shut. She tried to squirm away, but she was held tight, so tight in fact that she felt pain in her arms where her assailant held her. Horrified, she watched as Larry stepped out from behind the monument.

"Ah, Miss Von Harmon," said Larry, grinning at her with his crooked teeth. "I've been waiting for you. I see you got my message." He stepped closer to her, and Henrietta could smell his foul odor, her heart exploding in fear in her chest. "We were unfortunately interrupted the other night, but I find I can't quite get you out of my mind," he said, reaching out and tracing the curve of her breast. Henrietta recoiled at his touch, but she was held fast. "I don't think that's necessary anymore, do you?" he said to whomever was holding her. A knife then flashed beside her face, and she felt the point of it at the base of her neck.

"Don't even think about screaming," said a voice she recognized as Carlo's as he roughly released his hold on her. She stumbled a bit as she turned toward him, "I . . . I thought you were in jail!"

He smugly grinned. "Well, you were misinformed, then."

"What do you want with me?" Henrietta asked, shaking. Wildly, she looked again around the immediate vicinity but saw no one. Oh, why had she been so foolish! She should have taken Stan, though she wasn't sure that would have helped, anyway. In fact, she contemplated, it might have made it worse.

"I've already said, my little filly," Larry answered. "We were interrupted. And what I want, I generally get, so I've come back for you," he said, moving toward her. "I should have taken you that first time down in the tunnels. I almost did, you know. You're a very ripe peach,"

he said, tracing her bottom lip with a thin, skeletal finger, "that simply must be plucked and savored. Nice and juicy is how I like it."

"You're disgusting!" Henrietta said loudly, though inside a desperate panic had begun to radiate through her. She wasn't even sure she could move. There was no one to save her now. "You won't get away with this, you know!" she said, trying to sound brave.

Larry laughed. "Oh, very good."

"I know you killed Libby and Iris! You won't get away with that, either!"

"Seems I already have, my dear. And don't worry, I'll get away with this as well. Though I'll try not to let it go too far as it did with those two. I got a bit carried away with them. But you," he quavered, "I'd rather like to keep you around. Once won't be enough, I don't think," he said, reaching out and gripping her face with one hand, again revealing his raw brutality. "Get the car," he growled to Carlo, the quick change of tone to one of viciousness causing Henrietta to jump. Carlo immediately faded into the shadows that were growing all around them, Larry watching him go.

As he did so, Henrietta took the one second he was distracted by watching Carlo go and bit the hand that held her face, causing Larry to cry out in pain.

"Bitch!" he said, lifting his arm to backhand her. Instinctively, she turned her face and shut her eyes to absorb the blow, but instead she heard the hammer of a pistol being cocked.

"I wouldn't do that if I were you," came a deep voice beside her. She opened her eyes to see Clive standing next to Larry with the pistol to his head. "Take a step back from the girl," Clive said evenly, keeping the gun at Larry's temple as he slowly obeyed. Henrietta felt relief flood through her, but she remained frozen, unable to move as she tried to take in the fact that Clive was really standing there. Everything seemed to happen at once then, cops appearing out of nowhere, running toward the scene. Two of them grabbed Larry on either side and another had him covered with a shotgun. Two more came up dragging Carlo.

"Got him, boss!" they said gruffly. Carlo's head hung down as they dragged him along as if he had already been struck several times by his captors.

"Get him in the wagon," he shouted to them, "and take him downtown. You know what to do."

He turned his attention, then, slowly back to Larry. "Thought I'd find you here," Clive said calmly as he put his pistol back in his jacket holster. "You and your cockroach."

"I ain't afraid of you, copper. I'll be out before you get this one knocked up," he said, grinning wickedly at Henrietta. With a nod from Clive, one of the cops rapidly punched him in the gut, causing Larry to double over. Roughly they yanked his head up by the hair, then, and Henrietta winced when Clive punched him so hard in the face that blood exploded from Larry's nose. She thought she might be ill.

Clive stepped back calmly, though his breath was ragged. "Don't you ever talk to her again. Don't even look at her!"

he said commandingly. "And you won't be getting out. You'll hang for the murder of two innocent girls."

Larry struggled to stand. Though blood was pouring from what looked like a broken nose, he attempted a laugh. "They weren't so innocent, believe me." One of the cops punched him in the gut again. Clive watched him struggle.

"You're playing with the big boys now, copper," Larry sputtered, "and you'll live to regret it. Don't think the mob won't come after you for this. If I go down, you'll attract their attention."

"Oh, don't worry; I intend to," Clive said, regarding him coolly. "I'm not afraid of you. Take him away," he said, nodding toward the paddy wagon. He watched them drag Larry off a few paces before turning to Henrietta, who, indeed, felt she might collapse at any moment. The residual terror she felt coupled with an overwhelming sense of relief made her legs feel weak. Indeed, Clive caught her just as she was beginning to sink. "Miss Von Harmon—Henrietta," he said gently, putting his arms around her. "Are you hurt?"

She shook her head, unable to speak just yet, and he cradled her to him, burying his face in her hair and kissing her head softly as she began to cry. "Shhh. It's all over now," he said as gently, as if he were comforting a child. "I'm so terribly sorry you had to go through this, but I didn't see any other way. I had to make sure he was out of the picture for good, that you were safe."

Slowly she pulled back from him. "You knew? What do you mean? You knew he was still after me?" She reached in her pocket for a handkerchief but found none. Clive handed her a clean white one from his breast pocket and led her to the bench, which she sunk down onto. There were still cops scurrying to and fro, and Henrietta saw Jones signal to Clive from a little way off.

"One moment," he said, holding up his finger to her, and strode over to where Jones stood. Clive tipped his hat back and rubbed his chin as Jones spoke to him in low tones, gesturing out across the park. Clive nodded, pointed back toward the cars and then Jones ran off again.

Clive walked slowly back to where Henrietta sat huddled. He sat down beside her, resting his arm along the back of the bench. "I wasn't sure, but I had a hunch," he said, taking up the conversation as if he'd never left. "We had Carlo in custody, but we knew if we let him out, he'd eventually lead us back to Neptune. Sure enough, he did. I put it out that I'd left the state in search of Miss Shoemacher, hoping they'd make a move."

"So, you didn't really find Polly?" Henrietta interrupted, earnestly studying his face and noticing for the first time the heavy bruising that still haunted his left eye.

"I sent Jones down. First-rate sergeant, he is. Needs experience, though. He found her, like Clancy told you, with her aunt. But none too soon. Jones and the local authorities found some suspicious characters hanging about whom they had to round up. No doubt in Neptune's pay. Meanwhile, in custody, Alice Jenkins confessed that Mama Leone was indeed a supplier for Neptune's prostitution ring. That's how they got Libby and then this Iris. Polly got suspicious like she said and started snooping around."

"But surely Polly didn't kill Mama Leone?" Henrietta simply couldn't believe that.

"No, it wasn't Polly. She was planning to threaten her maybe, but it seems that Mama Leone was blackmailing Neptune, or attempting to anyway, saying she'd go to the police and spill the beans if they didn't pay her more cash than they already did. So Neptune sent guys to bump her off. Unfortunately, both Polly and Mickey witnessed it, so the search was on. Polly realized they were in danger, so she tried to find Mickey, but it was too late. That's when she decided to flee. It would have just been a matter of time before they found her. They almost did, really, except that Jones got there first."

Henrietta stared straight ahead. It was a lot to take in and sort through. "But we . . . we don't know for sure that Libby and Iris are dead?" she said hopefully, forgetting that Larry had basically just confessed to it. "Perhaps they ran away, too!"

Clive looked at her, his eyes full of compassion. "I'm afraid they really are dead," he said patiently. "Alice Jenkins told us where to look. They were both buried out back behind the Marlowe. My suspicions were first aroused when you told me about the tunnels. It was a hasty, slipshod job. Apparently, they were afraid to throw the bodies in the river in case they floated up downstream somewhere. I'm sorry, Henrietta," he said, putting his arm around her as she buried her face in her hands, crying again. The strain was becoming too much. Quietly she cried for a few moments until she became conscious that he was holding her and sat up straight, then, trying to collect herself.

"So, who really killed Mama Leone?" she finally asked.

"Jenkins says it was Carlo and another bouncer, Frankie," he said, gradually releasing her, "though they're not admitting to anything just yet."

"Then why let Carlo go?" Henrietta asked, confused.

"Because we figured he'd do something stupid, which he did. Instead of laying low, he weaseled his way back to Neptune who, it seems, didn't want to disappear into the woodwork without taking you with him. It was simply a matter of me following him."

"But I thought Clancy said you had a guy following me," she said, muddled.

"Correct. That would be me," he grinned.

"You? You've been following me for weeks and never let on?"

"Well, that would hardly have been effective, now would it?"

They were alone in the park, the rest of the cops having finally dissipated back toward the waiting cars and the station under Jones's direction. A quiet stillness had returned as if the police raid had never even occurred. Henrietta looked up at him hesitantly. "But I . . . I was . . . I thought you'd forgotten about me, or—"

"Didn't Clancy give you the message?" he asked worriedly. "I had to stage him taking your statement, you see. My God, he gets everything wrong! How he ever made the force, I'll never know," he said, running his hand through his hair. "He was supposed to tell you that I would contact you soon."

"Well, he did . . . honestly . . . but I—" She looked at the ground and then up into his hazel eyes. "I was starting to think that perhaps you hadn't really meant everything you said that night . . . that it was just the heat of the moment, or that maybe you regretted it," she faltered and searched his eyes. Finally, she spoke again. "Was there another reason why you stayed away?" she asked faintly.

"Can't you guess it?" he asked, reaching out and tenderly caressing the side of her cheek. At his touch, she felt a shiver run through her. The fact that he could be so commanding, so severe, even violent, with his enemies but so very tender with her was wildly attractive to Henrietta. As she sat, vulnerable, gazing up at him, he leaned across and softly kissed her, and she didn't resist. Emboldened, he kissed her again, harder this time, breathing deeply as he did so. Without thinking about it, Henrietta felt her body arch toward him, wanting to be closer to him, to melt together with him. His arms went around her, and he held her close to him as his lips left hers and began to travel instead across her cheek and then her neck. "Oh, Henrietta," he whispered into her hair.

He pulled back then, his eyes lingering on hers. "I was sincere in every word I said that night. And yes, perhaps I did stay away for another reason," he paused, taking a deep breath. "The truth is that I'm afraid of how much I love you. God knows I've tried to fight against it," he hurried on. "But I think I've loved you since that first dance at the Promenade. I kept telling myself that you were too young, too beautiful for someone like me, and I tried to hide my feelings for you, but, my God, it was hard. But then, the night at the Marlowe, when you said that you could have fallen in love with me, I. . . ." He paused here as if thinking. "I suppose I stayed away because I worried about what might happen next . . . that we might really be in love."

"Why is that a bad thing?" she asked, nearly inaudibly, fearing she already knew the answer.

He looked at her then with such wistful yearning. "Because I'm not right for you. I'm too old, for one thing."

"How old is too old?" she asked apprehensively.

"Thirty-five," he said with one eyebrow arched.

"That's not too old," she said, smiling shyly. For once, she had guessed correctly.

His gaze lingered on her again before he looked away. "It's not just that, it's—there are other things you don't know about me," he continued, hesitantly.

"Such as ?" she tried leading him, but he was silent. "Do you mean about your wife?" she asked quietly. She felt his body tense, then, and immediately regretted asking him about it, but she knew it would have to be said at some point.

"How?" he asked, stunned. Before she could explain, however, he had answered his own question. "It was Clancy, wasn't it?" he asked tiredly.

"Well—"

"I really am going to kill him," he muttered.

"Oh, please don't! He didn't mean to! He's terrified you'll put him on traffic duty," she said earnestly.

"Did he tell you everything? About the baby, too?"

"He did, yes," she said softly. "But perhaps *you* should tell me," she suggested, timidly touching his rough cheek. "I'm . . . I'm sure you loved her."

His eyes closed at her gentle touch and sighed. "I did. Yes. Very much. But I was very young then, and our time together was very short. It was before the war. When I came back, wounded, I was told they had both died."

Henrietta reached out and took his hand. "I'm so sorry, Clive. Really I am. It must have been terrible for you."

"Yes, it was for a long time. But life goes on, even though you don't want it to, and one day you find you're not . . . not quite so sad as you were the day before." He wavered for a moment, thinking, before he plunged ahead. "You know it all now, I suppose. I'm older than you, I've been married, fathered a child," he said, looking down at the ground and then back to her. "I've lived through the war, had my shoulder nearly blown off. I'm growing old and cynical, if you must know the truth. I'm not right for you in countless ways, and yet I can't seem to stop myself from loving you."

Whatever doubts Henrietta had had before, they were slipping away as she listened to him pour out his heart to her. His urgency and his need were almost overwhelming in their intensity, so much so that she could barely take it all in. She looked away, but he put his finger under her chin and gently drew her gaze to him. "For what it's worth, I love you more than I've ever loved anyone; I swear it," he entreated quietly.

Henrietta felt her heart melting; none of the objections he had put forward seemed to matter to her. All she wanted was to be with this man. "I love you, too, Inspector Howard," she whispered back. "I always have."

At this, Clive let out a rasping sort of noise, almost as if he were choking, and squeezed the hand he still held. "Oh, Henrietta, is it wrong to love you this much?" he asked, his voice strained. Without waiting for an answer, he went on. "Marry me," he said slowly, taking her other hand in his and studying her eyes intently. "Will you do me the honor of being my wife? Please say yes, Henrietta. I promise to make you happy; at least let me try."

"Oh, Clive," Henrietta said, her own voice catching. Her love for him in this moment was difficult to contain, and she could hardly believe what was unfolding. It was all so sudden, and it scared her a bit. "Clive," she began again. "We don't know each other very well, not really. Are you sure? Sure you want a girl like me? I'm not exactly respectable," her voice quavered. "My father . . ."

"Yes, I know all about that," he said, caressing her hand with his finger. "I've done some investigating, and I'm very sorry for what you must have suffered," he said, looking at her now with genuine sympathy.

She was so taken aback by his tenderness regarding her father's shameful act, something she was never allowed to speak about, that a small tear escaped her eye, and she had to bite her lip, fiercely, to keep from crying.

"Whatever was the source of, or the result of, your father's despair, it is not for you to feel ashamed," he said lovingly.

She began crying in earnest, and he swiftly reached for a fresh handkerchief and upon taking it out, delicately wiped her tears for her.

"Of course I'm sure about you," he said earnestly. "Henrietta, I need you. I've been so empty for such a long time, and there's nothing left now for me but to love you. I don't care about anything in your past. I'm asking you to be my wife," he said, tracing the line of her jaw with his finger. "If you'll have me, that is, such as I am. He searched her eyes again, almost desperately. "Will you marry me?"

With a bleary smile, Henrietta grasped the hand so very near her face. She wanted to give herself, all of herself, to this good man sitting before her, and just as he had wiped away her past almost as he had wiped her tears, she, too, wiped his past from her mind. "Yes, Clive, I will marry you," she said, looking steadily into his eyes and smiling gratefully, her heart bursting with love for him.

"Oh, Henrietta," he whispered as he leaned closer to her. "I promise to make you happy. I want to take all of your burdens away from you, if you will let me." He kissed her lips, and the electric current that surged between them was palpable. Clive felt a passion erupt in him as he held her, so long had it lain dormant, and it didn't help that the adrenaline was still coursing through his body from his encounter with Neptune. Normally he could maintain his composure, though in this moment with Henrietta he felt dangerously out of control. To his surprise she responded in kind, tentatively putting her hand behind his head as his arms encircled her, and running her fingers through his hair, electrifying him all the more. He began to kiss her deeply, more fervently than he ever had before, trying to take her all in.

As Clive began to cover her neck with kisses until she gasped, Henrietta's heart was racing, and a warmth had begun to spread like fire through her. She had never felt quite like this before. As his fingers found her top button and deftly undid it, she could not help but to elicit small murmurs, his kisses continuing down her chest, inching lower and lower until they reached the swell of her breast. His hands began to travel over her body, and she gasped anew when she felt his hand reach under her skirt, gently parting her legs. The passion wrought in his kisses and his touch overwhelmed her, but it scared her, too, despite the exquisite pleasure she was feeling. She was afraid of how pleasurable it was, of how much she didn't want him to stop, but a warning bell went off in her mind as she realized suddenly that this wasn't how she wanted it to happen, that this wasn't what she had always believed herself to be, even now, in Clive's arms, wanting more than anything to be loved by him in this way. Somehow, she understood that she had reached her own moment of crisis where she would be defined if not by him, then by herself, and she did not want to be the woman her mother imagined her to be.

"Clive . . ." she whispered urgently.

At the sound of her hesitation, Clive instinctively understood its source and came to his senses, pulling himself away as if in pain, breathing heavily. "Yes," he said hoarsely. "You're quite right. Not like this."

He sat back heavily and cleared his throat as Henrietta, still quivering, sat up and hurriedly began buttoning her blouse.

"I'm sorry, Henrietta. I shouldn't have done that; I . . . I got carried away," he said shamefully. "I don't know what came over me."

Henrietta, still shaking a bit, leaned toward him. "I thought you said you wouldn't take a woman to your bed that wasn't your wife," she smiled in an awkward attempt to be playful.

Painfully realizing what she was trying to do, he took her hand. "True enough," he said, smiling apologetically, "though soon you will be my wife, and for that I am very grateful."

Henrietta took the hand that held hers and brought it up to her lips and kissed it. The seconds passed as he looked at her and she at him.

"Whom should I ask for your hand?" he asked solemnly, finally breaking the silence that felt like it could go on forever, so happy were they both in just the other's presence.

"Mr. Hennessey, I suppose," she said, without really thinking about it, and was surprised by how quickly the answer had come out.

"The barkeep?" Clive asked, puzzled.

"Yes, he's . . . he's been very good to me. Kind of like a father," she said, embarrassed.

"Then I shall have a word with this Mr. Hennessey first thing in the morning," he said, adjusting his tie and running a hand through his hair. He stood up then, pulling her with him, wincing still from the beating he had gotten at the Marlowe.

As he slipped his arm through hers and led her across the park toward the entrance, Henrietta's heart was very full. Furtively, she glanced at him from time to time, unable to suppress her smile of joy. So much had happened. She couldn't believe that she was his, a girl like her, that she would soon be Mrs. Clive Howard! She was still shaking a bit from their abbreviated attempt at lovemaking, still tingling from his touch. She hoped she hadn't offended him and that he understood why she had wanted to stop what they both so obviously wanted. She wanted to explain, but she couldn't find the right words.

"You aren't angry, are you?" Henrietta asked unsteadily. "About before?"

"Of course not," he said softly, looking over at her out of the corner of his eye. "Except with myself," he added. "I . . . there's no excuse, really. Just that it's been so very long, and I'm quite mad for you. I find you intoxicating—irresistible. But it's more than that, of course. It's . . . well, forgive me," he said simply. "It won't happen again."

Henrietta blushed. "There's nothing to forgive."

"And I'm sorry, while we're at it, that you had to go through all of this."

Henrietta shuddered again at the thought of what she had endured under Neptune, but she made a valiant effort to shrug it off, though she suspected that it might take time. "Well, it brought me to you," she said thoughtfully, looking up at him, "so it was all worth it, I suppose." She leaned into him, then, and gratefully he bent and kissed the top of her head.

When they finally reached the North Gate, a lone policeman stood waiting to lock it. He tiredly saluted Clive as he and Henrietta walked past and pushed the creaking gate closed. As they walked along the littered street toward her apartment building, Henrietta couldn't help but wonder if it had all been real. It was as if they had been in an enchanted garden and now were back in the real world, where nothing was quite perfect. She sighed as she wondered how she was going to make this work; how could she be this man's wife and Ma's daughter as well? She tried to push those questions from her mind, not wishing to mar the happy moment.

"Happy?" Clive asked her, hearing her sigh.

"Very," she said, smiling up at him. They had reached her front door.

"You don't sound convinced," he said, glancing up toward her apartment as if he understood the source of her new anxiety.

"How could I not be happy with you?" she said, squeezing his hand, not knowing what to do next. She didn't want him to leave, didn't ever want him to leave her again, but—

"Don't you think I should meet your mother?" he suggested gently.

"Yes, I suppose so," she murmured. "They'll be terribly worried. I'm sure Texaco Town's over by now, and they wanted me to play rummy."

"Well, you're in luck, there. I'm an expert at rummy, actually."

"Something tells me I'm not sure I should believe you," she laughed.

"Well, you'll just have to trust me, won't you?"

Henrietta smiled warily. "I . . . I should warn you, Clive, it might not be pleasant. She—"

"I understand," he said, running his hand tenderly through her hair. "And I'm not afraid."

Henrietta willed her legs to not melt at his touch.

"I've faced far worse, believe me. You of all people should know," he grinned. "I think if the two of us can take on the likes of Neptune, we can take on your mother. Besides, you haven't met mine yet," he said with a wry grin.

Henrietta hadn't considered this and quailed at the thought. So much was happening so fast. As usual, though, Clive seemed to be able to read her mind. "We'll work it out," he promised calmly, his head tilted to the side.

Henrietta took a deep breath and put her hand on the doorknob, but then suddenly turned to him, remembering something. "Oh, yes, and Stan's up there, too," she said, not being able to suppress a mischievous smile.

"Pipsqueak?" he said, frowning. "Now that is a cause for concern," he said, his brow knitted.

Henrietta laughed. "Ready?" she said holding out her hand to him. "Ready," he said taking it, and together they went in.

ACKNOWLEDGEMENTS

The original version of *A Girl Like You* wouldn't have come into the world without the encouragement and support of Brooke Warner and She Writes Press, who first believed in this story and helped launch my journey as an author. I'm forever grateful for that beginning.

This new edition—and the relaunch of the entire Henrietta and Inspector Howard series—has been shaped by a talented team of creatives and professionals. Special thanks to **Kari Brownlie**, whose stunning cover design perfectly captures the mood and mystery of this book. Though several editors have worked on this story over the years, I want to especially thank **Susie Chinisci**, whose sharp eye and deep understanding of the series helped guide it into its final form. Likewise, thanks to **Danna Steele** of Dearly Creative, whose beautiful interior design breathes new life into these pages. And a big shout-out to **Lisa Dailey** of Sidekick Press for managing my website, and to **Yolanda Facio** for formatting my newsletter. Last but certainly not least, I'd like to thank **Jayne Entwistle**, my audiobook narrator, for bringing these characters to life in such a professional—and, might I say, charming—way.

A heartfelt thanks as well to **my beta readers and street team** for your unending support in helping me get these books out into the world. And to all of my readers—who now span the globe!—thank you for your enthusiasm, your reviews, your emails, and your love for these characters and the world they inhabit. It's a feeling unlike any other to have created a place others enjoy escaping into as much as I do myself.

Last, but certainly not least, deepest gratitude to **my family**—for their patience and love. Thank you for giving me the time and space to chase this dream, even when it meant living alongside a fictional cast of characters from the 1930s—and sometimes having to fend for yourselves for dinner. Special thanks go to my husband, **Phil**, who read more raw chapters than anyone else—so much so that he barely made it to the finished product. Thank you for your unwavering support and belief in me. It has made all the difference.

AUTHOR'S NOTE

A Girl Like You is a work of fiction, but Henrietta's roots are very real.

Henrietta is based on a woman I met while working in a nursing home—an 81-year-old firecracker named Liberty Adelaide Appleby, affectionately called "Addie," who, despite declining health, still carried herself with striking elegance and a mischievous twinkle in her eye. What struck me right from the beginning was her favorite phrase: "You know, once upon a time, I had a man-stopping body—and a personality to go with it!"

How could I *not* write about her?

Addie grew up during the Great Depression, the eldest in her family, and like Henrietta, was left to help support her siblings after her father died. From the age of fifteen until nearly seventy, she held dozens of jobs—many of which appear in this book: waitress, "Dutch Girl" at the 1933 Chicago World's Fair, hair-curler demonstrator, radio welder, bookie's girl, taxi dancer, and usherette at a burlesque theater.

She often told me that, due to her good looks, she didn't have a problem getting a job—even at the height of the Depression. It was *keeping* the job that proved harder, as she was frequently the target of unwanted overtures from predatory bosses who tried to corner her in supply closets or backrooms. Her response was to slap them—for which she was promptly fired. In my opinion, this took real courage, given that she was the breadwinner for her family in an economically depressed world.

She was a "nice girl," is how she put it—a fact apparently known by a small group of neighborhood boys who saw themselves as her protectors. Dutifully, they would wait by the El station or bus stop for her to return from late-night shifts and would then follow—at a not-so-inconspicuous distance—until she reached home safely. I desperately wanted to include this detail in the novel, but it proved too complex to manage in the narrative. So I combined the boys into a single loyal young man: Stanley Dubowski.

Much of Henrietta's early storyline mirrors Addie's real-life experiences, including her audition at the burlesque theater, which I recreated almost exactly from her telling. Once hired, she was indeed befriended and protected by a group of lesbian coworkers. One in particular—Didi, the inspiration for Lucy—became her closest friend and protector.

Eventually, though, Henrietta's story had to diverge to allow for more drama—namely, a mystery. To my knowledge, Addie was never drawn into a murder investigation. But who's to say she didn't once share a slow dance with a certain dashing, aloof detective?

Over the course of the series, Henrietta's world expands far beyond its origins in Chicago's gritty neighborhoods and into something uniquely her own. Still, this first book remains the beating heart of the series—grounded in one real woman's courage, resilience, and spark.

It was an honor to know Addie, and it's been an even greater joy to bring her spirit to the page.

BOOK CLUB DISCUSSION QUESTIONS

1. Henrietta is introduced as the breadwinner of her fatherless family, facing economic hardships and scarce jobs in 1930s Chicago. How do these circumstances and her family responsibilities influence her choices, particularly her decision to become a taxi dancer and then an usherette at the Marlowe? What do these choices reveal about her character and her definition of self-worth?

2. The phrase "a girl like you" is used repeatedly in the novel, often in contexts that question Henrietta's virtue or suitability for certain jobs. Henrietta herself grapples with societal expectations of a "good" woman versus the realities of her life. How does the novel explore themes of morality, judgment, and personal integrity in this era? How does Henrietta ultimately define "good" for herself?

3. Inspector Howard initially deceives Henrietta about his true identity and profession, later recruiting her for a dangerous undercover operation at the Marlowe. What are your thoughts on his methods? Do his intentions justify his deception and the risks he places Henrietta in, especially considering his later realization of her innocence?

4. Michelle Cox is praised for "masterfully recreating 1930s Chicago" and "bringing to life its diverse neighborhoods and eclectic residents, as well as its seedy side." How does

the pervasive economic hardship of the Great Depression influence the characters' motivations, their desperation, and the difficult choices they make throughout the novel? Consider how it shapes opportunities and dangers.

5. Henrietta moves from being a twenty-six girl at Poor Pete's to a taxi dancer at the Promenade, and finally to an usherette at the Marlowe. Compare and contrast the environments, challenges, and perceived dangers of each of these roles. How does each experience contribute to Henrietta's understanding of the world and her own capabilities?

6. Many characters in the novel engage in various forms of deception, including Henrietta (lying to her mother about her job), Inspector Howard (his identity), Polly (using an alias), and most notably, Larry (his true identity as Neptune). Discuss how these acts of deception, both personal and professional, impact the plot, character relationships, and overarching themes of the story.

7. The discovery that Larry, the seemingly "dimwitted" custodian, is the notorious Neptune, is a major plot twist. What was your initial reaction to this reveal? How does this change your perception of earlier interactions Henrietta had with Larry, such as his comments about Libby's dress or his behavior during the audition?

8. Henrietta and Clive's relationship evolves from initial suspicion and professional interaction to a deep, complex affection and love. What specific moments or interactions stand out in the development of their feelings for each

other? How do their different social backgrounds and personalities both challenge and strengthen their bond?

9. Discuss the roles and perspectives of other female characters such as Polly, Elsie, Mrs. Von Harmon, Lucy, Gwen, and Rose. How do their individual struggles, loyalties, and life choices reflect upon or contrast with Henrietta's journey and her understanding of women's roles in 1930s society?

10. Despite frequently finding herself in vulnerable or dangerous situations, Henrietta demonstrates remarkable agency and initiative. What motivates her to insist on continuing her undercover work at the Marlowe, even after recognizing the extreme dangers and Clive's desire to pull her out? How does her desire to "prove herself" to Clive intertwine with her genuine concern for Libby and Iris?

11. The novel highlights rigid class structures, with Henrietta's family having a storied but lost aristocratic past in Alsace-Lorraine. How do the family's past and current working-class status impact Henrietta's self-perception and her mother's worldview? How does the revelation about her mother's true family background challenge these established perceptions?

12. Describe the dramatic events leading up to Henrietta and Clive's rescue from Neptune. What role do unexpected allies play in their survival? What was Stan's role? Do you see him as a protective figure or a warning against settling for what's easy?

Coming next in the Henrietta and Inspector Howard series...

A RING OF TRUTH

A HIGH-SOCIETY SUMMER. A MISSING RING. A ROMANCE PUT TO THE TEST.

After accepting the proposal of the dashing Inspector Clive Howard, Henrietta is unexpectedly invited to spend the summer with his family—at their grand estate in Winnetka. While Clive returns to his duties in the city, Henrietta is left to try to navigate the rules and rituals of upper-class life—and the sharp eye of his disapproving mother.

When an elderly servant, Helen, insists a treasured ring has been stolen, Henrietta takes the accusation seriously—even as Clive dismisses it as merely confused ramblings of old age. Despite this, Henrietta persists in her own investigation, which raises Clive's ire. Feeling rebuffed and out of place, Henrietta returns to Chicago, only to learn that her younger brother Eugene has been arrested for theft.

As tensions rise at home, Henrietta and Clive must reconcile and decide whether their engagement can survive the sharp divide between their worlds. Regardless, the danger they thought was behind them isn't finished yet. Events soon draw Henrietta back to Highbury—and into far greater danger than she ever imagined. *Can she uncover the truth before it's too late—or will her new life slip away before it's even begun?*

Available now at your favorite retailer!

DID YOU ENJOY YOUR TIME WITH HENRIETTA AND CLIVE?

WANT MORE?

You can explore the entire series in my online shop! When you buy direct from me, you support me as the author—*and save money in the process.*

Available now at your favorite retailer!

STEP BACK INTO 1930S CHICAGO—ANYTIME YOU LIKE!

Sign up for my newsletter and stay connected! Each monthly issue includes a variety of personal updates, book news, fascinating tidbits from Old Hollywood, and the odd giveaway—plus first looks at new releases.

Whether you're here for romance, mystery, or a little old-fashioned charm, you'll be the first to know what's next.

Newsletter/Fun Stuff

OTHER TITLES BY MICHELLE COX

THE HENRIETTA AND INSPECTOR HOWARD SERIES

A RING OF TRUTH As Henrietta navigates her introduction to Inspector Howard's wealthy family, she unearths shocking secrets about her own past and finds herself caught in a dangerous web of deception and crime.

A PROMISE GIVEN Henrietta and Clive Howard travel to England for their honeymoon and get entangled in a local murder investigation, uncovering secrets about the Linley estate and Clive's cousin, Wallace.

A VEIL REMOVED Henrietta and Clive investigate the death of his father, seemingly an accident. But when they discover years of extortion by their arch-nemesis, a violent confrontation ensues.

A CHILD LOST Henrietta and Clive investigate the disappearance of an immigrant woman and her child, tracing both to an infamous asylum while navigating the unsettling prophecies emerge from a local psychic.

A SPYING EYE Henrietta and Clive return to Europe for a second honeymoon, but it takes a dangerous turn when British Intelligence recruits them to recover a missing art panel that Hitler believes contains a coded map to mystical relics of power.

A HAUNTING AT LINLEY At Castle Linley, Henrietta and Clive must unravel a murder, a supposed haunting, and a web of shocking family secrets to save the estate from ruin and expose the true culprit behind the sinister events.

A CHRISTMAS AT HIGHBURY Henrietta and Clive return to Highbury for the holidays only to find themselves swept into a festive whodunit when gifts (and a necklace) go missing at a glittering Christmas ball.

THE MERRIWEATHER SERIES

MATCHED IN MERRIWEATHER Forced to abandon her glamorous 1930s Chicago college life, Melody Merriweather returns to her small hometown to save her family's struggling general store, where she unexpectedly finds herself entwined in matters of the heart.

UNCOVERED IN MERRIWEATHER Kate Kerwyn, aka "Indian Kate" embarks on a quest to uncover her true family and identity, while Melody returns to Chicago to try to resurrect her old life.

STAND-ALONE TITLES

THE FALLEN WOMAN'S DAUGHTER Based on a true story, this novel chronicles the decades-long journey of a young woman who, after running off with a carnival barker in the 1920s, fights to reunite with her two daughters taken by the state.

ABOUT THE AUTHOR

Michelle Cox has always been obsessed with stories of the past and has spent a lifetime collecting them. She is the award-winning author of historical fiction, including the *Henrietta and Inspector Howard* series, *The Fallen Woman's Daughter*, and the *Merriweather Series*. She also pens the wildly popular "Novel Notes of Local Lore," a weekly blog chronicling the lives of Chicago's forgotten residents.

To date, her novels have won more than eighty international awards and have received acclaim from *Library Journal* (starred), *Booklist* (starred), *Publishers Weekly*, *Kirkus*, Book Life (Editor's Pick), *Foreword Reviews*, *Historical Novel Society*, and media outlets such as *PopSugar*, *BuzzFeed*, *Redbook*, *Elle*, *Brit + Co*, *Bustle*, *Culturalist*, *Working Mother*, and many more.

She lives in the northern suburbs of Chicago with her husband, an assortment of children who continually leave and then come back, and one naughty Goldendoodle. Unbeknownst to most, she hoards board games she doesn't have time to play and is—unsurprisingly—in love with both Cary Grant and Jimmy Stewart. She is also happily addicted to period dramas, big band music, and marmalade.

www.ingramcontent.com/pod-product-compliance
Lightning Source LLC
Jackson TN
JSHW021215011025
91881JS00007B/45